S0-ASI-672

WALLINGFORD PUBLIC LIBRARY
200 North Main Street
Wallingford, CT 06492

WITHDRAWN

Christmas in
Snowflake Canyon

Center Point
Large Print

Also by RaeAnne Thayne and available from
Center Point Large Print:

Hope's Crossing Novels
  Blackberry Summer
  Woodrose Mountain
  Sweet Laurel Falls
  Currant Creek Valley
  Willowleaf Lane

**This Large Print Book carries the
Seal of Approval of N.A.V.H.**

Christmas in Snowflake Canyon

RaeAnne Thayne

WALLINGFORD PUBLIC LIBRARY
200 North Main Street
Wallingford, CT 06492

CENTER POINT LARGE PRINT
THORNDIKE, MAINE

This Center Point Large Print edition is published in the year 2014 by arrangement with Harlequin Books S.A.

Copyright © 2013 by RaeAnne Thayne.

All rights reserved.

This is a work of fiction. Names, characters, places and incidents are either the product of the author's imagination or are used fictitiously, and any resemblance to actual persons, living or dead, business establishments, events or locales is entirely coincidental.

The text of this Large Print edition is unabridged. In other aspects, this book may vary from the original edition. Printed in the United States of America on permanent paper. Set in 16-point Times New Roman type.

ISBN: 978-1-61173-986-2

Library of Congress Cataloging-in-Publication Data

Thayne, RaeAnne.
Christmas in Snowflake Canyon / RaeAnne Thayne. —
  Center Point Large Print edition.
pages cm
ISBN 978-1-61173-986-2 (Library binding : alk. paper)
1. Christmas stories. 2. Large type books. I. Title.
PS3570.H363C47 2014
813'.54—dc23
                                            2013037557

A deep and loving thank-you to my parents, Elden and RaNae Robinson, for making each of my childhood holidays wonderful. Also, special thanks to a dear octogenarian aunt Betty Grace Hall—who constantly urges me to write faster so she can live long enough to see what happens to all my people.

Dear Reader,

I don't think any of you who regularly reads my books will be surprised to learn I love the holidays. I've written many stories centered around this time of year, when family and friends draw closer to share traditions, memories, music, food.

Despite all the glittery magic and shining joy, I'm sure I don't have to tell you the holidays can be chaotic and stressful, too—a time of unreasonable expectations and unrealized potential. Nothing will ever be as ideal as we imagine and for some of us (me!) that can be as hard to swallow as last year's peppermints.

But how boring is perfection, really? It is our flaws and our failings—and the dignity and grace with which we strive to overcome them—that make each of us beautifully human. This is the lesson both Dylan Caine and Genevieve Beaumont, the hero and heroine of *Christmas in Snowflake Canyon*, must learn.

This year I'm resolved to give myself a break. My tree can be a little lopsided, each ribbon doesn't have to be precisely measured and curled, nobody but me will know if I use store-bought cookie dough in my gifts to neighbors. Instead, I intend to take every occasion to pause, to breathe, to remind myself to savor the tiny joys of each day. It's my wish that you might do the same.

All my very best,

RaeAnne

Chapter One

If he had to listen to "The Little Drummer Boy" one more time, he was going to ba-rum-bum-bum-bum somebody right in the gut.

Dylan Caine huddled over a whiskey at the crowded bar of The Speckled Lizard, about two seconds and one more damn Christmas carol away from yanking the jukebox plug out of the wall. Some idiot had just played three versions of the same song. If another one flipped, he was going to knock a few heads and then take off.

His brother was now—he checked his watch—ten minutes late. The way Dylan figured, it would serve Jamie right if he bailed. He hadn't wanted to meet at the bar in the first place, and he certainly wasn't in any mood to sit here by himself listening to a bad version of a song he'd never liked much in the first place.

On this, the evening of Black Friday, the Liz was hopping. A popular local band was supposed to be playing, but from the buzz he'd heard around the bar, apparently the bass player and the lead singer—married to each other—had shared a bad Thanksgiving tofurkey the day before and were too busy yakking it up to entertain the masses.

Those masses were now growing restless. He no longer liked crowds under the best of circumstances, and a bar filled with holiday-edgy, disappointed music fans with liberal access to alcohol struck him as an unpleasant combination.

Somebody jostled him from behind and he could tell without turning around it was a woman. The curves pressing into his shoulder were a good giveaway, along with a delectable scent of cinnamon and vanilla that made him think of crisp, rich cookies.

His mouth watered. He'd been a hell of a long time without . . . cookies.

"Pat, where's my mojito? Come *on*. I've been waiting *forever.*"

The woman with the husky voice squeezed past him to lean against the bar, and from the side, he caught only an equally sexy sleek fall of blond hair. She was wearing a white sweater that was about half an inch too short, and when she leaned over, just a strip of pale skin showed above the waistline of a pair of jeans that highlighted a shapely ass.

The longtime Lizard bartender frowned, his wind-chapped face wrinkling around the mouth. "It's coming. I'm shorthanded. Stupid me, I figured when the band canceled, nobody would show up. Give me a sec. Have some pretzels or something."

"I don't *want* pretzels. I want another mojito."

She had obviously already had a mojito or three, judging by the careful precision of her words. The peremptory tone struck a chord. He looked closer and suddenly recognized the alluring handful: Genevieve Beaumont, spoiled and precious daughter of the Hope's Crossing mayor.

She was quite a bit younger than he was, maybe six years or so. He didn't know her well, only by reputation, which wasn't great. He had always figured her for a prissy little society belle—the kind of vapid, boring woman who wasted her life on a solemn quest for the perfect manicure.

She didn't look it now. Instead, she looked a little tousled, slightly buzzed and oddly delicious.

"If somebody plays another damn Christmas carol, I swear, I am going to *scream*. This is a freaking bar, not Sunday school."

"Hear, hear," he murmured, unable to hold back his wholehearted agreement.

She finally deigned to pay attention to any-thing but herself. She shifted her gaze and in her heavily lashed blue eyes he saw a quick, familiar reaction—a mangle of pity and some-thing akin to fascinated repugnance.

Yeah, he hated crowds.

To her credit, she quickly hid her response and instead offered a stiff smile. "Dylan Caine. I didn't see you there."

He gave her a polite smile in return. Completely out of unwarranted malevolence, he lifted what remained of his left arm in a caricature of a wave. "Most of me, anyway."

She swallowed and blinked but didn't lose that stiff smile. If anything, it seemed to beam unnaturally, like a blinking string of Christmas lights. "Er, nice to see you again," she said.

He couldn't remember ever having a conversation with the woman in his life. If he had, he certainly would have recalled that husky voice that thrummed through him, as rich and heady as his Johnnie Walker.

"Same," he said, which wasn't completely a lie. He did enjoy that little strip of bare skin and a pair of tight jeans.

"Are you visiting your family for the holidays?" she asked, polite conversation apparently drilled into her along with proper posture and perfect accessory coordination, even when she was slightly drunk.

"Nope." He took a sip of his whiskey. "I moved back in the spring. I've got a place up Snowflake Canyon."

"Oh. I hadn't heard." She focused on a point somewhere just above his right ear, though he noticed her gaze flicking briefly, almost against her will, to the eye patch that concealed a web of scar tissue before she jerked it away.

He fought the urge to check his watch again—or, to hell with Jamie, toss a bill on the bar for his tab and take off.

Though they certainly weren't society-conscious people like the Beaumonts, Dermot and Margaret Caine had drilled proper manners in him, too. Every once in a while he even used them. "Don't think I've seen you around town since I've been back. Where are you living these days?"

Her mouth tightened, and he noticed her lipstick had smeared ever so slightly on her lower lip. "Until three days ago, I was living in a beautiful fifth-floor flat in Le Marais in Paris."

Ooh là là. Le Marais. Like that was supposed to mean anything to him.

"Somebody should really do something about that music," she complained to Pat before Dylan could answer. "Why would you put so many freaking versions of the same song on the jukebox?"

The bartender looked frazzled as he pulled another beer from the tap. "I *had* to spring for that stupid digital jukebox. Worst business decision of my life. It's completely ruined the place. It's like karaoke every night. Here's a little secret you might not know. We have a crapload of people in Hope's Crossing with lousy taste in music."

"You could always take it out," Dylan suggested.

"Believe me, I'm tempted every night. But I paid a fortune for the thing. Usually I just end up forking over some of my tips and picking my own damn songs."

13

He finally set a pink mojito in front of Genevieve. She picked it up and took a healthy sip.

"Thank you," she said, her sexy voice incongruously prim, then gave Dylan that polite, empty smile. "Excuse me."

He watched her head in the direction of the gleaming jukebox, wondering what sort of music she would pick. Probably something artsy and annoying. It better not be anything with an accordion.

He checked his watch, which he really hated wearing on his right arm after a lifetime of it on the left. Jamie was now fifteen minutes late. That was about his limit.

Just as he was reaching into his pocket for his wallet, his phone buzzed with an incoming text.

As he expected, it was from Jamie, crisp and succinct:

Sorry. Got held up. On my way. Stay there!

His just-older brother knew him well. Jamie must have guessed that after all these months of solitude, the jostling crowd and discordant voices at The Speckled Lizard would be driving him crazy.

He typed a quick response with one thumb—a pain in the ass but not as bad as finger-pecking an email.

You've got five.

He meant it. If Jamie wasn't here by then, his brother could drive up to Snowflake Canyon to share a beer for his last night in town before returning to his base.

The digital jukebox Pat hated switched to "Jingle Bell Rock," a song he disliked even more than "The Little Drummer Boy."

"Sorry," the bartender said as he passed by on his way to hand a couple of fruity-looking drinks to a tourist pair a few stools down.

Dylan glanced over at the flashing lights of the jukebox just in time to see Genevieve Beaumont head in that direction, mojito in hand.

Uh-oh.

More intrigued by a woman than he had been in a long time, he watched as she said something impassioned to the professionally dressed couple who seemed to be hogging all the music choices.

He couldn't hear what she said over the loud conversation and clinking glasses wrapping around him, but he almost laughed at her dramatic, agitated gestures. So much for the prissy, buttoned-up debutante. Her arms flung wide as she pointed at the jukebox and then back at the couple. From a little impromptu lipreading, he caught the words *bar, idiot* and *Christmas carols.*

The female half of the couple—a pretty redhead

15

wearing a steel-gray power suit and double strand of olive-sized pearls—didn't seem as amused as Dylan by Genevieve's freely given opinion. She said something in response that seemed as sharp as her shoes, judging by Genevieve's quick intake of breath.

The woman brandished a credit card as if it was an AK-47 and hurried toward the digital piece of crap, probably to put in the Mormon Tabernacle Choir singing "Away in a Manger" or something else equally inappropriate for the setting.

Dylan chuckled when, after a quick, startled second, the mayor's genteel daughter rushed forward like a Broncos tackle, her drink spilling a little as she darted ahead, her body blocking the woman from accessing the jukebox.

"Move your bony ass," he heard the woman say, quite unfairly, in the personal opinion of a man who had just had ample evidence that particular piece of Ms. Beaumont wasn't anything of the sort.

"Make me," Gen snarled.

At that line-in-the-sand declaration, Dylan did a quick ninety-degree swivel on his barstool to watch the unfolding action and he realized he wasn't the only one. The little altercation was beginning to draw the interest of other patrons in the bar.

Nothing like a good girl fight to get the guys' attention.

16

"I have the right to listen to whatever I want," Madame Power Suit declared.

"Nobody else wants to listen to Christmas music. Am I right?"

A few nearby patrons offered vocal agreement and the color rose in the redhead's cheeks. "I do," she declared defiantly.

"Next time, bring your iPod and earbuds," Genevieve snapped.

"Next time be the first one to the jukebox and you can pick the music," the woman retorted, trying to sneak past Genevieve.

She shoved at Genevieve but couldn't budge her, again to Dylan's amusement—until the man who had been sitting with the carol-lover approached. He wore a dress shirt and loosened tie but no jacket and was a few years older than his companion. While he carried an air of authority, he also struck Dylan as similar to the bullies in the military who had no trouble pushing their weight around to get their way.

"Come on. That's enough, girls. What's the harm in a few Christmas carols? It's the day after Thanksgiving, after all."

"I believe this is between me and your girlfriend."

"She's not my girlfriend. She's my associate."

"I don't care if she's Mrs. Santa Claus. She has lousy taste in music and everybody in the place has had enough."

The other woman tried again to charge past Genevieve with her credit card but Genevieve blocked access with her own body.

"Do you have any idea who you're messing with?" He advanced on her, his very bulk making him threatening.

"Don't know, don't care."

He loomed over her, but Genevieve didn't back down. She was just full of surprises. On face value, he wouldn't have taken her for anybody with an ounce of pluck.

"She happens to be an assistant district attorney. We both are."

Oh, crap.

Genevieve apparently meant it when she said she didn't care. "I hate attorneys. My ex-fiancé was an attorney," she snapped.

The guy smirked. "What's his name? I'd like to call the man and buy him a drink for being smart enough to drop-kick a psycho like you."

Genevieve seemed to deflate a little, looking for a moment lost and uncertain, before she bristled. "*I* drop-kicked *him,* for your information, and I haven't missed him for a minute. In my experi-ence, most attorneys will do anything necessary to get their way."

"Damn straight," the woman said. She planted her spiked heel on Genevieve's foot hard and when the effort achieved its desired result— Genevieve shrieked in surprise and started to stumble—the woman tried to dart around her. But the former head cheerleader of Hope's Crossing High School still apparently had a few moves. She jostled with the woman and managed to slap away her hand still gripping the credit card before she could swipe it.

"That's assault!" the woman declared. "You saw that, didn't you, Larry? The stupid bitch just hit me."

"That wasn't a hit. That was a slap. Anyway, you started it."

"True story." A helpful bystander backed her up.

The woman turned even more red in the face.

"Okay, this is ridiculous. Let her pass. Now." Larry the Jerk reached for Genevieve's arm to yank her away from the jukebox. At the sight of that big hand on her white sweater, Dylan rose, his barstool squeaking as he shoved it back.

"Sit down, Caine," Pat urged, a pleading note in his voice. Dylan ignored him, adrenaline pumping through him like pure scotch whiskey. He didn't necessarily like Genevieve Beaumont, but he hated bullies more.

And she did have a nice ass.

"You're going to want to back down now," he said, in his hardest former-army-ranger voice.

The guy didn't release Genevieve's arm as he looked Dylan up and down, black eye patch and all. "Aye, matey. Or what? You'll sic your parrot on me?"

Dylan was vaguely aware of an audible hiss around him from locals who knew him.

"Something like that," he answered calmly.

He reached out and even with only one hand he was able to deftly extricate Genevieve's arm from the man's hold and twist his fingers back.

"Thank you," she answered in surprise, straightening her sweater.

"You're welcome." He released the man's hand. "I suggest we all go back to our drinks now."

"I'm calling the police," the woman blustered. "You're crazy. Both of you."

"Oh, shut up," Genevieve snapped.

"You shut up. You're both going to face assault charges."

"I might not be a lawyer but I'm pretty sure that wasn't assault," Genevieve responded sharply. "This is."

Dylan hissed in a breath when Genevieve drew back a fist and smacked the woman dead center in her face.

Blood immediately spurted from the woman's nose, and she jerked her hands up, shrieking. "I think you just broke my nose!"

The contact of flesh on flesh seemed to shock Genevieve back to some semblance of sobriety. She blinked at the pair of them. "Wow. I had no idea I could do that. I guess all those years of Pilates weren't completely wasted."

The words were barely out of her mouth when

the woman dropped her hands from her nose and lunged at her, and suddenly the two of them were seriously going at it, kicking, punching, pulling hair.

Why did they always have to pull hair?

Dylan, with only one arm and skewed vision, was at a disadvantage as he reached into the squirming, tangled pair of women to try breaking things up. Larry, without a similar limitation, reached in from the other side but the women jostled into him and he stumbled backward, crashing into a big, tough-looking dude who fell to the floor and came up swinging.

Everybody's nerves were apparently on edge tonight, what with dysfunctional family dinners, early-morning shopping misery, puking-sick musicians. Before he knew it, the guy's friends had entered into the fray and what started as a minor altercation over Christmas carols erupted into a full-fledged, down-and-dirty bar fight involving tourists and locals alike.

Dylan did his best to hold his own but it was harder than he expected, much to his frustration.

At one point, he found himself on the ground, just a few feet from the conveniently located jukebox power cord. He did everybody a favor and yanked it out before leaping to his feet again, just in time to see his brother wading into the middle of the fray, along with Pat and the three-hundred-fifty-pound Speckled Lizard cook,

Frankie Beltran, wielding a frying pan over her head.

"I can't leave you alone for a *minute*." Jamie grabbed him by the shirt and threw him away from the fight that was already abating.

His own adrenaline surge had spiked, apparently, leaving him achy and a little nauseous from the residual pain. He wiped at his mouth where one of the tourists—a big dude with dreads and a couple of tattoos—had thrown a punch that landed hard.

There was another new discovery that sucked. A guy had a tough time blocking with his left when he didn't have one.

"If you'd been here on time, you could have joined in," he answered.

"You ought to be ashamed of yourself, hitting a wounded war hero!" The woman who had started the whole thing had apparently turned her ire to the tourist who had punched him. Even though Pat tried to restrain Genevieve, she leveraged her weight back against the bartender to kick out at the dreadlocked snowboarder.

He wasn't quite sure how he felt about Genevieve Beaumont trying to protect him.

"How the hell was I supposed to know he was a wounded hero?" the snowboarder complained. "All I saw was some asshole throwing punches at my friends."

A commotion by the door to the tavern

announced the arrival of two of Hope's Crossing's finest. The crowd parted for the uniformed officers, and Dylan's already-queasy stomach took another turn.

Two people he did *not* need to see. Oh, this wasn't going to end well.

He had dated Officer Rachel Olivarez in high school a few times. If he remembered the details correctly, he'd broken up with her to date her sister. Not one of his finer moments.

If that wasn't enough, her partner, Pete Redmond, had lost his girlfriend to Dylan's older brother Drew. He doubted either one of them had a soft spot for the Caines.

He should have remembered that particular joy of small-town life before he moved back. Everywhere a guy turned, he stumbled over hot, steaming piles of history.

Rachel spoke first. "What's our problem here, folks?"

"Just a little misunderstanding." Jamie gave his most charming smile, still holding tight to Dylan. Predictably, like anything without a Y chromosome, her lips parted and she seemed to melt a little in the face of all of Jamie's helicopter-pilot mojo for just a moment before she went all stern cop again.

"They always are," she answered. "Genevieve. Didn't expect to see you here. You're bleeding."

She said the last without a trace of sympathy,

which didn't really surprise Dylan. Genevieve didn't have many friends in Hope's Crossing.

"Oh." For all her bravado earlier, her voice came out small, breathless. Rachel handed her a napkin off a nearby table and Genevieve dabbed at her cheek, and her delicate skin seemed to turn as pale as the snowflakes he could see drifting past the open doorway.

Rachel turned to him. "You're bleeding, too," she said, with no more sympathy.

"Oh, I think I've had worse," he said, unable to keep the dry note from his voice.

"This is all just a misunderstanding, right?" Jamie aimed a hopeful charmer of a grin at Rachel. "No harm done, right?"

"No harm done?" The woman holding a wad of napkins to her still-streaming nose practically screamed the words. She held up a hank of red hair Genevieve had pulled out from the roots, and for some strange reason, Dylan found that the most hilarious thing he'd seen in a long time.

"What do you mean, no harm done? I've got a court date Monday. How am I supposed to prosecute a case with a broken nose and half my hair missing?"

"Why don't you shave the rest?" Genevieve suggested. "It can only be an improvement. It will save you a fortune on hair spray."

"Can you really be as stupid as you look?" Larry shook his head. "We're district attorneys. Do you have any idea what that means? We decide who faces criminal charges. Officers, I insist you arrest both of these people."

Rachel didn't look thrilled about being ordered around. "On what charges, Mr. Kirk?"

"Assault, disturbing the peace, drunk and disorderly. How's that for starters?"

"It was just a bar fight," Jamie protested. "The same thing happens a couple times a week here at the Lizard. Isn't that right, Pat?"

"Don't bring me into this," the bartender protested.

"So are you pressing charges, Ms. Turner?" Officer Redmond asked.

"Look at my nose! You're damn right I'm pressing charges."

"Pat?"

The bartender looked around. "Well, somebody needs to pay for these damages. It might as well be Mayor Beaumont."

"Oh! That's *so* unfair!" Genevieve exclaimed. "If you hadn't bought that stupid digital juke-box, none of this would have happened."

"You probably want to keep your mouth shut right about now," Dylan suggested. "I'll pay for the damages."

He ignored Jamie's rumble of protest.

"That's all I care about," Pat answered, reaching out and shaking Dylan's hand firmly, the deal done. "Caine is right. We have bar fights in here a couple times a week. As long as somebody replaces those broken tables, I won't press charges."

"It doesn't matter whether you press charges or not. You still have to arrest and book them for assault," the prick of an assistant district attorney said.

"Sorry, Dylan, Ms. Beaumont, but I'm going to have to take you in." Despite her words, Rachel didn't sound at all apologetic.

"You can't do that!" Genevieve exclaimed.

Rachel tapped the badge on her chest. "This sort of says I can."

The officer reached around and started handcuffing Genevieve. With all her blond hair, silky white sweater and that little stream of blood trickling down her cheek, she looked like a fallen Christmas angel.

"Stop this. Right now," she said, all but stamping her foot in frustration. "You can't arrest me! My father will never allow it!"

"Believe it or not, there are still a few things around Hope's Crossing William Beaumont can't control."

Like most of the rest of the town, it sounded as if Rachel had had a run-in or two with Mayor Beaumont, who tended to think he owned the town.

"Why aren't you arresting her?" she demanded with a gesture to the assistant district attorney.

"She's the one who wouldn't stop playing the stupid songs on the jukebox. *And* I think she broke my foot with that hideous shoe."

Rachel seemed unaffected as she turned her around and started reciting her Miranda rights. Her partner turned his attention to Dylan.

"Turn around and place your hands behind your back," Pete ordered.

"I'll do my best, Officer," Dylan answered. He twisted his right arm behind his back and twisted his left, with the empty sleeve, as far as he could.

"Dylan," Jamie chided.

Redmond apparently realized the challenge. "Um, Olivarez, what am I supposed to do here?"

Rachel paused in mid-Miranda and looked at her partner in annoyance that quickly shifted to more of that damn pity when she looked at Dylan.

"You could always let me go," he suggested, fighting down the urge to punch something all over again. "I was only coming to the rescue of a damsel in distress. What's the harm in that?"

"Or not," she snapped, and before he realized what she intended, she reached for the cuff on Gen's left wrist and fastened the other side onto his right.

Oh, joy. Shackled to Genevieve Beaumont. Could he stoop any lower?

"You can't do this!" she exclaimed again. "I've never been arrested before. I can't believe this is happening, all because of some stupid Christmas carols."

"I like Christmas carols," Rachel said.

"So do I," Genevieve answered hotly. "Believe me, I do. But not on a Friday night when I only wanted a few drinks and some good music."

"You can explain that to the judge, I'm sure. Come on. Let's go."

She headed for the door, pushing her still-protesting prisoner ahead of her. Dylan, by default, had to go with them.

When she opened the door, a blast of wind and snow whirled inside, harsh and mean.

He was aware of Genevieve's sudden shiver beside him and some latent protective instinct bubbled up out of nowhere. "It's freezing out there. At least let the woman put on her coat."

Rachel raised an eyebrow at him, as surprised as he was by the solicitude. Genevieve apparently didn't even notice.

"That's right. I can't leave without my coat. And my purse. Where's my purse?"

"I'll get them," Jamie offered.

"Where are they?" Pete asked.

"I was sitting over there." She gestured toward her table. It seemed a lifetime ago that she had pressed her chest against his shoulder so she could bug Pat about her mojito. "My coat should be hanging on the rack. It's Dior. You can't miss it."

Jamie found the coat and purse quickly and handed them over. "I can't say this is how I expected to spend my last night of leave."

"Sorry."

"No worries. I'll call Andrew. He'll have you out in an hour or two."

The only thing worse than the lecture in store for him from Pop would be the similar one their older brother would likely deliver.

"If they send me to the big house, take care of Tucker for me, will you?"

Jamie threw him a look of disgust. "This isn't a joke, damn it. You're under arrest. These are serious charges."

"It was just a bar fight. Drew can handle that in his sleep. On second thought, Charlotte can take care of Tuck. He likes it at her place."

His brother shook his head. "You're insane."

He must be. Despite the indignity of being shackled to Genevieve Beaumont and hauled out through the biting snow to the waiting patrol car, Dylan was astonished to discover he was enjoying himself more than he had in a long, long time.

Chapter Two

This was a *disaster*. A complete, unmitigated catastrophe.

The rush that had carried her through the altercation—had she *really* punched a woman in the nose?—was beginning to ebb, replaced by hard, terrifying reality.

Her father was going to kill her.

Her mother was going to pop a couple of veins and *then* kill her.

She slumped into the seat, wondering just how her life had descended into this misery. A week ago, she had been blissfully happy in Paris. Long lunches with her friends at their favorite cafés, evenings spent at Place Vendôme, afternoon shopping on the Rue de Rivoli.

Okay, maybe, just maybe, she should have been looking for work during some of those long lunches. Maybe she should have tried a little harder to turn her two internships into something a little more permanent.

She had always figured she had plenty of time to settle down. For now, she only wanted to grab as much fun as she could. What else was she supposed to do after her plans for her life disintegrated into dust like old Christmas wrapping paper?

She had been in a bit of a financial hole. She would be the first to admit it. She liked nice things around her. She would eventually have climbed her way out of it.

How was she supposed to do that now, with a record? She slumped farther back into the seat, vaguely queasy from the scent of stale coffee and flop sweat that had probably seeped into the cheap leather upholstery along with God knows what else.

Her father would see her arrest as just more proof that he needed to tighten the reins.

She burned from the humiliation that had seethed and curled around in her stomach since that afternoon. Her parents were treating her as if she were twelve years old. She was basically being sent to her room without supper in a grand sort of way.

She should have known something was up when they sent her a plane ticket and demanded she come back to Hope's Crossing, ostensibly for Thanksgiving with them and her brother, Charlie. Stupid her. She hadn't suspected a thing, even though she had picked up weird vibes since she arrived home Wednesday.

Thanksgiving dinner had been a grand social affair, as usual. Her parents had invited several of their friends over and Genevieve had endured as

31

best she could and escaped to her room at the earliest opportunity.

Then this morning after breakfast, William had asked her to come into his study. Her mother had been there, looking pale and drawn. As usual, sobriety wasn't agreeing with Laura.

It certainly hadn't agreed with Genevieve as she had sat, sober as a nun, while William outlined the financial mess she was in and then proceeded to give her the horrifying news.

He was closing her credit accounts, all of them, and withdrawing her access to her trust fund.

"I've been patient long enough." His grim words still rang in her ears, hours later. "For nearly two years, I've let you have your way, do what you wanted. I told myself you were healing from a broken heart and deserved a little fun, but this is becoming ridiculous. It stops today. You're twenty-six years old. You graduated from college four years ago and haven't done a damn thing of value since then."

Her father had thrown her one miserable bone. Her grandmother Pearl had left her hideous house to her only son when she died in the spring. If Genevieve could take the house, fix it and sell it at value within three months, she could take the earnings back to Paris to seed the interior-design business she had been talking about for years.

And if she could turn a profit within the first

year of her business, her father would release the rest of her trust fund permanently.

William had been resolute, despite her best efforts to cajole, plead or guilt him into changing his mind. She was stuck here in Hope's Crossing —this armpit of a town where everyone hated her—throughout the winter.

Furious with all of them, she had packed her suitcase, grabbed the key to Pearl's house and left her parents' grand home in Silver Strike Canyon—the second biggest in town, after Harry Lange's.

Yet another big mistake. Pearl's house was far, far worse than she had expected. Was it any wonder she had gone to the Lizard with the intention of getting good and drunk?

True to form, she had taken a lousy situation and made it about ten times worse. She could only blame it on mental duress brought on by hideous pink porcelain tubs and acres and acres of wallpaper.

That was really no excuse. What had she been thinking? She didn't pick fights, take on annoying people, *punch* someone, for heaven's sake! She had just been so angry sitting there in the Liz, feeling her life spiral out of control, certain that she would have to spend the next several months in this town where everybody snickered at her behind their hands.

Now she was sitting in the backseat of a police

squad car, handcuffed to Dylan Caine, of all people.

He shifted in the seat and she was painfully aware of him, though she couldn't seem to look at him. He used to be gorgeous like all the Caine brothers—tough, muscular, rugged. They all had that silky brown hair, the same blue eyes, deep creases in their cheeks when they smiled. Keep-an-eye-on-your-daughters kind of sexy.

He was still compelling but in a disreputable, keep-an-eye-on-your-wallet kind of way. He hadn't shaved in at least three or four days and his hair was badly in need of a trim. Add to that the scars radiating out around his eye patch and the missing hand and he made a pretty scary package.

Each time she looked at him tonight—damaged and disfigured—sadness had trickled through her, as if she had just watched someone take a beautiful painting by an Italian master and rip a seam through the middle.

Yes, that probably made her shallow. She couldn't help herself.

He did smell good, though. When he shifted again, through the sordid scents of the police car, she caught the subtle notes of some kind of outdoorsy scent—sandalwood and cedar and perhaps bergamot, with a little whiskey chaser thrown in.

"I'm sorry you were arrested, but it's your own fault."

He scoffed in the darkness. "My fault. How do you figure that, Ms. Beaumont?"

"We are handcuffed together," she pointed out. "I think you could probably call me Genevieve."

"Genevieve." He mocked the way she had pronounced her own name, as her Parisian friends had for the past two years—Jahn-vi-ev, instead of the way her family and everyone she knew here had always said it, Jen-a-vive—and she felt ridiculously pretentious.

"You didn't have to come riding to my rescue like some kind of cowboy stud trying to waste his Friday-night paycheck. I was handling things."

He snorted. "Last I checked, *Genevieve,* that bitch looked like she was ready to take out your eyeball with her claws. Trust me. You would have missed it."

Like he missed being able to see out of two eyes? She wanted to ask but didn't dare.

"You wouldn't be here if you had just minded your own business."

"It's a bad habit of mine. I don't like to watch little cream puffs get splattered."

It annoyed her that he, like everybody else she knew, thought so little of her.

"I'm not a cream puff."

"Oh, sorry. I suppose it would be *éclair.*"

He said the word with the same exaggerated

French accent he had used on her name, and she frowned, though she was aware of a completely inappropriate bubble of laughter in her throat. It must be the lingering effect of those stupid mojitos.

"I believe the word you're looking for is *profiterole.* An *éclair* is oval and the filling is piped in while a *profiterole,* or cream puff, is round and the pastry is cut in half then some is scraped away before the rest is filled with whipped cream."

It was one of those inane, obscure details she couldn't help spouting when she was nervous.

He snorted. "Wow. You are quite a font of information, *Genevieve.* This evening is turning into all kinds of interesting."

She couldn't see his features well through the snow-dimmed streetlights but she was quite certain he was laughing at her. She hated it when people laughed at her—one of the biggest reasons she hated being here in Hope's Crossing.

Before she could respond, the vehicle stopped and she saw the solid, somehow intimidating shape of the police station outside the ice-etched window.

A moment later, the door on her side of the vehicle opened and Pete Redmond loomed over her. "You two having fun back here?"

Dylan didn't answer, making her wonder if he *had* been having fun.

"What do you think?" Genevieve tried for her frostiest tone. Pete had tried to ask her out once when she was home for the summer, before her engagement to Sawyer.

"I think you're in a pickle, Ms. Beaumont," he answered.

Oh, she could think of a few stronger words than that.

"I think we all need to suit up for the you-know-what to hit the fan after Mayor Beaumont gets that phone call," the female police officer with the split ends and the improper lipstick shade said as she helped pull Genevieve out of the backseat and Dylan, by default, after her.

Her stomach cramped again, just picturing her father's stern disapproval. What if he decided her latest screw-up was too much? What if he decided not to give her the chance to sell Pearl's house as her escape out of town?

She might be stuck here forever, having to look for excitement at a dive like The Speckled Lizard.

A sudden burst of wind gusted through, flailing snow at them, rattling the bare branches of a tree in front of the station. Gen shivered.

"Let's get you two inside," the female officer said. "This is shaping up to be a nasty one. We're going to be dealing with slide-offs all night."

Despite the nerves crawling through her, the warmth of the building seemed almost welcoming.

She had never been inside a police station.

Somehow she expected it to be . . . grittier. Instead, it looked just like any other boring office. Cubicles, fluorescent lighting, computer monitors. It could be a bland, dreary insurance office some-where.

She was aware of a small, ridiculous pang of disappointment that her walk on the wild side had led her to this. On the other hand, she was still shackled to the scruffy, sexy-smelling, *damaged* Dylan Caine.

The officers led them not to some cold interrogation room with a single lightbulb and a straight-backed chair but to what looked like a standard break room, with a microwave, refrigerator, coffee maker.

Yet another illusion shattered.

"Have a seat," Pete said.

"Can you take these off now?" Dylan raised their joined arms.

The female officer seemed to find the whole situation highly amusing, for reasons Gen didn't quite understand.

"I don't know about that," she said slowly. "We wouldn't want the two of you starting any more fights. Maybe we should leave it on a few more minutes, until we give Chief McKnight time to assess the situation."

Genevieve drew in a breath. The McKnights. She couldn't escape them anywhere in this cursed town.

"What about our phone calls?" Dylan said. "I need to call my attorney, who also happens to be my brother Andrew. I'm sure Ms. Beaumont wants to call her father."

"You don't speak for me," she said quickly. "I don't need to call my father."

"But you're going to need an attorney."

She was exhausted suddenly after the ordeal of the evening and the cut on her cheek burned. Her brain felt scrambled, but she said the first thing that came to her mind. "I'll use yours. Andrew Caine is my attorney, too."

Her father would find out about this, of course. She couldn't hide it. For all she knew, somebody had already told him his only daughter had been scrapping in a bar like some kind of Roller Derby queen. But she couldn't endure more of his disappointment tonight, the heavy, inescapable weight of her own failure.

"Seriously?" Officer Olivarez—now, there was a mouthful—looked skeptical. "You're sure you don't want to call Daddy to bail you out?"

"Positive." She looked at the two officers and at Dylan. "I think we can all agree, the last thing any of us needs tonight is for my father to come down here. Am I right?"

"I doubt anything you do will stop that," Dylan drawled.

He was right. Someone at the Lizard had probably already dropped a dime on her. Wasn't that the appropriate lingo? William was probably already on his way over but she wasn't going to be the one to call him.

"Andrew Caine is my attorney. End of story," she declared. "Now will you please take these things off?"

After a pause, the female officer pulled out a key to the handcuffs and freed them. Instead of elation, Genevieve fought down an odd disappointment as she rubbed the achy hand that had been cuffed with her other one.

"You can call your brother over there." Officer Olivarez gestured with a flip of her braid to a corded phone hanging on the wall.

Dylan headed over and picked up the phone receiver, and after an awkward moment where he tried to figure out what to do with it, he draped it over his shoulder so he could punch the numbers with his remaining hand.

Poor guy. Even something as simple as making a phone call must be a challenge with only one hand.

The two officers started talking about a sporting event Genevieve didn't know or care anything about. She couldn't hear Dylan's conversation with his brother, but judging by the way his expression grew increasingly remote, it wasn't pleasant. After a few minutes, he hung up.

"Well? Is he coming to get us out?"

"He'll be here. He wanted to know if we had been booked yet."

The two officers exchanged glances. "Chief McKnight wants us to hang on until he gets here. It's kind of a sticky situation, what with the district attorney's office being involved."

"What does that mean?"

"Once we book you, you have to go into the system," Pete Redmond explained, not unkindly, and she was a little sorry she hadn't agreed to go out with him all those years ago. "That means your arrest will always be on record, even if you're not charged."

"The police chief is on the phone with the district attorney, trying to iron things out."

"How long will that take?" she asked.

"Who knows?" Pete said.

He started to explain the judicial system to her but she tuned him out. He was saying something about bail hearings when she heard a commotion through the open doorway.

"Where the hell is my daughter?"

Merde. Any alcohol that hadn't been absorbed into her system by now seemed to well up in her gut.

Dylan gave her a careful look and shoved a garbage can over with his foot. "You're not going to puke on me now, are you?"

She willed down the gorge in her throat. "I'm fine. I won't be sick."

She was almost positive that was true, anyway.

"Good. Because I have to say, that would just about make this the perfect date."

An inelegant snort escaped before she could help it. Again, she blamed the mojitos, but her father walked in just in time to catch it.

He stood in the doorway and glowered at her, and she was filled with such a tangle of emotions, she didn't know what to do with them—anger and hurt and an aching sort of shame that she was always a disappointment.

"Genevieve Marie Beaumont. Look at you. You've been back in town less than forty-eight hours and where do I find you but in the police station, associating with all manner of disreputable characters."

Beside her, Dylan gave a little wave. "Hey there, Mayor Beaumont."

Some of her father's stiff disapproval seemed to shift to an uncertain chagrin for a moment and it took her a moment to realize why. She had heard enough in her infrequent visits home to know that Dylan was considered a hero around town, someone who had sacrificed above and beyond for his country.

"I didn't, er, necessarily mean you by that general statement."

"I'm sure," Dylan said coolly.

"Yes, well." Her father cleared his throat and turned back to Genevieve. "I'm doing what I can to get you out of here. I've already been on the phone with the district attorney to see if we can work things out with his people before this goes any further. I'm quite outraged that no one called me first. That includes you, young lady. I realize you haven't been in trouble with the law before but surely you know the first thing you should always do is call your attorney."

"You're not my attorney." Her words came out small, and, as usual, her father didn't pay her any mind.

He went on about his plan for extricating her from the mess as if she had said nothing.

"You're not my attorney," she said in a louder voice. "Andrew Caine is."

Her father didn't roll his eyes, but it was a close thing. "Don't be ridiculous. Of course I'll represent you."

"I thought attorneys weren't supposed to represent family members."

"That's people in the medical profession, my dear," he said indulgently, as if she were five years old. "Attorneys have no such stricture. If you would prefer, I can call one of my associates to represent you. Either way, we'll have these ridiculous charges thrown out and pretend this never happened."

She could just cave. It would be easy. Her father would take care of everything, as he had been doing all her life—as she had *let* him do, especially the past two years.

He couldn't have it both ways, though. He couldn't one moment tell her he was cutting her off financially to fend for herself and then still try to control the rest of her life.

"I have an attorney," she said, a little more firmly. "Andrew Caine."

Her father gave her a conciliatory smile that made her want to scream. "You're overwrought, my dear. I'm sure this has been an upsetting evening for you. You're not thinking clearly. Mr. Caine is a fine attorney, but how would it look if you had someone else represent you?"

As if she had finally found a little backbone?

She was spared from having to answer by the arrival of the police chief of Hope's Crossing, Riley McKnight.

William spotted him at the same time. "Finally!" he exclaimed and headed out to apprehend the police chief, leaving her and Dylan alone.

An awkward silence seemed to settle around them like the cold snow falling outside. "Wow. Your dad . . ."

"Is incredibly obstinate. Either that or he has selective hearing loss," she finished for him.

"I was going to say he's concerned about you. But those work, too."

She could feel her face heat. "He's tired of cleaning up my messes. Can you tell?"

"Caught a hint or two. What kind of messes, *Genevieve?*"

Oddly, she didn't mind his exaggerated French pronunciation of her name this time. It was actually kind of . . . sexy. "It's a very long and boring story." One she didn't feel like rehashing right now. "Listen, I *am* sorry you were messed up in this whole thing. I had a bit too much to drink and I guess I went a little . . . crazy."

"I would describe it as completely bat-shit, but that's just me."

"I did, didn't I?" It wasn't a completely unpleasant realization.

"I wish I'd thought to shoot some video of you punching that woman. I haven't enjoyed anything that much in . . . a long time."

She was glad, suddenly, that she'd given him something to find amusing.

"Thank you for trying to protect me."

He shrugged, looking embarrassed. "I would say *anytime* but I'm afraid you might take me up on that," he answered, just as Andrew Caine walked in.

"Take you up on what?"

"Nothing. Never mind. What the hell took you so long? Did you stop off for Thanksgiving leftovers at Pop's on the way?"

Andrew Caine looked very much like she remembered Dylan looking before his accident. Gorgeous. Brown hair, blue eyes, chiseled features.

Tonight, Andrew's short brown hair was

rumpled a little on one side and she wondered if Dylan's call had caught him in bed, or at least dozing on the couch while a basketball game played or something. His blue dress shirt was tailored and elegant but a little wrinkled, as if he had yanked it out of the laundry hamper at the last minute.

"Tell me why I never get calls about you during business hours. I ought to leave your ass in here overnight. Hell, I should leave you here all weekend. It would serve you right."

"Guess it's my turn for the annoying family lectures," Dylan murmured in an aside to her.

A little laugh burbled out of her; she couldn't help it, and he gazed at her mouth for a moment before jerking his gaze back to his brother.

"A bar fight at the Lizard. Really. Couldn't you try for something a little more original?"

Dylan shrugged and aimed his thumb at Genevieve. "She started it."

"Tell me you weren't fighting with Genevieve Beaumont." Andrew narrowed his gaze. "Pop is seriously going to kill you. And then Mayor Beaumont will scrape up what's left of you and finish you off."

"That's not what I meant." Annoyance flickered across his expression. "I haven't sunk that low."

"It was all my fault," Genevieve said. "I . . . lost my head and your brother stepped in to try to calm the situation."

"It obviously didn't work."

"Well, no," she admitted.

"What's this I hear about you scalping a county prosecutor and breaking her nose?"

She had actually physically attacked another human being. She flushed, hardly able to believe she had actually done that. She didn't know how to respond. Fortunately, Dylan's brother didn't seem to require a response.

"Never mind," he said. "I'm sure your father will fix things for you. Where is he?"

She gestured to the back of the police station. "He's talking to Chief McKnight. But he's not my attorney. You are."

The man's eyebrows rose just about to his hairline. "Since when?"

"Now. I want to hire you." Of course, she didn't have much money to pay him right now but she would figure something out.

"You really think your father will go for that?"

"I'm twenty-six years old. I make my own decisions." Most of them had been poor the past few years but she decided not to mention that. "I would like to hire you to represent my interests. That's all that really matters, isn't it?"

He studied her for a long moment and then shook his head. "Sure. Far be it from me to turn away business, especially when it's guaranteed to piss off William Beaumont. No offense."

"None taken," she assured him.

"I'm going to assume I'm entitled to some kind of referral bonus for steering new clientele your way," Dylan said.

Her new attorney frowned at his brother. "You can assume you're entitled to shut your pie hole and let me see if I can get you and your new friend here out of this mess."

Chapter Three

❋ ❋ ❋

"That's it? We're really free to go?"

An hour later, Jahn-Vi-Ev Beaumont looked at Andrew as if he had just rescued a busload of puppies from a burning building.

Dylan wasn't quite sure why that made him want to punch something again.

"For now. Between your father and me, we were able to work the system a little to get you both out of here tonight. You're still facing charges for felony assault. It's a very serious accusation."

"But at least I don't have to spend the night in jail. I couldn't have done that." She shuddered. "I don't even have any moisturizer in my purse!"

Dylan just refrained from rolling his eyes. He noticed Andrew was trying hard to avoid his gaze. "Maybe you should think of that next time before you start barroom fights," his brother suggested mildly.

"I won't be starting any more fights. You can be sure of that. I never want to walk into the Lizard again."

"Good idea. I can't guarantee you're not going to serve any jail time for this. Felony assault is a very serious charge, Ms. Beaumont."

To Dylan, this seemed like a lot of wasted energy over a couple of punches.

"I know."

"Your father says he can give you a ride home."

She looked through the glass doors to where Mayor Beaumont waited, all but tapping his foot with impatience. "Do I have to go with him?" she asked, her voice small.

"No law says you do."

"Can't you give me a ride to my car? I'm parked behind the bar."

Did she really think her attorney's obligation extended to giving his clients rides after a night in the slammer? And why was she so antagonistic toward her family? It didn't make sense to him. Seemed to him, the Beaumonts were the sort who tended to stick together. Just them against the poor, the hungry, the huddled masses.

"How much did you have to drink tonight? Maybe you'd better catch a ride all the way."

"Three—no, three and a half—mojitos. But that was hours ago. If you want the truth, I'm feeling more sober than I ever have in my life."

He had a feeling she would want nothing so

much as a stiff drink if she could see herself right now, her hair a mess, dried blood on her cheek from the cut, her sweater fraying at the shoulder where the district attorney must have grabbed a handful.

"Maybe you'd be better off catching a ride with your father."

"Would you want your father to give you a ride home from the police station right now?" she demanded of Dylan. When he didn't answer, she nodded. "That's what I thought. I won't drive, then. You can just give me a ride to my grand-mother's house. Either that or I'll sneak out the back and walk."

Andrew sighed. "I'll take you to your grand-mother's house. I have to drop my idiot brother off, too. But you can't just ditch your father. You have to go out there and tell him."

So much for his puppy-saving lawyer brother. Now she looked at Andrew as if he were making her pull the wings off butterflies. Dylan didn't have a whole lot of sympathy for her. *Don't do the crime if you can't do the time, sister.*

"Fine," she said and tromped out of the room in sexy boots that had somehow lost a heel in the ruckus.

The minute she left, Andrew turned on him. "Gen Beaumont. Seriously? I do believe you've hit a personal low."

"Knock it off," he growled. Funny. While he

might have said—at least *thought*—the same thing, he didn't like the derision in his brother's voice when he said her name.

"What were you thinking, messing with Gen Beaumont?"

"I was *not* messing with her." He didn't want to defend himself, but he also didn't want to listen to his brother dis her, for reasons he wasn't quite ready to explore.

"Yeah, I should have stepped back. It was stupid to get involved, but I could see that if I didn't, somebody would end up seriously hurt. Probably her."

"She's a walking disaster. You know that, right? From what I hear, she's been leaving a swath of credit-card receipts across Europe, embroiled in one financial mess after another."

His family was going to make him crazy. For months they had been nagging him to get out of his house in Snowflake Canyon, to socialize a little more, maybe think about talking to somebody once in a while besides his black-and-tan hound dog. But the minute he ventured into social waters, they felt compelled to yank him back as though he were a three-year-old about to head into a school of barracudas.

"Relax, would you? I'm not going to get tangled up with her. I know just what Genevieve Beaumont is—a stuck-up snob with more fashion sense than brains, who wouldn't be caught dead in public with someone like me. Someone less than perfect."

He heard a small, strangled sound behind him and Andrew's expression shifted from skepticism to rueful dismay. Dylan didn't need to look around to realize Gen must have overheard.

Shoot.

He turned, more than a little amazed at the urge to apologize to her.

"Gen."

She lifted her slim, perfect nose a little higher. "I'm ready to go whenever you are. I finally persuaded my father I didn't need a ride," she said to Andrew before turning a cool look in Dylan's direction. "I'll wait by the door. That way I don't have to be around someone like you any longer than necessary."

With one last disdainful glance she picked up her purse and her Dior coat and walked back out of the office with her spine straight and her head up.

"There you go. See?" Dylan said after she had left, shoving down the ridiculous urge to chase after her and apologize. "Nothing to worry about. Now she won't be speaking to me anyway."

"And isn't that going to make for a fun ride home?" Andrew muttered, shrugging into his own coat.

She refused to look at Dylan Caine as his brother drove through the dark, snowy streets of Hope's

Crossing. Since Thanksgiving had come and gone, apparently everybody was in a festive mood. Just about every house had some kind of light display, from the single-strand, single-color window wrap to a more elaborate blinking show that was probably choreographed to music.

"I'm living in my grandmother's house," she reminded Andrew from her spot in the second row of his big SUV that had a Disneyland sticker in the back window and smelled of peanut butter and jelly sandwiches.

"Got it."

"You know where that is?"

"Everybody knows where Pearl lived."

Genevieve looked out the window as they passed a house with an inflatable snow globe on the lawn featuring penguins and elves apparently hanging out in some kind of wintry playground. She thought it hideous but Grandma Pearl would have loved that kind of thing. She felt a pang of sorrow for the woman who had taught her to sew and could curse like a teamster, especially when she knew it would irritate her only son.

Gen had flown home for her funeral in April, wishing the whole time that she had taken time to call her grandmother once in a while.

Grandma Pearl's house squatted near the mouth of Snowflake Canyon on a wooded lot that drew mule deer out of the mountains. It was just as ugly as she remembered, a personality-less rambler covered in nondescript tan siding.

"You have the key?" Dylan asked.

"Yes," she answered, just as curtly.

He opened his door on the passenger side of the front seat. "You don't have to get out," she said quickly. "I don't want to be seen with you, remember?"

He ignored her and climbed out of the SUV and held her door open in a gesture that seemed completely uncharacteristic. She thought about being childish and sliding out the other side, but she figured she had already filled her Acts of Stupidity quota for the day.

Aware of his brother waiting in the car, she marched up the sidewalk to the front door, where she at least had had the foresight to leave a porch light burning before leaving for the bar.

"I'm good. Thanks. You can go now."

"Genevieve. I'm sorry you heard that."

"But not sorry you said it."

"That, too," he said.

She still burned with humiliation, though she wasn't sure why. Everyone saw her that way. Why did it bother her so much that he did, too?

"Forget it," she said. "I have. Do you think I really care about your opinion of me? After tonight, we won't have anything to do with each other. We don't exactly move in the same social circles."

"Praise the Lord," he said in an impassioned

undertone, and she almost smiled, until she remembered he despised her.

"Good night, Dylan."

"Yeah. Next time, try to have a little self-restraint."

She nodded and quickly unlocked the door, hurried inside and closed it shut behind her.

She had to will herself not to watch him walk back to his brother's waiting vehicle. Instead, she forced herself to focus on the challenge ahead of her—the horrible green shag carpeting, dark-paneled walls, tiny windows.

She was so tired. Exhaustion pulled at her, and she felt as if her arms weighed about a hundred pounds each. Mental note: lingering jet lag and adrenaline crashes didn't mix well.

She headed straight for the hideous pink bathroom and managed to wrestle her clothes off with those giant, tired arms then stepped into the shower.

At least she had hot water. Always a plus. Actually, the house had a few things going for it —decent bones and a fantastic location at the mouth of the canyon, to start. The half-acre lot alone was worth at least a couple hundred thousand. If she could transform the house into a decent condition, anything else would be a bonus.

She stood under the hot spray until the water finally ran out, then toweled off, changed into her favorite pair of silk pajamas and climbed into the bed, grateful for the sheets she had thought to bring down from her parents' house.

She could do this. Yes, it was overwhelming, especially on an extremely limited budget. Difficult, but not impossible.

If she pulled this off, she might be able to leave Hope's Crossing with a nice chunk of cash, at the very least, and maybe pick up a little hard-earned pride along the way.

She supposed it was too much to hope that she might even earn her family's respect—or anything but contempt from a tough, hardened ex-soldier like Dylan Caine.

Over the weekend, Dylan tried not to give Genevieve Beaumont much thought. He was surprised at how difficult he found that particular task.

He would think of her at the oddest times. While he cleared snow off his long, winding driveway in Snowflake Canyon with the thirty-year-old John Deere he had fixed up. While he went through the painstaking effort of chopping wood for the fireplace one-handed and carried it into the house—also one-handed. While he was sitting by said fire with a book on his lap and Tucker curled up at his feet.

Monday morning his cell phone rang early, yanking him out of a vaguely disturbing but undeniably heated dream of her wearing a demure, lacy veil that rippled down to a naughty porn-star version of a wedding gown made out of see-through lace.

His phone rang a second time while he was trying to clear that vaguely disturbing image out of his head.

"Yeah?" he growled.

"Cheerful this morning, aren't we?" His father's Ireland-sprinkled accent greeted him. "I suppose I might be a mite cranky, too, if I had spent my weekend on the wrong side of the law."

Dermot made it sound as if his youngest son had been riding the range holding up trains and robbing banks. Dylan imagined his father viewed the transgressions the same.

"Not the *whole* weekend," he answered, sitting up in bed and rubbing a little at the phantom pains in his arm. His now-narrowed world slowly came into focus. "Only Friday night. I spent the rest of the time shoveling snow. How about you?"

"You didn't come to dinner last night."

Dermot threw a grand Sunday dinner each week for any of Dylan's six siblings who could make it and their families. The combined force of all those busybodies was more than he could usually stand.

"I came to dinner on Thanksgiving, didn't I? I figured that would be sufficient. Anyway, it took me a couple hours to clear the snow and by then I figured you'd be eating dessert."

"Nothing wrong with coming just for the dessert. It was a delicious one. Erin brought that candy-bar cake you like so much and we had leftover pie from Thanksgiving."

His stomach rumbled at the mention of the signature recipe Andrew's wife made. "Sorry I missed that."

"She left a piece especially for you as she knows how you favor it. You can stop by the house when you're in town next."

That was an order, not really a suggestion, and Dylan made a face he was quite glad his pop couldn't see.

"I'm to give you an important message from your brother."

"Which one? I have a fair few."

"Andrew. He tried to call you earlier but couldn't get through. He said the call went straight to your voice mail, and he left orders for me to try again."

Dylan hadn't heard his phone but sometimes the cell-tower coverage up here could be sketchy. He checked his call log and saw he had three voice-mail messages, no doubt from Andrew.

"What's the message?"

"You're to meet him at the district attorney's office at noon. Don't be late and wear a tie if you can find one."

Now, *that* sounded ominous. He had always hated dressing up, something Pop and all five of his brothers knew. A lifelong healthy dislike had become infinitely more intense over the past year.

"A tie." Another of his many nemeses. He defied anybody to knot a damn Windsor one-handed.

"Do you have one?" Dermot asked when he didn't respond. "If you don't, I can run one of mine up to you."

"I can find one. You don't need to drive all the way up here." He didn't know whether to be touched or guilty that his father was willing to leave the Center of Hope Café during the break-fast rush to bring his helpless son a necktie.

"Did Andrew tell you *why* I'm supposed to meet him wearing a tie?"

"Nary a word. All I know is he was heading into court and ordered me to make sure I personally delivered the message. If you didn't answer your phone this morning, I was under orders to drive up Snowflake Canyon to drag you down. You'll be there, right?"

"I'm not five years old, Pop. I'll be there."

A guy might have thought multiple tours in Afghanistan would be enough to convince his family he could take care of himself.

Then again, since he had come home half-dead, they could possibly have room for doubt.

"See that you are," Dermot said. He paused for a moment, long enough for Dylan to accurately predict a lecture coming on.

"I'm disappointed in you, son. Surely you know

better than to find yourself in a fight at a place like The Speckled Lizard, no matter the provocation."

"Yes. I've heard the lecture now from both Jamie and Andrew, thanks, Pop."

"What were you thinking to drag that pretty young Genevieve Beaumont into your troubles?"

He snorted at the blatant unfairness of that. "Who dragged whom? You obviously didn't hear the whole story. I was minding my own business, waiting to share a drink with my brother. I can't help it if the woman is bat-shit."

"Watch your mouth," Dermot said sharply. "That's a young lady you're talking about."

He shuddered to think what Pop would say if he knew the kind of semipervy dreams Dylan was having about that particular young lady, crazy or not.

"Right. A young lady with a particular aversion to Christmas carols and a right hook that needs a little work."

"Ah, well. She's a troubled girl who could use a few friends in town. You treat her kindly, you hear me?"

When Dermot was riled, the Irish brogue he'd left behind on the shores of Galway when he was just a lad of six peeped out like clover in July.

"I hear you."

"Now you had best be hurrying along if you're to make it to meet your brother on time."

"Yeah. Message received. I'm up. I'll be there. I'm heading into the shower right now."

"See that you are." Dermot's voice was stern but he tempered it to add, "And I'll expect to see both of my sons here afterward for a bite and any news from court."

He hung up with his father and slid out of bed. After letting Tucker out with a quick check to make sure he didn't have to plow again in order to make it down to the main canyon road, he hurried into the shower, trying to pretend he wasn't wondering whether Genevieve would be there.

"No. Hell no. Are you freaking kidding me? That's the stupidest thing I ever heard. Absolutely not."

Through her own shock at the proposal Andrew Caine had just laid out for the two of them, Genevieve found Dylan's reaction fascinating.

"Geez, Dyl. Don't hold back," his brother said with a raised eyebrow. "Seriously, why don't you tell us how you really feel?"

"You want to know how I really feel? I feel like I've just been steamrolled."

"Come on. It's a hundred hours of community service. It's not like you're being sentenced to hard labor on the chain gang. I hope I don't need to tell you how far I've had to bend over in the last forty-eight hours to make this deal happen. You're lucky you're not serving hard time for assaulting two officers of the court."

Beside her, she was aware of Dylan's hand clenching on his thigh. Despite the evidence of his frustration, she couldn't help thinking he looked quite different from the disreputable hellion who had brawled at The Speckled Lizard just a few nights earlier. Though his hair still needed a trim, he had shaved off the stubble that had made him look so dangerous, and he wore tan slacks, a light blue dress shirt and a shiny hammered silver bolo tie that gleamed in the fluorescent lights.

She wouldn't have taken him for the cowboy sort but the look somehow worked.

"I'll do the community service," he growled to his brother. "I've got no problem with that. Just not there. This is a damn setup, isn't it? They got to you, didn't they?"

Andrew Caine looked slightly bored. "Who's *they?*"

"Charlotte and Smoke Gregory. Since the moment the two of them hooked up, they've been trying to drag me into this stupid Warrior's Hope business. I won't do it. Have the judge throw me in jail for contempt if you have to, but I'm not going out there."

"What's the problem?" Genevieve asked. "I think it's a fantastic deal! My father has been calling me all weekend to warn me I could be going to prison if I didn't let him take over my defense. I'm really glad I didn't listen to him."

"Thank you. It's always nice to hear from a client who appreciates all my hard work."

"You're welcome."

From what she understood, Andrew had worked some kind of attorney magic. They only had to plead guilty to misdemeanor assault and disturbing the peace charges and they would in turn be sentenced to a hundred hours of community service. If they were able to finish the hours before the New Year, their guilty pleas would be set aside and nothing would remain on their records.

"I'm not doing it," Dylan said, his jaw set.

"Don't be an asshat," his brother said. "How hard can it be? It's basically two weeks' effort to keep from going to jail. Only an idiot would refuse a sweet deal like this."

"I don't want to work at A Warrior's Hope," he said through clenched teeth. "Charlotte and Spence know that."

Genevieve didn't know much about the organization, though she had heard it started up this summer while she had been in Paris.

When she arrived at the airport before Thanksgiving, she had been surprised to find Charlotte Caine, Dylan's once-fat sister, at the baggage claim along with the town's disgraced hero, former baseball star Spencer Gregory, helping a guy in a wheelchair in a Navy cap pick up his luggage.

She wasn't sure what she found more stunning: how much weight Charlotte had lost or that she was apparently hooking up with Smokin' Hot Spence Gregory, at least judging by the way they held hands like a couple of teenagers at the movies and even shared a quick kiss in a quiet moment.

Her parents had treated Charlotte and Spence with stiff politeness, not bothering to hide their disapproval. She thought it was because of Spence's past but quickly found out otherwise. Spence had apparently been exonerated of all charges, something else she hadn't heard about in Paris. Instead, her father had spent the first ten minutes in the backseat of the car service grousing about A Warrior's Hope.

From their complaints, she figured out Charlotte and Spence had started the organization to provide recreational therapy to wounded veterans. Her father seemed to think Harry Lange was crazy to condone and even encourage it, which was one of the few times she had ever heard William complain about Harry.

She wasn't necessarily looking forward to helping out with the charity but it beat multiple alternatives she could think of, not the least of which was scrubbing toilets at the visitors' center.

"You don't have a lot of options here, Dylan," Andrew Caine went on. "The assistant district attorneys are pushing hard for jail time, especially since this isn't your first brush with the law in Hope's Crossing. Because I happen to be damn good at my job, I was able to talk them down off the ledge. Wounded war hero, bad press, yadda yadda yadda. This is a good deal. As your attorney and as your big brother, I have to advise you to take it. Both of you. You would be stupid to walk away."

"I'm taking it," Genevieve assured him quickly, before she could change her mind. Both of the Caine brothers shifted their gazes to her and she couldn't help compare the two. Even though he had cleaned up, Dylan still looked dangerous and rough, probably because of the eye patch, while Andrew had an expensive haircut and wore a well-cut suit.

He was just the kind of guy she should find attractive—well, except for the wedding ring, the reportedly happy marriage and the two kids.

Somehow she found Dylan far more compelling, though she was quite sure all either Caine saw when they looked at her was a ditzy socialite.

I know just what Genevieve Beaumont is—a stuck-up snob with more fashion sense than brains, who wouldn't be caught dead in public with someone like me. Someone less than perfect.

She pushed the memory away. "Do you, er, have any idea what kind of things we might be required to do?" she asked Andrew.

She didn't have a lot of experience with people with disabilities or, for that matter, with warriors of any sort. Unless one counted women fighting over the sales rack at her favorite department store in Paris, which she doubted anyone would.

"You'll have to work that out with Spence and his staff. From what I understand, they have another group arriving for a session in a few days, and because of the holidays, they are in need of volunteers."

"Sure. Why not," Dylan said shortly. "Might as well waste the time and money of everybody in town."

"*You* might think it's a waste of effort, but not everybody agrees with you," Andrew answered. "Most people in Hope's Crossing think it's a great program. They are jumping at the chance to help make a difference in the lives of people who have sacrificed for the sake of their country."

The attorney's voice had softened as he said the last part, Gen noted. He was watching his brother with an emotion that made her throat feel tight. Dylan looked down at the hand clenched on his leg.

"I don't claim to be as smart as you. I don't have a couple fancy degrees hanging on my wall. But be honest, Andrew. Do you really think a week in the mountains can make any kind of *difference* for guys whose lives are ruined?"

Was that how Dylan saw his own war injuries? Andrew's jaw tightened, and she knew he was thinking the same thing.

"A hundred hours," the attorney said instead. "You can finish that in a few weeks and put this whole thing behind you. Or," he went on, "you can stand by your belief it's a big waste of time and choose jail time instead. Before you do that, ask yourself if you really want to break Pop's heart by spending the first Christmas in a decade when you haven't been in the desert or the hospital, not with your family but in a jail cell."

For just a brief moment, she caught a tangle of emotions in Dylan's expression before he turned stoic once more.

"At least tell me the truth." His voice was low, heated. "This was Charlotte's idea, wasn't it? She and Spence won't back off. They've been riding me about this for weeks."

"Neither of them had anything to do with it," Andrew assured him. "If you want the truth, Pop suggested it. When he mentioned it, I thought it was a good idea and brought it up with the D.A. They ran with it."

"Remind me to take you off my Christmas list for the next twenty years or so," Dylan growled.

"Like it or not, you're in a unique position to help here," Andrew said quietly. "Charlotte, Spence . . . everybody can give lip service about what it takes to walk that journey to healing but you're right in the middle of it. You understand better than anyone."

Genevieve's face and neck felt hot as the

sincerity of the words seemed to arrow straight to her stomach.

She thought she enjoyed such a cosmopolitan life, but she suddenly realized she knew *nothing* about the world. She hadn't given men like Dylan a thought while she had been in Paris.

It made her feel small and selfish and stupid. He might think A Warrior's Hope was a waste of time, but she resolved in that moment on a hard chair in her attorney's office that she would do her best, even if the concept filled her with anxiety.

"Stand on your principles if you want," Andrew went on when his brother remained silent. "What do I care? I get paid either way, though I will point out that I'll be the one to get crap from Pop if you're enjoying the county jail's hospitality over the holidays."

"Yeah, boo hoo."

Andrew rolled his eyes. "Right. Or you can just yank up your skivvies, suck it up and keep in mind it's only for a few weeks. Lord knows, you've endured a hell of a lot worse than this."

That hand clenched again on his thigh, then he slowly straightened long fingers. She was certain he would stick to his guns and refuse to agree to the plea agreement and she didn't want him to. She hated the idea of him spending time in jail, especially when she knew the whole thing was her fault.

"What's the big deal?" she said quickly. "Like

your brother said, it's only a few weeks. It might even be fun."

"There you go," Andrew said dryly. "Listen to the woman. Lord knows, you could use a little fun."

She knew he was mocking her, that he probably thought she was some useless sorority girl out to have a good time, but in that moment she didn't care. Not if it meant Dylan Caine wouldn't have to spend Christmas in jail because of her.

The silence stretched out among the three of them like a string of too-taut Christmas lights, crackly and brittle, but after a long moment Dylan's shoulder brushed hers as he shrugged.

"Fine," he bit out. "A hundred hours and not a minute more."

The attorney exhaled heavily, and she realized he had been as anxious as she was. He had just been better at hiding it. "Excellent." Blue eyes like Dylan's gleamed with triumph. "I'll run these over to the courthouse and let the district attorney and the judge know you've both agreed. The paper work should be in order by Wednesday and you should be able to start the day after."

"Great. Can't wait for all that fun to begin," Dylan said.

"Someone from A Warrior's Hope will be in touch to let you know details about what time to show up."

"Thank you," Genevieve said. "I appreciate your hard work."

A small part of her had to wonder if her father or someone else in his firm might have been able to get all the charges dismissed, but she wasn't going to let herself second-guess her decision to have Andrew represent her.

"I've got some papers I'll need you to sign. Give me just a moment."

He walked out of the office, and she shifted, nervous suddenly to be alone with Dylan. The events of Friday night seemed surreal, distant, as if they had happened to someone else. Had she really been handcuffed to the man in the back-seat of a police car?

He was the first to break the silence. "I have to admit, I didn't really expect to see you here."

"Why not? Did you think I would have preferred jail? I've heard it's horrible. My room-mate in college was arrested after a nightclub bust for underage drinking. She said the food was a night-mare and her skin was never the same after the scratchy towels."

"I guess taking the plea agreement was the right thing to do," he drawled. "I wouldn't want to ruin my skin."

He almost smiled. She could see one hovering there, just at the corner of his mouth, but at the last minute, he straightened his lips back into a thin line. It was too late. She had seen it. He *did* have a sense of humor, even if she had to pretend to be a ditzy socialite to bring it out.

"What I meant," he went on, "was that I figured you would have second thoughts and go with your own in-house counsel. I can't imagine the mayor is thrilled you're letting a Caine represent you."

An understatement. She had finally resorted to keeping her phone turned off over the weekend so she didn't have to be on the receiving end of the incessant calls and texts.

"He didn't have a choice, did he? I'm an adult. He might think he can dictate every single decision I make, but he's wrong. He might be forcing me to stay in Hope's Crossing but that doesn't mean I'm going to let him strong-arm me in everything."

"He's forcing you to stay home? How did he do that? Cut off your credit cards?"

Right in one. Her mouth tightened at the accuracy of his guess. She was angry suddenly, at her parents for trying to manipulate her, at herself for finding herself in this predicament, even at Dylan. He had a huge, boisterous family that loved him. Even more, they seemed to respect him. She had witnessed both of his brothers trying to watch out for him while he only pushed them away.

She and Charlie hardly spoke anymore, both wrapped up in their separate worlds.

"None of your business," she answered rudely. "Spending an evening handcuffed together doesn't automatically make us best friends. Anyway, I'm still mad at you for what you said about me to your brother."

Again that smile teased his mouth. "As you should be. If you remember, I did apologize."

She made a huffing noise but didn't have the chance to say anything else after his brother returned.

An hour later, the deed was done.

"So that's it?"

"On the judicial end. Now we turn you both over to Spence and his team at A Warrior's Hope. You only need to fill your community-service hours. They'll give the judge regular updates on the work you do there and whether it meets the conditions of the plea agreement."

That wasn't so bad, she supposed. It could have been much worse. She could only imagine her father coming in and trying to browbeat the judge, who happened to be one of few people in town who stood up to William, into throwing out all the charges.

"Thank you," she said again to Andrew. "Dylan, I guess I'll see you Thursday at A Warrior's Hope."

He made a face. "Can't wait."

With an odd feeling of anticlimax, she shrugged into her coat and gathered up her purse.

"Wait. I'll walk out with you," Dylan said.

She and Andrew both gave him surprised looks. "Okay," she said.

Outside the courthouse, leaden clouds hung low overhead, dark and forbidding. They turned everything that same sullen gray. In the dreary afternoon light, Hope's Crossing looked small, provincial, unappealing.

She could have been spending Christmas in the City of Lights, wandering through her favorite shops, enjoying musical performances, having long lunches with friends at their favorite cafés.

Paris at Christmas was magical. She had loved every minute of it the year before and had been anticipating another season with great excitement.

Instead, she was stuck in her grandmother's horrible, dark house, surrounded by people who disliked her. Now she had to spend the weeks leading up to Christmas trying to interact with wounded veterans. If they were all as grim-faced and churlish as Dylan Caine, she was in for a miserable time.

"Where are you parked? I'll walk you to your car."

She blinked in surprise at the unexpected courtesy. "That midblock lot over by the bike shop."

"I'm close to that, too."

They walked in silence for a moment, past the decorated windows of storefronts. She would have liked to window-shop but she didn't have any money to buy anything, so she couldn't see much point in it.

"Your brother did a good job," she finally said, just as they passed Dog-Eared Books & Brew, the bookstore and coffee shop owned by Maura McKnight. "We got off easier than I expected. We could have been assigned to pick up roadside trash or something."

"Is it too late for me to sign up for that?" he answered.

She made a face. "What's the big deal? Why don't you really want to help out at the recreation center? Your brother's right. You understand better than anybody some of the challenges wounded veterans have to face."

The clouds began to spit a light snowfall—hard, mean pellets that stung her exposed skin.

He was silent for a long moment, snow beginning to speckle his hair, and she didn't think he would answer. She was just about to say goodbye and head for her car when he finally spoke. "I believe Spence and Charlotte had good intentions when they started the program."

"But?"

"Nobody else on the outside understands what it's like to have to completely reassess everything you do, everything you thought you were. I hate bolo ties."

She blinked at the rapid shift in topic. "O-kay."

"I hate bolo ties but here I am." He aimed his thumb at his open coat, where she could see the string hanging around his collar, with that intricate silverwork disk at the center. "Andrew ordered me to wear a tie for the hearing. I can't tie a damn tie anymore. After trying for a half hour, I finally just stopped at that new men's store over on Front Street and bought this. It was either that or a clip-on, and I'm not quite there yet."

She didn't know what to say, especially as she could tell by his expression that he was regretting saying anything at all to her.

She decided to go back to the fashionista ditz he called her. "Personally, I like bolo ties. They're just retro enough to be cool without being ostentatious. Kind of rockabilly-hip."

He snorted. "Yeah. That was the look I was going for. The point is, a couple of days playing in the mountains wouldn't have a lot of practical value when the real challenges are these endless day-to-day moments when I have to deal with how everything is different now."

She couldn't even imagine. "I guess I can see that. But don't you think there could be value in something that's strictly for fun?"

"I don't find too many things fun anymore," he said, his tone as dark as those clouds as they walked.

"Maybe a couple days of playing in the mountains are exactly what you need," she answered.

"Maybe."

He didn't elaborate and they walked in silence

for another few moments. As they walked past one of her favorite boutiques, the door opened with a subtle chime and a few laughing women walked out, arms heavy with bags.

She didn't recognize the blonde with the paisley scarf and the really great-looking boots, but the other one was an old friend.

"Natalie! Hello."

The other woman stopped her conversation and her eyes went wide when she spotted her. "Gen! Hi."

They air-kissed and then Natalie Summerville stepped back, giving a strange look to Dylan, who looked big and dangerous and still rather scruffy, despite his efforts to clean up for court.

"How *are* you?" Natalie asked. "I saw your mom at the spa the other day and she told me you were coming back for Thanksgiving."

Yet you haven't bothered to call me, have you?

Natalie had been a good friend once, close enough—she thought, anyway—that Genevieve had included her in her flock of seven bridesmaids. They had been on the cheerleading squad together in high school, had double-dated often at college, had even shared a hotel room in Mazatlán for spring break after junior year.

When she had been engaged, preparing to become Mrs. Sawyer Danforth of the Denver Danforths, Natalie had loved being her friend.

After Gen ended the engagement, she felt as if she had broken off with many of her friends, as well. Natalie and a few others had made it clear they didn't understand her position. She and Sawyer weren't married yet. Why couldn't he have his fun while he still could? She had overheard Natalie say at a party that Genevieve was crazy for not just ignoring his infidelity and marrying him anyway.

Sometimes she wished she had.

"Are you heading back to Paris soon?"

"I'll be here for a month or so. At least through Christmas."

She imagined word would trickle out in their social circle about her parents' mandate and her enforced poverty, if it hadn't already. Her mother was not known for her discretion.

"Great. Good for you."

"We should do lunch sometime," Genevieve suggested. "I hear there are a few new restaurants in town since I've been gone."

"Yeah. Of course. Lunch would be . . . great." Genevieve didn't miss that Natalie had on her fake voice, the one she used at nightclubs when undesirable men tried to pick her up.

"I'll call you," Natalie said, with that same patently insincere smile.

"Or I can always call you."

"My schedule's kind of crazy right now. I don't know if you heard but I'm getting married in

February. I think you know my fiancé. Stanton Manning."

He had been one of Sawyer's friends and cut from the same impeccably tailored cloth. "Of course. Stan the Man."

Her face felt frozen from far more than the ice crystals flailing into her. Natalie had been one of her bridesmaids, for heaven's sake, but hadn't bothered to even let Genevieve know she was engaged.

If she were fair, she would have to acknowledge that she hadn't been her best self during the humiliation of her marriage plans falling apart. She had been the one to drop all her friends first and flee Colorado as quickly as possible.

"I hadn't heard," she said now. "Congratulations."

"Thanks. I'm counting down the days. You know how that is."

Natalie's friend poked her and she flushed. "We're honeymooning in Italy. He has an uncle who owns a palazzo on the Grand Canal in Venice with stunning views. It's going to be *unbelievable*. Oh, and we've already bought a house together in Cherry Creek. You'll have to see it next time you're in Denver. Stunning. Just stunning. Six bedrooms, five bathrooms. It's perfect for entertaining."

"I'm very happy for you," she said stiffly.

Okay, so Natalie was living the life she had

expected, the one she had dreamed. Italian honeymoons, showplace houses, beautiful friends. She refused to let envy eat at her.

She gave Natalie another hug. "Seriously, I'm really happy for you. Be sure to tell Stanton congratulations from me, won't you?"

"Definitely." Natalie avoided her gaze and definitely didn't risk any glances in Dylan's direction. Her friend nudged her again and she gave that well-practiced smile again. "Well, we'd better go. We're meeting people at Brazen. See you, Genevieve."

" 'Bye," she murmured.

Only after they walked away did she realize she hadn't introduced Dylan. Despite the cold wind that seeped beneath her jacket and whipped her hair around, Genevieve could feel her face heat. A lousy mood was no excuse for poor manners.

He was gazing at her with an expression she couldn't decipher but one that made her squirm. "Oh. You're still here."

"So they tell me."

"You didn't need to wait. I can find my own way to my car."

As if to illustrate, she set off at a brisk pace toward the parking lot, still a few hundred yards away. She had only made it past one more storefront when her heel caught on a patch of ice and she started to flounder.

In a blink, he reached out to block her fall with his arm and his body. Instead of tumbling to the sidewalk, she fell against him and for a moment she could only stare up at him, that strong, handsome face now dominated by the black eye patch. He was still gorgeous, she realized, a little surprised. And he smelled delicious, clean and masculine.

A slow shock of heat seemed to sizzle inside her, and she couldn't seem to make her limbs cooperate for a long moment. He gazed down at her, too, until a car passed by on Main Street, splattering snow, and she remembered where they were.

What was *wrong* with her? She couldn't be attracted to Dylan Caine. She wouldn't allow it. Genevieve jerked away from him, her face burning, and made a point to move as far away on the sidewalk as she could manage.

He watched her out of that unreadable gaze for a long moment. "Let's get out of this snow."

They walked in silence the rest of the way, until she reached the cute little silver BMW SUV her parents had given her when she graduated from college. At least they hadn't taken that away, too.

At her SUV, she unlocked the door and he held it open for her. Just as she was sliding in, Mr. Taciturn finally found his voice.

"Can I offer a little friendly advice?"

Her stomach tightened. "In my experience, when someone says that, a person usually can't do much to shut them up."

And the advice was rarely friendly, either, but she didn't add that.

"Don't I know it. I was just going to suggest that you might endure your hundred hours of service a little easier if you can get over being chickenshit."

"Excuse me?"

"You know. The whole disgusted, freaking-out thing if one of the guys looks at you or, heaven forbid, dares to touch you only to keep you from falling on your ass."

Her face heated all over again. "I don't know what you're talking about," she said stiffly.

She certainly couldn't tell him she had freaked out because of her own inconvenient attraction.

"Goodbye. I'll see you Thursday," she said, then slammed her door shut, turned the key in the engine and sped out of the parking lot without looking back.

Chapter Four

❄ ❄ ❄

Three mornings later, Genevieve was still annoyed with Dylan, with Natalie, with her parents—with the world in general—as she dressed carefully for her first day at A Warrior's Hope. She really had no idea what to expect or what she might be asked to do, which made it difficult to determine appropriate attire.

She finally selected black slacks and a delicious peach cashmere turtleneck she'd picked up at a favorite little boutique in Le Marais. Probably overkill, but she knew the color flattered her hair and eyes.

Or at least it usually did. Unfortunately, it clashed terribly with the overabundance of Pepto-Bismol-pink in Grandma Pearl's hideous bathroom.

This was her least favorite room in the house. How was she supposed to apply makeup when this washed her out so terribly? If she could afford it, she would renovate the entire room, but she doubted her budget would stretch to cover new bathroom fixtures.

She was just finishing her second coat of mascara with one eye on her watch when chimes rang out the refrain of Handel's "Hallelujah Chorus." Grandma Pearl's ghastly doorbell. She shoved the wand back into the tube and hurried through the house, curious and a little alarmed at who might be calling on her this early in the morning.

"Good. You *are* home." Her mother beamed at her as soon as Genevieve opened the door.

"Mother! What are you doing here?"

"Oh, that awful doorbell! Why haven't you changed it yet?"

"I'm still trying to figure out how. Seriously, why are you here?"

"I'm on my way to the salon. When you were at the house the other day, I couldn't help noticing your nails. Horrible shape, darling. I thought I would treat you to a mani. I've already made the appointment with Clarissa. She had a tight schedule but managed to find room first thing this morning. Won't that be fun?"

Her mother gave her a hopeful look and Genevieve scrambled for a response. Since the end of her engagement—and the subsequent death of all Laura Beaumont's thinly veiled ambitions to push them both into the higher echelons of Denver society—Genevieve's interactions with her mother had been laced with heavy sighs, wistful looks, not-so-subtle comments about this gathering, that event.

Being married to one of the most financially

and politically powerful men in small Hope's Crossing wasn't enough for Laura. She had always wanted more. When she was engaged to Sawyer and she and Laura worked together to create the wedding of the century, Genevieve had finally felt close to her mother.

She had missed that closeness far more than she missed Sawyer.

"I can't," she said regretfully. "I'm starting my community service today."

Laura gave a dismissive wave of pink-tipped fingers that looked perfectly fine to Genevieve. "Oh, that. Well, you can just start tomorrow, can't you? I'm sure they won't mind. I'll have your father give them a call."

This was her family in a nutshell. Her mother didn't understand anything that interfered with her own plans, and when she encountered an obstacle, she expected William Beaumont to step in and fix everything.

When Gen's younger brother, Charlie, had been arrested for driving under the influence in an accident that had actually resulted in the death of one of his friends, William had been unable to prevent him from pleading guilty. Charlie had served several months at a youth corrections facility, and Laura hadn't spoken to her husband for weeks.

Now both of their children had been embroiled in legal difficulties. She imagined Laura found it much easier to pretend the whole thing hadn't happened.

"I don't believe it's that simple, Mother," Gen said. "It's court-mandated. I have to show up or I could go to jail."

Laura pouted. "Well, what am I supposed to tell Clarissa? She's expecting us."

How about the truth? That you see the world only the way you want to see it?

"Tell her I have another obligation I couldn't escape. I'm sure she'll understand."

Laura gave a frustrated little huff. "I was looking so forward to finding a moment to catch up with you. We hardly talk when you call from France. I can't say I agreed with your father's decision to cut you off financially. I tried my best to talk him out of it. I told him you were having a wonderful time in Paris, that you needed this time and why shouldn't you take it? As usual, he wouldn't listen to me. You know how he can be when he's in a mood. Still, I told myself at least this would give me the chance to spend a little more time with you, darling."

Her parents drove her crazy sometimes . . . she couldn't deny that. These past two years away had helped her see their failings more clearly, but she still loved them.

"I'm sorry. I wish I could go," she said, not untruthfully.

"I understand. You have to do what you

must. I'll see if I can reschedule for tomorrow."

"Mother, I'll be going to the center tomorrow, too. And the day after that."

"Every day?"

Laura obviously didn't quite grasp the concept of a commuted sentence. "I have a hundred hours of community service to complete in only a few weeks. Yes, I'll probably be going every day between now and Christmas."

"This is what happens when you decided not to have your father represent you. He could have had the whole misunderstanding thrown out."

Like Charlie's little "misunderstanding" that had killed one girl and severely injured another? William had been helpless to fix that situation. Charlie had taken full responsibility for his actions and had come out of his time in youth corrections a different young man, no longer sullen and angry.

"It's done now," she said. "I'm sorry, Mother, but I really need to go or I'll be late for my first day."

"Well, will you come back to the house instead of staying in this horrible place? Then I would at least have a chance to catch up with you in the evenings."

Again, her mother saw what she wanted to.

"I can't. My evenings will be spent here, trying to do what I can to prepare this house for sale. Dad didn't give me any other choice."

"He has your best interests at heart, my dear. You know that, don't you?"

"He might have *thought* he did. We have differing opinions on what the best thing for me might be."

Not that anything was new there. Her father had notoriously found her lacking in just about every arena. He thought she had been wasting her time to obtain a degree in interior design, nor could he see any point in the sewing she had always loved or the riding lessons she tolerated.

The only time either of her parents seemed to approve of her had been during her engagement.

"Will you at least go to dinner with us this weekend? With Charlie back in California for his finals week, the house is too quiet."

"I'll try," she promised. She ushered her mother out with a kiss on the cheek and firmly closed the door, practically in her face.

After Laura drove away, Genevieve hurriedly grabbed one of the totes she loved to make and headed out the door, fighting down a whirl of butterflies in her stomach.

For two days, she had been having second—and third and fourth and sixtieth—thoughts about this community-service assignment with A Warrior's Hope. She couldn't think of a job less suited to her limited skill set than helping wounded veterans. What did she know about their world? Next to nothing. Most likely, she would end up saying something stupid and offensive and none of them would want anything to do with her.

A hundred hours could turn into a lifetime if she screwed this up.

By the time she drove into the parking lot of the Hope's Crossing Recreation Center in Silver Strike Canyon, the butterflies were in full-fledged stampede mode.

She was five minutes early, she saw with relief as she climbed out of her SUV and walked into the building.

Construction on the recreation center had been under way during her last visit home for Pearl's funeral. The building was really quite lovely, designed by world-renowned architect Jackson Lange. Created of stone, cedar planks and plenty of glass, the sprawling structure complemented the mountainous setting well for being so large.

It also appeared to be busy. The parking lot was filled with several dozen cars, which she considered quite impressive for a weekday morning in December.

She wasn't exactly sure how A Warrior's Hope fit into the picture, but she supposed she had a hundred hours to figure that out.

The butterflies went into swarm-mode as she walked through the front doors into a lobby that wouldn't have looked out of place in one of the hotels at the ski resort.

She stood for a moment just inside the sliding glass doors, hating these nerves zinging through her. Spying a sign that read A Warrior's Hope at one desk, she drew in a steady breath in an effort to conceal her anxiety and approached.

The woman seated behind the computer was younger than Genevieve and busy on a phone call that seemed to revolve around airline arrangements. She held up a finger in a universal bid for patience and finished her call.

"Sorry," she said when she replaced the phone receiver on the cradle. "I've been trying to reach the airline for *days* to make sure they know we need special arrangements to transport some medical equipment when our new guys arrive next week."

"Ah." Gen wasn't quite sure what else to say. "I'm Genevieve Beaumont. I believe you were expecting me."

The woman looked blank for a moment then her face lit up. "Oh! You're one of the community-service people. Spence said you were coming today. Our computers have been down. No internet, no email, and wouldn't you know, our IT guy is on vacation. I've been so crazy trying to track down somebody else to help I forgot you were coming. I'm Chelsea Palmer. I'm the administrative assistant to Eden Davis, the director of A Warrior's Hope."

"Hi, Chelsea."

She didn't recognize the young woman and couldn't see any evidence Chelsea knew her—or *of* her—either.

"I don't suppose you know anything about computers, do you?" the woman asked hopefully.

Gen gave a short laugh. "On a good day, I can usually figure out how to turn them on but that's the extent of my technical abilities. And sometimes I can't even do that."

Chelsea gave her a friendly smile. She was quite pretty, though she wore a particularly unattractive shade of yellow. She could also use a little more subtlety in her makeup.

Gen certainly wasn't going to tell her that. Instead, she would relish the promise of that friendly smile. Around Hope's Crossing, she found it refreshing when people didn't know who she was. Here, many saw her as snobbish and cold. She had no idea how to thaw those perceptions.

She had loved that about living in Paris, where her friends didn't care about her family, her connections, her past.

"Thanks anyway," Chelsea said. "I'll figure something out. My ex-boyfriend works in IT up at the resort. He agreed to come take a look at things."

"Even though he's an ex?" She hadn't spoken with Sawyer since the day she threw his ring back at him.

"I know, right? But we left things on pretty good terms. He's not a bad guy. . . . He was only a little more interested in his video games than me, you know? I decided that wasn't for me."

"Understandable."

Chelsea's gaze shifted over Gen's shoulder and her face lit up. "Hey, Dylan! Eden said you would be stopping in this morning."

"And here I am. Hi. Chelsea, right?"

"One two-second conversation in line at the grocery store and you remembered my name."

Gen didn't like the way all her warm feelings toward the other woman trickled away. Friends weren't that easy to come by here in Hope's Crossing. She certainly couldn't throw one away because she was feeling unreasonably territorial toward Dylan, even if *she* had been the one shackled to the man.

She didn't blame Chelsea for that little moment of flirtatiousness. Dylan still needed a haircut. Regardless, he looked quite delicious. Even the black eye patch only made him more attractive somehow, probably because the eye not concealed behind it looked strikingly blue in contrast.

She thought of that moment when she had nearly fallen on the ice a few days earlier, when he had caught her and held her against his chest for a heartbeat.

And then the humiliation of his words, basically accusing her of being so shallow she recoiled in disgust when he touched her, which was *so* not true.

"Genevieve." He again said her name as her Parisian friends did and for some strange reason she found the musical syllables incredibly sexy spoken in that gruff voice.

"Is that how you say your name?" Chelsea asked in surprise. "I thought it was Gen-e-vieve."

She managed to tamp down the inappropriate reaction to the man. "Either way works," she said to Chelsea. "Or you could simply call me Gen."

"Thanks. I'll do that."

The young woman turned her attention back to Dylan. She tucked her hair behind her ear—her *pointy* ear, Gen thought, before she chided herself for her childishness in noticing. She was a horrid person, as superficial as everyone thought.

"We're all so excited you're finally coming to help us," Chelsea said. "Eden has been over the moon since she heard about your, er, little brush with the law."

"Good to know I could make everybody's day," he said dryly, but Chelsea didn't appear to notice.

"It's going to be *perfect,*" she exclaimed. "You're going to be great! Exactly what we need."

She had said nothing of the sort to Genevieve, yet another piece of evidence in what she was beginning to suspect—that her presence was superfluous here, an unnecessary addendum. The organizers of the program wanted Dylan to help out at A Warrior's Hope because of his own perspective and experience. She, on the other hand, was little more than collateral damage.

"Where is Eden?" she finally interjected.

"She's at the pool with Spence and our new program coordinator, Mac Scanlan."

"I thought Eden was in charge," Genevieve said.

"Technically, she is. She's the executive director, in charge of fundraising, planning, coordinating events etc. We just hired a new person to actually run the activities. He's spending the day familiarizing himself with the facilities. She told me to send you to the pool the minute you both arrive."

Which had been several minutes earlier, but who was counting?

"Thanks," Genevieve said.

"I'm supposed to make you ID badges first, but we'll have to do that later, when my system is back in action. You know where to go, right? Through the main doors there and down the first hall."

Dylan seemed reluctant to move. Apparently Genevieve would have to take the lead. She followed Chelsea's directions, aware of him coming up behind her.

"You made it," she said to Dylan as they entered the hallway.

"You didn't think I'd show?"

"Given your general reluctance to this whole idea, I guess I wouldn't have been surprised if you had decided you'd rather go to jail."

"I'm still not discounting that possibility."

She smiled a little. "I don't even know what I'm doing here. Chelsea's right. You are in a far better position than anybody else, especially me."

"So everybody says. I'm not seeing it."

"You know what it's like to be injured in battle, to have to rebuild your life."

"Right. I'm doing a hell of a job, aren't I?"

Genevieve flashed him a quick look. "Better than I would in your situation," she answered truthfully.

"You would probably start designing a fashion line for one-armed pirate wannabes and go on to make millions of dollars."

She laughed. "The only one-armed pirate wannabe I know doesn't seem particularly interested in fashion."

He gave her a mock offended look. "What do you mean? I wore a bolo, didn't I? I thought I was going for the hipster look."

"Or something," she answered.

He snorted but said nothing as they moved toward the door at the end of the hall where she could see the flickering blue of water.

"You were wrong the other day," she said when they nearly reached it.

He paused and gave her a curious look. "You'll have to be more specific. I'm wrong about a lot of things."

She fiercely wished she hadn't said anything but she couldn't figure out a way to back down now.

"Er, you implied I flinched away when you touched me—that I was, I don't know, disgusted or something because you're, er, missing your arm. That wasn't it. You just . . ." Her voice trailed off.

"I just . . ." he prodded.

"You make me nervous," she said in a rush. "It has nothing to do with any eye patch or . . . or missing hand. It's just . . . you."

His eyebrow rose and he studied her for a long moment, so long she could feel herself flush. "How refreshingly honest of you, Ms. Beaumont."

"I just didn't want you to think I'm—What's the word you used? Er, chickenshit."

He laughed as she pushed open the door to the pool area and the sound echoed through the cavernous space.

Several people congregating beside the pool looked over at the sound and Genevieve recognized Spence Gregory and Dylan's sister, Charlotte, as well as a man in a wheelchair and another woman she didn't know.

"I wasn't sure you would make it," Spence said to Dylan when they reached them, holding out his hand. After a slight pause, Dylan took it.

"Why does everybody keep saying that?" he asked.

"No reason." Charlotte hugged him and he gave her an awkward sort of pat with his right arm.

"I'm so glad you agreed to do this," his sister said.

"You made it impossible for me to refuse, didn't you?"

"Don't blame me. It was all Pop's idea, and Andrew's the one who ran with it. Though I probably should confess that Spence *might* have mentioned to Harry Lange how much we'd like to have you volunteer here and I believe Harry *might* have mentioned it to Judge Richards during one of their poker games."

Charlotte stepped away from her brother and gave Genevieve a cool smile. "Hello, Genevieve. We're glad you agreed to help, too. We have a strong core of volunteers already, but we're always glad for more."

Genevieve had enough experience with polite falsehoods to recognize one when she heard it. She supposed she shouldn't be surprised. Charlotte probably blamed her for her brother's troubles in the first place.

"I'm happy to help." She was an old hand at polite falsehoods herself.

Spencer Gregory stepped up. "Good to see you again. I didn't have the chance to say hello when we saw you at the airport last week."

He really was gorgeous up close. She didn't follow baseball but she knew Smokin' Hot Spence Gregory was a nickname given only in part for the man's fastball. Oddly, despite those long lashes and that particularly charming smile, he didn't make her nerves flutter at all, unlike others in the room she could mention.

"My father loved to tell business associates from out of town how you used to be our paper boy."

"I hope I was a good one."

"The best, according to my father."

Spence smiled and gestured to the other two people. "Dylan, Genevieve, this is Eden Davis, our executive director, and Mac Scanlan, who just started this week as our program coordinator."

"What is your role at A Warrior's Hope?" Genevieve asked, trying to keep things straight in her head.

"I'm the director of the entire recreation center. A Warrior's Hope is only one part of what we do here."

"But it was his idea and he's the fundraising genius behind it." Charlotte smiled with far more warmth than she had shown Genevieve. Spence aimed that charmer of a grin down at her, and even if she hadn't seen them together at the airport, she would have easily picked up that the two of them were *together.*

The once-fat-and-frumpy Charlotte Caine was

involved with Smokin' Hot Spence Gregory. She still couldn't quite believe it.

"It's become Charlotte's baby, too. She organizes all the volunteers."

"What do you think we'll be doing?" she asked. "I'm really good at filing, correspondence, that kind of thing. And I've had a little experience with fundraising for a few charities my family supports."

"Just for the record, I'm not good at any of those things," Dylan offered.

Charlotte gave her brother a sly smile. "I've got just the project for both of you. Yesterday Sam Delgado, our contractor, and his crew put the finishing touches on several cabins for our guests. The first group to use them will be coming in first thing Monday morning. Before they arrive, we need to decorate the cabins for Christmas. That's where you two come in."

Chapter Five

This was his version of hell.

Yeah, he had spent a combined total of six of the past ten years in the Middle East through his various deployments, four of those in direct combat. He was a trained army ranger, sent in to dangerous hot spots for difficult missions.

He had seen and done things that kept him up nights—and had spent months in rehab, a very special kind of misery.

He would rather go back to living in a tent where the sand seeped into every available crevice, wearing seventy-five pounds of gear in a-hundred-twenty-degree weather without showering for weeks, than endure this torture his wicked sister had planned for him.

He stood in a large storage room in a back corner of the recreation center surrounded by boxes and crates.

"Isn't there something else I could be doing right now?" he asked, with more than a little desperation.

"I can't think of a thing," Charlotte said cheerfully. "We want these cabins to be perfect, a home away from home for these guys—and one woman—while they're here. We want to make this a perfect holiday."

He wanted to tell his sister she was wasting her time, but he had already tooted that particular horn enough.

"We'll do a fabulous job. Don't worry." Genevieve beamed with excitement. Why shouldn't she? This was probably right up her alley. Hang some lights, put up a few ornaments. Nothing so uncomfortable as actually *talking* to any wounded veterans—present company excluded.

He remembered what she had said earlier—that he made her nervous and it had nothing to do with his physical disfigurements.

He didn't believe her. Not really. How could he? She was a perfect, pampered little princess and he was scarred and ugly. They were Beauty and the Beast, only this particular beast couldn't be twinkled back into his old self, the one without missing parts.

"I'm sure you will, Genevieve," Charlotte was saying. "You have such an instinctive sense of style. When I heard about your little, uh, legal trouble, I knew you would be perfect to help us get the cabins ready for their first guests."

Genevieve looked surprised and flattered at Charlotte's words. "I graduated with a degree in interior design," she said. "Eventually I hope to open my own design firm."

"Then you really are perfect."

"I'll do my best. I saw some really beautiful lights in Paris. They had these little twinkly snowflakes and each one was unique. They were stunning. You don't have anything like that, do you?"

Charlotte pressed her lips together to keep in the smile he could see forming there. "We didn't buy our lights in Paris this year," she said with a dryness he wasn't sure Gen would catch. "You'll have to be content with the cheap ones from the big box store."

"I suppose we can make those work," she answered.

"You'll have to, I'm afraid."

"What about the trees?"

"Also from a big box store. But they're all prelit, which is a big plus."

"We'll make it wonderful. You'll see. Won't we, Dylan?"

"Wonderful," he repeated. Why did he suddenly feel as if he'd been dragged by a couple of high-school cheerleaders to help decorate for a homecoming dance?

He could really use a beer right about now.

"Aren't you supposed to be working?" he asked Charlotte, mostly to change the subject from snowflakes and Christmas trees. "Who's running Sugar Rush while you're here bossing around the reprobate help?"

Her haughty look rivaled anything Genevieve Beaumont might deliver.

"I have a staff, you know. They're very qualified to run the place without me."

"Even at Christmas, the busiest time of year?"

"Even then. I took today and Monday off so I can help Eden and Spence get everything ready for the group coming in next week."

She glowed whenever she talked about the things she loved: their family, her gourmet candy store in town, A Warrior's Hope . . . and Spencer Gregory and his daughter, Peyton.

He still wasn't sure how he felt about Spence and Charlotte together. When they were growing up, the man had been one of his closest friends. They had gone on camping trips together, played ball, even double-dated a time or two.

Their lives had taken very different paths in the years since Spence's mom used to work at Pop's café, Dylan's to the military and Spence's to a life of fame and riches—and eventual scandal—in Major League Baseball. Dylan still wasn't convinced the guy was good enough for his baby sister but it was obvious the two were crazy in love.

"I hope this doesn't sound rude," Genevieve said, "but I have to say it. You look completely *amazing.*"

Charlotte looked startled. "Thank you. Why would that be rude?"

"Just because . . . you know. How you were before."

Charlotte had always been amazing, as far as Dylan was concerned. Kind and funny and generous. Trust Genevieve not to be able to see past a few extra pounds.

"I just think it's fantastic. It must have been so difficult to lose all that weight when you spend all day surrounded by all those empty calories at your store," she went on. "How did you do it?"

Charlotte looked a little disconcerted by the blunt question. "Willpower, I suppose." Her gaze flickered to Dylan then back to Gen.

"The truth is, when Dylan almost died last year, I realized how off track my own life had become. While he lay in a hospital bed fighting to survive, I realized my own unhealthy habits were slowly killing me. I had been given the precious gift of life and I was wasting it. Dylan's challenges had been thrust upon him, but I was choosing mine every day. It was pretty sobering."

How had this become about him? Dylan shifted, wishing he could still tell his sister to shut up—though even when they were kids, if Pop had heard him, he would have had to scrub dishes at the café for a week.

He didn't like to think about that miserable time when antibiotic-resistant infections had ravaged his system and left him as weak as a baby —and he especially didn't like Charlotte giving Genevieve one more reason to see him as an object of pity.

He jumped up. "I'm going to start hauling some of these boxes down to the cabins."

"Oh, you don't have to do that," Charlotte said. "I can grab a couple of the guys who work at the recreation center to help."

"This is why I'm here, isn't it?"

Before she could argue—something his little sister had always been very adept at—he stacked a couple of boxes and lifted them with his arm, bracing them against his chest with his prosthetic.

"Don't be a stubborn jerk," she said. "I'm sure

there's a dolly or cart or something. You don't have to carry all these boxes down to the cabins by yourself."

"I've got it," he snapped and walked out before either she or Genevieve could stop him.

It was going to take him the whole damn afternoon to carry all the boxes down but he didn't care. He would take monotonous physical exertion any day over seeing that pity in Genevieve's eyes.

When he returned from carrying the first load of boxes to the five small cabins along the river, he found Genevieve and Charlotte loading a couple of wheeled carts with more boxes.

He frowned. "You didn't think I could carry them on my own?"

"This is about efficiency," his sister answered. "I won't let you spend four of the remaining hours you owe us schlepping boxes back and forth when the three of us can do it this way in a few trips."

Okay, she had a point, though he didn't want to admit it.

"Fine," he muttered, then directed his efforts to stacking the carts better for maximum-load capacity.

He ended up pulling one of the heavily laden carts while Genevieve and Charlotte maneuvered the other one together and he tried not to notice the nice rear view that had landed him in this mess in the first place.

He had to admit, his sister was right—as usual. They had all the boxes transported to the cabins and dispersed among them in only an hour, with Charlotte directing where everything should go.

The log structures weren't anything fancy, maybe a total of about six hundred square feet each. They seemed well laid out, with a large living area combined with a kitchen then two separate bedrooms and a roomy bathroom. Probably because they were so close to the river and the inherent flood potential, the cabins were built above grade but the cleverly designed landscaping created a natural wheelchair ramp into each one, which made it far easier to roll the carts to the porches.

The decor inside was what he considered Western chic—a lot of antlers, rich colors, cowboy themes. Each had big windows to provide warm natural light, with sweeping views to the river on one side and the mountains on the other.

"That should be the last of it," Charlotte said as they carried the final box inside the cabin farthest from the main building.

Genevieve pulled off her fluffy mittens and looked around at the space. "Goodness, it's tiny. There's hardly room for a Christmas tree in here," she exclaimed.

Charlotte looked amused. "This is bigger than most base housing. Am I right, Dylan?"

He shrugged. He had always rented off-base when he wasn't deployed. Sometimes a guy needed a break from the life. "The whole place would fit inside your bedroom, right?" he asked Gen.

She frowned, giving the matter serious consideration. "My room at my parents' house, maybe. But I lived in much smaller places in Paris. You wouldn't believe how tiny the flats there are—and how much they charge for them. It's really quite absurd."

He didn't comment since his only experience with Paris was a layover once when he was en route to a mission in Central Africa.

"I was planning to put the trees up there in the corner between the sofa and love seat."

Gen moved to the spot and slowly revolved with her arms out, gauging the space. "That should work."

Charlotte glanced at her watch. "Actually, let me rephrase. I was planning on the two of *you* putting the trees up there. I've got to run."

A ridiculous little spasm of panic burst through him, in no small measure at the idea of being alone in these cozy little cabins with Genevieve.

He had to wonder if his sister wanted a little payback for her frustration with his attitude these past months since he had returned to Hope's Crossing.

"You two should be able to handle this without

any problem. These are the keys to all six cabins. As you saw when we dropped off the boxes, the layout is the same, only the furniture and colors are different. You can set up the Christmas trees in the same spot in all of them. Just lock up when you're done. See you."

She left in a rush, leaving behind a long, agonizing silence.

Yeah. Definitely his version of hell. He couldn't imagine a deeper misery than an afternoon putting up Christmas decorations with Jahn-Vi-Ev Freaking Beaumont—even if she did look particularly lovely in a fancy little tilted knit hat that matched her scarf and roses in her cheeks from the past hour's exertion.

She gave him a sideways glance, and he thought he saw nerves in her gaze. Maybe she wasn't any more thrilled about being in an enclosed space with him right now.

She should be nervous. He was feeling particularly . . . predatory right about now.

"This is *tons* better than the things I expected we might have to do, don't you think? I mean, putting up Christmas decorations is fun. I thought I might have to, I don't know, help with therapy or something."

She tended to chatter when she was nervous. Under normal circumstances, that would have set his teeth on edge, but with Gen, he actually found it . . . endearing, though he wasn't quite sure why.

"Have you ever put up a Christmas tree before?" he asked gruffly.

She looked at the long box with the tree label. "Um. No. You?"

He shook his head. "I haven't spent a Christmas stateside in seven years—except for last year, when I was in the hospital."

"I'm afraid we're going to be in trouble. I've never needed a tree of my own. I came home from Paris for Christmas the past few years and never wanted to go to all the trouble to put one up since I was coming home anyway. Before that, my sorority mother or roommates always took care of it."

"Well, we're both obviously underqualified for this job. We'd better let Eden know she'll have to find some other criminals to help her out."

He supposed it *had* been a while since he had felt like joking about much of anything, and apparently he was out of practice, at least judging by the uncertain look Genevieve was sending him.

"Oh. We'll figure it out. Don't you think?"

Sure, they could figure it out. How hard could it be? But he had only one hand that worked and he couldn't imagine that would make the process easier.

After much debate that morning, he had ended up wearing one of his prosthetics. He didn't like either of them but this one was slightly less annoying than the other. He had also packed his Leatherman multitool, invaluable when driving in changeable Colorado weather situations, where a guy never knew what might happen.

Now in resignation, he pulled out the Leatherman and used it to rip the tape on the Christmas-tree box. Once open, the contents just looked like a big pile of green bristly branches.

Genevieve peered over his shoulder. "Is that the way it's supposed to look? It seems kind of . . . smushed. That can't be right."

"Let's hope it bushes out after we pull it out. Give me a hand here."

Together, they lifted the pieces out, power cords trailing, and set them side by side on the wood flooring of the kitchen.

Genevieve studied the sections then nudged one with her foot. "This looks like the biggest one. Don't you think it goes on the bottom?"

He fought a smile at her serious contemplation of the task at hand. "Good guess."

After struggling to figure what went where for a few more moments, Gen discovered a sheet of directions concealed under packaging in the box. The rest of the assembly went off without a hitch.

He maneuvered the tree into the corner where Charlotte had indicated, which had a conveniently located outlet. He crouched down and plugged it in and the seven hundred white lights lit up the small space.

"Oh. Look!" she exclaimed softly. "It's beautiful!"

He was looking, but not at the tree. The flickering lights reflected in her eyes and she seemed to glow from the inside out, with all that blond hair and the deliciously soft sweater that clung to her.

He was staring, he realized with dismay.

"Even for a cheap department-store tree?" he asked, his voice more caustic than teasing.

He was sorry for the words when her expression of joy seeped away and her features closed.

"I'm not saying a designer tree wouldn't look more real but this one will do for here."

He fought the ridiculous urge to apologize for shattering the magic like a cheap glass ornament. "Great. One down, five more to go."

An hour later, each of the cabins had a Christmas tree in the corner. They had developed a certain rhythm to it. He would open the box, she would separate the pieces and they would work together to assemble them. By the last one, she didn't clap her hands with glee when he tested the lights, only fluffed out a few of the crinkled branches.

"Now we can decorate them," she said. "What a relief they're already prelit. My dad used to complain so much about his struggles to string lights on the tree."

He had a tough time picturing the starchy

mayor with his hands covered in sap, trying to twist Christmas lights around tree branches.

"I would have thought the Beaumont family hired somebody to do that kind of menial labor."

She leaned back against the kitchen counter, a pensive, almost sad look in her eyes. "We hired a decorator after we moved into the new house in the canyon when I was ten. In the early days when we lived over near Miner's Park, we always decorated it ourselves. It used to be a wonderful family time. The first Saturday afternoon in December, we would go up to Snowflake Canyon and cut down our Christmas tree. My mom would make hot chocolate and we would all bundle up and set out. Charlie was always so cute in his snowsuit."

It matched a lot of his own memories and he was aware of a familiar, hollow pain. His mother had died of cancer when he was a teenager, and he still sometimes fiercely missed her softness and warmth.

"After my dad would wrestle with the lights for a couple of hours, we would spend all evening hanging the decorations, making sure each strand of tinsel hung just so."

His mom hadn't been nearly as fastidious. Their tree had always been one big haphazard jumble of keepsakes, photographs, sloppy ornaments made by little hands. A glorious, magical shambles.

The Christmas after Margaret died, none of

them had felt much like celebrating. A few days before Christmas, Charlotte had begged Pop to get a tree. He remembered finding her in the living room in tears with boxes of ornaments open around her.

Teenage boys weren't always the most emotionally sensitive creatures, but he had done his best to comfort her and had ended up helping her decorate the tree the best they could.

Come to think of it, that had probably been the last ornament he had hung.

"Yeah, I'm afraid tree decorating isn't really my thing," he said. "Since you seem to be all over it like sugar on a doughnut, maybe I'll go search out Eden and see if she wants to put me to work doing something else."

Anything else.

"You'll do no such thing." She frowned at him. "I can't decorate six trees by myself! They have to be done today and they have to be *perfect*."

"I really think this is a job you can handle better by yourself."

She narrowed her gaze. "Now who's being, er, chickenshit?"

He didn't want to do this. The very idea of spending even five minutes hanging Christmas decorations just about made his toes curl. But he was no coward.

He looked at the sprawl of boxes, at the bare Christmas tree, at the lovely woman standing in front of him with a barely suppressed crackle of excited energy at the prospect ahead of her.

He sighed and accepted his fate. "Fine. Where do we start?"

Genevieve could think of far worse things than decorating six cute little cabins for the holidays.

As they started opening boxes to see what she had to work with, she wondered if adding a few festive touches to Grandma Pearl's house might brighten up the place.

Her grandmother had adored Christmas. Every year, she had turned the outside of her house into a blinking, tacky wonderland. Plastic Santas, snowmen, polar bears. Gen hadn't wandered into the storage room in the basement yet, but she could only guess that it would probably still be stacked high with boxes containing Pearl's huge crèche collection.

Her grandmother probably had a hundred different manger scenes. The Holy Family in a shelled-out coconut she had bought on a trip to Hawaii, a teak-carved set a friend carried home on her lap from Australia, chiseled ebony from Ghana dressed in tribal clothing.

A few were elegant, even artful, but most were tacky, brought home from Pearl's extensive travels to Branson, Mount Rushmore, Florida, Las Vegas.

And her grandmother hadn't been content to

collect alone. From the time Gen was a little girl, her grandmother would give her a new Nativity set each year. She used to love decorating her bedroom with them, touching each figure, setting them around her bedroom. After she became a teenager, she had gotten tired of the hassle of it.

Maybe she would pick a few of her favorite sets from Pearl's collection—*not* the one that featured Homer and Marge Simpson, certainly—and set them out while she was living in her grand-mother's house.

The garland for the tree in this cabin was made of red wooden beads strung together. It probably wouldn't have been her choice, but it fit the cozy setting.

She draped it carefully then stood back to gauge the results. "Does that look good?" she asked Dylan.

Her dour companion gave a cursory look. "Sure. Fine."

She sighed. They had been doing this for only twenty minutes and it felt like forever, especially with this uncomfortably awkward silence between them.

She would far rather be doing this with some-one else. Eden, Charlotte. Even Mac.

"We ought to have some kind of Christmas music," she said suddenly.

"I won't sing, if that's what you're getting at."

She wouldn't be surprised if he sang beautifully, judging by his low, melodious speaking voice. At least when he wasn't grumping and grousing at her.

"I wouldn't dare ask," she retorted, stepping away from the tree and heading toward the well-outfitted entertainment center against the wall. She turned on the TV and found, as she suspected from the dish she had seen on the roof, that the cabin was connected to a satellite system. She flipped through channels until she found a station streaming Christmas music. A jazzy version of "Jingle Bells" filled the small space.

"Correct me if I'm wrong," Dylan said after a moment, "but isn't Christmas music what got us in this mess in the first place?"

"It's all about the venue, right? It wasn't appropriate at The Speckled Lizard on a night when I wanted to get sloppy drunk and stupid, but for decorating a Christmas tree, it's perfect."

He started indiscriminately tossing green and red balls on the tree. All her aesthetic senses recoiled from such haphazard decorating, but she forced herself to bite her tongue. She wasn't in charge here. He could decorate however he wanted. At least he was helping.

"Why did you want to get sloppy drunk the other night?" he asked after another silence that somehow didn't seem as uncomfortable with the Christmas music in the background.

"It's a long story."

He gestured to the tree and the overflowing boxes. "We've got nothing but time, sweetheart."

She knew he meant nothing by the endearment. Still, it helped her answer without the customary bitterness that ate away at her whenever she thought about her father's ultimatum.

"I'm not exactly thrilled about being back in Hope's Crossing."

He chuckled. "No kidding?"

"That afternoon, my parents gave me an ultimatum. I have to stay here until I manage to flip my grandmother's house, which is a complete nightmare. It's going to take me *forever.* Pearl had absolutely no design sense whatsoever."

"What do you mean? When we were kids, we always begged Mom and Dad to drive us past your grandmother's house to see her Christmas light display."

She shuddered. "Her *hideous* Christmas light display, you mean."

"Kids don't care about things like that. The bigger and brighter the better as far as the younger set is concerned."

"And some in the older set. Grandma Pearl, anyway. Her house is . . . well, something to behold. I packed my suitcase and moved in after my little chat with my dear parents. After just an hour, the magnitude of the task at hand sort of . . . smacked me in the face and I needed the escape."

"Ah. That explains a lot. In other words, it was an interior-design crisis. You should have explained that to the judge. 'Yes, I punched that woman, Your Honor, but there were extenuating circumstances. Two words—*shag carpeting.*' "

She laughed, amazed at further evidence that Dylan Caine had a sense of humor. "You can joke about it, but you wouldn't be laughing if you saw the place. Every time I walk through the door, I feel like I'm entering a time warp, discoing back to the seventies."

"I'm sure it's not that bad."

"Oh, it is."

She told him about some of the low points— the layers after layers of wallpaper, the tile in the bathroom, the blue carpet in a couple of the bedrooms.

"Where are you going to start?"

He seemed genuinely interested—either that or he was only trying to stave off boredom while they decorated the tree.

"I should really gut the place and start over, especially the bathrooms and the kitchen, but I don't have any kind of budget. I'm going to focus on fixes that are cheap. I'm renting a steamer to take off the wallpaper. I figure I can paint for the cost of a couple buckets."

"You ever painted a room?"

She made a face. "I have a degree in interior design. I know how to paint a room."

"You know how, but have you ever actually done it?"

"For your information, we had to as part of our course work." She didn't add that four of her fellow students had worked together on the assigned project, redecorating a few rooms at a group home in Denver for people with developmental disabilities.

She had mostly cleaned brushes and picked up lunch for the other three, but she figured she had absorbed enough information through the experience that she could pick things up as she went along.

"I'm a long way from painting, anyway. It's going to take me *weeks* to steam off the wallpaper."

"Weeks, huh?"

"I'm not kidding. I counted six layers of wallpaper. I think every time Pearl was in a mood, she would slap up another design on top of what was already there."

She went on about her plans for the house, and before she realized it, the tree was finished. She had jabbered the entire time, barely aware of it.

He was going to think she was the brainless debutante everyone else did.

"Sorry to ramble." To her astonished horror, she could feel heat soak her cheeks and knew she must be blushing. "I tend to get carried away."

"I didn't mind," he said gruffly. She had the

strangest feeling he wasn't only saying the words to be nice. Dylan Caine was many things but she wasn't sure *nice* was among them.

"Well, I'm sorry anyway. See what being alone in that house for only a few days is doing for me? I'm turning into my grandma Pearl, ready to talk anybody's ear off."

"If you don't mind, I've got two of those for now and I'd like to keep it that way, all things considered."

How could he joke about his missing parts? She did not understand this man.

Needing a little distance, she took a look around the cabin and decided on a whim what else was needed.

"I'm going to go outside and cut some evergreens to arrange on the mantel, along with the lights your sister was talking about. That will make it perfect in here."

He looked wary. "Fresh pine boughs weren't on Charlotte's list."

"This is what you call improvisation," she said with a smile.

His gaze shifted to her mouth and stayed there for just an instant, long enough for heat to bloom inside her and her thoughts to tangle like strings of Grandma Pearl's Christmas lights.

She grabbed the pair of scissors Charlotte had provided them for cutting ribbons and hurried outside into the December afternoon.

The cold mountain air slapped more than a little sense back into her.

Any attraction to Dylan Caine was absolutely ridiculous. Two people could not be more opposite. He was gruff, rough-edged, slightly dangerous. He had seen things, probably *done* things she couldn't even imagine, and he had the battle scars to prove it.

She was, in his words, a cream puff. Why would a man like him ever be interested in her?

What had she done in her life that had any meaning? Beyond the project to help that group home where she had made only a halfhearted effort, what had she ever done for someone else?

Oh, her family donated to various charities. Her mother sat on some philanthropic boards in town and helped out with a few causes.

Those were her parents' efforts, desultory as they might be.

The past two years, Genevieve had spent in self-indulgence and self-pity. She was really rather tired of it.

Even if her parents hadn't reined her in, she wanted to think she soon would have come to that realization on her own—but she would have done it in her lovely little flat in Le Marais, not stuck here.

She sighed as she clipped another pine branch. She didn't have any business being attracted to the compelling, dangerous Dylan Caine, but they could at least be friends. She might be as crazy as Grandma Pearl but she thought he had enjoyed listening to her talk about the house.

She had a feeling maybe he needed a friend as badly as she did.

As much as he loved his baby sister, right now he wanted to wring her neck.

Was this what he had come to? Of all the assignments she might have found for him, why the hell would she put him to work hanging Christmas decorations with Genevieve Beaumont? Did she think he wasn't capable of anything more?

He glowered as he carried a couple of the empty boxes outside to the porch to be hauled away later.

It didn't help anything that when he looked at Gen, all he could see was someone beautiful and perfect, with a whole world of possibilities ahead of her. She might be going through a tough time right now—though, really, did she think dealing with her grandmother's ugly house was the worst thing that could happen to a person?—but life would even out for her. Her parents would probably come around and she would return to Paris to her life of frivolity and fun.

He shoved a smaller box into another one a little harder than he'd intended and it ripped just as Genevieve returned to the porch with her arms full of evergreens.

"Sorry it took me so long but I tried to cut from the side of the trees that faces away from the recreation center and the cabins."

"Won't those turn brown before Christmas?" Even from here, he could smell them—tart, crisp, citrusy.

She frowned and looked down at the boughs in her arms. "My parents always have a fresh-cut wreath and it's good from Thanksgiving until New Year's. I think they should be okay for a few weeks, don't you?"

With her cheeks flushed from the cold and her nose an even brighter pink, she looked fresh and sweet and not at all like the snobby bitch he wanted to believe her. She was also as unreachable as the Christmas star on top of the sixty-foot spruce in front of City Hall.

His stump ached suddenly from the cold and the exertion.

"How should I know?" he snapped, suddenly pissed at the whole damn world. "Do I look like a freaking expert on Christmas decorating?"

Her eyes went wide at his sudden attack, and her breath hitched in a little. He saw surprised hurt in her eyes for only an instant before she composed her lovely features into that cold, supercilious expression he was beginning to suspect she donned for self-protection.

"Sorry," she answered, her voice icicle-cool. "My mistake. Forget I asked your opinion."

She brushed past him on her way inside, stirring the air with the thick scent of pine mingled with the vanilla-and-cinnamon scent that was hers alone.

He probably should apologize for his bad temper, but he decided to let things ride. Better she think he was a bad-tempered bastard.

"I'll start opening the boxes in the next cabin over," he said curtly.

"Fine."

He might as well have been invisible for all the notice she paid him as she started arranging pine branches on the mantel.

After a moment, he turned and stalked down the sidewalk to the cabin next door.

He found the garland in the first box he opened. He should probably leave it for her to hang when she finished in the other cabin, but as he gazed down at the coil of intertwined thin ironwork stars of this one, he felt a ridiculous urge to atone somehow for hurting her feelings.

He picked it up and started draping it around the little tree, trying his best to imitate the artful way he had seen her hang the garland in the first cabin. It was harder than it looked, though he wanted to think he had done a passable job.

When she finally came in sometime later, her nose was a little pink, her eyes slightly swollen. She looked as if she had been fighting tears—or maybe even giving in to them—and his stomach felt hollow.

"I know. It looks terrible," he muttered.

Not only that, but hanging the garland by himself hadn't been nearly as enjoyable as decorating the other tree had been with both of them working together.

"I didn't say that."

"You didn't have to." He could either be miserable and short-tempered or he could try to get along with her. They still had four-and-a-half trees to go. It didn't have to be *complete* torture.

"I'm obviously not as gifted in this arena as you are," he said gruffly.

"Few people are," she said, voice smart as she stepped forward to reposition one section of garland.

She smelled delicious, he couldn't help noticing again as she nudged him out of the way so she could move another loop of garland.

He had to stop picking up those things, he told himself.

She was the perfectly beautiful Genevieve Beaumont, pampered and adored princess.

He was . . . not.

"There. That should do it," she said. "You had the basics down. Now it's only a matter of finessing the details, see?"

In her naturally husky voice, the benign words sounded vaguely sexual.

"Yeah. I can see that," he said. "That looks much better."

She offered a hesitant smile and his heart gave a hard little tug.

Kissing her right now would be a really terrible idea. The worst. So why couldn't he stop thinking about it?

He shoved away from the wall. "Since you're obviously better at this, why don't you finish up here and *I'll* go cut down some evergreens for this cabin and the others."

"Can you—" she began then stopped. Could he what? Clip the branches? It would probably be a little harder than it should be, especially with only a pair of scissors instead of pruning loppers, but he didn't doubt he could handle it.

"Yes," he said firmly. He held out his hand and she handed over the scissors, still looking a little doubtful.

He grabbed his jacket and waited until he walked outside to shrug into it and then headed toward the thick trees near the river.

He should have brought Tucker with him, he thought as he did his best with the scissors. The coon dog loved to be outside and adored any kind of running water. Sometimes he thought Tuck must have a little water dog in him, as much as he loved chasing skeeters in the little stream that trickled through Dylan's land in Snowflake Canyon.

He stacked the boughs he cut next to a little snow-covered bench beside the groomed trail that ran alongside the river. After he cut what he gauged the appropriate amount of pine boughs for the remaining five cabins, he returned to the bench for the rest.

No rush, he thought. They would be decorating the rest of the day. He figured he deserved five minutes to himself after being around Genevieve all morning.

He used one of the pine branches to sweep snow off the bench and then sat in the quiet little woods, listening to the river's music and the mournful wind in the treetops.

After only a few moments of peace, he heard the crunch of boot steps in snow and tensed, assuming Genevieve had come looking for him.

"It's restful here, isn't it?"

He jerked around at the male voice to find Spence Gregory walking toward him. So much for his mad special-forces skills. The ambush had taken more from him than several good friends and a few things he rather needed.

"Not bad," he answered. "It's a little cold this time of year for meditating on the meaning of life, but it will do."

Spence smiled as he crossed the last few feet between them, wiped off snow on the other side of the bench and sat down. "Don't you have some community service you're supposed to be doing?"

He should probably be embarrassed to be caught slacking, but something told him Spence understood. If he didn't, well, too damn bad.

"Just taking a breather. Genevieve wanted pine boughs to decorate the mantels." With his thumb, he pointed to the pile beside him.

"Sorry. I wasn't riding you," Spence assured him. "How's that working out? Genevieve Beaumont, I mean. I don't know much about her, but Charlotte seemed to think she would try to wiggle out of her sentence after the first hour."

He fought down his immediate urge to defend the woman, who had been working her butt off since they arrived. Just the fact that he *wanted* to defend her to his friend seemed wrong on multiple levels.

"She's fine," he said shortly. "I, on the other hand, am ready to poke one of those pointy star ornaments in my other eye. Come on, Spence. Can't you find something else for me to do? This is a nightmare assignment."

Spence gave a solemn look that didn't fool Dylan for a second, especially when he caught that little gleam of amusement in his friend's eyes. "I'm sorry. I tried, I really did, but Eden and Charlotte tell me decorating the cabins has to be the priority for now, at least until the new group arrives next week. After that, you'll have plenty of other things to fill your hours."

"Can't wait," he muttered.

He wasn't looking forward to any of it. He suspected Spence and Eden and the rest expected him to magically bond with the other veterans, simply because they had a small thing in common. He wasn't seeing it and really wished he could figure out a way to wriggle out of this whole thing.

"It should be fun," Spence said. "We've got a great group coming in. A couple of marines and the rest are army. None of them has been on skis or snowboards before."

He hadn't been skiing since his accident. It ought to be interesting to see how he would do on the turns when he could only plant one pole. He saw a lot of right turns in his future.

"You're wearing one of your prosthetics," Spence said after a minute.

Not his favorite topic of conversation. "For now. The thing is a pain in the ass. Or stump, anyway."

"How is your pain level these days? Charlotte worries about you."

Something else he didn't like to talk about. More than a year after the amputation, he had become used to the occasional phantom aches.

Unfortunately, he wasn't sure he would ever become accustomed to waking up each morning and seeing that empty space starting a few inches below his elbow.

"I'm fine," he said, rising and scooping up the

greenery in one motion. "I'd better take these back before Gen has to come looking for me."

Spence gave him a curious look and Dylan realized using the shortened version of her name probably sounded far too familiar.

His friend said nothing, though, only nodded. "You probably don't want to keep a woman like her waiting."

Dylan scooped up the branches and headed through the snow back to the cabins.

Chapter Six

"So. What do you think?"

Several hours later, the pale afternoon sun filtered in through the cabin windows, illuminating the cheery scene inside—the decorated tree, the red and green ornaments she had hung on ribbons in the windows, the mantelpiece covered in some of the cut pine boughs with white pillar candles popping through as well as a few scattered gold stars and little twinkly lights.

He had just finished hanging more greens that Gen had shaped into a wreath and adorned with red ribbons and more of those glittery gold stars.

The mission furniture in this cabin featured simple oak and wrought-iron accents, sparely elegant lines and simple design. With the ribbons weaving through the entwined elk-antlers chandelier above the small dining room, every inch of the cabin seemed festive and welcoming, even to his untrained eye.

He looked around at all the work they had both done with an odd sense of satisfaction. "It will do," he said.

She was silent and he saw her face fall. "Oh," she said.

He wasn't quite sure why until he realized that what he considered pretty high praise—especially given that he expected most of the guys participating in A Warrior's Hope would just be grateful for a comfortable bed—probably came across as faintly damning.

He cleared his throat and tried again. "You don't need me to tell you the place looks great," he said gruffly. "All six cabins are perfect. You did a good job."

Color seeped into her cheeks. "Thanks. You were really a huge help, too."

He doubted that. His job seemed to mostly consist of doing what he was told—hanging this ornament here, that ribbon there. He had to wonder what any of the guys in his unit would say if they knew he was putting up holiday decorations because of a bar fight over Christmas carols.

He hoped like hell they never found out.

"From here, it looks like the star on top of the tree is a little bit crooked," he said. "I'll see if

I can straighten it out. Where's that step stool?"

She tilted her head with a frown that made her look a little like a puzzled kitten. "Are you sure? It looks okay to me."

"What do you mean? You don't trust the opinion of the man with one eye?"

Her color deepened and she looked flustered. "I didn't say that."

"Where's the stepladder? I'll adjust the star, and if you don't think I'm right, I can move it back where it is now."

"Sure. Okay."

She brought the small stepladder over. He climbed up and tweaked the star slightly, aligning the horizontal points until they looked level to him.

He stepped down again and went to stand by Genevieve. "Is that better?"

She tilted her head one way and then the other, then shifted to face him.

"You were right! It *was* crooked. Wow, that's *tons* better."

He had to chuckle at her reaction, as if he had just single-handedly—yeah, punny—saved Santa's sleigh from enemy combatants.

"I do what I can," he said modestly.

She smiled back at him and a subtle, seductive intimacy seemed to stretch between them, fragile and bright like those glass ornaments gleaming in the windows.

This wouldn't do. He cleared his throat. "I guess that about wraps things up for our first day. Eight hours down, ninety-two something to go."

"Oh, don't remind me." She looked daunted at the prospect of the hours stretching out ahead of them. He couldn't blame her for that.

"Sorry. For now, you should focus on what we accomplished today," he said. "More like what *you* accomplished. I'm sure everyone who stays here will feel welcome in Hope's Crossing."

She nudged his shoulder. "We did it together. We make a pretty good team, Caine."

She smiled, soft and pretty, and a fierce need twisted in his gut. For hours, he had been working closely with her, had been trying not to be intoxicated by the cinnamon-vanilla scent of her, had listened to that contralto voice talk about everything and nothing.

It was more than a guy could take. He wanted to kiss her. Right here, surrounded by all this holiday hoopla. He wanted to lick that sweet bottom lip, to trace his thumb over the arc of her cheekbones, to tangle his fingers in her hair. . . .

He gazed at her and the moment seemed to freeze like the river's edge. It might have been the reflection of the lights from the tree—or maybe his overactive imagination—but he thought he saw something flicker in her eyes, something warm and almost . . . welcoming.

He leaned down an inch, not sure if he had the

stones to take the chance and cover the rest of the distance between them. In the second or two while he was still trying to make up his mind, the door to the small cabin opened, sending a cold rush of air washing over him.

"Here you two are!"

Charlotte's voice effectively shattered that crystalline moment. Gen eased away from him, color rising on her cheekbones.

Yeah. He was going to strangle his sister one of these days.

"Hey," he said, trying for a casual tone.

Charlotte's gaze slid between him and Gen, and he saw concern there before she quickly masked it. Great. He had just given her something else to worry about.

"I checked every cabin and finally found you in the very last one."

"Funny. Seems like it might have made more sense to start with the one that had all the lights on."

She made a little-sister sort of huff. "Yes, but that would have been too easy. Besides, this way I got to look at all the other cabins. I was amazed. They look fantastic! The real greenery was a fantastic touch."

"Don't look at me." Dylan pointed to Genevieve. "It was her idea."

"You cut down most of the branches," Gen said, quick to give him credit where it certainly wasn't due.

"Yeah, but I wouldn't have had the first clue where to put them. That was all you."

"I get it," Charlotte cut in before Gen could add anything else. "It was a team effort. A great one. The cabins turned out better than I imagined —so good, in fact, I need to grab my camera and take some pictures for the website."

"I can do that, if you want," Genevieve offered. "Photography's kind of one of my things. I have a high-resolution digital SLR and a wide-angle lens that would really help capture the whole cabin."

Charlotte made a face. "I have no idea what half of that meant, so I guess that indicates you're far more qualified than I am to take pictures."

"I can bring it tomorrow, if you'd like."

His sister smiled. "That would be fantastic. In fact, if you don't mind, why don't you plan on bringing it with you every day while you're here? We have a small digital camera and one of those GoPro cameras to capture live action when the guys are out on activities, but we could always use a few more photographs taken by somebody who knows what she's doing to use on the website and in our brochures."

"Sure. No problem."

Charlotte took another look around the cabin, focusing on all the clever little touches Genevieve had incorporated.

"I can't believe you're already done," Charlotte

said. "I was afraid it might take the entire week-end to finish decorating all six of the cabins."

Gen had been a bit of a taskmaster but he really hadn't minded. "Does that mean we don't have to come tomorrow?" he asked, only half joking.

Charlotte made another one of those sibling noises of disgust. "Nice try. You're not getting off that easily. We have a million things to do before the new group arrives Monday."

Yeah, he was afraid of that. While they had been working on these cabins, it had been easy to focus only on the task at hand, not the bigger picture.

"This wasn't so bad, was it?" Charlotte asked.

"It had its moments," he answered. Including the one she had interrupted before anything could really begin. "Are we done here?"

"Yes. Actually, that's why I came looking for you, to let you know you could wrap things up and go for the day."

"Great." He grabbed his coat. "See you tomor-row."

He suddenly had a fierce craving to be sitting by his fire with a beer and the quiet, undemanding company of his dog.

Genevieve watched Dylan rush off as if he couldn't stay here in this small cabin another moment. His sister watched him, too, a little frown rippling her forehead.

He had obviously reached the end of his patience

with her. She wasn't sure how he'd endured her mindless chatter as long as he had.

He had almost kissed her. If Charlotte hadn't interrupted them, Gen knew he would have. She wasn't sure what she found more surprising, that he had thought about kissing her—or that she had wanted him to. For hours, she had been thinking about it, wishing for it.

This was completely ridiculous. She was crushing on Dylan Caine—shaggy, cranky, *damaged* Dylan Caine.

He was the exact opposite of the sleek, polished men she usually dated. Men like Sawyer, who used to put almost as much care and attention into his wardrobe and appearance as she did.

Maybe that was what drew her to Dylan, that he was so very different from her norm. He had done things she couldn't begin to imagine. He was tough, hard. Genuine. Unlike Sawyer, who had dreams of following in his father's congressional aspirations, Dylan was the sort of man who could never be a politician because he would say just what he thought, to hell with the consequences.

"Is he always so . . . abrupt?" she asked his sister now.

Charlotte watched after her brother. "I can't believe he made it this long, if you want the truth. I honestly thought he would be climbing the walls after the first hour. Was he a bear all day?"

Gen thought of that moment when he had

stomped outside to gather more pine boughs. He had been gone a long time, so long she had been ready to go search for him in case he'd fallen in the river, when he returned with his arms full of greenery. After that, he had been more relaxed and comfortable, as if those few moments out in nature had centered him or something.

"He had his moments," she said. "I think mostly we managed to tolerate each other. He let me jabber on about whatever, inanities, really, though every once in a while I let him slip into those brooding silences of his."

His sister gave a surprised-sounding laugh. "How thoughtful of you."

Gen shrugged. "I figured it was the least I could do for a returning war hero and all."

When Charlotte laughed again, Gen wanted to bask in the warmth of it. She liked the other woman. In their interactions that day, she had been kind to her, even though Gen could tell she had great reservations about Genevieve's ability to contribute to A Warrior's Hope.

As far as she remembered, Charlotte had never been outright rude to her but she was usually cool—probably because Genevieve had never been particularly nice to her.

She thought of Natalie suddenly and the gulf between them now and felt a wave of loneliness. She had a few close female friends in Paris and she missed them fiercely.

She pushed it away. Once she straightened out her life and sold the house, she could return to Paris and her friends there.

"The problem is," Charlotte answered thoughtfully, "I think we've all indulged those brooding silences for too long, until now Dylan is more comfortable with his own company than engaging in polite conversation. He prefers to hide away at this dilapidated old cabin up in Snowflake Canyon where he doesn't have to talk—or *listen*—to anyone."

Gen didn't want to contradict his sister but she wasn't sure that was true. When she thought about it, Dylan seemed to want her to keep talking. In a strange sort of way, he had almost seemed . . . *soothed* while he listened to her ramble on about living in Le Marais: her favorite candlelit bistro, the pâtisserie she loved, the best museums.

When she ran out of things to talk about and lapsed into silence while they worked, he would target a well-placed question about other countries in Europe she had visited, people she knew there, her plans for Pearl's house, and she would start up again.

Her throat hurt from all that talking, but she was pretty sure he had enjoyed listening to her more than he probably would admit. He had smiled several times and had even chuckled a time or two at one of her stories involving her elderly neighbor and the very large dog who shared her very small flat.

"I'm really hoping that being forced to work at A Warrior's Hope will, I don't know, help drag him out of himself, you know?"

Again, she didn't want to contradict his sister after really only a day spent in the man's company, but she knew a little about interfering family members. "I'm sure you have good intentions and want to help him. But really, if he enjoys being on his own in Snowflake Canyon and isn't hurting anybody by it, that's his call, isn't it?"

Charlotte blinked a little and Gen wished she hadn't said anything. She didn't want to ruin any chance she might have of a friendship with Charlotte. After a moment, the other woman's expression turned pensive.

"That's exactly what he says."

"He should know, don't you think?"

"I suppose you're right. I just can't imagine he's happy up there."

"Again, his call."

"You might be right," Charlotte said. "It's never easy watching someone you care about make choices you can't accept are good for him."

Was that how her parents felt? Were they acting out of a position of concern and not manipulation? She wasn't quite ready to accept that yet.

"Do you have a place to store all these empty boxes?" she asked.

"I was going to have a couple of the guys carry them back to the storage room in the main building, but we might as well take care of it. Do you mind helping me haul them back before you take off?"

"The carts should be down here somewhere. We can probably get them all in one trip."

Together, she and Charlotte loaded the empty boxes onto the two utility carts.

"Thank you again for all your hard work," Charlotte said after they pulled the carts back to the recreation center and stacked the empty boxes in the storage room.

She had accepted early in the day that her sweater was likely ruined. It was too bad, too, as it was one of her favorites. She supposed that served her right for ever being silly enough to think she could wear peach cashmere to work.

"I'm thrilled with the way the cabins look," the other woman said. "It's so much better than I ever imagined."

"You're welcome. Decorating is right up my alley. It's too bad you don't have a hundred more. That would probably fill the rest of the hours, wouldn't it?"

Charlotte laughed and Gen thought how pretty she was now that she had lost all that weight. No wonder Smokin' Hot Spence Gregory was dating her.

As soon as the thought flitted across her brain,

she felt vaguely ashamed of herself for focusing on the superficial. She needed to train herself to look beyond appearances. Really, Charlotte had always been quite lovely, for a large girl.

"I'm afraid you've met and exceeded all our decorating needs. I'm sure we can find plenty of other things to keep you busy, and very few of them should be completely miserable."

"Something to look forward to," Genevieve said with a smile, picking up her purse. "I'll see you tomorrow."

She was almost to the door when Charlotte called her back. "Do you have plans tonight? I'm getting together with some friends for dinner. You could join us if you want."

For a moment, she didn't know what to say. She was a little embarrassed at how excited she was by the invitation. She thought of all those lovely long lunches in Paris when she and her friends would talk about food and fashion, history and even a little politics.

She found it difficult to come up with the perfect balance in her response. She didn't want to come across as giddily overenthusiastic, but she didn't want to be a snotty bitch, either.

Apparently, she mulled it too long. At her lingering silence, Charlotte's friendly smile slid away. "Well, if you want to come, we're meeting at Brazen, the new restaurant that opened this summer in the old firehouse at the top of Main Street."

"Brazen." Alex McKnight's restaurant. All her good feelings dissolved.

"Have you been there? The food is fantastic and the ambience is wonderful, with gorgeous views of downtown."

Alex would be there, and perhaps even her sister Maura. Maura's daughter, Sage, might even show up. The McKnights tended to run in packs.

Every time she thought about the family, she had a sick, greasy feeling in her stomach—part anger, part shame. She had treated them horribly. She knew that. She had been cold and downright mean, and she knew her mother had been worse.

Still, she couldn't help wondering if they had all been laughing at her behind her back for being so stupid she didn't know her fiancé was sleeping around during her entire engagement, with one of the McKnights and with many others.

"I'm sorry. I can't tonight. Maybe another time."

"Sure. It was last-minute anyway. I'm sure we'll have another chance."

She wanted to say yes. She would like to be friends with Charlotte—and not because she had developed a serious crush on the woman's brother. She liked her, and heaven knew, she could use a friend in Hope's Crossing since it appeared all her old crowd didn't have room for her anymore in their busy lives.

As much as she would like to go to dinner with

Charlotte tonight, Gen knew she couldn't. Sometimes, the past dug in with sharp claws and wouldn't let go, no matter how hard a person tried to pry it loose.

He would rather be tortured than admit it, but by the afternoon of his second day working for A Warrior's Hope, Dylan almost wished he had a few more ornaments to hang.

Instead, he was in a large storage room behind the building with Mac Scanlan, the program director for the organization, trying to organize and inventory the huge volume of equipment, much of it apparently donated.

He didn't mind the work so much as the company. Mac seemed like a decent enough guy for a United States Navy combat diver, but he was chatty as hell.

Where Dylan hadn't minded Genevieve's prattle the day before—okay, he had actually enjoyed some of it—Mac was driving him crazy, asking questions about his deployments, his injuries and his recovery process.

Though he didn't give many precise details, Dylan picked up that he had lost the use of his legs during a covert operation during Gulf One when an underwater explosive had detonated at the wrong moment.

"That looks like all the regular skis," he said shortly after they had tallied a vast collection, some new and apparently donated by Brodie Thorne's sporting-goods store and some really nice gently used high-dollar equipment donated by people in town. "You've got enough here to open a ski swap."

"Good to have options so we can fit all sizes and abilities," Mac said. "Growing up here, you've probably got skis of your own, don't you?"

"Somewhere at my pop's house. I haven't been up in a few years."

"You're coming with us next week, though, aren't you? We plan to hit the slopes at least a couple times."

The guy was relentless about encouraging Dylan to participate in the activities of A Warrior's Hope.

"I'll cross that bridge."

"No reason you can't ski one-handed," Mac said. "Hell, I can do it with no legs. I've got a little ski seat I sit on. It's boss. Or you could snow-board. You can probably rip it up on a board."

He had never had much patience for snow-boarding. Maybe he was a snob because he had always liked the purity of skiing, but he might have to reconsider.

"Yeah, maybe," he answered, which had become his answer to everything Mac threw at him.

For the past two hours, the man had seemed determined to wrest more out of him than a couple of syllables at a time and Dylan had become equally determined not to let him.

In the midst of the battle of wills, all he could think about was how much he had actually enjoyed the day before with Genevieve.

She had yammered on just as much as Mac and about far more ridiculous things. If he ever went to Paris, he wouldn't need to read a guidebook. She had told him more than a guy would ever have to know. Hell, he even knew exactly which shops sold her favorite scarves and which tried to pass off knockoffs from China as genuine antique Lyonnaise silk.

For some reason, he had enjoyed listening to her far more than he did being smacked in the face with all the things he couldn't do anymore.

The room was filled to the brim with sports equipment. Baseball bats, tennis racquets, climbing gear, canoes. Much of it was designed for use by people with various physical limitations.

He hated those adaptations.

All he could see when he looked at the rows of skis, the golf clubs, the fishing poles were all the things he had left behind. He wanted his old life back, when he could grab a fly rod any damn time he felt like it and head for a nearby trout stream to be alone with the current and the fish and his thoughts.

"You live in one of the most gorgeous places I've ever been, and that's saying something," Mac was saying. "What kinds of things do you like to do for fun?"

The man just wouldn't let up.

"Oh, you know. This and that," he said shortly. Right now he didn't do much, mostly puttered around his land in Snowflake Canyon, messing with the tractor, repairing the chicken coop that had been there when he moved in, tossing a stick one-handed for Tucker when they were both in the mood.

"After I was hurt, I spent the first five years in a bottle," Mac said into the silence. "Didn't want to do a damn thing."

Dylan tensed. Apparently the program director had been talking to Charlotte, who seemed to think he was turning into some self-pitying alcoholic. He wasn't. He knew when to stop and forced himself to do it, even when he didn't want to.

"That can happen," he said, hoping that would be the end of it.

It wasn't.

"One night I went out for a drive while I was loaded and crashed this really sweet van with hand controls the VA bought for me. Ended up with a broken arm and some cuts and bruises, but I was lucky I didn't kill anybody else. Nothing like wrapping a van around a tree to sober you up fast. I realized while I was stuck in the wreckage waiting for the fire department to cut me out that I wasn't ready to go. I could still think and talk and breathe, so why the hell was I feeling so sorry for myself? I went to AA, cleaned up my act, went back to school on the government's dime. Five years ago I met the love of my life, Luisa. She was a nurse at the VA and still has the most beautiful eyes I've ever seen. I told her so, she went out with me and we've been married for four years. She had a couple kids with her first husband who died a few years before I met her, so now I get to be a dad, too. Funny how life works out, isn't it?"

"Hilarious," Dylan muttered.

"It's been a great ride, man. I wouldn't change a thing."

He didn't believe that for a second. If Mac had a chance to go back to the moment before that underwater bomb exploded, Dylan didn't doubt he would do it in a heartbeat.

Just as Dylan would give anything to go back and redo a few of his own decisions the day his world changed.

"How's it going in here?"

He looked up to see Eden Davis in the doorway.

"We're just about wrapping up the inventory," Mac said. "I wanted to check the snowshoes you were telling me about. I think that's about all I have left."

"Think you can handle that yourself?"

"I should be able to."

"Great. I need to steal Dylan for a minute," she said. "We just finished buying the grocery staples to supply the cabins, and I think

Genevieve could use some help sorting them and stocking the cupboards." He wasn't sure he really trusted himself to be alone with Gen in the cabins again. On the other hand, it beat the hell out of the alternative.

"You're the boss," he said.

"We took everything to the cabin closest to this building. You'll find her."

"Sure."

He headed down the trail through a light, pretty snowfall that gently landed on the pines, trying to tell himself his little surge of excitement was due to the reprieve Eden had granted him from listening to more of Mac's stories. It couldn't have anything to do with Genevieve.

He rapped on the door of the cabin, though he wasn't really sure why, since she didn't live there, then pushed open the door when she bade him come in.

"Oh. Dylan. Hi."

He registered how lovely she looked today, in a far more practical cotton shirt than the fuzzy peach sweater she had worn the day before. He had seen her only briefly that morning when they had both picked up their ID badges from the front desk, before Eden sent them in different directions.

Somehow he had forgotten that silky fall of hair; her soft mouth; the high, elegant cheekbones.

He forced himself not to stare, looking instead

at the boxes and bags of groceries that covered just about every inch of the cabin.

"That would be a little food."

She tucked an errant strand of hair behind her ear with a frazzled sort of gesture. "I know, right? We filled three carts and spent a small fortune. You would not *believe* the price of milk these days."

"I do drink milk occasionally," he murmured. "Since I don't currently have a cow, I do have to purchase it."

"Oh. Of course. I guess I'm still thinking in liters and euros instead of gallons and dollars. It's hard to make the translations in my head."

"Understandable." He looked around at the bags of groceries. "So what is the plan here?"

"We bought the same thing for each cabin—cold cereal, snacks, that kind of thing. We'll have to divide everything evenly and then put it all away in the cabins."

He could think of worse tasks. Inventorying recreational equipment, for instance. "Let's unload everything onto the table and the bar and group the items together, then we can divvy things up into a couple empty boxes for each cabin."

"That's exactly what I was thinking. I hope we've got enough boxes."

They set to work stacking piles of items together. When six boxes were emptied, he set them along one wall and started dispersing one of each item to the boxes.

She didn't seem as talkative today. He missed her chatter, though he would rather be dragged behind a pair of those skis than admit it.

"Eden said we don't have to come in tomorrow," she said after several moments. "That will be nice. I have a million things to do, including a trip to the hardware store that will probably take me hours. I have so many things to buy for the house."

Here was the chatter he had missed.

"Oh?"

"I'm hoping to get some of the wallpaper down tomorrow and start painting. We'll see if I make it that far since it's my only day off for a while. Eden told me to expect a crazy day on Monday, shuttling the new guests here from Denver and helping them settle in. She said expect a ten-hour day."

"Can't wait," he muttered.

She paused in distributing bunches of bananas in the boxes. "I don't think it's been that terrible so far. In fact, I've quite enjoyed it."

"It's been less than two full days," he pointed out. "And you spent most of that time decorating and shopping. That's not really out of the norm for you, is it?"

He regretted the rather snarky words as soon as they were out, especially when her mouth tightened and she looked down at the bananas as if they were dipped in diamond dust.

"Now, if only we can spend a few days having our hair done and getting a massage, it will seem like every other day for me," she said quietly.

He sighed, feeling like the jackass that he was. "Sorry," he muttered. "That was out of line. You've worked hard."

He wasn't sure whether she accepted his apology or not as she picked up another bag and started sorting bagged baby carrots into the piles in silence.

"Tell me something," she finally said. "Were you this cranky before you, er, were injured?"

The unexpected question startled a laugh out of him. "Before I left my hand in an ambush in Helmand Province? I don't know. Probably."

She was quiet, her head angled to one side as she watched him. "You were in an ambush?"

He didn't want to talk about this. Hell, he didn't like *thinking* about it, though memories of that fateful evening would always haunt him.

Mac had been trying to weasel the information about his injuries out of him all morning, and he hadn't wanted to reveal a damn thing. For reasons he couldn't have explained, he wanted to tell Genevieve.

"Yeah. We were on the hunt for a group of insurgents responsible for several bombings focusing on girls' schools. They were killing their own people, just because a few girls wanted to learn how to read. We had solid information that the insurgents were in one particular village, so we were doing a house-to-house search."

He was quiet, focusing on the small bag of clementines in his hand, crisply orange and sweet smelling.

"Everybody in the whole village was acting suspicious. We knew we were onto something. Finally, somebody directed us to this cluster of houses, all connected to each other, on the outskirts of town. We were clearing it room by room when I found this kid. He couldn't have been more than twelve."

The kid—barefoot, big dark eyes—had a weapon, a big old Kalashnikov probably left over from the Soviet war.

Dylan should have shot him on sight but those big dark eyes had looked terrified as hell. He had tried to talk to him in his limited Persian and then had tried Pashto, trying to assure the kid they wouldn't hurt him if he handed over the weapon.

Instead, the kid had watched out of those big eyes, saying nothing. Dylan knew now he had only been waiting until the rest of the unit moved within range before he detonated the suicide bomb strapped beneath his robes, taking down the whole dilapidated series of buildings.

"What happened?" Gen asked softly.

"He was one of the insurgents."

"The little boy?"

He nodded. *There you go, Princess Jahn-Vi-Ev. That's the real world for you, at least in some of the planet's nastiest neighborhoods.*

"Beneath his robes, he was strapped with a shitload of explosives, which he detonated as soon as he could achieve maximum kills."

She made a soft sound of distress that seemed to drive sharp splinters into his heart. "Oh, no."

He should stop now. He had told her enough. She didn't need to hear the rest. He wouldn't tell her about the eighteen hours he had spent buried under rubble, listening to his friends' gurgling last breaths. Or the rabid fear that the rest of the insurgents would be the ones to dig him out and how much pain they would inflict once they found him.

He didn't need to tell her everything, but once he started, the words just seemed to ooze out of him like raw sewage.

"I lost five good friends that day. Good men and good soldiers. When more of our guys in the area finally dug me out, everybody kept telling me how lucky I was to survive. A miracle, they said. I've got to say, I'm not convinced."

Especially since he knew his stupid soft heart had been responsible for the whole FUBAR. He should have blasted the kid when he'd had the chance. The explosives would have gone off and Dylan still would have gone down but everybody else would have been out of range of the worst of the damage.

She had turned pale, clutching a jar of salsa to her chest as if it were her firstborn. "Oh, Dylan." Her voice sounded ragged, thin. "I'm so sorry."

He shrugged. After one quick look, he shifted his gaze back to the clementines and their sweet citrus scent that drifted in the air, unable to bear the pity in her eyes.

"I expect you'll hear worse from the guys who come through the program," he said. "My story is pretty classic, all things considered."

"Do you . . . ? Are you still in pain?"

Her question took him by surprise. Few people asked him that. The ambush had been more than a year ago.

"Is that why I'm a grouchy bastard, you mean? Because I'm nobly and heroically coping with my battle scars?"

She made a small sound, not quite a laugh—but he wouldn't have expected that after the grim story he had just shared. "I didn't say that," she said as she moved closer to him to set the salsa in one of the boxes.

"That's not why I'm grouchy," he said. "But yeah, sometimes I feel a twinge or two."

The eye actually bothered him more than anything. Once in a while, he had headaches that made him want to rip off half his face, but he didn't want to tell her that.

"I'm so sorry," she said again. This time she rested her hand on his, where he still clutched the bag of fruit, and he wanted to drown in the warmth of her eyes.

He would never be able to eat an orange again without thinking of this moment, her fingers soft against the back of his hand, the heat of her seeping into him, the tug of emotions in his chest.

He wanted desperately to kiss her again, even though he knew it was completely idiotic. She was a pampered princess. Perfect hair, perfect clothes, perfect makeup, while he was a broken-down wreck of a man with no job, no prospects, nothing except a great dog and an equally broken-down wreck of a house.

He jerked his hand away and shoved the bag of fruit into one of the boxes. "Everybody's sorry. That doesn't ease the pain one damn bit, now does it?"

She gave him a long look. "No. I guess you're right. Biting everybody's head off is probably a much better pain reliever."

He almost smiled at her sarcastic response but managed to bite it back. He still couldn't believe he had shared that with Genevieve Beaumont, of all people. He hadn't told anyone in his family those details. Why her?

Needing to put a little emotional and literal distance between them, he focused on the task at hand. "Looks like we've sorted everything. I'll take one of these boxes over and start putting things away in the cabin next door. You can start in this one, since you're here."

Without waiting for an answer, he lifted the heavy box using his arm and propping it on the prosthetic. Ignoring the pain that was a little more than the twinge he had told her, he headed outside and away from her as quickly as he could manage it.

Chapter Seven

Her cell phone rang just as she was climbing into her SUV to make the short drive from the recreation center back to her grandmother's house at the mouth of the canyon.

She was so exhausted, she just wanted to rest her head against the steering wheel and sleep for a few days.

She hadn't slept well the night before, troubled by angst that kept her awake and then night-mares when she finally did manage to close her eyes. Even if she hadn't already been feeling as if her bones were coated in lead, the afternoon with Dylan had been emotionally draining.

Every time she thought of him lying injured

under rubble or grieving for his friends afterward, she wanted to cry. She *had* cried a few tears in the bathroom after he left the cabin but had quickly rinsed her eyes and then applied a few artful brushstrokes of makeup to conceal the evidence.

She couldn't imagine what he had endured. It seemed so real, so raw, completely out of her realm of experience. They were total opposites, as she had thought many times, which made this odd, tangled connection between them so disconcerting.

She knew he was attracted to her, but he didn't seem at all motivated to do anything about it. Maybe he wouldn't. He apparently preferred to ignore the currents zinging between them.

She only wished that she could do the same.

Depressed suddenly, she pulled out her phone and looked at the caller ID.

The mayor—just about the last person she felt like talking with right now. She wasn't at all in the mood to listen to her father lecture her about all the many ways she was wasting her life.

She turned off the sound and sent the call to voice mail. As she started the SUV, the phone vibrated with a second call, also from her father.

He would keep this up all day until she answered. Her parents were experts at relentless erosion tactics, wearing her down until she finally gave in.

Once in France, she had forgotten to charge her phone overnight and her battery died. Her mother had ended up calling poor old Madame Archambault—her neighbor with the big dog— and insisted she climb the three flights of stairs to Genevieve's flat to make sure she wasn't lying comatose from carbon-monoxide poisoning.

Intoxication au monoxyde de carbone.

She could turn her phone off, but if she did that, she suspected William might very well be waiting for her at Grandma Pearl's house by the time she drove down the canyon. She would rather talk to him on the phone than in person any day.

With a heavy sigh, she connected the call. "Hello, Father."

"Genevieve. Darling. There you are!"

"Yes," she answered. For a brief moment, she ached for the surreal but wonderful relationship they'd developed when she was engaged, when both of her parents had seemed to think she could do no wrong. For once.

"I dropped by your grandmother's house today but you weren't there."

Court-ordered community service, remember that? Of course he didn't.

"I'm sorry I missed you," she lied.

"I let myself in and took a look around."

He threw the words out between them like a dead rodent. Though he didn't add anything else, she heard the subtext anyway. *You haven't done much, have you?* No. She hadn't. She had been there only a week and had spent most of that time having estimates done and figuring out her budget. And staying out of jail.

"If you had waited until I was there, I could have showed you around and told you some of my plans."

"Your plans." He said the words mildly but, again, subtext was everything. They smacked of so much derision, her chest actually hurt.

"Now that I've done the initial survey work, I'm going to start taking the wallpaper down in a few of the rooms tonight. I'll be bringing in someone to strip the cabinets in the kitchen and I've picked out the new flooring."

"That all sounds . . . ambitious."

"It's going to be great when I finish. Just wait."

"I'm sure," he answered. "I had forgotten how small and depressing my mother's house was. Are you certain you wouldn't like to stay in your own room here while you're working on the renovations?"

She really longed for her little en suite bathroom with the jetted tub and the steam shower, but she wasn't going to cave on this. "Positive. I'm fine."

"If you change your mind you know you're always welcome."

"Thank you."

"The reason I called, actually, is that I have some good news."

"Oh?"

She could use a little good news right now after the difficult day.

"Yes. I had lunch today with Judge Richards. He indicated he might be amenable to changing the terms of your plea agreement."

"Change the terms." For a long moment, she didn't know what else to say.

"Yes. He's not willing to reduce your community-service hours but he says he has no problem with changing the venue to somewhere a little more . . . appropriate. Somewhere like the library or the fine-arts museum."

The words took a moment to sink through her exhaustion. Change the venue. Library or museum.

A few days ago, that would have been an immensely appealing offer.

"Why would Judge Richards be willing to do that?"

"It took some doing—I won't lie to you, but let's just say I called in some favors."

She could almost hear her father preening on the phone. She hated when he pushed his weight around town, especially on her behalf. It was more proof that he didn't think her capable of anything on her own.

As much as she might cringe at his efforts, she was also fiercely tempted by them. Volunteering at the library or the museum would be so easy.

She could be done by Christmas and would enjoy being surrounded by books or precious artworks. Both the library and the art museum offered safe, serene environments, far removed from the kind of gritty details she had heard today.

The internal war only lasted a moment before shame washed over her for even being enticed. She thought of Dylan and everything he had lost and the courage it must take him every single day to climb out of bed and face the world, given his new limitations.

She could borrow a little of his strength and carry on with the current arrangement.

"I appreciate your efforts on my behalf, Father, but that's not necessary," she said quickly, before she could change her mind. "I'm content with the agreement as it stands."

"You don't know what you're saying." Her father's voice was slightly impatient—and more than a little patronizing. "Think this through before you make a hasty decision you'll regret later. Wouldn't you be more comfortable spending your hours at the library than working with rough soldiers who aren't fit to do anything worthwhile anymore?"

Appalled, she moved the phone away from her ear and stared at it. She wanted very much to hang up the phone. She loved her father but sometimes she didn't understand how he could be so callous, bordering on cruel.

"Yes. I would probably be more comfortable doing something more in my element," she said. "But maybe I'm tired of being comfortable."

"Now, Genevieve . . ."

He was ramping up for another lecture, she knew, and she didn't want to hear it.

"I've got to go," she said quickly. "I'm driving through the canyon and I'll probably lose you. Thank you for trying, but I signed a plea agreement and I intend to stick by it."

She hung up quickly before her father could start in again and turned her phone completely off so he couldn't try calling her back. She wasn't nearly as tired now as she backed out of the parking space and headed for the main road.

It was amazingly empowering to make a decision she could feel good about, for once, and she wouldn't let her father take that from her.

The moment he drove up to his childhood home on Winterberry Road, Dylan knew he shouldn't have come.

The driveway was chock-full of vehicles and he ended up parking his old pickup behind Spence's Range Rover on the street.

He usually tried to avoid these Sunday dinners like the plague, but Pop's birthday was the next day. He kind of felt obligated to make an appearance. He loved his family, but they were easier taken in small doses. Having everybody together like this made for a loud, boisterous scene. He always ended up with a headache that lasted hours.

Still, after he shut off the engine, he sat in his truck for a long time, until Tucker whined a little and rested his chin on Dylan's thigh.

"Yeah. I know. We're here, right? We might as well go in."

He opened his door, dread heavy in his gut, and started up the sidewalk. The weather matched his mood, darkly ominous. Winter storm clouds obscured the tops of the mountains and the air smelled of impending snow. While nothing was falling yet, weather forecasters were predicting a few inches that night.

Despite the grim evening, Pop's house looked warm and inviting, with a big Christmas tree in the window dressed in thick gold ribbons and a hodgepodge of ornaments.

Charlotte had probably set it up for Pop, who was usually too busy this time of year to worry much about Christmas decorations while he catered holiday parties all around town.

"You're going to behave yourself, right?" he said to Tucker. The dog gave him a patient, what-do-you-think? sort of look. Dylan sighed and pushed open the door.

A wave of noise, heat and sumptuous smells just about knocked him off his pins. Roast beef, if he wasn't mistaken, and some of Pop's glorious mashed potatoes, as well as something chocolatey.

Tucker was completely at home here on Winterberry Road since he had lived here with Pop—and Charlotte, until she'd bought a house of her own—during Dylan's various deployments. The dog immediately headed to what he and his siblings had always called Mom's company room to plop down on his favorite spot by the gas fireplace that oozed out heat. A minute later, a rat-skinny little Chihuahua raced in and started licking Tuck's big, jowly face.

"Tina! Come back!" A little dark-headed boy ran after the Chihuahua, followed by Pop's plump tabby, who always acted more like another dog than a cat.

When his nephew Carter—his brother Brendan's son—spotted the coon dog, joy exploded on his four-year-old features.

"Tucker!" He clapped his hands and hurried in to throw chubby arms around the dog's neck. When Tina—his brother Drew's dog—decided she had spent long enough greeting Tucker, she scampered off, and Carter toddled after her with a cheery giggle.

Pop's Sunday dinners were always like this. Chaos and chatter, kids and animals chasing each other, delicious smells seeping out of the kitchen.

Curled up in a corner chair beside the fire was one of his favorite people on earth, his niece Faith. She had a book on her lap, her legs tucked up beside her, and was wearing a cute little fluffy white snowman sweater that somehow made him think of Genevieve, until he pushed away the thought.

"Hey, Faith."

Her smile was soft, pretty, genuine. She looked at him without any kind of expectations, which was particularly refreshing in this family where everybody seemed to have some.

"Hi, Uncle Dylan. I knew you were here because of Tucker. Did Grandpop know you were coming?"

He pretended to grimace. "Oops. I think I forgot to mention it to him. Do you think he'll have enough food?"

"You know he will. He always makes *tons*." She gave him a comforting sort of smile, looking so much like her mother that his heart gave a sharp twist for this poor motherless little girl and her brother, the little imp currently on Chihuahua patrol.

"What are you doing in here by yourself?" he asked.

"I got this book yesterday and I want to finish it. It's *so* good. It's about cats and they live in the forest and hunt together and talk to each other and stuff. You should read it!"

He smiled. "Sounds like it's right down my alley," he lied. "Maybe you could lend it to me when you finish."

"Sure," she said generously.

Right now he had a powerful desire to sit on the uncomfortable sofa by the fire while Faith read her book about cats beneath a big framed photograph of the whole Caine family under different circumstances.

There was his mom, sweet and pretty, though even then he could see signs of the cancer she fought for two years. And there was Charlotte, chubby and cute, and Pop with considerably more hair.

And him. He was there, too, a cocky-as-hell, good-looking teenager, smiling and whole.

"I wish I'd thought to bring along a book. I would sit here with you and read."

"You can borrow one of Grandpop's."

His chuckle sounded rusty but she didn't seem to mind. "Maybe I'll find one and come back when everybody starts getting too loud in the other room."

"Sure." She smiled happily at him, and his heart ached all over again for Brendan and his family.

"I guess I'd better go tell your grandpop happy birthday."

"Okay."

He kissed the top of her head, remembering the pictures she would color and send him every week during his long hospitalization. Some weeks they were the only thing that carried him through.

Knowing he couldn't delay anymore, he steeled himself and walked back to the huge great-room addition off the kitchen that he and his brothers had helped Pop build the summer he was twelve.

As he expected, the scene was chaos—a few people sitting at the table talking, a couple of boys cheering at a football game on the big-screen TV, still others—Pop included—working in the open kitchen.

His oldest brother, Patrick—a banker in Denver who must have driven out with his family for Pop's birthday—was the first to notice him.

"Well. Miracles never cease. Look who decided to come down from his mountain to be with us mortals."

Everybody snapped to attention at the grand announcement, including Pop, who looked beyond thrilled.

"Told you he would come," Charlotte said smugly. Dylan was almost certain money exchanged hands in a few corners.

They didn't need to make it seem as if he was a recluse. It hadn't been that long since he had come to one of the infamous Caine family Sunday dinners—and he'd been here on Thanksgiving, for heaven's sake.

"You know this doesn't count toward your community service, right?" Spence asked from the table where he was apparently hard at work snapping beans. Pretty humble work for somebody who should have been in the Baseball Hall of Fame.

"Yeah, yeah. Hey, Pop. Happy birthday."

He leaned in and gave his father an awkward, one-armed hug. Dermot threw his arms around Dylan's waist and hugged him back. "My birthday is complete now that you're here," he said when he pulled away, his eyes a little damp.

"Yeah, forget about Jamie and Aidan. Who needs them?" he said.

"We're calling Aidan on Skype later," Charlotte said. "He'll be here next week for Christmas anyway. And Jamie was just here for several days. He took Pop to Le Passe Montagne for his birthday before he left."

"I guess that counts. Smells great in here." He mustered a smile for Erin and Carrie, his two sisters-in-law—married to Drew and Patrick, respectively. Pop always did most of the work in the kitchen, even for his own birthday party, but Charlotte and the sisters-in-law all shared matriarch responsibilities.

He was grateful his brothers had married good women. The men in his family seemed to have inordinately good taste—and then worked hard to deserve their wives.

"How long before we eat?" he asked.

"As soon as you get over here and stir the gravy," Pop growled.

"There are nearly twenty people crowded into this house. I just got here. Why do I have to stir the gravy?"

"That's why," Dermot said briskly. "Because you just got here. Everybody else has been helping already. You know the rule in my kitchen."

"If you want to eat, you have to work," all the Caine siblings said in unison.

He sighed but moved obediently to the stove, picking up a wooden spoon from the drawer. Everything smelled delicious. His stomach growled. He probably hadn't had a decent meal since that Thanksgiving dinner—not counting the leftovers Pop had sent home with him.

He had cooking skills. All of them did. Dermot wouldn't have allowed his children to grow up without them. Their parents had taken that motto seriously—with seven children, they had to be organized and efficient in splitting the workload.

Pop had also made sure they all took a turn working at the café. He and Spence used to wash dishes together, back in the day.

His limited culinary skills had come in handy during a few meals when they only had MREs. He always kept a few extra spices in his ruck to dress things up.

He supposed he ought to start cooking more. TV dinners and a few doggie bags of food Dermot sent from the café just weren't enough all the time. He didn't really have a good excuse for why he didn't, other than he didn't feel like it most of the time.

When Pop judged the gravy to be ready—others might be in on the prep, but he always had the final vote—they all jostled to find spots to eat.

Even without Jamie and Aidan, the Caines overflowed the big twelve-place dining table. A second long folding banquet table had been set up in the sunroom for the kids.

He enjoyed the meal and even enjoyed the company. He was grateful to be seated between Erin and Carrie. Erin taught third grade at one of the two Hope's Crossing elementary schools while Carrie was a pediatrician in Denver.

They talked over him mostly about their Christmas preparations, which presents were already wrapped, the gifts they were giving to neighbors. He was content to listen to them and also grateful not to have attention focused on him for once.

His luck ran out just as the meal was winding down.

Erin was the first to go in for the kill. "So, Dylan. How are things going with your service work at A Warrior's Hope?"

He set down his fork, the last few bites of his lusciously juicy roast beef losing a little of its savor. "Fine, so far."

"The real work will start tomorrow, when our

new guests arrive," Charlotte said from across the table.

He wasn't looking forward to that, but he supposed he would survive.

"How are things with Miss Priss of the mighty right hook?" Brendan asked.

"You mean Gen Beaumont?" he asked, a little more testily than he should have.

"Yeah," Brendan said. "You ready to strangle her yet?"

For a brief instant, his gaze connected with Charlotte's, and he saw that shadow of worry there again. She hadn't said anything to him since that moment the other day when she had walked into the cabin just as he was about to make the momentous mistake of kissing Gen. He had been waiting for a lecture, but for once his baby sister was minding her own business.

"Not yet," he murmured.

"I would be. From what I understand, she is a holy terror. The other guys at the station house were talking the other day about a time when she crashed her car into the ladder truck when she was about sixteen, I guess. It was a brand-new convertible and the ink was hardly dry on her license. I guess she hit the truck while trying to back out of a parking space at the hardware store during the Fill the Boot fundraiser—and then she threw a fit. The guys shouldn't have parked right there. It was all their fault. Blah blah blah.

You would have thought the world had ended and the whole volunteer fire department had purposely set out to park in a spot they knew she would stupidly back into—like a big fluorescent green ladder truck was invisible. I guess her tantrum was pretty legendary."

"Now, Brendan Thomas. That will be enough of that," Dermot said firmly from the head of the table. "I'll not have you speaking poorly about Miss Beaumont."

He wasn't sure why his father jumped to Gen's defense but he wouldn't complain about it. At least this way, he wouldn't have to do it.

"Why can't he talk about her?" Erin asked. "Dylan wouldn't even be in trouble with the law if not for her. Isn't that right?"

"Whatever happened to lawyer-client privilege?" he muttered to his brother, across the table.

"Drew didn't say a word about what happened, as much as I nagged him. I heard the whole story out of Charlotte when we went to String Fever for their annual holiday bead fair—where I spent entirely too much money, by the way."

"Thanks," he muttered to Charlotte.

"You should probably know Genevieve is a frequent topic of conversation at String Fever, especially since her ill-fated but gorgeous wedding dress is still on display in the store."

He didn't want to ask—nor did he want to think about her engagement to some jackass who had probably been perfect for her. Except, maybe, for his little habit of impregnating teenagers.

"Everybody was talking about this latest escapade of hers," Charlotte went on. "Word was already out that you had been involved, so people pressed me for details. You'll be happy to know, I glossed over most of the finer points."

"It wasn't *entirely* her fault. I should have minded my own business. Like a few others I could mention in this family," he said pointedly to Charlotte, though he could have been addressing the room as a whole, or at least all those over eighteen.

"I'm still blaming her," Erin said. "I agree with Brendan. She's bad news. She and her mother donated some books to the school library a few years ago and insisted on a full-fledged assembly so they could receive proper recognition from the school for their generosity."

Something told him Laura Beaumont had been the driving force behind that one, though he supposed he could be completely wrong about the situation.

"She's been a really good help so far at A Warrior's Hope," Charlotte said. "In fact, she and Dylan spent all day decorating Christmas trees in the new cabins. You should see them. They're beautiful."

The whole room seemed to descend into silence at that pronouncement and everybody stared at him. A few jaws might have even sagged.

Even Brendan looked amused, and it took a lot to make that happen these days.

"Excuse me," he murmured. "Did you say . . . Christmas decorating?"

"Yes. They did a really good job, too," Charlotte said.

"Do you even have a Christmas tree at your own cabin?" his thirteen-year-old niece Maggie —named for their mother—asked him with interest.

Dylan felt heat crawl up his cheeks and hoped to hell he wasn't actually blushing.

"Yeah," he growled. "Tucker and I put it up weeks ago. And then we held hands, er, paws and sang Christmas carols all night long."

"Really?" Faith looked wide-eyed at him.

He shook his head at her, feeling kind of bad for being grumpy around her.

"That's what you call sarcasm, honey," Brendan said to his daughter. "Your uncle Dylan is something of an expert at it."

True enough.

"I haven't gotten around to putting a Christmas tree up this year," he answered her more gently. "It's just me and Tucker. There's not much point, especially when I can always enjoy your grand-pop's tree when I need one."

Faith seemed to find that a terrible tragedy. Her chin even quivered. "You could always put up a little one. I have one in my room you could borrow, if you want."

He mustered a smile for her, touched to the depths of his hardened, sarcastic, miserable soul. "I appreciate that, honey. I do. I'll tell you what. I'll try to cut down a little one from the forest around my place."

That seemed to satisfy her and he was grateful Brendan didn't bring his kids up to Snowflake Canyon very often for her to check the veracity of that particular claim. He had no intention of cutting down a tree. Decorating six cabins for A Warrior's Hope had rid him of absolutely any desire for a tree of his own. Not that he ever planned to put one up in the first place.

"Genevieve is a beautiful decorator," Charlotte said. "I'm not sure how she pulled it off but she made each one of the cabins magical."

"With Dylan's help, of course." Spencer made sure to emphasize this point, grinning broadly, until Dylan wanted to pound him. If the man didn't seem to fit in so effortlessly with the family and wasn't so obviously crazy about Charlotte, he might have tried, old friend or not.

"Genevieve Beaumont is a nice girl," Dermot insisted. "She always has a kind word for me when she comes into the café. I'll admit, I can't always say the same about her mother, but they're two different people."

He didn't want to talk about Genevieve. He

bluntly changed the subject to one he knew would best distract his father. "So, Pop, I bumped into Katherine Thorne the other day."

"Did you?" Dermot seemed inordinately interested in cutting his delicious roast beef with pinpoint precision. Dylan was sure he wasn't the only one of his siblings amused by the color that rose on his father's cheeks. Pop and the elegant city councilwoman must hold the record for world's slowest courtship. It mostly consisted of a lot of hem-hawing around and Dermot pretending he didn't blush every time she walked into the café.

"She and I seem to be on the same schedule for grocery shopping. I see her at the market just about every time I go. If you want me to, I can give you a call next time I'm heading that way and you can meet us there."

Charlotte and Brendan, the only ones really paying attention to the conversation, both snickered, and color rose over Dermot's weathered features. "You all think you're so funny."

"Yes. Yes, we do," Dylan said. Teasing his father about his crush was one of the few things that made him happy these days.

"Well, you're not. Katherine is a lovely woman and I'm happy to count her as a friend. That's all there is to it."

Dylan wanted to say the same about Genevieve but decided the circumstances weren't at all comparable.

Chapter Eight

After dinner, he helped clear the table and even managed to make polite conversation with just about everybody while they all worked together to clean the kitchen—all except Pop, who played a game with the grandkids in the great room.

As long as he could remember, the Caine family tradition had held that Pop—and Mom, before cancer took her when he was a teenager—would fix the meal and the kids would clean it up together. All these years later, they still fell into the same habits.

He had never minded much. They would tease and joke and sometimes taunt each other, but the work went fast with seven children.

Growing up in a big family had advantages; he couldn't deny that. He had always known one of his brothers would have his back, whether with playground bullies or on the ball field.

There were also negatives. He couldn't deny that, either. Everybody seemed to think he—or she—had a right to know his business and then offer an opinion on it. Since his injury, that had become more obvious.

As he might have expected, Charlotte managed

to corner him just as everybody was wrapping up the dishes.

"I'm so happy you came for Pop's birthday," she said with one of her customary hugs. He loved all his siblings but had a special spot in his heart for her, not only because she was the only girl and they all looked out for her but also because the two of them had been the last Caine kids home while their mother was dying of cancer.

They all shared the grief over Margaret Caine's passing but he and Charlotte had probably felt it most keenly. Unlike their older brothers, they hadn't started moving on with their lives yet or had the distraction of new adventures or challenges.

They had been in this house, forced to try to comfort each other as best they could and to step in where needed to help Pop.

He still had memories of walking downstairs in the middle of the night on more than one occasion and finding Pop sobbing by himself in the dark.

The experience had bound them together as nothing else could.

"I'm not a complete hermit, contrary to popular belief," he said to her now. "I do get out once in a while."

"I've seen you more this last week than I think I have since you've been back in Hope's Crossing."

He grunted and returned their mom's beloved gravy tureen to the top shelf of the cupboard.

"I so wish Aidan could have come for Thanksgiving while Jamie was home on leave. It's been forever since we've all been together."

"Never satisfied, are you?" he teased.

She smiled a little as the group playing a game with Pop in the other room suddenly erupted in laughter.

"You haven't been completely miserable so far working at A Warrior's Hope, have you?"

"Not *completely.*"

She rolled her eyes at the heavy emphasis he placed on the word, as if he had been mostly miserable but had somehow endured.

"I'm asking in all seriousness," she said. "I don't want you to hate it. If you don't think you can stand it, I'm sure Spence could work with the court system to find somewhere else for you to fill your community-service hours. The legal system probably doesn't care where you do it, as long as you fill the requirements. You could maybe even do something else at the recreation center without us having to go through the system. Sign out basketballs or something."

He gave her a long look. "I love you, sis. You know I do. But if I live to be two hundred years old, I will never understand you."

She made a face. "Why do you say that?"

"From the minute you and Smoke came up with the crazy idea for A Warrior's Hope, you've been nagging me to help. How many times did you come up to my place to bug me about it?"

"A few," she muttered.

"More than a few, as I recall. I do believe it's come up every time I've seen you in the past six months. You finally got what you wanted, with the help of a little blackmail and one night of stupidity, and now you're trying to weasel out of the deal."

"I am not weaseling out of anything! I want you there. I just . . . don't want you to feel forced."

Siblings could drive a guy crazy like no one else. He sighed. "I *was* forced. We both know it. I didn't have a choice in the matter. Not really. I can't say I'm thrilled to be volunteering there, but now that I'm into it, I don't want to switch canoes midstream. Change skis halfway down the hill. Whatever metaphor you want to use. I just want to finish my obligation and be done with it so I can go back to my mountain."

"Good. I'm glad you're sticking it out. I'm sorry you've been stuck with Genevieve the first two days. Once the session starts next week, I'll make sure the two of you aren't always assigned the same jobs."

He wanted to tell her not to do that, that he didn't really mind working with Gen, but he had a feeling Charlotte would be quick to miscon-strue any such claim.

"Whatever," he said, in what he hoped was a casual tone.

To his relief, one of the twins—Patrick's teenage boys who were almost as tall as Dylan —came in to grab a soda out of the refrigerator and ended the conversation.

Dylan managed to stick it out for another hour, until Pop opened all his presents, before the noise and crowd started to press in on him. He found his coat in his parents' old bedroom and shrugged into it, then went in search of Tucker. Last time he checked, the old dog had been blissfully getting the love from Maggie, Peyton Gregory and Eva, Drew and Erin's daughter.

They were still there, unfortunately, which meant he couldn't quietly slip away.

"Tuck, come on. Home. Sorry, girls."

The dog gave him a disgruntled look but lumbered to his feet and padded over to him.

"You can't be leaving already," Dermot protested. "You haven't had dessert. Erin made a cake and I baked a huckleberry pie just for you."

Since his father didn't even know he was coming, he doubted that, but he didn't want to argue with the man on his birthday.

"I'll take some home, if you don't mind, but I should really head up the canyon before the storm hits."

He had a garage just off the main road where he stored a snowmobile for those times the snow was too deep for his pickup until he plowed, but he would rather not have to use it. Beyond

181

that, the canyon road to his house was twisty and could be tough to navigate in bad conditions, especially when his night vision and nocturnal driving skills weren't the greatest with only one working eyeball and one hand.

"I don't know why you have to live clear up there by yourself, especially in the winter," his father said. "I've all these empty bedrooms, you know. And what's more, I'd be lying if I said I didn't miss that rascal hound of yours."

"I like it up there," he answered quietly. "Even in the winter. When it snows, the silence is absolute."

Dermot looked at him for a long moment then gave a smile tinged with sadness. "I told myself I wouldn't badger you about it. I know you find peace up there and I understand it. But I'm your father. It's my job to worry, especially with winter upon us."

His father would worry in the middle of a blazing summer afternoon. That was just who he was.

"Don't fret about me, Pop. I'm fine. Better every day. Thanks for dinner."

"Stop a minute in the kitchen so I can ready your pie."

He followed his father and leaned against the counter while Dermot set a large piece in one of the café's to-go boxes he always kept at home for the family to package leftovers.

"Thanks," he said when Pop finished, but to his surprise, Dermot slid another piece of the pie in a second box. "I'm sure you won't mind doing a favor for your old man on his birthday."

"What kind of favor?" he asked, wary at the sudden crafty look in his father's eyes.

"Oh, not much. I'd like you to drop a piece of that huckleberry pie to your Christmas-tree-decorating friend Genevieve. Her grandmother's house is right there at the mouth of the canyon, isn't it? It's on your way home. Won't be any trouble at all."

"Pop. Really?"

"I'll have you know, Genevieve loves my pie. She stops into the diner for a slice whenever she's in town from her travels. She even brought that troublemaking fiancé of hers in before she had the good sense to drop him. I never liked him, I can tell you that."

Dermot closed the lid of the box and tucked in the tab closure. "You'll take it for me, won't you? I've a feeling she could use a bit of cheering up. From what I hear, she and her family are on the outs. That can't be easy on a young lady during the holidays."

Had Charlotte been talking to Pop? Or had Dermot picked up some kind of hint while the conversation had revolved around Genevieve that Dylan's feelings for the woman were a big, tangled mess?

He should say no. That would be the wisest course. He could use the weather as an excuse, even though he knew he had a few hours before the storm was supposed to even start.

On the other hand, what would it hurt? He could stop by, say hello, drop off the pie and be on his way in only a few moments.

Besides, after listening to her ramble on about the horrors of her grandmother's house, he was more than a little curious if the place was as bad as she said.

"Yeah. Sure. I can take her a slice of pie."

"While you're at it, you might as well take her some of the mashed potatoes and roast beef, as well. She can warm it for her dinner tomorrow."

She had to say, she had spent more pleasant Sunday nights.

Removing layer after layer of hideous wall-paper from the dining-room walls was a much more arduous task than she'd expected. In her home-improvement naïveté, she had expected the steamer machine she had rented from the hard-ware store would make everything sheer away, ripple after ripple of ugliness, but the reality wasn't nearly as cheerful.

After three hours of work, her arms ached, her hair was a frizzy mess and she had only finished one depressingly minuscule section of wall.

"Come . . . on . . . and . . . move!" she muttered,

trying to budge the massive buffet where Grandma Pearl had kept her best china. She only needed to push it away from the wall a few feet but even that seemed an impossible undertaking.

She drew in a deep breath and shoved with all her energy. It moved about an inch at the same moment, ironically, that the "Hallelujah Chorus" doorbell rang out through the house.

She froze, muscles twitching. Oh, she hoped that wasn't her parents, stopping in for a pleasant visit. In the mirrored top to the buffet, she caught her reflection. It wasn't pretty. A fine sheen of moisture clung to her skin. The hothouse humidity in here from the steamer had contributed to most of it, along with a considerable amount of perspiration.

Her hair was coming out of the pony holder she had shoved it into and any makeup she had applied earlier that day had long ago dripped away.

Maybe it was the Angel of Hope, the mysterious benefactor in Hope's Crossing who went around doing nice things for people. Paying utility bills, delivering bags of groceries, leaving envelopes of cash for needy families.

Maybe the Angel was dropping off some miraculous gift to help her finish de-wallpapering.

Not likely.

The doorbell rang again. She pushed a bedraggled strand of hair out of her eyes, fiercely tempted to ignore the summons. How could she possibly face anybody in her current situation? She could just imagine her parents' reaction if they unexpectedly came calling on her.

She could hide out in here. On the other hand, every light in the house was on, music was blaring and the curtains were open. Whoever it was could probably hear her and see movement through the windows.

With a sigh, she found the remote to turn down the speakers, wiped her sticky hands off on a rag and headed to the door.

Grandma Pearl didn't have anything as modern as a security peephole, though she did have a chain. Genevieve pulled the door open just wide enough to see who was sending Handel chiming through her house—and just about fell over.

A girl could use a little warning about these things. When she considered all the people she might have expected to see on the other side of the door, Dylan Caine wouldn't have even made the list. Yet there he was, looking completely gorgeous in the light from her porch, dark and forbidding.

He had a couple of boxes of what looked like takeout from his dad's café in his hand, she noticed through her shock as she fumbled with the chain and opened the door wider. For some reason, she thought he looked completely uncomfortable to find himself on her doorstep.

So why was he here?

Though his ranch coat hung on his frame as if he'd lost weight since he bought it, he still had rather delicious muscles. She had noticed that while they were working together at A Warrior's Hope.

She glanced behind her at the dining room and then back at him, making an instant decision she had a feeling she would regret.

"What a coincidence. You're just the guy I need right now."

She grabbed his arm and dragged him across the threshold then closed the door behind him against the December cold that hung heavy with impending snow.

"Am I?" He blinked a little, though she didn't know if he was trying to adjust to the light or her enthusiasm.

Okay, maybe she had been too hasty. She suddenly remembered how awful she must look, bedraggled and damp.

She pushed it away. If she wanted to finish this project, she didn't have room to let vanity stand in the way. "Yes. I desperately need a hand."

He held up both arms, including the empty sleeve. "Yep. I'm your guy, then."

She made a face. "You know I meant it as a figure of speech. What I really need is a strong back. I'm trying to move a piece of furniture that I swear feels like it's bolted down. Can you help me?"

He looked back at the door and then at her. "I guess I can spare a minute." He held out the boxes in his hand. "Where would you like this? I just came from Sunday dinner with my family and my pop wanted me to drop off some leftover roast beef and mashed potatoes for you. Don't ask me why. I have no idea. And pie. Huckleberry. He says it's your favorite."

She gazed at the boxes, her stomach rumbling a little at the realization that she hadn't eaten since a late breakfast.

"How kind," she exclaimed. Her insides completely dissolved into soft, gooey warmth—whatever hadn't already melted from three hours with a wallpaper steamer. "You know, I would marry your father if he were a few years younger."

His mouth quirked just a little. Not quite a smile, but close. "Apparently, he's quite fond of you, too. Who knew? He might even marry you back, if he wasn't already head over heels in love with Katherine Thorne."

"Katherine? Really?" She thought of the elegantly proper city councilwoman who used to own Claire McKnight's bead store.

Katherine's granddaughter Taryn had been severely injured in a car accident a few years ago, a passenger in a truck driven by Genevieve's brother, Charlie. Charlie had been drinking when he climbed behind the wheel, and the ripple effect of that one decision had affected countless lives.

Even before the accident, Genevieve had always had the vague feeling Katherine disliked her. Perhaps she was someone else who only saw her as a brainless, snobbish debutante.

"I hadn't heard they were dating," she said now to Dylan.

"Oh, they're not. As friendly as he might be to customers at the café, Pop is actually on the shy side when it comes to women. He might get around to asking her out before they're both in their seventies."

She smiled. These little flashes of Dylan's sense of humor always seemed to take her by surprise.

"If it doesn't work out between them, I'll be waiting to snatch him right up," she said. "I'll just take this in the kitchen for dinner later. Leave your coat on the chair there."

He obeyed with a faintly amused look and followed her into the kitchen. As she placed the takeout containers in the refrigerator, he took a good look around at the harvest-gold, severely outdated appliances, the cheap dark cabinets, the orange-patterned carpeting—ew!—on the floor.

"Didn't I warn you it was hideous?"

"It's not so bad."

She stared at him. "To somebody used to living out of a tent in the desert, maybe."

He again had that faint smile, that tiny easing of his harsh features. She found it amazing how that slight shift in his expression could make him so much more approachable.

"It has four walls and a window, anyway," he answered. "And electricity."

"Don't forget running water. I guess you're right. Why would I need to change a thing?"

This time his smile was almost full-fledged. That smile was a dangerous thing, only because it made her want to wring it out of him, again and again.

"If I had my way, I would like to gut the whole thing and start over. Travertine counter-tops, stainless-steel appliances, custom cherry cabinetry. Unfortunately, my budget for this entire house project is minuscule to nonexistent. I can afford new paint for some of the rooms but that's about it."

"Don't you have some designer purses or last season's clothes you could sell online?"

As she hadn't expected to be forced to live here for weeks on end, she had left most of her things at her apartment in Paris. She supposed she could have a friend ship them over or liquidate there but she would need them when she was ready to return to her life in Le Marais.

Of course, she did have her little side business nobody knew about, the purses she had started sewing for fun.

She had started making them as a bit of a joke. Her friends in Paris had loved them and on a whim one night she had had a few extras delivered to Maura McKnight's bookstore, just to see if she could sell them.

To her shock, the first order of a half dozen had sold within a week and Maura had written a letter to her mystery supplier, seeking more.

Gen had sent her ten more and they had also sold out. She had decided she should stop there, though Maura had sent multiple letters to the PO Box she had forwarded to her in Paris, requesting more.

She would have to sew all day and all night for weeks and sell everything she made in order to earn enough profit to even afford a square yard of travertine countertop.

"I'm going to have to be content with doing what I can to freshen the place up on a shoestring. I really don't know why I'm bothering. Whoever buys it will probably tear the whole place down to build some mega vacation house anyway."

She looked around at the kitchen, so familiar to her from her childhood, and a little sadness seeped through her. Despite the aesthetic affront, she had many pleasant memories of her grandmother here.

When she was young, she used to stay overnight with Pearl. Her grandmother would make her luscious hot chocolate with whole milk and chocolate chips—oh, the calories!—and they would watch game shows and try to beat each other to the answers.

Pearl had taught her how to sew at this very kitchen table, on her old Singer. She'd made aprons and hot pads and even a few wraparound skirts that had been quite cute.

She pushed away the memories that clung like cobwebs.

"Come on. I'll show you where I need help." She led the way to the dining room next door.

He looked around at the section she had worked on and the curls of wallpaper scrapings that littered the floor. "This looks fun."

"I don't know why Grandma Pearl was compelled to change her wallpaper every other week. And of course, she didn't bother to take off what was underneath—she just slapped up another layer. I swear, every time she changed her hair color, she decided to change the walls, too."

He chuckled a little, and the rough sound sizzled along her nerve endings.

"So where do you want the buffet?"

"I just need to push it a few feet from the wall into the middle of the room so I can work behind it. The two of us should be able to manage it, don't you think?"

He looked a little doubtful and held up his empty sleeve. "Keep in mind, one of us has a little bit of a liability."

She frowned. "Why do you always feel as if you have to point that out?"

"I don't," he said. A little defensively, she thought.

"You've mentioned it twice since you showed up on my doorstep five minutes ago. Do you think I'm going to forget? I know you lost an arm, Dylan. That doesn't mean I think the rest of you is worthless."

As soon as she said the words, she wished she hadn't. His eyes widened and he looked as if she'd just smacked him in the back of the head with the wallpaper steamer. He must think she was an idiot. She really, really hoped he didn't pick up the signs that she had developed a serious crush on him.

"If you take that side, I'll try to move it from here."

He complied. Even with one arm, he had far more strength than she did and was able to push his side several feet to her six inches—and then he moved over and pushed her side, as well.

"That should be far enough. If I have to shove that thing another inch, I'm afraid I'll have a heart attack."

"Or at least break a nail."

She held up her hands. "I've got no nails to break right now, courtesy of all that Christmas decorating we did. I'm going to be in serious need of a manicure if this keeps up."

"Yeah. Same here."

"Thanks. I don't know what I would have done

if you hadn't shown up. I probably would have left a buffet-shaped square of wallpaper right there and painted around it. I can't believe how heavy that thing is. It must be solid oak."

"Or maybe your grandma Pearl hid gold bricks in the bottom."

"Wouldn't that be the answer to my prayers? Don't think I haven't gone through every drawer and cupboard in the house looking for old bond notes, hidden cash bundles, gold doubloons. Whatever. So far, no luck."

"I guess that means you're stuck in Hope's Crossing for a while."

She wasn't quite ready to look at the reasons why she didn't find that prospect as depressing now as she might have a week ago.

He looked around. "So what color are you painting the room?"

"I haven't decided yet." She was surprised he asked and had a feeling he was, too. "Hey, I can show you the paint cards and you can help me choose."

"No, really. That's okay—"

She ignored him and grabbed the samples she had picked up from the paint aisle of the hardware store. "I think I'm painting neutral tones through the rest of the house but I wanted something with a little more splash here. I'm thinking a neutral on three of the walls and then something rich on the big one where we moved the buffet."

Though he looked as if he would rather be painting his own fingernails, he dutifully looked at the chips. After a long moment's scrutiny, he pointed to one on the edge of the pile.

"I like this one. Cocoa Heaven. A nice warm brown."

Remarkable! She grinned at him. "You have good taste, Dylan Caine. That's exactly the one I was going to choose. Why did you pick that one?"

He shrugged. "It just reminded me of my dog. He's got a spot on his back exactly that color."

She laughed hard at that; she couldn't help herself. He smiled, too, and the moment seemed to pull and stretch between them. Her heart seemed to give an almost-painful squeeze.

"I should probably go," he said after a pause.

She looked away, flustered at these ridiculous feelings she couldn't seem to control. "Oh. Right. And I've got hours of steaming off wallpaper ahead of me."

He started for the door, stopped for a moment and then turned back around. "Do you need help? I can probably spare an hour or so for you. It might help the work go a little faster with two of us."

She stared at him, shocked by the offer. He looked as if he wasn't quite sure why he had made it—and perhaps was already regretting it—but she didn't care. She was deeply grateful, both at the help and that he seemed to want to spend more time with her, or at least wasn't in a big rush to hurry away.

"I could definitely use a hand."

"Good thing I've only got one, then." He winced. "Sorry. Habit."

Grandma Pearl got a cat from the animal shelter once who hid under the bed and hissed and lashed out a paw, hackles raised, if anybody tried to get close. Her grandmother had explained the cat had been badly abused by a previous owner, and as a result, attacked instinctively before anybody could strike first. Gen wondered if Dylan pointed out his disability in the same sort of protective mechanism.

With love and care, Mr. Fuzzy had eventually learned to trust Grandma Pearl enough that he lost his bristly ways with her and even most of the time with Genevieve. She had to wonder whether Dylan might ever do the same.

"Do you mind if I bring in my dog?" he asked now. "He's out in the truck, since I only thought I was running in for a second."

She wasn't a huge fan of dogs, but what could she say after he'd offered to help her? "Um, sure."

"I'll be back in a second."

She watched him go, pretty certain he wouldn't be lured to her side with a little catnip and a mouse toy.

"You'll have to be on your best behavior, Tuck," Dylan said to his dog as they walked toward Gen's door. "No scratching at fleas, no jumping up on anybody, no leg-humping. I have a feeling Genevieve hasn't had a lot of experience with a couple of mongrels like us."

Tucker gave him a doleful look out of those big droopy hound-dog eyes and then gave the musical *wooo-wooo* bark his breed was famous for, the song some compared to a choir of angels and others found the most annoying sound in the world.

It was all a matter of perspective.

If he had a single brain cell left in his head, he would just start the truck again, back out of her driveway and head up the canyon. He had no business manufacturing excuses to spend more time with Genevieve Beaumont.

He had no idea why he had. One minute, he had been ready to walk out the door, the next the offer to help had gushed out of him.

Gen made him do the craziest things. Again, no idea why. Bar fights, decorating Christmas trees, stripping wallpaper. What the hell was wrong with him?

He didn't understand any of this—he only knew that she seemed to calm the crazy. He had the strangest feeling of peace when he was with her, as if all the chaos inside him, the anger and bitterness and regret, could finally be still.

She must have been waiting for him to come back. The door opened the moment he rapped on it.

Her eyes grew wary as she looked at the big dog, who reached past her hip. She reached a hand out to offer a tentative pat on Tuck's head. Sensing a sucker, his dog turned those sad, please-love-me eyes in her direction and nudged at her hand as if he hadn't just spent two hours at Pop's getting attention from all the girls.

Gen scratched behind one floppy ear and Tuck's eyes just about rolled back in his head.

"Wow. He's . . . big. I'm used to smaller dogs. My mom has a bichon frise."

He wasn't quite sure what that was, though an image of a little white ball of fur stuck in his head. His dog was big and brawny, with broad shoulders and that morose face.

"Don't worry. He's a big softy. Aren't you, Tucker?"

At his name, the dog barked a little, nothing too prolonged, as it could be, but Genevieve still looked startled.

"What kind of dog is Tucker?"

"A black-and-tan coonhound. It's quite an honorable breed. George Washington actually had many of them, including the most famous—Drunkard, Taster, Tipler and Tipsy."

"A proud heritage indeed," she said. "Do you, er, hunt raccoons?"

He barely managed to keep from snorting. What kind of good old boy did she think he was? On the other hand, he drove a dilapidated pickup truck and his coat had definitely seen better days.

"No. I actually got him when I was stationed in Georgia. Somebody dropped him and a couple others in his litter by the side of this little backwoods road. I just about hit him one night driving home from visiting a friend but managed to swerve just in time. Instead, I hit a mile marker post and scraped up the fender of a really nice Dodge Ram pickup truck, too. I found homes for the other puppies, but by then Tucker and I were pretty good friends."

He gave the dog an affectionate scratch. Maybe he did have a bit of good old boy in him. His favorite moments were long, lazy summer evenings on the porch of his house watching the shadows stretch over the mountains and the world go dark while Tuck dozed at his feet.

He doubted Genevieve would appreciate knowing Dylan found the same peace with his dog that he did listening to her chatter.

"Does he need anything? Some water or, I don't know, some peanut butter on a cracker or something?"

He shook his head. "My nieces and nephews have been giving him treats under the table all evening, none of it good for him. He probably just needs a warm place to take a nap."

As if on cue, the dog headed to a patch of carpet in the living room in front of a heater vent, circled a few times to claim it as his and then stretched out.

Once the dog was settled, Gen turned back to Dylan. "How much experience do you have with a wallpaper steamer?"

"About as much as you've had with black-and-tan coonhounds, I imagine."

She smiled, tucking a stray lock of hair behind her ear. He liked seeing her this way, with her hair a little tousled, her skin flushed, her face fresh and natural.

She would probably look just like this after making love.

Everything inside him seemed to shiver, and he had to take several sharp breaths to regain control.

"I've been thinking about the logistics here," she went on, "and I think it would be best if you direct the steamer while I scrape off the wallpaper."

He could handle that, as long as he could keep these inappropriate sexual thoughts at bay.

She frowned. "You're not really dressed for this. It's a messy job. I'm going to be sticky with wallpaper glue and little shreds of paper for weeks."

Pop didn't strictly have a dress code for his Sunday dinners, but he didn't appreciate his family showing up in any old thing, either. Dylan had worn a blue long-sleeved oxford to dinner, with the sleeve pinned up over his stump.

He should have worn the prosthetic arm. As painful as it could be some days, it wasn't quite as unsightly as that empty sleeve.

"It's fine. It will wash."

"Just take off your shirt. I can see you're wearing a T-shirt underneath. You can just work in that and then change back into the other shirt when we're done."

He shifted, wondering what he had gotten himself into. He ought to tell her to forget this whole thing. He hated dressing and undressing with one hand. It was awkward and uncomfortable, especially trying to shrug out of a shirt. He also didn't wear short sleeves much anymore, even in the summertime.

"Sure. Okay," he finally muttered. Feeling stupid, he did his best to unbutton the shirt without looking like a three-year-old learning to undress himself and then pulled it off and hung it over the same chair with his coat.

She was watching him, her eyes wide and her color high. Morbid fascination, he might have thought, except she seemed to be looking more at his chest and his shoulders than the empty spot below his left elbow.

"Where do we start?" he asked.

She cleared her throat and tucked another strand of hair behind her ear. "Um. This is the steamer."

She turned it on. Tucker looked up through the doorway at the whining noise then dropped his head again, the lazy old thing.

A hose led from the main machine on the floor to a rectangle panel about the size of a notebook. Tendrils of steam curled out of it.

Gen handed that part to him. "Just hold the plate against the wall to moisten the paper and release the glue, section by section. I'll come along behind you and try to find an edge to lift away with the scraper."

After a few moments, they fell into a comfortable rhythm. Working vertically, he would steam a piece for a moment then she would scrape that while he moved to the next area. By necessity, they had to stay close together, the steam from the machine swirling around them in an oddly intimate way. He was hyperaware of his body—each pulse of blood through his veins, each inhale and exhale.

He was also aware of her, the flex and release of her biceps as she worked, the way she nibbled her lip as she scraped away at a particularly difficult spot, how her T-shirt molded to her chest . . .

"Oh. I almost forgot," Gen said after a few moments. "I had music going while I worked. I turned it off to answer the door."

She pulled a tiny silver remote out of the pocket of worn jeans and aimed it at a small speaker unit in the corner. Some kind of weird music eased out, lots of accordion and mournful French that sounded like something out of a smoky Paris jazz café.

He raised an eyebrow. "Really?"

Her expression turned rueful. "What can I say? Sometimes I'm in a mood. What would you prefer?"

His music tastes were all over the place but lately he mostly enjoyed classic rock. It might help keep his mind off enjoying a little *ooh là là* with her.

"Got any CCR or Stones?"

"I can make a playlist."

She fiddled with the MP3 player attached to the speakers, and a moment later, Mick and the gang started in on "I Can't Get No Satisfaction."

Perfect.

The work was physically demanding but not disagreeable. He had already found at his house in the canyon that deconstruction—tearing down in order to rebuild—could be oddly satisfying. The experience was the same here.

Together, they made good progress. After maybe half an hour, they finished the second wall. She stopped and shook out her arms.

"Why don't we trade places for a while?" he suggested. "Your arms are probably killing you."

"But I can always switch if one gets tired," she said, her expression solemn.

Something bleak and grim lodged in his chest. "Don't feel sorry for me, Gen," he said quietly. "I feel sorry enough for myself."

He grabbed the scraper away from her and set to work on the section he had last steamed.

After a charged moment, she picked up the steamer. "So I'm thinking about ripping up the carpet next," she said. "I pulled up the tacks in one corner and it looked as if it had hardwood underneath. I have no idea how to refinish floors but I read an article this afternoon online and it didn't sound all that difficult. You have to start with tearing out the carpets, obviously, and then you remove all the tacking strips, which sounds like an awful job. I can't imagine how gross it will be under the carpet. I might have to rent a floor sander but they have those at the home-improvement store."

She started chattering about finishing wood floors, about buying new hardware for the kitchen cabinets, about all the other things she planned to do on the house—many of which she had already told him up at the cabins, but he didn't care. The words surged over and through him, edged with an oddly poignant sweetness that left no room for the bitter.

She knew.

Somehow she knew how much he liked listening to her talk about anything and every-thing in that throaty, sexy voice.

She couldn't possibly understand why. Even he wasn't sure he comprehended why her conversation filled some gaping chasm inside him, how focusing on the mundane details helped keep all the ugliness at bay.

A fragile sort of tenderness seemed to twist and writhe around them like the steam, easing its way around all that ugliness, scraping him bare just like he peeled away her wall.

He faltered in his steady movements but quickly recovered. He couldn't let himself have feelings for her. Now, *that* was a freaking disaster in the making. He pushed it away and focused instead on the story she was telling him about a trip she took to the wine country of the Loire Valley with some friends.

Before he knew it, she had jabbered her way around the entire room. His arm throbbed from the relentless scraping, but it was a good kind of sore, earned through hard work and effort.

"I guess that's the last of it," she wound down enough to say and turned off the steamer. The music on the media player had stopped, too, without either of them being aware of it.

The room suddenly seemed far too quiet.

"I can't tell you how much I appreciate all your help, Dylan. You've saved me so much time and energy. Thank you."

"You're welcome," he said gruffly, wondering what the hell was wrong with him that he actually felt more centered and calm after an hour of scraping wallpaper layers off a wall with Genevieve Beaumont than he had from sharing dinner with the people he loved most in the world.

"I must have yakked your ears off."

"You didn't. See? Still here." He tugged at an earlobe and she smiled a little.

She tucked that errant hair behind her ear again. Her fingers were long and slender—elegant, even with her battered manicure.

He should leave. Now. The warning bells sounded in his head but he ignored them. Instead, he crossed the small space between them, leaned down and took what he had been thinking about since the moment he walked into her grandmother's ugly house.

Chapter Nine

❄ ❄ ❄

On the crazy scale, kissing Genevieve Beaumont topped out at "Are-you-out-of-your-freaking-mind?"

He knew it intellectually in the tiny sliver of his brain that could still function at that level, but he ignored it. This just felt too right, too perfect. It had been so damn long since he had felt the wonder of a woman's kiss—the soft sweetness of her breath mingling with his, the press of her curves against his chest through thin cotton, the urgent churn of his blood.

Other than a shocked inhale, she didn't react for a few seconds, then he felt the slide of her arms around his neck and she returned his kiss with delicious intensity.

His mouth moved on hers, wondering how he could possibly have forgotten how delicious that surge of blood, that edgy hunger could feel.

She tasted sweet and minty, with just a hint of that vanilla scent that surrounded her. She made a soft, sexy sound in her throat and he deepened the kiss, unable to believe she was here next to him, her mouth warm and enthusiastic against his.

Their mouths fit together perfectly. In his experience, that wasn't always the case. First kisses could be awkward affairs, trying to figure out what to move where, but this . . . This was better than any of the increasingly heated dreams he'd been having about her since that memorable night at The Speckled Lizard.

She made another sexy sound and drew her hands up around his neck. He had to be closer to her. Without thinking, he went to wrap his arms around her. Both arms.

She faltered a little, just a tiny stiffening, but he felt the sudden tension and ice crackled through him.

He had forgotten. For one brief, amazing moment, he had completely forgotten the vast gulf between them.

He jerked away, his breathing ragged and his heart pulsing in his chest like the first time he'd jumped from a plane in Airborne School.

"You . . . didn't have to stop."

She sounded breathless, and she looked absolutely delectable—her lips slightly swollen, her cheeks flushed, her eyes dazed. He was almost positive she had been just as into the kiss as he had been.

It was the *almost* there that slayed him.

What if she hadn't been? What if she had only been playing along to protect his feelings, so he didn't feel like an ass for kissing her? They were friends, of a sort. She knew more about him than his family by now.

He knew she had a much softer heart than she let on—maybe she didn't want to hurt his feelings by showing her revulsion.

He grabbed his shirt off the chair in the entryway and shoved his stump through the sleeve, out of sight. He was aghast at his sudden urge to plow his fist through the walls they had just scraped.

He mustered as much calm as he could. "We both know that was a mistake."

"Do we?"

She seemed genuinely confused. How could she act all innocent, as if nothing out of the ordinary had happened, as if the world hadn't suddenly shifted, as if she could see nothing wrong in the kiss?

"For the next few weeks, we're obligated by the court system to work together. How will we do that when things are funky between us?"

"Why would things be funky over a simple kiss?"

It hadn't been simple. To him, the kiss had been magical. Hearts and flowers and choirs of angels singing. Okay, they were naughty angels, yeah, singing about tangled bodies and slick skin and losing himself inside her, but singing nonetheless.

He wasn't about to admit that to her, not when she was acting as if it meant nothing. A simple kiss. Huh.

"Don't worry. It won't happen again. My stump and I won't disgust you anymore."

"Who says you disgust me?"

"Your body language did. Come on, Gen. Don't pretend. I felt how you flinched away when I accidentally touched you."

Her color rose a little higher. "You're imagining things."

"Am I? Go ahead. Touch it." He unpinned his sleeve and shoved the cuff up, extending his arm as far as it would go.

"This is stupid."

She looked at him and at his arm, the puckered edge, the scars. He saw something in her eyes, something deep and troubled. Oddly, it didn't look like disgust. After a pause when she made no move forward, he yanked the sleeve down again and shrugged into his coat.

"Yeah. It is stupid," he said quietly. "So was kissing you. It won't happen again."

She opened her mouth to respond, but he cut her off. "Come on, Tucker."

The dog rose, stretching his hind legs first and then his front before he padded sleepily over to Dylan.

"Wait. You don't have to leave."

He gave her a long, solemn look. "Your wallpaper is down. You should be all ready to paint now."

She chewed her lip. "Dylan—"

"Good night, Gen. See you tomorrow."

After a long pause she sighed, still looking troubled. "Thank you for your help. You saved me a great deal of time and energy."

He nodded, whistled to his dog and headed for the door.

That had to rank among the strangest hours of her life.

Gen stood at the window watching Dylan's battered old pickup drive away through the snow that had begun to flutter down, coating the roadway with a thin layer that reflected white in his headlights.

She thought of working beside him as they removed the wallpaper, of that strangely sweet mood, tenderness and affection and that sexual awareness that had swirled around them like the steam.

And then that kiss.

Everything inside her shivered at the memory of his mouth on hers, firm and demanding, of the scent of him, masculine and outdoorsy. In all her twenty-six years, no kiss had ever stirred her like that.

As usual, she had ruined everything, startled by the unexpected feel of his unnaturally smooth arm against her back where she had expected another hand.

He thought she had been repelled. She didn't know how to tell him she hadn't found anything disgusting, only different. If he had given her another minute or two, she would have touched him when he'd demanded it. She hadn't been able to find the nerve, not with him watching her so intently. She had been too busy being over-whelmed with compassion and sorrow for all he had endured.

She closed her eyes, tasting him on her lips again, sweet and sexy. She wanted to savor the moment, especially given his determination that it had been a mistake that wouldn't happen again.

Why would he want to kiss her again? What could she possibly have to interest a man like

WALLINGFORD PUBLIC LIBRARY
200 North Main Street
Wallingford, CT 06492

Dylan? He thought her some kind of empty-headed party girl who only cared about fashion and design.

She sighed and began cleaning up the mess left in the dining room. Shredded paper, sticky with wallpaper paste, covered the floor in piles.

Remodeling a house was sloppy and dirty and hard.

Kind of like her life felt right now.

Once again, Grandma Pearl's annoying Hallelujah doorbell rang just as she was giving her hair a final brush.

Thus far, she hadn't had a single visitor worthy of such a gleeful announcement. She might have been happy to see Dylan the night before but by the time he left, she certainly wasn't singing the man's praises.

Luck still wasn't with her. She opened the door with the security chain in place and saw only a faux-fur coat so authentic-looking she sometimes wondered if it was real.

She wanted to close the door again, lock it tight and sneak out the back. Too bad she instantly saw a few obvious problems with that. For one thing, she wouldn't be able to back out her BMW without smashing her mother's Mercedes SUV in the driveway. For another, eventually Laura would find her, and she was quite sure she wouldn't like dealing with the consequences.

After fumbling with the chain with fingers that felt graceless and awkward, she pulled open the door. "Mother. Here you are again, bright and early."

"I know. Crazy, isn't it? I decided on a whim last night to drive into Denver to finish some last-minute Christmas shopping. When your father and I were in Switzerland in August, I bought a really lovely sweater for my friend Annamaria—you know, that nice tennis pro I've been working with lately. But she told me last month she's expecting a baby. Can you believe that? I certainly can't give her a size-four sweater now, when she won't be able to wear it for a whole year."

"That is a quandary."

"I've shopped in every store in Hope's Crossing without finding anything I think she would like, but I'm sure I'll be able to pick something up in Denver."

"Well, good luck."

Her mother pushed her way into the house and pulled off her leather driving gloves. "I thought perhaps you could come with me, darling. We haven't spent nearly enough time together since you've been home from Paris. Wouldn't it be fun to have lunch at the Brown Palace and walk through our favorite shops?"

Laura gave her a strangely tentative smile. She seemed almost . . . desperate for Genevieve to go with her.

"Oh, I can't. I have to work at the center today. I wish you had called before driving over here," she said, surprised that she meant the words and that she actually felt a little regret at having to refuse.

Her mother pursed her lips. "Again? Didn't you work several days last week?"

Gen fought back a sigh. Despite having a workaholic husband, Laura seemed to think the rest of the world existed just to fill her own leisure hours. She couldn't always have been this way. The Beaumonts were not wealthy when she was little, only for the past twenty years or so.

"I really am sorry, Mother, but I have to finish a hundred community-service hours by January. I've completed sixteen, which still leaves me eighty-four to go. I'm probably going to have to go every day until Christmas."

"It's ridiculous. That's what it is! I don't understand how your father could let this happen. He said he would fix it. He talked to the judge! I thought everything was settled. You did absolutely nothing wrong. I don't understand how you can let yourself become a virtual slave to that . . . that wounded-soldier outfit."

"I'm not a slave. And Father did talk to the judge. While he couldn't reduce my time, I did have the option to go somewhere else for the rest of my hours. I chose not to because I have committed to A Warrior's Hope and right now they need me."

She doubted her mother would understand that particular concept.

"You could call in sick. Surely they won't make you come in to work if you're under the weather."

"True, but I'm not under the weather," she pointed out.

"You could tell them you are," her mother persisted. "Everyone deserves a little holiday. I was so looking forward to having a day of shopping, just the two of us. Girls' day in the city. It's just what we both need."

Even if she didn't have to go to the recreation center that day, she couldn't have spared the time to shop with money she didn't have in Denver. Not when she had this horrible house hanging around her neck like a hideous scarf.

"I can't, Mother. They're expecting me today at A Warrior's Hope. We have new guests arriving, which is apparently a stressful time, and I'm in charge of decorating for the welcome reception."

Anticipating the task ahead of her after Charlotte asked her Saturday, Gen had even bought some supplies the day before around town and gathered more from nature. She couldn't wait to see how they turned out. She didn't mind the decorating part of things, but she was more than a little nervous about meeting a roomful of wounded veterans and their families. Would they all be bitter and angry like Dylan? Anxiety fluttered through her.

"Come on, darling. Someone else could do that for you," Laura pressed. "We haven't had a moment together since you arrived. I'm anxious to catch up and find out about all those French men you've been dating."

She didn't have much to tell in that direction. She had dated a few. While she had inevitably been entranced by their charm and wit, she hadn't had a silly girlish crush on any of them. None had made her chest tingle or her stomach twirl with nerves like Dylan Caine did.

She swallowed. "I can't."

Laura heaved a sigh. "I suppose I'll have to spend the day in Denver by myself."

If she didn't know better, Genevieve might think her mother sounded almost . . . lonely.

On impulse, she stepped forward and kissed her mother's cheek. Laura smelled of Estée Lauder makeup and the Annick Goutal perfume she always wore. "I'll have an afternoon off either Wednesday or Thursday. Perhaps we can go to lunch here in Hope's Crossing. Several new restaurants have opened since I've been back. If that doesn't work out, let's definitely plan on brunch Sunday."

"I have a hair appointment Wednesday and a luncheon party at the country club Thursday. I'll make reservations for Le Passe Montagne for Sunday morning. Charlie is coming home this week after his finals so we can all go together."

"Deal."

Her mother hugged her and then stepped back. She looked around the house, her carefully constructed nose wrinkled with distaste.

"This house. It's terrible. It looks like you're living in a war zone! I don't understand why you can't just sell the place as is. Whoever buys this land will probably tear this horrible house down."

Though she suspected her mother was right, she still felt a pang of regret she didn't quite understand. She hated the house, too, though the funkiness was growing on her. She didn't want to contemplate the idea of someone razing it.

If that was the eventual outcome, she still wanted to pour as much as she could afford, financially and physically, into making the house presentable. The better the house looked, the more she could make in profit from the sale.

Her mother probably couldn't understand that, especially as *she* wasn't the one fighting for a future. Laura had always hated this place, only in part because of the outdated decor that Grandma Pearl refused to change.

Laura and Grandma Pearl hadn't really gotten along. Her grandmother had had little patience for her daughter-in-law's social ambitions, and Laura had had even less for Grandma Pearl's loud, gaudy, sometimes abrasive personality.

"Oh. Look at that," Laura exclaimed. "You've

taken down that atrocious wallpaper. That must have been a job by yourself."

She thought about letting the false impression stand but something compelled her to honesty. "I wasn't by myself. I had help. Dylan Caine came over last night and worked with me to strip the walls."

Her stomach tingled again as she remembered that kiss that had happened right about where her mother stood.

Laura frowned. "Which Caine brother is that? There are dozens of them."

"Only six, Mother. He's the youngest son."

Laura looked baffled for a moment, trying to put the pieces together, and then her eyes widened. "Dylan. He's the one who lives up in Snowflake Canyon. The one who lost his arm."

"Yes," she said calmly. "That's the one."

Laura stared at her. "Why would you have him help you? What can he even *do* without an arm?"

Kiss her until she couldn't remember her name, for one thing. He had amazing skills in that direction, but she was quite certain her mother wouldn't appreciate that particular insight.

"Plenty of things. Just about everything." Whether he wanted to believe it or not. "He was amazingly helpful last night. I honestly couldn't have managed without him."

Her mother's frown deepened. "Is there . . .

something going on with you and Dylan Caine your father and I should know about?"

Heaven forbid. Her parents didn't need to know *anything* about whatever might be going on with her and Dylan. Not that there was anything to know.

"Why would you say that?" she countered.

"As I am remembering things now, he's the one who got you into trouble, isn't he? Yes. I remember now. He was in that bar fight with you. And now you tell me he came over on a Sunday night to help you with home renovations. What am I supposed to think?"

How would her family react if she started seeing Dylan? He was so vastly different from Sawyer, her parents' ideal of a potential mate for her. Where Sawyer had been cultured, polite, polished and adroit, Dylan was rough, shaggy. Dangerous.

Her parents would probably totally freak. Her dad would start blustering around about bad boys and silly girls; her mother would shriek and ask what all her friends would think.

Charlie would be cool about it. Since his time in juvenile detention, she sometimes thought her little brother was just about the most grounded person in the family.

Not that it mattered how they might react, since it was the most hypothetical of questions. He had kissed her, yes, but swore it wouldn't happen again.

On that depressing note, she ushered her mother

to the door. "You don't need to worry about me and Dylan Caine, Mother. We're friends, that's all. That's why he helped me last night."

Laura didn't look convinced. She opened her mouth to argue, but Genevieve wasn't in the mood to talk about Dylan another minute and especially not with her mother.

"I'm sorry but I've really got to go. I'm already late. Have a great time in Denver. Love you, Mother."

Before Laura could protest or shove one of her black leather boots in the frame, Genevieve managed to close the door and lock it tight.

Chapter Ten

❄ ❄ ❄

This was becoming a habit.

Genevieve adjusted a fold of garland on the seventh Christmas tree she had decorated for A Warrior's Hope then eased back a little to admire the results.

This one—located in the main reception room just off the lobby of the recreation center, with equally stunning views of the mountains—was bigger than those in the cabins. While the tree already had a few basic decorations, they were sparse and lackluster.

Saturday she had bought jute and spray paint at the hardware store and then had stopped into the craft store for a roll of burlap and ribbon.

Just before scraping wallpaper Sunday, she had gathered some bare branches from Grandma Pearl's yard, laid them flat in the garage and spray-painted them with a little silver. Not too much, just a hint.

She had felt more than a little silly spending money she didn't really have, but she was pleased with the results.

As this room with its big river-rock fireplace and wide windows would serve as the main gathering spot for everybody, she had wanted it to be as warm and welcoming as their cabins. The program participants shouldn't want to only spend all their time in their individual spaces.

"Oh, wow. This looks fantastic, Genevieve."

From her perch on top of a ladder, she glanced down to find Dylan's sister watching from the doorway. She looked smart and pretty in tan slacks and a pale blue sweater.

"Do you think so? I was afraid the silver branches were too much."

"Not at all. They're perfect. It sets just the right tone, I think. Not too fancy, with a focus on nature." She moved farther into the room and looked around at the table decorations Gen had thrown together to be reused throughout the week, a mix of flowers donated from the florist in town, the burlap and more of those spray-painted branches.

"All I can say is, it was a lucky thing for A Warrior's Hope that you decided to get into a bar fight at the Lizard."

Gen gave a rueful smile. "I do what I can."

"And we appreciate it." Charlotte gave her a warm look that made Gen glow more than the eight hundred lights on the tree.

"I don't have your aesthetic sense, that's for sure," the other woman continued. "Seriously, have you ever thought about being an interior decorator?"

"Yes, actually." She climbed down from the ladder and was grateful to be on solid ground again. She really didn't like heights. "I graduated from college with a degree in interior design. I'd like to open my own company someday."

"You'll be wonderful at it," Charlotte assured her.

"Thank you."

"I came to tell you they're only fifteen minutes away. Spence just called from the road with a status update."

"Great," she lied, nerves crashing around in her stomach like drunken butterflies. "I had better finish up in here, then, and put away all the supplies."

"I can help you with that."

"You don't have a million other things to do?"

"At this particular moment in time, no. Amazingly enough. Everything is done, as far as I know. Alex and her crew are on the way from Brazen with dinner. We'll have the welcome reception and then dinner, then let everybody settle in after their day of traveling. Tomorrow the fun starts in earnest."

That was a matter of perspective. "Will you be here the whole week?"

"I wish. Unfortunately, I've still got a store to run. Sugar Rush is crazy-busy this time of year, with everybody wanting custom orders at the last minute. I'll be here on and off most of the week. Eden, Chelsea and Mac should have everything under control, with all the other volunteers that come and go. Plus you and Dylan, who will be here full-time."

She hadn't seen the man since he'd left her house the night before after that stunning kiss.

"I guess Dylan went to help with the airport pickups," she said since his sister brought up his name. She tried to inject a casual tone into her voice, but she was afraid she failed when Charlotte flashed her an intent look.

"He wasn't very happy about it, but yes. Spence talked him into going with him."

What would Charlotte say if she knew about that stunning kiss—or that Genevieve fiercely wanted more?

"What would you like me to do during the

welcome reception?" she asked, quickly changing the subject.

"Just try to make everyone feel comfortable. That's all. Change can be overwhelming to some of these guys, especially the few we have with head injuries, and the logistics of traveling can be stressful. The first night, we just try to relax and let them settle in, become familiar with the place, that sort of thing."

Those nerves snarled in her stomach again. This part was easy. Hanging a few ornaments, wielding a can of spray paint, arranging some flowers.

Interacting with people who had been through hell was a different situation entirely.

On the other hand, she liked Dylan and had been able to get along fine with him, with only a few faux pas. She would just try to treat the others as she did him.

Except for the serious-crush part. Oh, and the kissing.

The guests of A Warrior's Hope arrived at the recreation center in three separate vans. Eden, in her hyperorganized way, had emailed Genevieve —and everyone else, she assumed—a list of everyone attending this eight-day-long camp, as well as photos and a quick biographical sketch and which family members they would be bringing as guests.

The two men using wheelchairs were easy to

identify. One was young with blond hair and an open, fresh-faced demeanor. Army Corporal Trey Evans hailed from Alabama, she knew, and had limited use of his legs after a spinal-cord injury. He was also the only warrior attending without any family members.

In quite startling contrast, the other man using a wheelchair must be Army Sergeant Joe Brooks. He was surrounded by family—a wife, Tonya, Gen remembered from the bio, who was just about the most beautiful woman Gen had ever seen in person, and two adorable girls with hair in a flurry of braids, Marisol and Claudia. One of the girls sat on his lap and the other one held her mother's hand as they walked in beside the chair.

She knew two of the men had suffered brain injuries. They were a little harder to pick out, until she remembered one was coming with his parents. Judging by the way an older couple fussed around a tall, good-looking man with a buzz cut, she guessed that was Marine Lance Corporal Robert Augustine and his parents, Robert Sr. and Marie.

She found the other one, Ricardo Torres, and his wife, Elena. When Eden sent his bio picture, Gen had thought he reminded her of one of her friends in Paris. Now she saw the similarity was even more pronounced. That would help her remember his name.

Lieutenant Pam Bryant was quite easy to pick

out, as well. She was a pretty, compact woman with severe scarring over one side of her face who walked with a pronounced limp. Beside her was her fiancé, Kevin.

The last group to come in had to be Marine Lance Corporal Jason Reid and his wife, Whitney, who carried a little boy who was probably about three.

They were all talking together and laughing, though a few seemed tired and Jason Reid had a stony expression that discouraged conversation.

What did she have to talk about with any of these people anyway? She knew nothing of what they had endured. Feeling awkward and superfluous, she stood in one corner, trying to gather the courage to mingle.

Eden and Mac moved through the crowd, handing out appetizers, drinks, snacks for the children. Even Dylan was deep in conversation with Pam Bryant.

Etiquette and manners had been drilled into her from the time she used to go to dance class. She knew it was the height of rudeness to stand here in the corner. She had to make some kind of effort. By avoiding interactions, she likely appeared rude and snobbish, exactly how people perceived her.

What was she supposed to say to any of them? The old social nicety of seeking points of commonality seemed ludicrous under these circumstances. What could she and these battle-scarred men—and Lieutenant Bryant—who had seen and done so much, possibly have in common? It seemed ridiculous to even try making faltering conversation.

She stood shifting her weight from foot to foot, gazing out the window to avoid eye contact, wishing she were anywhere else on earth.

Finally, after about ten minutes, one of the men took the matter out of her hands.

"Hey there. What's so interesting out there?"

She turned to find the younger man in the wheelchair had approached without her realizing. Trey Evans, she remembered. Up close, she could see he was about her age, with sun-streaked hair and quite handsome features. Not Dylan-gorgeous but enough to make most women a little flustered.

"It's not a matter of something else being more interesting than present company. I'm just a little . . . out of my comfort zone."

"Aren't we all, darlin'."

She had to smile at his easy charm and Southern drawl.

"You don't like Colorado?"

"Never been here. All I can say is, you all sure know how to bring it when it comes to mountains and snow."

"We do our best."

He held out a hand. "I'm Trey Evans. You can probably tell I'm not from around here. I'm originally from Wetumpka, Alabama."

She could feel herself relax. He was just a kid who had lost a great deal. She shook his hand. "Hi, Trey. I'm Gen Beaumont. Welcome to Hope's Crossing. I hope you enjoy your stay. I'm actually from here, though I've been living in Paris until recently. Do you know which cabin you're in yet?"

"No idea. Why?"

She felt stupid for asking. "I helped decorate them for the holidays last week. They all have different themes and I have a few of my favorites. I was just curious which one you would be staying in."

"So you're, what, the staff decorator or something?"

She could feel more tension seep away. This wasn't so bad. She could handle small talk. "Something like that. Mostly, I do what they tell me."

Except for the part about relaxing and making everyone feel comfortable. So far, that was a big fail on her part.

"You're the general dogsbody, then."

"I don't have any idea what that means, but, um, sure."

He laughed, taking a sip of the drink he had somehow managed to prop on his lap when he wheeled over. "My grandpap used to call me that when I was a kid and would spend the day at his store being his grunt. Running for change to the bank, sweeping the floors, grabbing him another coffee next door. It means errand boy. Gofer. Whatever you want to call it."

"That would be me." Something in this young man's casual friendliness appealed to her, maybe because it presented such a sharp contrast to Dylan's general surly reticence. "If you want to know the truth, I'm here for court-ordered community service."

He nearly spilled his precariously balanced drink. She saw him catch it just in time, eyes wide, though some dribbled over the lip of the cup onto his slacks. "Community service? Wow. Didn't expect that one. Seriously?"

She scooped up a napkin from a nearby table and handed it to him. "Do I look like the kind of girl who would lie about something as embarrassing as that?"

His long scrutiny wasn't flirtatious, only friendly, edged with a daub of sadness she didn't quite understand given their lighthearted conversation.

"No. But I have to say, you don't look like the kind of girl who would be here on court-ordered community service, either. What did you do? Let me guess." He narrowed his gaze. "Shoplifting."

"I beg your pardon." She sniffed. She had many faults, but she considered herself an honest person in general and disliked deception in others. She'd broken an engagement over it, for heaven's sake.

"No?" He set his drink on a table and wheeled around her adeptly, trying to see her from a different angle. "How about . . . tax evasion."

"Not even close."

Dylan had moved closer, she saw, and was now in conversation with the Augustines about six feet away. When she glanced over, she found him watching her interaction with Trey out of the corner of his gaze—quite a trick, when one eye was covered by that ever-present black eye patch.

She turned back to Trey, suddenly enjoying herself much more than she expected. "Do you want to hear the ugly truth?"

"Oh, hell yeah. Lay it on me."

She smiled, leaned in close and tried for her best bad-girl voice. "I started a bar fight and ended up busting the nose of the assistant district attorney."

Trey laughed so hard some of the other guests looked over with curious looks—including Dylan, whose expression was far more inscrutable.

"I would have paid good money to see that."

"Sorry to disappoint you, but I don't intend for there to ever be a repeat performance. It was purely a one-off. I learned my lesson. The next time some idiot decides to play every conceivable rendition of 'The Little Drummer Boy' on the jukebox of the worst dive in town, I plan to pay my tab and leave."

He laughed again, so hard that Lieutenant Bryant and her fiancé approached.

"What's so funny over here?" the woman asked.

"This is Gen Beaumont. She was just telling me a story about breaking a woman's nose over Christmas carols."

Lieutenant Bryant grinned. "Wow. Remind me not to sing 'Jingle Bells' around you."

At first, Genevieve was uncomfortable looking at that scarred face that must have once been quite pretty, but after a few moments' conversation, she relaxed, especially when the other woman commented about how much she loved her sweater and asked where she could find one.

Gen launched into a conversation about her favorite of the few shopping spots in town, which drew the attention of Tonya Brooks and Elena Torres. Before she knew it, she was offering to take the women on a shopping expedition into town if it could be arranged.

Perhaps this wasn't such a bad way to spend her community-service hours after all.

Chapter Eleven

If he hadn't seen it with his own eyes, he wouldn't have believed it.

While he did his best to make conversation, fighting the urge to escape to his canyon retreat with every breath, Genevieve held court in the corner. She seemed to have charmed just about everyone who had come in contact with her. Every time he turned around, the group was laughing. More often than not, Gen was in the middle of it.

He wasn't quite sure what to think about that. He supposed he should have expected it from a socialite like her. When she put her mind to it, she could probably charm whomever she wanted.

He wasn't sure what switch had been flipped after about the first ten minutes of the gathering, when she had stood in the corner looking awkward and immensely uncomfortable, but now she seemed relaxed and outgoing.

The more she relaxed, the more his tension escalated. For a guy who had lived as a virtual hermit for months, all this socializing left him as edgy as his chickens in a windstorm.

He was wondering how much longer he had to stay when his sister came over with a plate of appetizers she handed him.

"I haven't seen you eating anything. You've got to be hungry, aren't you?"

"Not really."

"Eat. You'll feel better."

Apparently she had inherited the need to feed from their father, who was never happy unless he was cooking up something delicious. He knew she wouldn't let up until he took the plate, so he gave in to the inevitable, even though he felt stupid propping the plate in the inside crook of his left elbow. He had worn one of the prosthetics today. While it could be useful for some tasks, holding a small appetizer plate wasn't among them.

"Thanks for helping with all the airport pickups today. Spence said you were a great help with loading all the luggage."

"I don't recall being given much choice in the matter. Spence basically told me to get my ass in the van."

"You could have stayed here and helped Genevieve decorate, since you're so good at it now."

He glowered at her. It was a good thing he loved her. She would be annoying as hell otherwise.

Genevieve's throaty laugh sounded from the corner, easing through him like a sultry jazz saxophone.

He turned, almost against his will, remembering the magic of having her to himself the night before, that voice soothing him.

That kiss that had left him aching and hungry.

"She's turning out to be rather a surprise, isn't she?" Charlotte said, following his gaze.

"Why do you say that?" he said, his voice gruff. He was really, really grateful his sister couldn't read his mind right now.

"You know what Laura Beaumont is like," Charlotte said with a shrug.

"Not really. I haven't lived in Hope's Crossing in years."

"Don't you remember how exacting she used to be when she would come into the restaurant when we were kids? She demanded perfection. I can remember once when I worked at the diner one summer during college, she made me fix the same Cobb salad three times. Each time, something stupid was wrong. The croutons weren't crisp enough, the tomatoes were wilted, the onions tasted off."

She grinned suddenly, looking young and mischievous, a rarity for a girl who had grown up too quickly after their mother's death. "Here's something funny. The fourth time, I just rearranged the very same salad she had just turned up her nose at and took it back to her table, and she declared it perfection, finally."

"Oh, man. I hope Pop didn't catch you doing that."

"No. He would have been livid about not giving the customer what she wanted. I never did figure out how he could always be so tolerant of her fussiness." She paused. "But then, that's Pop for you. He's entirely too patient when it comes to some people."

By the pointed way she said that last part, he was guessing she meant him. True enough. He hadn't made things easy on their father.

"Anyway," Charlotte went on, "during the process of planning her wedding, Gen gained a reputation in town as basically being a carbon copy of her mother. Nothing was ever good enough for her. My friend Claire, who owns the bead store, was charged with hand-beading the bodice of this incredible wedding gown Genevieve ordered from a designer back East. It took months for Genevieve to agree on the pattern and then more months for Claire to get it just right in her eyes. And then, of course, she had to do it all over again after Genevieve's brother and some other teenagers vandalized Claire's store and destroyed it."

He vaguely remembered hearing something about that in connection with a tragedy that had affected the town some years ago during his second-to-last deployment.

"I'll admit, I don't know her well, especially since she's been gone the last few years, but she has always struck me as someone who demands perfection," Charlotte went on. Though she didn't give him that same pointed look, the implication behind her words was obvious.

Perfection didn't come in the form of a broken-down ex-soldier who could barely hold an appetizer plate.

"She's different somehow. Not what I imagined," Charlotte went on. "She's worked really hard since she's been here. She spent all day today decorating this place by herself. She even brought a lot of supplies with her, things she must have prepared ahead of time. I would never have expected that."

He remembered their kiss the night before, her soft, eager response, the silk of her hair sliding through his fingers.

As far as he was concerned, that had been as close to perfection as anything he had known. Hot and sweet at the same time. He had been awake most of the night, staring at the flames in the fireplace and wishing things could be different.

"Can I have everyone's attention?"

Though diminutive, Eden Davis could really project her voice. Everybody looked up, even the kids who were playing in a corner with some toys someone—probably Charlotte—had provided.

"It's been a long day for everyone and I'm sure you would like to relax a little in your cabins for a while before dinner. Your bags should be waiting in your assigned lodging. A staff member will show you the way and help you settle in. The plan is to meet back here at seven for dinner. I promise, you're in for a treat. One of the premier restaurants in this area is providing the meal for you tonight. Brazen is fantastic. It's got phenomenal reviews. I know you'll enjoy it. So we'll see you back here just before seven. Bring an appetite. Could I have all the Hope's Crossing staff up here for a moment?"

Dylan didn't consider himself staff but Charlotte grabbed his elbow and basically dragged him forward. Eden quickly started handing out assignments and instructions.

"Dylan, do you mind helping Trey to his cabin? Genevieve, will you escort Joe and Tonya and their girls?"

Genevieve nodded, though he could tell she was uncomfortable at the prospect. It couldn't be the wheelchair, since she had been completely at ease with Trey. What made her uneasy?

The youngest little Brooks girl beamed up at Genevieve and reached for her hand. After a long pause, she took it, though with obvious wariness. He nearly chuckled. Of course. She wasn't used to kids. In her perfect little society world, she probably hadn't had many interactions with children.

That was one area where he, on the other hand, was completely at ease. Coming from a big family with an overabundance of nieces and nephews had given him plenty of experience with kids.

He almost offered to trade assignments with her and then changed his mind. The corporal didn't need more opportunities to fall head over heels—or wheels, in this case—for Gen.

He approached Trey, who was chatting up Chelsea, the office manager.

"Guess you get to be my tour guide," Trey said.

"Yeah," Dylan said.

"I'll see you later, Chelsea," the kid said.

She waved and Trey started wheeling toward the door that led to the cabins.

"You need help or anything?" Dylan asked.

"Naw. Just hold the door and point me in the right direction."

"Left," he said.

Trey wheeled outside and headed in the direction of the cabins.

"Man, it's gorgeous here," he said. "Only mountains I've seen this big were the Hindu Kush, and they weren't nearly this pretty."

"Except in springtime," he answered.

"No shit."

Trey was silent as they moved toward his cabin, the closest to the recreation center. It was the first one he and Genevieve had decorated together.

"Smoke Gregory said you were a ranger. You lose your hand in Afghanistan?"

He wanted to tell the kid to mind his own damn business, but he didn't have the heart to stomp on all that open friendliness. More power to the guy for not letting bitterness eat away at him.

"Helmand Province. Twelve-year-old insurgent with a suicide pack."

"Oh, man. That's rough. Kandahar for me. Firefight. Got hit by three rounds. My battle rattle stopped most of it but I caught one in my spinal column just below my flak."

Bad business, there. He wondered how Trey was coping, but that wasn't the kind of thing guys asked each other outside group therapy or something.

"Rehab's a bitch, am I right? I do the exercises,

but six months later, I don't know how much good it's doing. My left leg still works but it's weak. At least I can walk with crutches when I have to. The other one might as well be fake, all the good it does me. Sometimes I think a fake leg might even be better. I could put weight on it then, you know?"

"Flesh and blood is better than a prosthetic any way you slice it. So to speak," he muttered.

Trey chuckled as he wheeled up the ramp. "I'll take your word on that."

Dylan helped him with the door and made sure all his luggage was inside waiting for him.

"There's food in the lower cupboards. Should be within reach."

"Thanks."

He felt a little bad about leaving the kid here by himself, especially where everybody else had some kind of family or loved one for support.

"Anything else you need before I take off?"

Trey shook his head. "I should be good. Thanks." He paused. "This is a nice thing you're doing here."

"Not me," he said, quick to disabuse him of any idea to the contrary. "Charlotte, the bossy blonde, is my younger sister and Smoke is an old friend. They dragged me along. I'm only here because I'm doing community service."

Trey looked first surprised and then amused. "No kidding? Seems to be an epidemic of that around Hope's Crossing."

"You must mean Genevieve. We were arrested together."

"Same bar fight?"

He relived that fateful punch and almost laughed out loud. The more he came to know Genevieve, the more funny and completely out of character that moment seemed.

"Yeah. And the same crooked defense attorney —who also happens to be my older brother— arranged this plea deal for us both."

"Doesn't matter why you're here, I suppose. It's still a good thing. And I've got to say, Hope's Crossing might turn out to be more interesting than I expected."

"It has its moments," Dylan answered. "See you later."

" 'Bye."

Dylan headed out into the afternoon sunlight that reflected diamonds in the snow, his mind still on the conversation.

Trey might be young and fairly wet behind the ears but he was right about one thing. There was more to Hope's Crossing than some pretty storefronts and a gorgeous setting. There was pain and sorrow, humor and grace.

He had spent his time since returning to town hiding away in Snowflake Canyon, content to be alone in the mountains. While he was busy feeling sorry for himself and thinking his world had ended, others in similar circumstances had somehow managed to move forward.

He had to wonder what they had figured out that he hadn't yet.

"I'll tell you what A Warrior's Hope needs most. A hot tub."

Genevieve issued her heartfelt declaration to Eden Davis, riding alongside her on a big chestnut mare. They were bringing up the rear of the large group heading up a trail to visit what was supposed to be a spectacular iced-over waterfall.

She looked up the trail, overhung with pines on either side that randomly dropped cold little clumps of snow on them.

"I mean, this is beautiful, magical, a winter wonderland. Yadda yadda yadda," she said to Eden. "I just have to think, if I'm aching this much after a morning cross-country skiing and a half hour on horseback, how much worse must some of the guys feel?"

"I know. Believe me, I know." Eden rotated her shoulders, looking cute and still perky, her cheeks rosy beneath a shiny white Stetson she had probably purchased new just for today's outing. "A hot tub is definitely on the list. We can always use the hot tubs inside by the pool when we get back to the recreation center, but I would really like a few outside. After our first session in early fall, I wrote a grant for a couple. We have the funding, but the ground froze before we could run the electricity for the project. That will be first priority when the snow melts, I promise."

That wouldn't help Genevieve. Not when she needed one *now*—and they still hadn't reached their destination. Then she had the whole ride home to endure.

Every single muscle in her body ached, right down to her fingers from gripping first telemark poles and then the reins—not to mention priming her dining-room walls long into the night.

She wasn't a completely inexperienced rider. Her mother had insisted on lessons even though Gen hated heights and had always been uncomfortable on horseback. Her horse today was quiet and good-tempered, with a soft, easy gait that would have made riding her a joy if Genevieve hadn't already been stiff from her other activities that day and the night before.

She was achy enough that she was almost tempted to drive to her parents' house after her day ended here at the foundation to soak in theirs.

"It's been a fun day, though, hasn't it?"

"Yes. I think everyone enjoyed it so far," she answered. That morning, they had left early to go cross-country skiing on the groomed trail that ran beside the river and up into U.S. Forest Service land.

The guests of A Warrior's Hope seemed to have all enjoyed it, especially when they skied around a bend and spied a huge moose standing in a hot springs across the way, steam rising up around him and moss dripping from his antlers.

They barely returned from that excursion and had time for a quick, deliciously hearty lunch catered by Dermot Caine's café before they loaded everybody up and took off to the Silver Sage Riding Stables in Snowflake Canyon for an afternoon on horseback.

It was really a beautiful area, with towering pines and spruce and steep-sided mountains angling down to a glittery, half-frozen river running through the canyon floor.

"How much longer before the falls?" she asked Eden.

"We're nearly there, I think."

"Yep," answered Jake, their guide from the ranch—who seemed even more taciturn than Dylan, though she wouldn't have believed that possible. "Not far now."

The creek beside the trail seemed to bubble and hiss beneath a layer of ice. They turned a bend in the trail and suddenly the falls were there ahead of them.

Gen gasped. She couldn't help it. It was spectacularly beautiful, a gnarled, twisting column of unearthly blue ice that rose at least a hundred feet into the air.

"Wow," she whispered.

Some of the guests climbed off their horses to stretch and have a better look. She saw Dylan didn't dismount, just walked his horse a little away from the group. Was he worried about the difficulty of climbing off the horse without the use of both hands?

He lived up here somewhere in Snowflake Canyon. Spence had pointed out his driveway on the way.

"Climbers come from miles around to strap on crampons and reach the top," Eden said. "I'm going to do it sometime, I swear."

"You mean you didn't bring climbing gear?" Pam Bryant and her fiancé actually looked disappointed.

"Not this time," Eden said. "We can try to come back before you leave if you want."

"Not me," Gen muttered with a shiver. She couldn't imagine anything worse than climbing up a tower of ice with nothing but frozen air between her and serious injury.

"You're not ready to try your hand?" Trey Evans had maneuvered his placid gelding beside her. He was another who hadn't dismounted.

"I'm perfectly happy to stay on solid ground, thanks very much."

"Yeah, I'm with you." He smiled, looking young and rather sweet in the pale afternoon sunlight. "I've got to say, you folks sure know how to throw a winter around here. This is something to see."

"Are you enjoying yourself?" she asked.

"Sure." He answered perhaps a little too

promptly. "It's nice not to be cooped up in a rehab facility all day long. Everybody here is super-nice. Oh, and the cabin's great. Did I tell you that? You did a good job with the decorations. Last night, I sat by a fire and enjoyed the lights on the tree. I even listened to Christmas carols and enjoyed the lights on the tree. Not 'Little Drummer Boy,' " he hastened to add.

She gave a rueful smile. "Nobody believes me when I tell them I generally have no problem with that song. I quite enjoy it under the right circumstances. I just wasn't in the mood for it that night."

"I'm just teasing you," he answered. "Not about the cabin. That's still really nice. In fact, I asked Spence and Eden if I could maybe stay here for a couple of extra days after the session ends. I'm moving into a new apartment in San Antonio when I get back, but it won't be available until after the New Year. All my things are in storage, and I'd rather just stay here if I can."

She frowned, saddened to think about him staying here at the recreation center by himself for the holidays after all the others had left. "Don't you have family somewhere to spend Christmas with?"

"No family. Never knew my dad, and my mom died of an overdose when I was little. My grandpop raised me, but he died, too, when I was fourteen. I was in foster care until I graduated from high school and enlisted."

Oh, poor man. As crazy as her family made her, at least she knew they loved her and would be there if she needed them. She would see them on Christmas Eve. They would have a delicious dinner, maybe play games. Sometimes they attended church services in town.

"You should have a great holiday here in Hope's Crossing," she said, trying for cheerfulness even when sadness seemed to seep through her. "On Christmas Eve just after dusk there's a candlelit ski down the mountainside up at the resort. Everybody in town joins in to ski or just to watch the procession. It's really beautiful."

"That sounds nice. I would offer to join in, except I can just picture me skiing into the person in front of me and starting a domino effect down the whole mountainside, candles tumbling every-where."

She laughed at the picture he painted. The sound made her horse sidestep a little but she brought it back.

"Do that again."

"What? Lose control of my horse?"

"That laugh," Trey said. "You remind me a lot of . . . a girl I used to know."

"Somebody you cared about," she guessed.

He gazed at the frozen spill of water. "We were supposed to be getting married this month. This week, actually."

She stared at him, shocked, even as a rush of

sympathy surged through her. She didn't know what to say, which was stupid since she knew exactly how it felt to go through months of planning to hitch her life to someone and then to have to watch all her expectations implode.

"You remind me a lot of her. Not just your laugh, but other things. She has the same color eyes and her hair was a lot like yours, except shorter. Even her name is similar. Jenna, instead of Genevieve."

"Jenna what?"

"Jenna Baldwin. She was a schoolteacher at an elementary school near the base where I had basic training. We met at a church service and hit it off right away. She was about the prettiest thing I'd ever seen."

Though he smiled as he spoke, she sensed his light expression hid much deeper emotions.

"Since you're here and Jenna isn't, I guess that means no wedding bells."

"Yeah. We broke things off . . . after."

"After what?"

His mouth tightened. "After I was injured."

She frowned, shocked even though she had half expected the answer. First he had lost so much physically and then emotionally. It seemed the height of unfairness. How could any woman walk away from this kind, friendly young man so callously?

"I'm sorry," she said quietly as a cold wind

slithered through the trees, rippling the boughs.

"It's not your fault," he said.

"Well, I hope this Jenna and I are nothing alike, other than our laughs and our similar names," she said tartly.

He looked startled. "Why would you say that?"

For some reason, she was strangely aware of Dylan, who waited nearby on his horse, the reins loosely clasped in his hand, for everybody else to mount up and start down the mountainside.

Though he didn't appear to be paying attention to their conversation, something told her he was listening.

"I hope I wouldn't have destroyed any chance for a future with someone I care about because of something out of his control."

She looked up and met Dylan's gaze. Something glittery and bright sparked in his gaze, but he quickly bent down to say something to his horse, though he didn't move away.

He probably hadn't heard them anyway. And what would it matter if he had?

"Take me, for instance," she went on. "I'm a pretty shallow girl. I've never denied it. I can't say I'm proud of that fact, but I'm not afraid to face reality. I like nice clothes. I love having a facial. I'm careful with my hair and makeup. I like to look good and I work hard to make sure I do."

"And you look real nice."

She made a face. "I wasn't fishing for compliments, but thank you. I just wanted to make the point that as superficial as I might be about some things, I would hope that if I loved a man, I would be more concerned about his character and about the way he treats me than about what the world might see as a few physical imperfections."

The words seemed to spill out from somewhere deep inside her—she wasn't sure where—but as she spoke them, the truth seemed to pound hard against her heart.

Had she changed so very much in such a short time or had that conviction always lived inside her?

What she said to Trey was truth, as well. She had always considered herself superficial. She'd dated Sawyer originally because he was beautiful and because her friends told her they made a perfect couple.

Because all seemed so shiny and bright on the surface, she had overlooked many glaring flaws just beneath it. He was childish when he didn't get his way; he could be petty to anyone who crossed him; he liked to make cutting remarks about just about everyone, even their so-called friends.

She had been so focused on the perfect fairy-tale romance that she had ignored all the signs. As she sat atop a shifting horse while a cold wind knuckled its way under her coat, she wondered, not for the first time, if she would have been able to go through with the wedding, even if she hadn't found out that Sawyer had fathered a child with Sage McKnight.

Perhaps she had only seized on the first major excuse that came along not to marry him. Maybe she finally had reason to fix what her heart had been telling her all along was a mistake.

"For the record, she didn't dump me."

It took a moment for Trey's words to pierce her distraction. "She didn't?" She frowned. "Wait a minute. You dumped *her?*"

"Let's just say I spared her the trouble." He offered a lopsided smile that held no humor. "I knew it was only a matter of time before Jenna figured out she deserved better than a lifetime stuck with a guy who couldn't even walk her down the aisle."

"You hit first." It was Mr. Fuzzy all over again, crouching under the bed and spitting and clawing at anybody who came close. "You didn't want to give her the chance to be the one to break things off."

She wanted to yell at him and ask what the hell was wrong with him. How could he be so selfish that he would push away somebody who cared about him?

"I just spared us both a lot of trouble," he answered. "It would have happened eventually."

"You don't know that."

He looked down at his legs, dangling in the

stirrups. "Come on. Look at me. What kind of woman would want to spend the rest of her life dealing with this?"

"You must not have really loved her, then."

Trey narrowed his gaze at her, and she suddenly remembered that for all his good humor, this was a dangerous man trained in combat. "You don't know anything about it." His voice was suddenly as hard as that frozen waterfall. "You have no idea how much I loved her."

"I don't," she said after a moment. "I just know if I had been your fiancée I wouldn't have let you push me out of your life without a fight. I would have stuck to you like gum in hair."

He didn't say anything for a long moment. Genevieve was aware of Eden ushering everybody back to their horses and helping those who needed it to mount again.

"She doesn't know where I am," Trey finally said, his voice so low she almost didn't hear him over the jingling of tack and the heavy breathing of the horses.

"You didn't tell her you were coming to A Warrior's Hope?"

"No. Before that. I broke things off with her six months ago, the night before I was being transferred to a rehab facility in Texas. I made sure nobody told her where I was headed."

"All this time, she hasn't known where you are?"

With Facebook and Twitter and email, she couldn't believe the woman couldn't have found him, but maybe Trey had stayed off the grid. Closed out his email account, stayed off social networks, changed his phone number.

If a person didn't want to be found, she imagined it couldn't be that difficult to make it happen.

"No," he answered. "It was better this way."

Better for him, maybe. Not for the woman he had shoved out of his life like a pair of mangy old sweats. She opened her mouth to tell him so, but Eden's loud call froze her words.

"We should probably start back before those snowflakes get any bigger," the director said. "Everybody ready to go?"

"Yep," Trey said, urging his horse forward and effectively ending their conversation.

Chapter Twelve

❄ ❄ ❄

I would hope that if I loved a man, I would be more concerned about his character and about the way he treats me than about what the world might see as a few physical imperfections.

Genevieve's words seemed to circle around inside his head like Tucker settling onto the rug beside the fire on a wintry night.

He couldn't push them away. They just echoed there, in all their idealistic glory.

It was a nice thing to say in theory, all noble and well-meaning. She probably liked to believe she was above petty, superficial things like physical infirmities. But the first time one of her snooty friends made some kind of crack about pity dates and taking her charity work a step too far, Genevieve would probably shatter like a Christ-mas ornament caught under a horse's hoof.

On the other hand, she surprised him at every turn. Just when he figured he had her pegged, she did something unexpected, like befriend a young corporal from Alabama.

He needed to stop thinking about her. His task here was to get through the next week or so with a minimum of trouble and then move on with the rest of his life.

"How are you holding up?"

He glanced over as Spencer Gregory moved his horse along the trail beside Dylan's.

"Fine. Better than you. If you looked any more stiff on the back of a horse, we could spray-paint you gold and set you out in front of the library to replace that statue of old Horace Goodwin nobody likes."

Spence only grinned at the insult. "Yeah, riding isn't my best thing. I would blame my old baseball shoulder injury but, well, given the current company, that would just make me sound like an asshole."

Dylan's own laugh surprised him—and Spence, too, apparently, though he quickly hid it. Dylan had missed his friend over the years. They had been close in high school but had gone their separate ways when he had enlisted and Spence had been drafted to play Major League Baseball.

"Don't worry about me," he said now. "I'm doing fine. Haven't been on a horse in more years than I can remember and I'll probably ache in places I can't politely discuss, but so far, so good."

"Great."

Spence was quiet for a long moment as they rode along through the puffy snowflakes that clung to the horses' manes.

It wasn't an uncomfortable moment. In fact, though he would rather be tied to the saddle and dragged behind this horse than admit it, Dylan was actually rather enjoying himself. The steady, calming rhythm of the horses, the scenery, even the cold air blowing in his face—all of it contributed to an unexpected sort of peace.

He couldn't let Spence know that, not unless he wanted to hear a resounding *I told you so.*

He had been pretty damn antagonistic about A Warrior's Hope and the futility of anybody thinking they could help guys who had endured hell with a week spent in the mountains, but he couldn't deny he could feel a little of his own tension trickle away.

It was only the surroundings, he told himself. The sweet citrus scent of the pines, the cold mountain air, the expectant weight of impending snow in the air.

He tried to tell himself he would have had the same reaction working on his property just a mile or so away from this trail, but the argument fell flat.

"I've been looking for a chance to talk to you," Spence said after another moment.

Spence gripped the reins tightly, shoulders tense where Dylan's had begun to relax.

"Oh?" he asked, suddenly wary.

"Charley tells me I don't need to clear anything with the family but, well, you and I have been friends a long time and it feels right to let you be one of the first to know."

"To know what?" He had a strong suspicion he didn't want to hear the answer.

"I've asked your sister to marry me. She said yes."

Spence spoke the words with a sort of stunned disbelief, as if he were still trying to wrap his head around the whole thing. Despite his own squeamishness—he would probably never be crazy about his sister with *anybody,* and thinking about her with a close friend was just too weird—Dylan almost laughed.

This was Smokin' Hot Spence Gregory, who had women throwing themselves at him everywhere he went. He gave every appearance of a man completely flummoxed by love.

He was glad, for both of them. Charlotte had come a long way in her life. She had worked hard to remake herself and she deserved to be happy. When he thought about it, Spence had done the same. He had taken a chain of his own bad decisions and fate's bad breaks and turned them into something good.

"Congratulations," he said.

"I hope you mean that and aren't secretly wishing you could knock out a few of my teeth."

"I'm keeping the teeth-knocking-out in reserve. You know Charlotte has six older brothers. I figure you're either crazy in love or insanely brave to take her on, knowing if things go south you'll have every single one of us to deal with."

Spence was quiet, his features soft. "The first one you said. I love her, more than I ever imagined it was possible to care about somebody else."

Spence Gregory had once had everything a guy could want. He had once been a sports hero with an incredible fortune and a stunning supermodel for a wife. He drove fabulous cars, he had multiple houses, he was on magazine covers and on TV commercials hawking everything from cell-phone providers to sports drinks.

Not once, in all those years, had Dylan been jealous of the man. Right now, though, listening to

Spence talk about what he and Charlotte had together, Dylan was aware of a sharp pinch of envy just under his breastbone.

His own life stretched out as cold and empty as that snow-covered mountainside.

"Good," he said gruffly now. "Just make sure that doesn't change."

Spence smiled. "Charlotte is it for me, man. I promise you that."

Behind them, he suddenly heard Genevieve give that delicious, husky laugh at something.

At the sound, that edge of envy turned to a funny little flutter that instantly horrified him.

No. No way. He would never be stupid enough to fall for someone like Genevieve Beaumont— even if he was drawn to her far more than he knew was good for him.

"Will you slow down? I need to talk to you."

Back at the recreation center an hour later, Dylan paused on his way to the storage building. He wanted to ignore Genevieve's call but that would be rude and probably wouldn't accomplish anything other than to make her speed up to catch him.

He turned with more than a little wariness and shifted the weight of the mesh bag filled with riding helmets. Her cheeks and nose were rosy from the cold, and she wore a really ridiculous little pink stocking cap with a puff on the top that perfectly matched her designer parka and gloves.

He had been grateful they rode back to the rec center in separate vans, half hoping he could avoid her the rest of the afternoon—or at least that weird little clutch in his stomach whenever he saw her.

"Let me help you with that," she said, reaching for the bulky, awkward bag of helmets.

"I've got it," he said sharply.

At his tone, she backed off, hands in the air. "Sorry. Do it yourself."

"I will," he retorted, feeling about as mature as his nephew Carter right about now.

Without breaking stride, he continued on his way to the equipment storage building, and she walked double time to keep up with his longer legs.

"So I need some advice and I think you just might be the best person to give it to me."

Right now, all he wanted was to be sitting by his fire with his dog at his feet and a stiff drink in his hand—something he suddenly realized he hadn't had much of since he started at A Warrior's Hope.

He hadn't missed it, either, come to think of it.

"You need my advice, hmm. That can't be good."

She made a face as she reached to open the door of the storage building.

Dylan set down the bag of helmets and flipped on the lights, trying to ignore the rows of adaptive equipment that seemed to mock him.

"Where do these go?" she asked.

He had spent entirely too much time in here with Mac helping with inventory and knew more than he wanted about the organization system. "That shelf against the wall."

He carried them over and set the bag on the empty space provided for it.

"This is really quite amazing, isn't it?" Genevieve looked around the space, filled floor to ceiling with equipment. "I mean, A Warrior's Hope just started and they've already got all this . . . stuff."

"Spence is really good at getting donations and grants. Some of it is donated equipment from people in town but a lot of it was donated by the manufacturers because of his contacts."

"That's really great."

"Yeah. I guess. What did you need to talk to me about?"

She sighed. "I need your advice about Trey."

His arm suddenly ached, and he realized he was trying to clench a fist that didn't exist anymore. He relaxed his arm and walked out of the storage room and back into the soft snowflakes.

"You want advice about Trey from me."

"Yes, from you," she said impatiently, hurrying after him.

"Don't know what I can tell you. You obviously have another conquest there."

She rolled her eyes. "I'm not looking for a conquest. I like him. He's a sweet kid."

That sweet kid had been injured in a vicious firefight in Afghanistan and had probably seen things Genevieve Beaumont couldn't imagine in her darkest nightmares.

"Sure. Okay."

"Here's the thing," she went on. "He has a fiancée. *Had* a fiancée, I should say. He dumped her after he was injured."

He had heard some of their conversation near the frozen waterfall.

I would hope that if I loved a man, I would be more concerned about his character and about the way he treats me than about what the world might see as a few physical imperfections.

He pushed the words away again. "Yeah. That's not a big surprise. A lot of relationships can't survive the kind of life change Evans is dealing with."

"Did you have a girlfriend when you were injured?"

The question took him by surprise. He'd had a couple of girlfriends in the past, but nothing that had ever developed into more than casual. The best that could be said about his dating relationships was that he enjoyed lighthearted variety.

"Nobody serious."

"Well, Trey did, apparently. Her name is Jenna Baldwin and she sounds lovely. I want to find her and I need your help."

He stared at her. "Why the hell would you want to do that? And why would you ever think I'd help you?"

The little yarn puff on the top of her beanie flounced as she gave him a *duh* sort of look—though she probably wouldn't have called it anything as uncouth.

"Because he needs her. It's Christmas and he's all alone. He has no parents, no siblings, no one."

Dylan, by contrast, had too damn many people constantly asking how he was. Every time he turned around, Charlotte or Pop or one of the brothers was in his space, checking on him.

"So?"

"He met her when he was doing his basic training, but I don't know where that was."

He knew. That very day at lunch, he and Trey had talked about Fort Benning, as both had been stationed there around the same time.

"She was a schoolteacher near the base. Before I do an internet search, I just want to make sure I'm in the right region of the country."

"What makes you think she's still in Georgia?"

Her features lit up. "Georgia? Oh, thank you! That helps a *ton*. At least it gives me a place to start."

Crap. He was an army ranger trained to withstand torture. How could he have given that up so easily? Maybe because of those delectable rosy cheeks or the scent of cinnamon and vanilla that seduced his senses—or maybe just the fact that when she talked to him in that husky voice, he could barely manage to string together a coherent thought.

"I don't suppose you're willing to forget I said that, are you?"

She grinned as they walked toward the recreation center again. A few stray snowflakes glimmered on her cheeks and he wanted to lick them off. . . .

"No," she answered. "But I might be willing to forget you're the one who told me."

"She could have moved. She could have married someone else. What makes you think she wants to be found?"

"I don't know. Maybe she doesn't."

"They did break up, after all," he pointed out. "I don't see her here."

She stopped walking. "He dumped her the night before he was leaving for another rehab facility. Get this—he left without giving her a forwarding address. I think that's terrible, don't you?"

He didn't answer but Genevieve apparently didn't need a response.

"I just want to let her know where he is and how he's doing. What she does with that information is her business."

He saw the potential for a whole wall of trouble to come crashing down. If he were Evans and had broken up with a woman for whatever reason, he would be severely pissed if somebody stepped into the middle of things.

"Don't do this, Gen. Just butt out."

"I have to try. What can a phone call hurt?"

"This is none of your business. Let it go."

She frowned. "But you should have seen his face when he talked about her. His eyes went all soft and warm. He said my laugh reminds him of hers. I just feel so terrible when I think about him being all alone on Christmas. Wouldn't it be the most perfect holiday if we could help them find each other again?"

If this Jenna Baldwin was at all like Genevieve, all light and laughter and energy, he could certainly understand how Trey Evans could have been in love with her.

He didn't want to crush her romantic bubble—which, he had to admit, he found more than a little surprising, given her own less-than-ideal relation-ship history—but he couldn't let her pursue this crazy idea.

"There is no *we* here. I don't want any part of this. This is a huge mistake," he warned. "Mind your business, Gen. Trust me. Don't stick your pretty little nose into matters of someone else's heart. Ask the assistant district attorney how uncomfortable nasal-reconstruction surgery can be."

Uneasiness flickered in her gaze for just a moment, then she shook her head, once more the determined, indulged woman whose parents had likely never denied her anything she wanted. "Oh, stop. You're just trying to scare me."

"With good reason. Is it working?"

"No," she declared, her jaw set. "You didn't see his face. He loves her."

"So what? A man can be crazy in love with a woman, but that doesn't mean they're at all good for each other."

She gazed at him, not breathing, eyes wide, and he was oddly reminded of times when he would be leading a patrol and would become keenly aware of the world around him, all his senses on hyper-alert.

Just now he could hear the wind in the treetops and the far-distant laughter of someone on the trail on the other side of the river and the sound of a car with a bad muffler pulling out of the parking lot.

The moment seemed frozen like that eerily blue waterfall, scattered droplets suspended in space and time.

"I know," she finally said, her voice almost hushed. "I know that. I just . . . I want to make a phone call to tell her where he is. She must be worried about him. I'll just let her know he's safe and sound. If she doesn't want anything to do with him, so be it. It serves him right. I think it's cruel of him to leave like that, just sneak away in the night without giving her the chance to prove her love."

"You're going to be sorry," he warned.

"What else is new?" she muttered. "I'm sorry about a lot of things."

Nothing he could say would change her mind. He suddenly knew it. Gen Beaumont was an unstoppable force when she wanted to be—and apparently, right now she had a goal and wouldn't let anything sway her from it.

"When this comes back to bite you in the ass, just remember I tried to warn you."

She didn't stick her tongue out at him, but he had a feeling it was a close thing. "And when I bring together two people who love each other and help them find their happy-ever-after, you remember that I was absolutely right all along and that I did a wonderful thing, while you stood there with your callous, bitter, shriveled old soul, prophesying doom and gloom."

At her impassioned words, he laughed. He couldn't help himself. The sound was rough and rusty, startling a magpie that must have been overwintering in the tree above Gen's head. As he flew off, a huge clump of snow fell from the branch he vacated and landed right smack-dab on the little puff of her beanie and trickled down her cheek, which only made him laugh harder.

She narrowed her gaze at him, and before he realized what she intended, she scooped up a handful of snow and chucked it at him. By sheer luck, the loose snowball hit him on the cheek just below his eye patch. Ice crystals clung to his skin, so cold it stung, but it was somehow life-affirming, too, in a weird sort of way.

"My shriveled, bitter old soul and I did not appreciate that," he said, wiping it away with the sleeve of his coat.

She was fighting a smile, he could see, even as she pulled off her hat to shake the snow out. She had serious hat hair but he still wanted to run his fingers through it. . . .

"Tough," she retorted. "You deserved it. You probably trained that bird to dump that snow on me, didn't you?"

"Yes. I have a whole battalion of forest creatures waiting to obey my every command."

"Figures."

A little snow clung to the arch of her eyebrow and stuck in her hair and he couldn't resist reaching out, brushing it away.

When he lowered his hand, she swallowed hard, and he could feel his pulse race at the expression in her eyes.

Genevieve Beaumont was staring at him as if he was all she wanted wrapped and waiting under her Christmas tree. He desperately wanted to kiss her. Just toss that hat into the snow, reach out and capture her cold lips with his.

He could warm her. Warm them both. Judging by their kiss the other night, if he touched her again, they would soon be generating enough heat to melt the whole mountainside.

No. He couldn't kiss her. He was no better for Genevieve Beaumont than Trey Evans was for his Jenna.

He shoved his hand in his pocket to keep from reaching for her and stepped away, back to safety.

"That looks like the last of the snow. I'll try to keep my forest minions out of your way."

"Thanks," she mumbled.

He turned abruptly and headed back toward the recreation center. Only when he was almost there did he see his sister standing by the window inside, watching the whole interaction.

Chapter Thirteen

❄ ❄ ❄

"Where's my mommy?"

A question designed to spark panic in all but the most calm of hearts. Genevieve looked helplessly down at the little girl beside her, gazing up at her out of big, distressed dark eyes.

"She's still out there on the mountain, Claudia. Remember? We talked about this. She's skiing with your daddy and with your big sister. Your dad has a very cool chair he gets to ski on. You and I are having fun here with our hot chocolate and our coloring."

"I want my mommy."

And Genevieve thought things had been going so well. She was far from an expert on children and could probably count on one hand the in-depth interactions she'd had with any. Volunteering to stay behind with little Claudia Brooks had really been an act of self-protective desperation. When confronted with two things that scared her—the terrifying height of ski lifts or the only-slightly-less-terrifying prospect of a few hours entertaining a very cute little girl—she had picked the one with the least potential to cause death or serious maiming.

It had seemed like the smart choice, but now, a few hours in, she was running out of ways to entertain Claudia, who seemed to be growing increasingly restless.

"They should be back soon," she said, a little desperately. "Should we put our coats on again and take a walk outside so we can look for them?"

They had walked out twice and had watched Joe Brooks in his sit-ski once. Later, they found Tonya and Marisol riding the magic carpet, a beginner conveyor-belt lift that worked much like an airport moving sidewalk only going uphill.

"No outside." Claudia stuck out her bottom lip.

Okay. Genevieve scanned the little corner of the ski lodge they had taken over as their base. Her gaze landed on the almost-new box of crayons. "We could color another picture for Mommy and Daddy."

"No."

She pointed to her tablet computer and its fabulous entertainment offerings. "How about a game? Or we could watch another *Sesame Street*?"

Claudia's cornucopia of colorful barrettes quivered as she shook her head, braids flying. The girl really was adorable, with those huge eyes and dimples and all that beautiful café-au-lait skin, like her mother. Hanging around with her for the past few hours had really been quite entertaining.

There had even been a minute or two—when Claudia had insisted on sitting on Gen's lap while they read a Dr. Seuss book she hastily downloaded on her tablet—that Gen had felt a strange, soft, completely unexpected tenderness tug at her heart at the small, warm weight in her arms.

Claudia had this funny habit of playing with Gen's hair when she sat on her lap, almost as if she didn't know she was doing it, twisting it around and around her finger.

Just now, Gen was running out of options. She picked up Claudia's cute doll, all dressed up in a darling aprés-ski outfit of her own, and danced her a little in the air, side to side. "We could play with Penelope more. I bet she's getting tired of just hanging around, doing nothing," she tried.

"No."

That bottom lip started to quiver ominously, and panic skittered through Genevieve.

Okay, what would you like to do? she wanted to demand, but she knew that wouldn't accomplish anything except to make them both more frustrated.

Claudia yawned widely and blinked her eyes. Gen wanted to give herself a head slap. Oh. Of course. Little creatures sometimes needed naps. She should have realized.

The crowded, noisy ski lodge didn't seem the ideal place for a snooze, and Gen had no idea how to accomplish that particular feat amid all the bustle.

She finally settled into a comfortable armchair in a fairly secluded corner near the window, providing beautiful views up the slopes, then held her arms out to Claudia. "Why don't you sit right here and I'll tell you a story."

After a pause, Claudia grabbed her doll, ski parka and all, and climbed onto Genevieve's lap and promptly shoved her thumb in her mouth. Wishing for a warm, cuddly blanket, Gen settled for pulling her wool coat over both of them.

"Once upon a time, there was a beautiful princess who lived in a castle set on a huge hill," she began.

Claudia pulled her thumb from her mouth and pointed out the window. "That hill?"

"Why, yes. I believe it was. This princess didn't like snow and she really hated waking up with icicles hanging from her toes. Her days were spent trying on new dresses or brushing her hair or painting her toenails."

Claudia held out her little hand to show the vibrant pink polish there. Though barely three, the girl was definitely a fashionista.

"And painting her fingernails," Genevieve said with a smile. "She thought she was happy with her life. Surely no other princess lived in such a beautiful castle and had such stunning dresses to wear or could paint her toenails such spectacular colors. But one day the princess woke up. After shaking the icicles off her toes, just like usual, she started to try on another new dress and realized she didn't want to wear any of the dresses in her closet. They were beautiful and she still loved the bright colors and the silky feeling when she slid them on her head. But when she was wearing one of the dresses, she couldn't climb a tree or ride her horse or do somersaults down the mountainside, end over end until she reached the bottom."

Claudia smiled a little, though her eyes were half-closed as she listened. Genevieve lowered her voice to a slow, soothing cadence and proceeded to spin a tale about the princess's longing for adventure, for something more, and the silly steps she took to find it.

After a few more moments, she looked down to find Claudia's eyes closed, her chin drooping onto her chest. Gen stopped talking in the middle of telling about the princess trying to fly and just enjoyed the moment.

She had never really envisioned having children. Oh, eventually she supposed it would have been required of her and Sawyer, to carry on the Danforth legacy, but that sort of future had seemed nebulous at best, years in the future.

Now, as she held this darling little girl in her arms, she had a fierce urge for a child of her own. Someone who would love her as she was and wouldn't find her lacking.

Perhaps a little boy with vivid blue eyes. . . . The thought made her blush and quickly shy away from thoughts of Dylan Caine.

After a few moments, her arms started to ache. She shifted in the chair for a more comfortable position and was relieved when Claudia slept on. She thought about trying to settle the little girl on the adjacent sofa but she was afraid of waking her. This worked for now.

She might have dozed, but she wasn't sure how long. When she woke, her arms were just about numb and Charlotte Caine was coming toward her.

"How's it going in here?" Dylan's sister asked.

Genevieve pressed a finger to her mouth and pointed to the sleeping girl.

Charlotte winced. "Sorry. I didn't notice she was asleep," she whispered.

"She dozed off a little while ago."

Charlotte took the vacant seat on the sofa. "How did you get roped into babysitting duty?" she whispered.

"Nobody roped anybody into anything. I offered. The truth is, I was kind of glad of the excuse to stay in the warm lodge. I'm not supercrazy about skiing. It's a height thing."

Charlotte snickered softly. "Don't you find that a little ironic, considering your father was one of the original founders of the ski resort?"

Her father had been savvy with investments, saving enough from his fledging law firm to throw wholehearted support behind Harry Lange when he came up with the crazy idea of building the Silver Strike resort, which was now a huge industry that had become the driving force of the Hope's Crossing economy.

She shrugged. "Maybe. I can't help it. I've never really liked skiing. Sawyer used to make me go with him and I was always miserable."

She instantly wished she hadn't said that when Charlotte gave her a surprised, sympathetic look.

"What about you?" she asked quickly. "You're not skiing?"

Charlotte shrugged out of her parka. She wore a turtleneck underneath that revealed a curvy, attractive figure, a far cry from what she used to look like.

"I injured my ankle this summer, and it's still not as strong as I'd like it to be. It's aching a little,

273

so I figured I would take it easy. I went down a few runs but decided that was enough."

As she tossed her parka over the arm of the sofa, the light glimmered off a huge ring on her left hand. Gen had heard whispers that Charlotte and Smokin' Hot Spence Gregory were taking their relationship to the next level. She wouldn't have believed it if she hadn't seen them together the past few days. They were really quite cute together.

For a moment, she was tempted to confide in Charlotte about her thus-far-fruitless effort to find Trey's ex-fiancée. She hesitated, not eager to hear Dylan's sister tell her it was a lousy idea, too.

After a few hours of internet searches the night before, she had found an email address from an obscure school directory at an elementary school near Fort Benning, but she couldn't locate any kind of corresponding phone number. She had sent an email, not sure if it was even the right person or if the account was still open, but she hadn't had a response yet.

Before she could ask the other woman her opinion about the wisdom of continuing the search, Charlotte spoke. "I'm glad I caught you alone for a minute, actually," she said, her voice serious. "I need to ask you something."

Gen's arms tensed around the little girl in her arms. Claudia wriggled a little in her sleep, and Gen realized what she was doing and relaxed.

"Oh?" she asked, trying for studied casualness.

She had visions of her asking some kind of embarrassingly awkward question, like *what are you doing, kissing my brother?*

"I was wondering if you have plans tonight," Charlotte asked.

As usual, her plans revolved around Grandma Pearl's house. She had finished painting the dining room the night before and had thought about adding a second coat if it needed it. If not, she would continue with the endless effort of steaming off wallpaper in the other rooms.

Considering her biceps throbbed and her hair felt permanently frizzed from that particular activity, she welcomed any excuse to have a break from it.

"Nothing that can't wait. Why?"

Charlotte fiddled with a loose thread on the wristband of her sweater. "I'm supposed to go to a Christmas party tonight—women only—and was wondering if you might like to come with me. It should be a lot of fun. There's always good food and wonderful company."

After Genevieve had shut Charlotte down the last time she asked her to a social event, she would have thought the other woman wouldn't ask her again.

She didn't want to turn her down again. She had a feeling their fledgling friendship would die a quick, painful death if she did.

"Sure," she said, before she could talk herself

out of it. "A Christmas party with girl talk sounds fun, especially if it means I don't have to steam wallpaper off the wall for a few hours."

Charlotte smiled, looking relieved. "Oh, I'm so glad. I was hoping you could make it, even though it's short notice. The party starts at seven. Why don't I pick you up at quarter to, at your grandma Pearl's house?"

"That sounds great. Thanks."

Charlotte smiled again and settled into the sofa, her eyes on little Claudia.

"I've always considered myself a pretty good judge of character. As a result, I'm not often surprised by people. You are turning out to be . . . different than I expected."

She wasn't quite sure how to respond. "Are you saying there's a chance maybe I'm not the spoiled bitch everybody thought?"

Color climbed Charlotte's cheeks and she gave a shocked little laugh. "I didn't say that."

"You don't have to say it," Gen said. "I know how people see me. That I insist on my own way, that I'm demanding, that I ran roughshod over the town leading up to my grand society wedding that never happened."

Charlotte didn't deny her claim—confirmation in itself. "You have to admit, you were Bridezilla on steroids."

"Or worse," she muttered.

She hated looking back on that time. She

couldn't really explain it, to Charlotte or to herself. That time nearly two years ago seemed a lifetime away. When she looked back, that person seemed like someone else entirely.

"In my heart, I think I knew I was making a huge mistake," she finally said. She wasn't sure why she felt compelled to confess this to Charlotte, but somehow the moment seemed right, here in the lodge, with the soft weight of a sleeping child on her lap.

She admired Charlotte. More than that, she *liked* her. By asking to spend time together that evening, Charlotte was offering her a tentative friendship and Gen didn't want to screw it up. She wanted to tell her about how things had been during her engagement, if only to explain that wasn't all she was.

"I tried to convince myself things were fine. As I look back, I think I had to focus on making sure every detail of the wedding was flawless— down to the pattern on the china and the hemline on the flower-girl dresses—so that I didn't have to face the emptiness of our relationship. I guess maybe I thought if we had the ideal fairy-tale wedding, the marriage would have to be perfect, too. Stupid, isn't it?"

Charlotte didn't say anything for a long moment. When she did, her question was startling in its boldness.

"Do you have feelings for my brother?"

Gen inhaled sharply, emotions jumbling through her so quickly she didn't know how to sort them out.

"Sorry. Don't answer that. It's none of my business. Spence told me to stay out of things and here I am barging in anyway. It's just . . . I saw you yesterday by the river. I saw him laughing. Do you have any idea how long it's been since I've seen him laugh like that?"

"I . . . No."

"Forever. Oh, he'll smile once in a while, and he does give this terrible, hard laugh I hate. Genuine laughter, though, has been missing since he came back."

Again, she didn't know what to say. Not the most auspicious beginning to a friendship, when she was either spilling her innermost secrets or completely clamming up.

"He almost died, you know," Charlotte said, her mouth tight and her eyes glimmering. "At one point, the military doctors told us to prepare for the worst as the infection ravaged through him. But he was stronger than they gave him credit for. I always knew he was. He came through it, even though they couldn't save his eye."

She had wondered about his vision. He sometimes referred bitterly to not having a hand but she had rarely heard him discuss his eye.

"He's been through so much. Though he doesn't talk about it, I know he carries the weight of terrible things inside him. He lost five good friends in the explosion that injured him and for a while this summer, I was afraid he . . ." Her voice trailed off and her mouth pressed into a line.

"That he what?"

She didn't answer. "I want so much for him to be able to find joy again. To laugh like he used to. To move forward with his life."

"I want that, too," Gen said.

"I hope you mean that," Charlotte said. For being the sweet owner of a candy store and someone Gen had always considered quiet and unassuming, the other woman's voice was suddenly as sharp as the edge of a newly waxed ski.

"If you hurt him, Gen Beaumont, I swear to you I will find some way to make you pay. I don't know how yet, but I'll figure something out."

The very sincere threat might have made her shudder if she wasn't so touched at the love Charlotte had for her brother.

She wanted to tell the other woman Genevieve didn't think she had anything to worry about. There was little danger of Dylan ever giving her any power to hurt him, not when he kept his feelings so tightly locked up and pushed her away at every opportunity.

"Is that the reason you invited me to the Christmas party tonight?" she asked, more amused than offended. "You want to befriend me so you can keep an eye on me and make sure

I'm not going to break your brother's heart?"

Charlotte gave a surprised-sounding laugh. "I wish I were that clever. I'm afraid I had planned to ask you to the party before I saw the two of you together yesterday afternoon."

"Ah. Well, don't worry about Dylan. For one thing, I'm pretty sure he can take care of himself."

"He *thinks* he can, anyway."

She smiled but quickly grew serious, a sudden ache in her chest that had nothing to do with the little weight resting against it. "For another, even if I had feelings for him—which I'm not saying I do—he's made it quite clear he doesn't feel the same. We're friends. That's all."

Charlotte looked as if she wanted to discuss the issue further, but to Gen's relief, Tonya Brooks came in with a tired-looking Marisol. By some rather spooky instinct, Claudia awoke upon her mother's approach, and the moment was gone.

The first burst of panic didn't hit until Charlotte parked her little SUV on Main Street.

"Where is this party?" Genevieve asked.

She suddenly didn't want to hear the answer.

"At Dog-Eared Books & Brew," Charlotte said nonchalantly, opening the hatch of her SUV then walking around to lift out a basket of Sugar Rush treats. "Our book club has a big Christmas party every year, and this year we're each supposed to bring someone new."

Dog-Eared Books & Brew. Maura McKnight Lange's store.

Dread lodged in her stomach, hot and greasy. Oh, she was an idiot! Why hadn't she bothered to ask before? She should have figured it out! She had no real explanation for such airheaded negligence, except she had been flattered at the invitation and very much wanted Charlotte to be her friend.

She knew Charlotte was friendly with the McKnights. That was the very reason she had declined her dinner invitation the week before, because she had worried about going to Brazen and having to face the owner, Alex McKnight.

She should have *known,* darn it. Her mind raced as she frantically tried to figure a way out of this without completely alienating Charlotte. Maybe she could feign illness. It wasn't a complete lie—she was feeling fairly nauseous right now and her head was beginning to throb.

She was bound to see Maura Lange there—and perhaps even her daughter, Sage.

She shivered from more than the chill of a December evening. She didn't know how to face them, not after the way she had acted.

The whole thing made her feel so small and stupid and she hated it. Yes, Sage had slept with her fiancé just months before their wedding, knowing perfectly well he was engaged. Yes, she had become pregnant with Sawyer's baby. It still infuriated her, humiliated her.

Deep inside, some terrible, narcissistic part of her couldn't help wondering what Sage had that *she* hadn't.

She couldn't deny Sage was pretty in a granola-eater sort of way. She had dark curly hair, dimples, the pretty green eyes all the McKnights seemed to share. But she wore hideous clothing designed more for comfort than fashion—Birkenstock sandals, leggings, loose T-shirts with funny, tacky little sayings on them. She hardly ever bothered with makeup and she always had her nose in a book. And she was young! Not even twenty when she and Sawyer slept together.

That horrible night when Gen found out Sage was pregnant and that Sawyer was the father, she hadn't doubted the girl's story for a moment, even though her mother tried to convince her Sage and the rest of the McKnights were lying.

Sawyer had never denied sleeping with her, and Sage had been too miserable about the whole thing, acting as if she would have preferred any other man on the planet to be her child's sperm donor.

Genevieve hated thinking of her reaction. She had been angry, yes, but that burning, aching humiliation had been paramount. She had done everything she could to give the man a perfect wedding, to prove she would be the ideal wife for someone with political aspirations beyond Colorado.

Her efforts had been for nothing. Despite doing all she could to show she could make him happy, Sawyer had still preferred a little Hobbit granola-eater who probably didn't even shave her legs—and worse, her very public pregnancy ensured that every single person in town knew it.

How could she go inside that bookstore and be polite to Sage's mother and aunts and grandmother, when she had spent nearly two years being hateful and small to all of them?

"I should have asked where the party was and who might be there," she finally said. The best basis for a friendship was honesty, right? "You know the McKnights won't want me in there."

Charlotte glanced over with a startled look. "Why not?"

"Oh, I don't know," Genevieve said dryly. "We haven't been on the best of terms since Sage McKnight gave birth to my fiancé's child."

Charlotte gave that a dismissive wave of the hand not carrying the basket of goodies, a sort of *oh, that little thing* kind of gesture. "It will be fine. You'll see. Alex and Mary Ella and Maura are wonderful. I promise, everyone will be happy to have you there."

For a moment, she let herself believe in the pretty picture Charlotte painted, but the reality wasn't quite as rosy. Otherwise good people could still hold grudges—and in this case, they had reason to be upset with her.

"Just come for a while," Charlotte said. "If you're having a terrible time, I'll take you home, I promise."

She looked down the sidewalk at the small, puffy flakes under the streetlights. Surely she was tough enough to handle a few raised eyebrows, wasn't she? She liked Charlotte and admired—and envied—the way she had reinvented herself. Gen wanted to be friends with her, for reasons that had nothing to do with the woman's frustrating brother.

If she gave in to her fears and asked Charlotte to take her home, she had a feeling she would be shoving the door closed on any chance of friendship between them.

"You're right. I'm probably overreacting. Let's go."

She held the door open for Charlotte and followed her inside.

The warmth of the store embraced them. Dog-Eared smelled of coffee and ink, quite an appealing combination. She was reminded of a favorite bookshop in Le Marais, a crowded little place on Rue St. Paul.

Charlotte led her through the store to a corner where various plump armchairs had been gathered together to make a private seating area. The chairs were all filled. As she expected, her appearance there was met with a few shocked stares—notably from Ruth Tatum, Claire

McKnight's mother, and from Alex McKnight, Maura's younger sister and Sage's aunt.

Maura looked shocked, too, but she hid it quickly and gave a welcoming smile that Genevieve assumed was meant more for Charlotte than her. A quick look around told her Sage wasn't present.

"We're supposed to bring a friend, right?" Charlotte said cheerfully. "Genevieve has been doing such great things at A Warrior's Hope. She's been amazing. After all her hard work, I thought she could probably use a night out."

She hadn't felt this socially awkward ever.

"Come in. Grab a plate of food," Mary Ella Lange, recently married to Harry Lange, insisted to both of them.

"I hadn't heard you were back from your honeymoon," she said politely to Mary Ella.

To her astonishment, her retired high-school English teacher blushed like one of her students. "Yes. We had a wonderful two weeks in Southern France. It was so sunny and beautiful. Harry would have liked to stay longer, but we both wanted to be here to spend Christmas with our family."

She relaxed a little. France, she could discuss. "I love that area. I do hope you spent time in Paris while you were there. You can't visit France without wandering through the Arènes de Lutèce or Le Jardin du Luxembourg."

"We spent a few nights there, but Paris is a bit crowded and noisy for Harry's taste."

She wanted to say something derogatory about Harry's taste if that were truly the case, but she decided that probably wouldn't go over well with his new bride.

"It can be. But it can also be wonderful," she said. She and Mary Ella spent a few more moments discussing favorite spots in France. Evie Thorne chimed in about places she had visited, and after the first few moments, Genevieve could feel the tension in her shoulders begin to relax. Everyone was being surprisingly kind to her.

"I understand William has you fixing up Pearl's house to sell," Katherine Thorne, Evie's mother-in-law, said after a few moments. "How is it going?"

"I'm finding there's a little more to it than I expected." She launched into a description of how many layers of wallpaper she had steamed away, like a time capsule of her grandmother's various tastes and moods at the moment. Katherine even laughed at a few spots and asked her questions about her plans for the house and she relaxed further.

This wasn't so bad, she thought. In fact, she was actually enjoying herself. The rolling music of female conversation reminded her of long afternoons in her favorite café, talking with her Paris friends about anything and everything.

Genevieve was enjoying herself—that was, until she walked over to the refreshment table for more of the fantastic brownies Alex McKnight had brought—she figured she could work it off with painting—and bumped right into Maura Lange, who had just emerged from a back room with a new plate of party food.

The other woman did a bit of a double take before she bustled around the table, making room for the new plate and straightening up the other dishes.

Finally, Genevieve decided to just shoot the elephant in the room.

"How is Sage these days?"

Maura tensed, freezing for a moment before picking up a few stray napkins. "Wonderful," she said shortly. "Why do you ask?"

"Just curious."

Some small, petty part of her wanted to ask if she had slept with anyone else's fiancé lately, but that would just be rude. And beneath her.

"How's the baby?" she asked instead. She hadn't given much thought to the child that came from Sage and Sawyer's one-night affair but after playing with the sweet Claudia all day, little creatures were on her mind.

Maura didn't appear to appreciate the question. "My *son* is now eighteen months," she said, her tone sharp. "His name is Henry and he is very, very loved by his parents and his older sister."

Of course. Maura and her husband, Jack Lange, had adopted Sage's baby as their own. It couldn't have been an easy situation for any of them. She knew Sawyer had signed away any rights. After she stopped taking his phone calls, he had emailed her to tell her so, as if that might make some difference in his own culpability.

Did Sage view the boy as her own or as a younger brother? When she looked at Henry, did she see the smarmy, cheating son of a bitch Gen once thought she would spend the rest of her life with?

For an awkward moment, Genevieve stood at the refreshments table, not knowing quite what to say. Finally, she decided to follow the example of Charlotte, who seemed unfailingly kind.

"I'm glad he could have a good home, with people who love him," she said softly. None of what had happened was the child's fault.

Maura seemed startled by that, enough that she seemed to thaw a little. "We're the blessed ones. He's a complete joy."

She should probably stop there, take her plate of appetizers back to her seat and let the matter drop. But she had come this far. She was actually having a civil conversation with Maura Lange, and neither of them was throwing any food at the other. Yet.

"I believe I owe you and your family an apology," she said quickly, before she could lose her nerve.

"Oh?"

"After . . . I canceled the wedding, I guess I needed a scapegoat. It was easier to, um, blame your daughter than to admit my own mistakes. I wasn't very subtle about my anger."

"No. You weren't."

At Maura's discouraging expression, Genevieve faltered and would have let things rest there. Her mother would have brazened through the whole thing, acted all these months as if nothing had ever happened between them. That was probably what she *had* done while Gen had run away to Paris, just carried on as normal.

Genevieve wasn't Laura. She never would be, she realized. She needed friendship and respect and suddenly wanted to do whatever necessary to earn it.

"I was wrong and . . . I'm sorry. Will you please convey my apology to Sage? Contrary to the way I may have acted, I don't believe she was completely responsible for the whole mess. Sawyer certainly played a huge role and . . . I did, as well."

Well, she had at least succeeded in surprising Maura. The other woman stared at her warily, as if trying to figure out what angle she was playing.

"I was wrong to say what I did about her, publicly and privately. Will you please let her know?"

"I . . . Yes. Of course. I'll tell her what you said."

"Thank you."

She was about to return to her spot on the edge of the sofa when Maura, in turn, surprised her.

"I couldn't help noticing your bag when you came in."

Heat washed over her. The bag. Oh, no! She had completely forgotten she'd grabbed one of her hand-sewn pieces since the accent color of it so perfectly matched the salmon of her sweater. Maura was bound to recognize it as the same general style of the dozen or so bags she had anonymously shipped to Dog-Eared Books & Brew to sell.

"Did you?" she said, trying for a casual smile. "It's fun, isn't it?"

"Yes. I have one myself that's very similar. May I ask where you found it?"

Again, her mind did a frenzied workout as she tried to come up with an answer that wasn't a complete fabrication. "Paris," she finally said, honestly enough, though she didn't add exactly where: in her apartment, in the tiny spare bedroom/craft room where she hung all the others she had created.

"You don't happen to know where I could find more, would you? I had a few for sale in my store a few months ago and everybody wanted one."

Gen could feel her cheeks turn pink with pleasure and pride. She wanted to tell Maura she had made them but she didn't dare. Not now, when things were still awkward between them.

"I . . . I don't," she stammered. "I'll keep an eye out and let you know if I see any."

"Yes. Please. I made a nice profit from them and would definitely be open for more."

"Okay."

Flustered and off balance now, she decided she didn't have any appetite. She set her plate back on her chair, grabbed the bag in question and escaped to the restroom.

She fixed her hair quickly and applied a new coat of lipstick. Mostly, she just used the moment to collect her composure again. When she was ready, she left the ladies' room and headed through the shelves toward Charlotte's book-club party.

The sound of someone saying her name halted her footsteps.

"What were you thinking to invite Genevieve Beaumont?"

Gen's stomach contracted suddenly at the condemnation in the voice, which she now recognized as Ruth Tatum, Claire McKnight's mother.

"Everybody agreed to bring someone new, remember? Maura brought her pediatrician. Evie Thorne brought Brodie's new office manager. The whole point was to make the book club more inclusive."

"That was a stupid idea in the first place. Whoever thought of it? Probably Claire."

"Yes, it was my idea, Mother," Claire said. "It's

been wonderful to have fresh faces to talk to, new stories to hear. I think we sometimes tend to stick with our own little group and don't always make others feel welcome."

"Why do we need to? Things were fine," Ruth groused. "Anyway, couldn't you find anyone better to bring than Genevieve Beaumont?"

Any warm glow she might have been feeling at trying to make things right with Maura—at holding her own at this party and even trying to form tentative new friendships—seemed to shrivel and die a painful death.

"Stop it, Mom."

"I'm only saying what everyone else is thinking," Ruth Tatum protested. "You all know what Genevieve's like. She's an ice-cold bitch. It's no wonder her fiancé slept around. He was probably desperate for a little warmth."

"That's enough," Claire said sharply, but Genevieve didn't wait to hear more. All the remembered humiliation and hurt of that terrible time after her engagement ended came surging back and she thought she might truly be sick.

Trying not to give in to the further mortification of tears, she pushed around the bookshelf. "That's right," she said bitterly. "I'm the coldest bitch in Hope's Crossing. Sawyer couldn't wait to sleep with anyone who wasn't me."

Why had she even tried to be friends with these small-minded, provincial women who refused to think maybe a person could change?

She wanted to stomp and yell and throw books off the shelves at them. *I never wanted to come to your stupid book-club meeting anyway. You're a bunch of insulated, illiterate rustics who look at Paris and see crowds and noise instead of light and beauty and magic. I feel sorry for all of you.*

Instead, she swallowed down all those words—most of them not even true—and tried for some small semblance of the dignity and strength she wished she had shown after her engagement ended.

"Will you excuse me?" She grabbed her coat, grateful she already had her purse, and drew on the example of her father's pompous haughtiness as she marched toward the door.

She didn't look back, though she heard the shocked, echoing silence that met her pathetically melodramatic exit.

As she might have expected, Charlotte hurried after her, stopping Gen just before she yanked open the door and walked out into the cold.

"I am so sorry, Genevieve. Ruth Tatum is a cranky old biddy. She always has been. If she wasn't Claire's mother, I don't think we could tolerate her."

Apparently old bitches were more bearable than the young ones.

"She only said what everyone else was thinking. I knew this was a mistake before we ever walked in. I should never have come. I should have asked you where we were going. We both know I don't belong here in Hope's Crossing."

"Please. Come back. Everyone will feel so terrible if you leave."

She glanced over at the women in the corner and was rather surprised to see Ruth cornered by Claire and Katherine Thorne, of all people. She couldn't hear what they said, but judging by the way Ruth had her arms folded defensively and the animated expressions of the other two, it looked as if they were scolding her.

Surprising, yes, but not enough to compel her to return to that vipers' den.

"I'm sorry, but . . . I need to go."

Charlotte looked as if she wanted to argue, but after a long moment, she nodded. "I understand. Let me grab my coat and I'll give you a ride home."

"No. You don't have to leave because of me. It's not far. I don't mind walking."

Charlotte suddenly looked as obstinate as her brother. "Don't be silly. You came here as my guest. I'm not going to let you walk home in the snow."

The random flakes of earlier had turned into a steady snowfall. Already half an inch covered the roadway.

The idea of walking through it didn't appeal to her, especially in her heeled boots.

"Fine," she said. "I'm sure you'll understand if I wait outside."

Charlotte chewed her lip as if she wanted to continue urging Gen to stay at the party. After a pause, she nodded. "I'll be right back."

Genevieve pushed through the doors, into the cold air. The pelting snow was like a wake-up call.

Had she really thought she could make friends here in Hope's Crossing, where everyone would probably always see her as the person she had once been?

More depressed than she had been in a long time, she walked a little distance up the street and suddenly caught a distant chord of music coming from a side street.

Without waiting for Charlotte, she impulsively took a few more steps until she could look down the street and see the lights of The Speckled Lizard.

The site of her downfall.

She glanced back at the bookstore, sending out a different, warmer sort of glow. It was far more appealing, except for the women inside, who were probably chattering like angry magpies about her.

Suddenly, she desperately wanted to be in a place where people didn't care about her history, about her mistakes. Charlotte would understand.

She increased her pace and hurried toward the tavern without looking back.

Chapter Fourteen

❄ ❄ ❄

"Oh, man. Did you see that? Why didn't he just run the reverse?"

"Good question," Dylan muttered to his brother Brendan. An even better question: What the hell was he doing in a crowded bar watching a bowl game with Pop, his brothers and a few friends when he could be sitting by his fire, enjoying the quiet solitude of Snowflake Canyon?

That had been his plan until he made the mistake of stopping at Brendan's to pick up Tucker, who had hung out there that day while Dylan was busy at A Warrior's Hope. Brendan, who rarely asked him for anything, had invited him along to The Speckled Lizard to catch the game.

He hadn't had the heart to say no, not when Brendan seemed in the mood for company—and because he owed him for volunteering, along with Peyton Gregory, for dog-sitting duties so Tuck didn't have to spend the whole day with only the chickens for company.

He hadn't realized the whole family was coming. Pop. Andrew. A few friends. It was a regular party.

"You need another drink?" Pat asked.

He shook his head. "One crappy, watered-down whiskey ought to do it for me. Thanks."

Pat, the bartender, glowered at him. "You said you wanted rocks. I gave you rocks."

"And half the river, too," he muttered.

"Have another drink," Andrew urged. "Or are you afraid you might get wasted and deck somebody again? We're here with the chief of police. He'll keep things cool."

"Don't be so sure." Riley McKnight made a face. "You steal another one of my pretzels and I might throw your ass back in jail."

"Warning duly noted."

"Anybody want to play a little pool during half time?" Brendan asked.

"Sure," Riley said.

Andrew slid off his chair, always up for a challenge. "Yeah, I'm in."

"What about you, son?" Pop asked.

He shook his head, forcing a smile. Billiards used to be one of his favorite things, but he hadn't quite figured out how to manage holding a cue one-handed. He'd seen somebody online who had crafted a wooden cue rest to attach to an amputated arm to help with control and aim. It looked interesting. Maybe he would try to work on that over the Christmas holidays. He had always enjoyed woodworking and had been thinking about trying his hand at it.

"It's been a long day. I should really take off and—"

The door flew open behind Brendan in a swirl of snow and wind, and the rest of the sentence dashed out of his head, lost in the shock of seeing Genevieve Beaumont there.

She looked like an ethereal angel framed in the light of the doorway with that crown of blond hair and her pale wool coat and hat.

"Uh-oh. Here comes trouble," Riley said. "Careful, Dylan. I was only joking about hauling you back to jail. I'd really rather not."

She was upset. He wasn't certain how he knew, but her eyes were shadowed and her mouth trembled a little as she looked around at the mostly male crowd assembled to watch the bowl game.

When her gaze landed on him, her mouth made a little O and a vast relief spread over those lovely features, so unexpected and humbling it made his chest ache.

She headed straight for him. "Dylan! I didn't know you would be here. I can't *begin* to tell you how happy I am to see you."

He was aware of his brothers exchanging glances and didn't miss the mix of curiosity and worry in his pop's eyes. Unfortunately, he could guess what they were all thinking.

He cleared his throat. "What's going on? I thought Charlotte was taking you to her book-club party."

"She did. I left."

Her chin started to wobble again, and he knew

she would hate it if she broke down here in the middle of the bar. There was definitely a story here and he wanted to hear it—but not when half his family listened in with avid interest.

"Let's grab a table," he growled.

Ignoring the speculative looks aimed in their direction, he pushed his way through the crowd and found a secluded spot in the corner. Either Pat was overly concerned about the trouble the two of them might cause together, given recent events, or the small bar staff was also curious about what Genevieve Beaumont was doing at a dive like the Lizard on a Wednesday night. They had barely sat down when Nikki, one of the tavern servers, showed up tableside.

"Can I get you two something?" she asked.

"I really, really want a mojito," Gen said. "But I'd better just have a mineral water."

"Dylan, anything for you?"

"I'm good."

She rolled her eyes at the paltry order, slapped down a cardboard coaster and napkin and headed toward the bar.

After she left, Gen fidgeted with the coaster and refused to meet Dylan's gaze.

"You going to tell me what happened?" he finally asked.

"I'd rather not," she muttered, focusing on the pool table where it looked as if Andrew was cleaning up, as usual.

"You might as well tell me. I'm trained in interrogation, you know."

She finally did meet his gaze, her delicate eyebrow arched nearly to her hairline. "Well. That explains a lot."

"Such as?"

"You're always trying to make me spill my innermost thoughts. It's a bad habit, soldier."

He wanted to tell her he wasn't a soldier anymore. He wasn't much of anything right now. "My family would tell you I was born naturally nosy. With five older brothers, there were always interesting secrets to discover."

The group around the pool table suddenly exploded in cheers, probably because Brendan had aced a particularly difficult shot to pull ahead of Andrew the pool shark.

Genevieve followed the sound, her eyes wide and envious. "I'm interrupting a family thing," she murmured.

"Not at all. Brendan just asked if I wanted to come to the Liz and watch the game for a bit. I don't have great reception at my place when snow gets in the satellite dish, so I decided what the hell."

"You can go back to the game. I'm fine. I don't need a babysitter. I'll just drink my San Pellegrino and go home."

He liked looking at her. Even when she was distressed, she was so lovely it was almost unreal,

300

until a person came to know her. Then he could see the little flaws. A tiny mole on her jawline she concealed with makeup, one ear that was a fraction lower than the other one, a tooth slightly out of alignment when she smiled.

Those little imperfections made her real and endearing. His chest suddenly felt a little tight, clogged by a strange, thick emotion he didn't want to identify.

He had watched her the past week as they worked together at A Warrior's Hope. He didn't think he had been the only one surprised by Genevieve Beaumont. She had been sweet and warm, treating the guests with the perfect mix of lighthearted teasing and respect. The wives all seemed to like her and even the children were drawn to her.

That afternoon he had walked into the lodge and found her sitting on the sofa in earnest conversation with Charlotte and Tonya Brooks, one of the cute little Brooks girls snuggled on her lap, all braids and big eyes and adorable smiles.

His chest had felt the same way then, kind of thick and sluggish.

Maybe he was coming down with something.

Because he had been watching her so intently these past few days, he didn't need her to confirm something had upset her. She wasn't the soft, sweet Gen he was coming to know. There was an edgy brittleness about her, as if she would shatter like an icicle falling off a roof if some-body slammed a door too hard.

"Come on," he pressed. "Tell me what's wrong."

She gave him a haughty look he was coming to realize was simply another defense mechanism. "If this is an example of your interrogation skills, I have to tell you, I'm not impressed. You're not being particularly persuasive. So far, all you've done is order me to talk in that bossy tone. I suppose there's a slim chance you might eventually wear me down but, let's be honest, that could take all night."

He fought a smile he didn't think she would appreciate right now. "How about if I threaten to start another bar fight? Would that do the trick? I'm always looking for an excuse to go after one of my brothers. Annoying bastards, the lot of them."

"I've learned my lesson. If you started throwing punches, I would just sit here primly with my hands folded in my lap, minding my own business."

He snorted. He would believe that when he saw it.

"There's always a chance I might be able to help the situation, but not if you won't tell me what happened."

She opened her mouth to answer, but Nikki returned with her mineral water and a glass of ice and she closed her mouth again. He wanted to growl with frustration.

She drank the water straight from the bottle, ignoring the ice, then wiped at her mouth daintily with the napkin.

"Something happened at the book-club party, obviously."

"Wow. You *are* good," she said dryly.

"Oh, I've got skills you can't begin to guess at," he answered.

"No doubt," she murmured. It was probably just the low lighting in The Speckled Lizard, but for a moment, he was almost positive her gaze flicked to his mouth, sending instant heat curling through him.

He did his best to douse it. "You never know. I might even be able to help with whatever's bothering you."

She fretted with the bottle. "It's nothing. Just . . . I didn't belong there. I knew it before I walked in. Ruth Tatum even said so. She had some harsh words for Charlotte since she's the one who invited me."

"Seriously? That's why you came in here looking like somebody kicked your dog?"

"I don't have a dog."

"Okay, like somebody kicked *my* dog, then. Do you really care what Ruth Tatum said? She's a cranky bitch and always has been. It's no wonder her husband was going to leave her for a cocktail waitress."

Her finger traced the painted lizard on the

coaster. "Funny. That's just what she said about me."

"What?"

"That Sawyer slept around because I'm such a bitch. That he must have been desperate to find a little warmth wherever he could."

"She said that? See? Ruth is not only a bitch but a *crazy* bitch."

Her mouth lifted just a little but quickly sagged at the edges. "She's not wrong. I was terrible during my engagement. Bridezilla on steroids. That's what your sister said."

He frowned, thinking he might need to have a talk with Charlotte if she was calling people names like that. "However you might have acted in the stress of planning a wedding, that's no excuse for what your asshole of a fiancé did to you, humiliating you like that. You said yourself, you're far better off without him."

"I am. I know that. We would have made each other miserable and probably would have divorced within three or four years—if we could have lasted that long. By then we might have had a child or two to add to the mess."

He thought of her that afternoon with the little Brooks girl in her arm, how sweet and patient she had been with her.

"Forget about him. And Ruth Tatum, too. She's not worth wasting a minute on."

She sighed. "Do you want to know what makes me most upset?"

Not really. He just wanted to fix the whole thing and make it all better for her. "What?"

"Before I overheard her, I had been enjoying the party. I was talking to people, listening to their stories, having a good time. But then I heard what Ruth said and nothing else mattered. I let one person's opinion have too much power over me. I've always been that way. I became what my parents wanted of me, what Sawyer wanted. I've never bothered to become who *I* want to be."

"And who would that be?"

"I don't know yet," she said, so softly he had to lean in to hear. "But I think I'm closer to finding out."

He wanted to kiss her, right here in the middle of The Speckled Lizard. And wouldn't that send his family into an uproar?

She winced suddenly. "I should probably text your sister. She was going to give me a ride home, and I sort of ditched her outside the bookstore. What's her number?"

The image of her fleeing into the night like Cinderella would have made him smile if she wasn't so distressed over the whole thing.

"Here. Just use my phone. She's in there, though not under Bossy Little Sister, as she should be."

He pulled his phone out of his pocket and held it out to her. Her hand brushed his as she took it from him. Her fingers were cool from holding the chilled water bottle, and he wanted to fold them in his and tug them against his skin . . . .

He really, really needed to stop thinking like this. They were friends, that was all.

Her thumbs quickly flew over the screen of his phone, then she handed it back to him. He was curious enough to read the message:

Gen here. I'm with Dylan. Don't worry. Sorry I'm a baby. I'll see you tomorrow.

"You still need a ride home. Let me say goodbye to Pop and my brothers, and I'll drop you off on my way up the canyon."

"Why don't any of you Caines think I can walk six blocks by myself?"

"Maybe because it's dark and it's snowing."

"So what? I don't mind walking home. You don't need to leave your game on my account."

"I told you, I was just about to take off before you came in. These long days of recreating are kicking my butt."

She smiled a little, as he intended. Her mood seemed lighter, and he considered that just about his biggest achievement of the day.

"I'll be right back."

She nodded and sipped at her water as he headed for the billiards table.

"I'm taking off," he said.

"With Genevieve Beaumont." Pop's words were a statement, not a question.

He saw Brendan and Andrew exchange looks that made him want to pound both of them.

"I'm only giving her a ride home," he said.

"Good for you," Andrew said. "It's about time you, er, gave somebody a ride."

He was in his brother's face before he even thought it through, ready to go. "You want to say that again?" he snarled.

"That's enough," Dermot said in a long-suffering voice. "Settle down, boys."

Andrew looked startled. "Sorry. I didn't mean anything. I like Genevieve. It took guts to stand up to her father the way she did."

She had guts. She just couldn't seem to see it.

"She needs a lift home. I'm giving her a lift home. That's all."

"Okay, we get it. Go, already."

"I will."

Genevieve joined him at the billiards table with a hesitant smile for his family. He was glad she was oblivious to the currents zinging around.

He wasn't sure what to think when she kissed Dermot on the cheek. "Thank you for the pie the other night," she said. "It was just what I needed."

"Good. When you've got a hankering for another, just let my boy know and I'll be sure to bake one special for you."

"Thank you."

She looked as touched as if Dermot had just offered her keys to a new BMW.

Dermot could see how sweet she was. If his father could be so astute, Dylan had to wonder why everybody else only saw the prickles—including Genevieve herself.

Chapter Fifteen

They walked outside to more snowfall, big plump flakes that had added at least a few inches to the sidewalk.

"I'm parked the next block over," he said. "Sorry for a bit of a walk."

"I don't mind."

The Christmas lights hanging on just about every downtown business glimmered against the snow, cheery and festive. Hope's Crossing really was a pretty town this time of year. Most times of year, if he were honest. The restaurants and stores still open seemed to be doing a good business. A little foot traffic spilled out onto the sidewalks and everybody seemed to be in a good mood.

It was a far cry from the dust and grit and bleakness of Afghanistan.

With the sidewalks a bit slick, Genevieve slipped her hand into the crook of his arm for support—his good one, as he was always careful to position himself so the left arm was on the other side.

He could feel the heat of her, even through their layers of clothes and outerwear, and he wanted to soak it in.

"Your family is really close, aren't you?" she asked after a moment.

"Yeah. We were always pretty tight-knit, you know? A lot of camping trips, vacations to the coast when Pop could get away from the café. That kind of thing. After our mom died, I think Pop worked extra hard to make sure we didn't drift apart. The older brothers were in college or in the military, but Pop tried to get us all in one place at least a couple times a year. He was an early adopter of technology and even has a private family blog. He used to post at least once a week with information about what everybody was doing. With social media, that's even easier now."

"Your dad is wonderful. You're so lucky. I mean, I know my parents love me and everything, but it's not the same."

He thought about her own family—stiff and pompous William, picky, perfectionist Laura. Compared to what she came from, he *did* feel fortunate. Damn lucky. He had never spent a moment on the earth without knowing he was loved.

"Big families can be good in a lot of ways, but they can be a pain in the ass, too. Everybody thinks he has the right to stick his nose in your life. And try having five older brothers to follow in every sporting activity you ever wanted to participate in. I can't tell you how many times I had to sit and listen to coaches rave about Patrick's three-point percentage or Bren's rushing stats or Jamie's RBIs. It was enough to give a guy a complex."

She smiled a little. "I doubt that. I seem to recall seeing your name on a few awards in the trophy case at school."

That cocky kid who thought the world was his to conquer seemed a lifetime away now.

"Here's my truck," he said. He never bothered to lock the doors, so he reached and opened the passenger side for her. It was a climb up, so he supported her elbow as she stepped in, wishing for the first time since he returned that he had bothered to drive something that wasn't twenty years old, run-down and smelling like dog.

The engine turned over immediately—one of the reasons he still drove this one and not some shiny new thing he'd be afraid to take up the gravel drive to his place.

"I'll just be a second," he said, reaching for the scraper behind the seats. Because the snow was soft, light as cotton puffs, he only needed to brush off what had accumulated on the side and rear windows for visibility. The wipers would take care of the front.

By the time he climbed in, the heater was already blowing out warm air. Yeah, it might not look or smell like much, but he did love this truck. It got the job done.

They encountered little traffic as he pulled out of the parking lot and headed toward the mouth of the canyon and her grandmother's house.

Just about every house was decorated for the holidays. Everybody seemed to be in on the effort to punch up the pretty: little sparkly lights along roof lines or in shrubbery, a big Christmas tree in the window, a family of cheerful snowmen in one yard.

Everything looked magical, especially in the midst of a snowfall that seemed to mute all the colors and merge them together.

They were nearly to her grandmother's house when Genevieve's phone rang. Her ring tone sounded like a jazzy number from *A Charlie Brown Christmas*, which he found inordinately sweet.

She pulled it out of the pocket of her coat and looked at the caller ID.

"Unknown," she said but answered it anyway.

"Hello?" After a moment of silence, she frowned and said the word louder.

"Must have been a wrong number," he said.

"Maybe. I could swear someone was there. Weird."

She shoved the phone back in her pocket as he pulled up in front of her grandmother's house. For some reason, it didn't seem as ugly as he'd first thought. The porch lights were on, and he could see some little twinkly Christmas lights in the front window.

"I finished painting the dining room last night," she said. "Come see."

His fingers tightened on the steering wheel. He wasn't so certain that was a good idea. The more he was with her, the more he was struggling to keep his hands—*hand*—off her. But he knew she would see his refusal as another rejection, on top of an already-painful night.

"For a minute," he finally said. "And then I'd better pick up Tucker. He's been over at Brendan's house all day and is probably ready to go home."

"Why has he been at your brother's place?"

"It's stupid, but when I'm going to be gone all day, I don't like leaving him alone up at the house by himself."

"Will he cause trouble? Chew the cabinets or rip apart all your pillows?"

"Nothing like that. He's a good dog. I just don't like thinking about him being lonely up there by himself."

He also didn't like thinking about her being here in this dark house by herself, alone and unhappy, but, again, didn't think she would appreciate being compared to his dog.

"You're a very sweet man, Dylan Caine," she said.

Any argument he made to that would sound as ridiculous as her statement, so he just glowered at her and climbed out of his pickup to open her door.

Genevieve led the way up the snowy sidewalk, aware of Dylan walking beside her with all the enthusiasm of a man heading to a torture chamber in the desert somewhere.

She sighed, wishing she had simply thanked him for the ride and said good-night. She did not understand this man. Sometimes he acted as if he enjoyed her company, savored it, even. The next minute, he would back off so quickly it made her head spin.

Tonight was a prime example. He had been extraordinarily kind to her at The Speckled Lizard, though. She would never forget the vast, aching relief that had swept over her when she walked in and saw him sitting at the bar, big and strong and comforting, as if fate had led her exactly where she needed to be.

He had offered just what she needed—a listening ear, a little wise counsel and a big heaping plate of perspective.

She couldn't believe she had rushed out of the bookstore in such a huff. Dylan was right. Ruth Tatum was a cranky bitch. What did Genevieve care what she thought? The truth was, she really didn't—but she did care what the others thought.

Charlotte and Claire McKnight and Maura. She had wanted them to like her, to see that she was trying to change.

Ruth's words had only reinforced how fruitless that effort was. She had a well-earned reputation around town. In Hope's Crossing—like any community, she imagined—becoming something different, something *more,* than what people perceived her to be was a Herculean task.

Her hands trembled with the cold as she tried to unlock the door.

"Need some help?" Dylan asked.

"No. I've got it. It can be sticky." She wiggled the key just right and the door swung open into her house. She flipped on the light and held the door open for him. As he moved inside, she wondered how he had become so dear to her in such a short time.

Until a few weeks ago, she hadn't given the man more than a second's thought. Someone—her father, perhaps—had mentioned the gravity of his injuries in passing during one of their phone calls. She remembered a little pang of sadness for kind Dermot, but that had been about the extent of the attention she paid Dylan in years.

What would her parents think if they knew a gruff wounded army ranger had become her dearest friend in Hope's Crossing?

Forget her parents. What would *Dylan* say if he knew?

"You put up some Christmas decorations. I thought you weren't going to."

"No Christmas tree, you'll notice. My brain hit tree-overload the other day decorating the one at the recreation-center meeting room."

He smiled a little and looked around the living room at the various crèches she had set out—a few above the mantel, a handful more along the big front windowsill, more spilling across the ugly round oak side tables.

"It looks nice."

She had to admit, the Nativity scenes were lovely, especially with the strings of fairy lights she'd scattered around them.

"I suppose I found a little Christmas spirit after all. It seemed a shame not to have anything. I found these in boxes in the crawl space the other night."

"That's a few Nativity sets."

"You don't know the half of them. There's probably a hundred in boxes up there. Grandma Pearl loved them. She collected them from all over, the kitschier the better. I tried to pick the best of the lot to bring down."

She touched a finger to Mary's robe on one of her favorites, a finely wrought porcelain set where the figures each had realistic faces. "From the time I was a little girl, each year she would give me another Nativity set. When I was little, I used to love setting them around in my room. After I turned about twelve, I stopped doing anything with them, but she kept giving them. Every year, without fail. They're probably boxed up somewhere at the house or else Mother threw them out."

She was sorry now that she hadn't truly appreciated the tradition. Living in this house was giving her a new perspective on her grandmother—as well as a deep sorrow that she hadn't made more of an effort to forge a better relationship with Pearl as an adult.

"Come on. Let's go see the dining room," she said, tired of her maudlin mood.

She led the way, flipped on the lights and stood back to enjoy the way the new sage green around three of the walls brightened the room. She also particularly liked the accent wall, which Dylan commented on, too.

"You did paint that wall brown. It's nice. Comforting. Amazing, how a little paint can make such a change."

"Thanks. I agree. It makes me want to hurry and finish the other rooms. I definitely think it will help the house's resale value, even if the prospective buyers end up tearing it down."

He gave her a long look, but she couldn't read the expression in his eye. Not for the first time, she wondered if his thoughts might be easier to read if not for the patch.

"Why are you in such a hurry to leave town?"

he asked. "I mean, why couldn't you start an interior-design business here? I would think Hope's Crossing has as much need for your services as anybody in Paris. More, even."

Was his mouth tight like that because he disliked the idea of her leaving? she wondered. Or was he just annoyed at having to bring her home?

"You're right. I'm sure I could stay busy here, especially with all the second homes in town and the new construction. But think about it. How could I even contemplate staying? I told you what happened at the party tonight."

"You really want to build your life around one old crank's opinion?"

"What does it matter to you where I end up starting a business? I would have thought you would be happy to see the last of me. Will you miss me?"

It had been a daring question, only half-teasing. She was tired of not being able to figure out what he was thinking, where she stood with him.

He faced her, a stark expression on his still-handsome features that made her catch her breath.

"Yes," he answered, his voice gruff. "I'll miss you. More than I should."

She swallowed, her face heating. Before she could respond—or even react, beyond initial shock, he quickly changed the subject.

"You could be happy here, Gen. Not everyone is like Ruth. You know that. Anybody who thinks you're spoiled and selfish doesn't know you. You haven't given them the *chance* to know you. You get all stiff and bristly and people mistake that for arrogance and disdain."

Yes, there was truth to that. She had come into town with her defenses raised, in part because of her parents' ultimatum but also because she hated being the subject of whispers and stares, as she had been after her engagement ended.

"Maybe they won't like what they find," she whispered.

"Maybe not," he said, just as quietly. "But you should at least give them a chance to discover the Genevieve that I see."

She gazed at him, standing inside her dining room with the scent of fresh paint swirling around them. He was extraordinarily compelling, even more gorgeous, perhaps, than he would have been without his injuries.

The eye patch, the prosthetic on his arm—she remembered how she had been slightly afraid of those things when she first met him that night at the bar, but now they were badges of honor to her. Signs of his courage and his strength, of the great sacrifices he had made and the challenges he would endure the rest of his life.

Something profound inside her shifted, slid away, revealing absolute, unadorned truth.

She was falling in love with him.

The sweetness of it rushed over her, fierce and

strong. Yes. Of course. She should have realized. She was falling in love with Dylan Caine.

The emotions fluttered in her chest, so powerfully real she couldn't believe she had missed them all this time.

She didn't give a thought to how crazy this was or think about the dangers in risking another rejection that night. She only stepped forward, lifted up on her toes and kissed the edge of that unsmiling mouth.

He froze for just a moment, and she waited in breathless anticipation, her mouth pressed against his and her blood pulsing loudly in her ears.

Kiss me back. Please kiss me back.

She was terrified he would push her away once more, but then he yanked her hard against his solid strength and returned the kiss with fierce intensity.

His mouth was firm, insistent—hot and delicious with a tiny hint of whiskey, and he kissed her with an edge of desperation.

Oh. My.

She wrapped her arms tightly around him, pressed against him from shoulder to thigh. She wanted him everywhere, the strength of him, the intoxicating taste and scent and feel.

She had never felt anything like this before, this wild, aching rush of heat and need and hunger.

Yes. Only Dylan.

What an amazing difference these fragile, tender feelings made. She almost wanted to cry. It felt so perfect and so right to be here in his arms—as if everything inside her had only been waiting for this man, this moment.

He made a low, incredibly sexy sound in his throat and deepened the kiss. She shivered as a fresh torrent of emotions surged like an avalanche pouring down the mountainside, sweeping away everything in its path—the past, her insecurities. Nothing mattered but Dylan.

She wasn't sure if she was the one who moved first or if he did but somehow they were back in Grandma Pearl's living room with the little strings of fairy lights the only illumination. He was still wearing his coat and she pulled him out of it and then they were on the sofa, body against body, just as she craved.

He was hard everywhere. All this time she had thought him too lean, with the build of a man who had lost weight in recent months and needed a few good meals at his father's café to bulk up again.

He might be lean, but now she realized he was all muscle, unyielding and tough. He kissed her mouth and then trailed kisses to her throat and farther, to the skin bared by the V of her sweater. She arched up, wanting more, wanting everything.

She had always hated Grandma Pearl's sofa but now she was seriously considering a change of mind. The wide cushions she had thought so uncomfortable gave them plenty of room to lie side by side, a distinct advantage so he didn't have to put all his weight on one arm. Instead, he could use that hand to explore, his fingers tangling in her sweater as he bared her skin just a few inches at the waist.

There was no trace of the reluctant Dylan now. He was everywhere, his lips, his tongue, his fingers. He wedged one strong thigh between hers and she arched against him, setting off another wild avalanche of sensations.

She tangled her fingers in his hair, her mouth pressing against everything she could reach. Perfect. The moment was perfect, with the snow fluttering down outside, the lights twinkling, this man she loved in her arms.

And then her phone rang.

She froze as that silly Christmas song rang out from the coat she had thoughtlessly slung over a chair.

"Ignore it," she mumbled, her mouth pressed to the deliciously warm skin along his jawline. "It's nothing."

The sofa didn't offer much room for him to roll away but somehow he managed to put space between them anyway. "It might be."

"I don't care who it is. I don't want you to stop. Kiss me again, Dylan. Please."

The light only filtered across half of his features,

the side without the patch, and she saw hunger and need reflected in his gaze, and then to her great relief, he kissed her again, almost as if he couldn't help himself.

After only a moment, though, he jerked away.

"Stop, Gen."

"Why?"

He was only inches away from her, so close she could see each spiky eyelash around that beautiful blue eye.

"I haven't been with a woman in . . . a long time. I won't want to stop at a few kisses and a little touchy-feely on your grandmother's ugly sofa."

Her insides trembled at the way he was looking at her, as no one else ever had. As if she were everything he had ever wanted.

"Okay," she whispered. She could barely think straight with him looking as if he wanted to eat her alive—yes, please—but she managed to answer with quite remarkable coherence, under the circumstances.

"I've got a bedroom. It has really nice bedding, too. I brought it from Europe."

"Not a good idea."

To her dismay, he sat up on the edge of the sofa, both legs back on the ground.

She deliberately misunderstood him. "Oh, believe me, it was. You should have seen what my grandmother left on the beds. Polyester sheets and those awful bumpy chenille coverlets."

She gave a shiver that wasn't completely feigned. Without his heat against her she was cold, suddenly, even though Grandma Pearl's furnace worked perfectly well.

He studied her, and to her surprise, after a brief hesitation, his mouth quirked up a little on one side. That she could make him smile, even when the air was thick with tension—sexual and other-wise—filled her with effervescent little bubbles of happiness.

"I meant the two of us ripping up those parti-cular sheets together. That's *not* such a great idea."

The finality in his voice was even more chilling than walking barefoot through that snow. There he went, pushing her away again.

"Is this about your hand? Because, I promise, it doesn't matter. When you're kissing me and touching me, I can only think about the parts you're using, not anything that might be missing."

A muscle flexed in his jaw, that heat rekindled in his gaze. She thought for a moment he would kiss her again but then he sighed.

"I'm damaged, Gen. Not just the outside. The whole package."

He rose to his feet, his expression one of regret and sadness and lingering hunger, and reached for the coat she had thrown on the floor.

"You're not damaged to me," she said, climbing to her feet, as well. "I think you're . . ."

Perfect. Wonderful. The man I love.

"The best person I know," she finally whispered.

It sounded stupid, but she didn't know how else to tell him everything he was coming to mean to her.

"If that's the case, you seriously need to widen your circle of acquaintances."

He reached for her hand and squeezed it gently. "I'm shaking right now because I want you so much, but I'm not going to sleep with you, Gen."

"Why not?"

She wouldn't beg, even though she really, really wanted to.

"Neither one of us is in a good place for this."

"The bedroom is right down the hall," she pointed out.

"You know that's not what I mean." He frowned. "You're vulnerable and upset because of what happened earlier tonight. I get that. But I can't be the man you need. You deserve someone . . . better. Someone without all the garbage that comes with me."

"I don't want anyone else."

Okay, maybe she *would* beg.

That muscle in his jaw tightened again, and he rubbed at his forehead just above the patch. "You say that now, but if we made love, you would regret it. I would hate that. I'm sorry, Gen. I can't do this. Good night."

Before she could argue, before she could even react, he was out the door.

After the door closed behind him with grim

finality, she couldn't seem to move. She sat on the edge of Grandma Pearl's horrid sofa—which she now hated all over again. Her emotions were battered, numb, confused, as if she had just ridden out a tornado.

She loved Dylan Caine, and he had just made it painfully clear he wouldn't let himself feel the same.

Once more, she wasn't enough.

What was she supposed to do now?

She didn't have any idea how she could just go on with her life, when everything had changed so monumentally.

How could she go back to A Warrior's Hope in the morning and face him as if nothing had happened, as if her heart hadn't just been stripped bare and turned inside out?

Even more unsettling, how could she go back to Paris now and throw herself into a new life and new career when everything she had suddenly discovered she wanted was right here?

Chapter Sixteen

❄ ❄ ❄

She looked horrible, and this time she couldn't blame the pink tiles in Grandma Pearl's bathroom.

Genevieve gazed into the mirror, gradually reaching the grim realization that no amount of clever makeup magic could fix the effects of a sleepless night. She had tried to go to bed after Dylan left but had ended up climbing back out, throwing on work clothes and stripping wallpaper in the second bedroom until the early hours of the morning.

She did her best, even though she still didn't know how she would possibly face him. With any luck, she could persuade Eden she needed an assignment far, far away from him all day. Perhaps he would decide he'd rather serve jail time after all than be forced to spend more time with her.

So he didn't want her. She could deal with it. Hadn't she been trying to convince herself she was stronger than she'd always given herself credit for?

She sighed and returned her concealer to her makeup bag. After a little more magic, she decided she would do. Though the smudge of shadows remained under her eyes, nobody should be able to see that her heart was broken.

Finally ready, she shrugged into her coat and felt the weight of her phone in the pocket. Suddenly she remembered the call the night before that had ruined everything. She had never bothered to see who was calling.

Probably her mother trying to make plans for another day of shopping, in her oblivious way.

She thought about ignoring it but at the last moment decided to check the caller ID.

She scrolled through the numbers and saw it read Unknown. Whoever it was had left a message, though.

She retrieved the voice mail. As she listened, her eyes grew wider and her heart started to pound. She jotted down the message and let her excitement push away everything else—for now.

None of her exhilaration had faded by the time she hurried into the recreation center. If anything, the phone call she made after that message had only ratcheted things up a notch. She was giddy with nerves and excitement—okay, and lack of sleep, too.

She suddenly had a little insight into the way the town's Angel of Hope must feel, doing nice things for others. What a baffling concept—that when she was helping someone else, her own troubles and pain seemed more manageable. The sorrow was still there, simmering just under the surface, but she didn't have time to wallow in it. Not when she had a new purpose.

That pesky heartache had a way of pushing itself back into the forefront, though, especially when she walked into the recreation center and immediately spotted Dylan walking in from the other direction.

Fresh hurt and rejection sliced at her, throbbing and raw. She drew in a breath, pushing them down again, and forced a smile.

"You look like you're in a good mood," Dylan said.

"The *best* mood."

He looked a little taken aback. Had he expected her to come in all mopey and morose? If she hadn't had that amazing phone call, she might have been.

"So did you get a ten-million-dollar offer on Pearl's house?"

"No. Something even better."

"Oh?"

She had to tell somebody before she exploded from the excitement, and Dylan was the logical person. He had known her plans from the beginning. If not for his information leak about Fort Benning, she probably would never have been able to find what she needed so quickly.

She gave a quick look around to make sure they wouldn't be overheard, then leaned in close.

"I heard from Jenna Baldwin."

Instead of the reaction she'd hoped for, all she received from him was a blank look.

"You remember. Trey's girlfriend. The schoolteacher from Fort Benning."

"Ah."

"She was so happy I emailed her with my number. You should have *heard* the joy bubbling out of her. She's been trying to find him for months. And get this! She was able to get a last-minute flight and she'll be here tomorrow afternoon!"

He didn't respond for a long moment.

"Oh, Gen. What have you done?" he finally said.

She frowned at the note of dismay in his voice. "What do you mean, what have I done? This is the perfect outcome. She will come out here, he will see how very wrong he was to push her away and they'll live happily ever after."

"You are *completely* delusional."

After he'd put her through the misery of the night before, he actually had the nerve to call her names, to pop the little bubble of happiness that was the only thing keeping her upright and functioning right now?

"And you're the most cynical person I've ever met!" she retorted.

"Yeah, sorry if my life hasn't been all caviar and walks down the Champs-Elysées."

Five minutes ago, she had been so excited, filled with anticipation at doing something right for once. This was supposed to be her own little Christmas gift for a young man who desperately deserved to find some happiness. Now Dylan, Mr. You Don't Need My Garbage, was spitting all over her joy.

"You think my life is so perfect?" She wanted to smack him, but instead she settled for curling her hands into fists and folding them across her chest. "I'm broke. I've got no friends. My own family thinks I'm out of control. I'm serving community-service hours with *you,* for heaven's sake. Yeah, some rosy picture."

"It could be a hell of a lot worse."

"I know that. I'm not a complete idiot. What did I do that was so terrible? I thought I was doing something nice for two people who love each other. I even paid for half her airfare out of my emergency fund since the cost of the last-minute flight was out of a schoolteacher's budget."

"Oh, Gen."

Something warm and soft flitted across his expression but quickly disappeared again, replaced by that stony mask that filled her with self-doubt.

"You're right. It was a stupid idea. The whole thing will explode in my face and be one more screw-up in the loser column, along with maxing out my credit cards and being stupid enough to break the nose of the assistant district attorney."

To her horror, her voice wobbled a little on the last word. She swallowed hard and forced back the angry tears that threatened. Or maybe they weren't angry. Just more of the regular, garden-variety sad kind.

"Don't worry. I'll make sure Trey knows you had nothing to do with it."

"Nothing to do with what?"

She turned around to find the man in question had wheeled up to them without her hearing. Oh, Lord. What was she supposed to do now? She wanted to surprise him. If she told him Jenna was coming the next day, it would ruin every-thing, but she couldn't think of a way to back-track.

To her astonishment, Dylan—Mr. Cynical him-self—came to her rescue.

"You caught me. The plan is to go out on the snowmobiles this morning. They've got a couple with hand controls and I was trying to arrange things so you could have the most powerful one, since I remembered you were talking about how much you liked to race motorcycles before you were injured."

He had her six. Wasn't that what she'd heard the veterans call it when somebody watched their back? Though he objected to what she wanted to do, he still stepped up to help her out.

Was it any wonder she was crazy in love with him?

"Wow," Trey said, surprise in his voice. "Thanks, man. That's really nice of you."

"Yeah, that's me," Dylan drawled. "I'm nothing if not nice."

He gave Genevieve a hard sort of look. To her relief, Eden and Mack and the others joined them and the moment was gone.

By the end of the day, she was exhausted from trying not to burst with nerves.

Every time she came within range of Trey, she had to think of a hundred different distractions to keep from accidentally blurting out the news about Jenna.

Whenever she was near *Dylan* she had to do the same thing—mostly to keep from bursting into tears.

At least she didn't have to add Charlotte into the mix. She hadn't seen Dylan's sister since ditching her at the bookstore the night before. Over lunch, she had heard Spence tell Chelsea that Charlotte had too much work at her candy store and probably wouldn't make it until the dinner meal.

To her relief, Eden must have sensed some of her anxiety. Instead of sending her out while the families went cross-country skiing again, she assigned Gen to work inside the recreation center—away from everyone else, thank heavens. She was to finalize arrangements for the closing reception to be held Sunday night and work her decorating magic on wrapping some farewell gifts the rest of the staff had prepared for the guests and their families.

Everyone was leaving Monday. So much could happen between now and then. She really hoped the outcome of her actions would be a positive one.

She was just tying the ribbon on the last gift— another outfit for cute little Claudia Brooks's doll Penelope—when Spencer Gregory walked into the room off the lobby she had commandeered.

He was so movie-star gorgeous, it always took her by surprise. Smokin' Hot Spence Gregory. During her time working for A Warrior's Hope, she had come to realize he seemed completely unaware of it.

"Here you are. Looks like Eden has you working hard."

She smiled. "She's good at keeping me busy. I'm nearly done. Is everyone back?"

"Not yet. Mac called and said they were heading this way."

"I need to wrap this up—so to speak—and hurry to hide everything."

"We can stow them in my office."

"Okay. I'm almost done here."

"Need help?"

"No. I think I've got it."

He leaned against the table to watch, and she had to wonder again why, as great-looking as he was, he didn't make her stomach jump with nerves like Dylan did.

"So I was just looking through the paper work and realized you and Dylan have made a lot of headway on your community-service hours this week. A few more of these ten-hour days and you'll have finished your obligation to the court and to us."

"I guess that's right."

"I imagine you'll be glad to see the last of this place."

She should be excited to move forward and devote her attention to finishing the work on Grandma Pearl's house. Instead, she found herself unaccountably depressed. She had enjoyed her time here, more than she ever expected.

"It hasn't been bad. Actually, I've really liked working here. Thank you for giving me the chance."

He looked surprised. "You're welcome."

Though she had been in Paris, she knew Spence had come here in the midst of scandal, his name blackened by his wife's untimely death, by his own prescription-drug addiction, by a drug-trafficking scandal that had turned out to be a frame-up.

His life had changed radically since coming back to his hometown.

"Can I just tell you," she said on impulse, "I think it's a wonderful thing you've done here. A Warrior's Hope is a fantastic program. You're changing lives here. This morning I watched Ricardo Torres on the snowmobile with his wife, and they were having a wonderful time together. The first day they arrived, it seemed as if she barely spoke to him. And it was so great yesterday to watch Trey and Joe racing each other down the mountain on their adapted ski seats. Really, the whole program is quite remarkable."

"Thank you, Genevieve. I appreciate you saying that." He gave a rueful smile. "I wish you could convince your family. Your father, especially. Did you know he's trying to pull our conditional use permit?"

She stared. "I'm sure that's not true."

"According to Mayor Beaumont, the Hope's Crossing recreation center should be used only by the residents of Hope's Crossing, not by any Tom, Dick or Harry with a hard-luck story."

Oh, sometimes her father made her *crazy*. "I'm sorry. I'll try to talk to him, but I should warn you, I don't carry a lot of credit with my family right now."

"I'm not too worried about the whole thing, especially since we've got Harry Lange on our side. He and Mary Ella are two of our biggest donors. Your dad might complain about our mission here and make noises about trying to shut us down but I doubt he'll openly defy Harry."

"No. He won't."

He smiled at her, and again she wondered why she didn't feel the same tingle as she did when a certain wounded ranger gifted her with his rare smile.

"So Charlotte told me what happened at the book-club party last night."

She had almost forgotten Ruth Tatum, with everything else on her worry plate right now. Now that he mentioned it again, her face burned with remembered mortification. She avoided his gaze, focusing instead on tying the last bow on the present and arranging a little angel ornament in the folds.

"Not one of my happier moments."

"For the record, Charlotte was very upset about it. She wanted to rush right over to your house to make sure you were all right, but then Dylan called her and yelled at her for letting Ruth mouth off about you like that."

Oh. He did that? The little snowmen on the wrapping present seemed to blur and quiver as her eyes filled. She quickly blinked the tears away, wondering what his sister thought about her running to Dylan from the bookstore—and about Dylan leaping to her defense.

"None of it was Charlotte's fault. I never blamed her."

"She still felt terrible. Everyone did. You shouldn't worry about Ruth Tatum, you know."

She set the present on the pile with the others. "Yes. So everyone tells me."

"Can I share a little wisdom learned from hard experience?"

"I . . . Of course."

"I know what it is to be the object of people's dislike. Trust me. I've had more than enough experience coping with misconceptions."

She could only imagine how difficult it must have been to live under a cloud someone else had created. He had endured far worse smears to his reputation than a miserable mistake of an engage-ment.

The difference was, the allegations against him had been false, while she really *had* been a cold bitch.

"When things were at their worst for me, I learned to just keep my head up and do my best to hold on to my pride and my dignity."

"Thank you for the advice. I appreciate it."

"You're welcome. Are you ready to start hiding things away?"

"I guess we need to, unless we want everybody to find their presents early this year."

He picked up an armload and started down the hall. She followed him with her own arms full.

"For the record," she said as they returned for another load, "I'm glad things worked out for you the way they did. You and Charlotte seem very happy together."

His smile was bright, filled with such joy that sharp envy pinched at her. "We are. In fact, we're getting married next summer."

"Congratulations."

She meant the words. She liked and admired Charlotte and could tell she already loved Spence's daughter, Peyton.

For a moment, she was tempted to tell him about Trey's ex-fiancée flying in the next day, but Dylan had filled her with such anxious doubts she decided to keep her mouth shut for now.

Chapter Seventeen

❆ ❆ ❆

By noon the next day, she was a nervous wreck. Throughout the morning, Jenna had been texting her to update her on her travel progress.

In Chicago.
Ready to board connection.
Landed in Denver.
Renting a car.

She had texted back travel instructions and encouraging words, but now that the critical moment was approaching she could hardly breathe around her anxiety.

She should have texted Jenna to board the next plane back to Atlanta and forget the whole thing.

She couldn't bear this suspense. She really hoped Trey would be thrilled to see the woman he loved, would realize his mistake in pushing her away. She tried to focus on their conversation about Jenna that had started the whole thing. He had spoken of her with such tender emotion—and she had seen the loneliness in his eyes as he looked at all these other family units.

That was what she hoped would happen.

At the same time, she was very much afraid he would be furious and find the whole thing a cruel scheme aimed at snarling his life.

"How much longer before the fireworks show?" Dylan asked when they walked inside the recreation center for the lunch catered by one of Brodie Thorne's restaurants.

They hadn't spoken privately since the morning before and simply the sound of his voice filled her with longing. She firmly tamped it down.

"I hope there won't be fireworks, except the romantic kind."

He made a gruff, cynical sound, sending ripples of worry through her all over again.

"It won't be long now. She's about fifteen miles outside of town."

"Funny. For someone trying so hard to earn her cupid wings, you don't sound very excited."

She gave a weak smile, wishing with all her heart she had never sent that email. "Life was much safer when I only cared about myself."

To her astonishment, he reached out and took her fingers in his. "You know anything about physics?"

"Not really. I think I skipped that class for cheerleading practice."

He probably had no idea how much courage his slight smile gave her. "I'm sure you've heard Newton's first law that an object in motion tends to stay in motion."

"I did pick that up somewhere. Again, maybe cheerleading practice. And an object at rest tends to stay at rest, right? In other words, I should have just minded my own business and left well enough alone."

"It's too late for regrets, Gen. You set the boulder tumbling down the hill. Now you just have to wait and see which way it's going to land."

"What if it crashes onto my head?"

He squeezed her fingers, then to her further astonishment, he reached out and tucked a strand of hair behind her ear and gave her a heartbreaking smile. "Then you can fit right in with the rest of us bruised and broken souls."

She didn't know how to convince him she didn't see him as broken. He was a good man. Rough around the edges, maybe, and certainly cynical. But she had watched him this week with the others. Though he claimed in the beginning he wanted nothing to do with A Warrior's Hope, she had seen him exhibit amazing patience to everyone coming through the program. He was playful with the children, kind to the spouses and parents and understanding with the wounded veterans.

She wanted to tell him all the things she had discovered about him but this didn't seem the moment, not when she knew Jenna Baldwin would arrive any moment.

"He's going to hate me, isn't he?"

He sighed. "Maybe. Not much we can do about that now. But even if he's furious, I hope some part of him understands you thought you were doing something in his best interest."

He paused. "It's too late now, anyway."

She followed the direction of his gaze to find a young woman standing in the doorway with a hopeful, nervous expression on her pretty, sweet-natured face.

Dylan squeezed her fingers again. "Guess it's showtime."

In thirty-six hours of fretting, why hadn't she planned ahead enough to arrange a more private reunion between the two of them?

She still could. Trey had gone outside with a couple of others to photograph the bull moose that had lately taken to hanging around the recreation center, browsing on whatever water plants were still alive in the icy river.

She could head Jenna off, move her to a more private setting and then bring Trey in when he returned.

Amazing, how calming a plan could be.

She hurried over to greet the woman. To her surprise, Dylan walked over with her, despite his objections to the whole thing. She wanted to hug him, deeply grateful for his strength and support.

"Hi. You must be Jenna. I'm Genevieve Beaumont. This is Dylan Caine."

Jenna was even prettier up close, delicate and lovely, though her features were strained and she had circles under her eyes that looked as if they had been there for some time.

She twisted her fingers together. "Hello." She smiled nervously, looking fresh and sweet—all the things Genevieve wasn't. Why on earth had Trey ever said she reminded him of this gentle-looking woman? Yes, their hair color was the same and they both had the same blue eyes, but that was the only resemblance.

On impulse, she reached in and hugged the woman. After the past thirty-six hours, she felt as if she knew her well. Gen was certainly invested in the success of this little endeavor, financially and emotionally.

"How was your flight?"

Jenna gave a shaky little laugh. "To be honest, I have no idea. I feel like I've been in a daze since I spoke with you yesterday. Everything has happened so quickly. I . . . How can I ever thank you?"

Don't thank me yet.

"Don't worry about that."

Jenna craned her neck to look around the room, where Elena and Ricardo and the Augustines were still eating lunch. "Is he here? I don't see him."

Dylan spoke up. "He just stepped out a moment ago. We've had a moose wandering around the grounds for the last few days and several guests went out to take pictures of it down in the river. He should be up any minute now. Can I take your coat? Would you like something to eat or drink?"

Warmth stirred in her chest at this sweet, noncynical side of Dylan he showed so rarely.

"I . . . Thank you." She handed him her coat. "Some water would be good. I'm afraid I couldn't eat breakfast or lunch. I've been so nervous all day, I haven't been able to swallow anything."

"I'll be right back."

Dylan walked over to the table where the food had been set out buffet-style.

"I'm so anxious, I can hardly breathe."

"Everything will be fine. You'll see." She had nothing to base that particular statement on except hope, which seemed pretty flimsy right now, all things considered.

"What if he doesn't want me here? What if he hasn't reconsidered anything and still won't give me a chance?"

Genevieve shared the very same fear, but she couldn't say that now, in front of this young woman who seemed so pale, fragile as an antique blown-glass ornament.

"Then he will be making a terrible mistake."

Jenna rested a hand on her arm. "Thank you for this, Genevieve. Everything you've done."

She thought about her life merely a month ago in Paris, shopping and decorating her apartment,

343

sewing what she wanted, visiting with friends. All the things she thought were so important. That time seemed a world away—and not merely geographically.

One afternoon when she had nothing else to do, she had wandered into a gallery in the Sixth Arrondissement and had watched an artist create an exquisite papier-mâché sculpture, taking a simple wire-mesh frame and adding strip after strip of adhesive-soaked paper until the result was a thing of substance and beauty.

She wanted to think she was like that sculpture, in the process of adding her own layers upon layers. She was a different person than she had been a month ago. She wouldn't go back. She couldn't.

"You're welcome," she murmured, giving Jenna another hug.

Dylan returned with the water glass. "Why don't we see if we can find a quiet room somewhere for Jenna to wait, away from the crowd?"

"Yes. I think the office next to Spencer's should be available."

Gen started for the door. Before she made it more than a few feet, she heard voices and laughter in the hall and realized they had acted too late. Everyone was returning from outside. She could hear Trey's voice and realized how horribly wrong this could all go, throwing Jenna at him like this, without warning, in front of everyone.

She wanted to stand in front of the woman, to shield her from view and from Trey's wrath.

Pam and her fiancé Kevin, walked in first, holding hands, as usual. Joe and Tonya came in next, Claudia riding in her favorite place of honor on her father's lap and the quieter Marisol walking beside her mother behind the wheelchair.

Behind them came Trey, wheeling in with his usual cheerful smile.

Gen was aware of Jenna's sharp inhale beside her. Out of the corner of her gaze, she caught the other woman's expression: stark longing and love and sorrow, all jumbled together.

She could certainly relate to that.

He hadn't noticed them yet. "Man, I've never seen a moose that close before. I can't believe the size of that guy. I really thought he was going to come after you."

Tonya snorted. "Are you kidding? He wasn't even close. I was still at least thirty feet away from those big antlers. Anyway, you should see how fast I can move when I have to."

Joe's laugh was warm and infectious. "She's not kidding. Just a few weeks ago, Marisol wandered off for a minute at Walmart. Tonya was a blur racing through those aisles. Found her in the book section, of course. Where else?"

His voice trailed off when he must have realized Trey wasn't listening to him—he was staring at the woman standing numbly beside Genevieve.

He wheeled a few feet in their direction, almost as if he couldn't help himself, then stopped when he was still several yards away.

"Jenna! What is this?"

Genevieve's heart was in her throat. She couldn't read anything on his features—not pleasure or anger or anything. It was like staring at that papier-mâché sculpture.

Jenna gave him a wobbly smile. "Hi, Trey. You look great."

"You look . . . here."

"Yes." She swallowed. "Merry Christmas."

"*Why* are you here?"

Since he hadn't moved beyond those first few feet, Jenna walked toward him, her hands still twisted together in front of her.

No one else but Dylan knew exactly what was going on, but somehow they must have sensed something significant was happening. Everyone fell silent, even the little ones.

Trey was usually so affable and good-natured. Just now, though, his jaw was tight, his mouth unsmiling. He looked every inch the hardened soldier.

"Why are you here?" he repeated, his voice harsh.

"To see you," she whispered. "To . . . I don't know, make you see sense."

"Sense." The word came out hard, sharp, like a rock striking a tree trunk.

"Yes." She moved forward and spoke softly. "I missed you, Trey. So much."

For just a moment, he gazed at her with raw yearning before his expression shuttered again.

"How did you find me?" he demanded.

She didn't answer, but her gaze subtly shifted to Genevieve before turning back to Trey. "Does it matter? I had to come. Sunday was supposed to be our wedding day. December twenty-second. I still have all the invitations."

"You should have burned them," he said harshly.

Her chin trembled a little, but she quickly firmed it again, earning even more of Genevieve's respect. She wasn't sure she could face a man who had dumped her, especially in front of nearly a dozen witnesses.

"You can run away all you want, Trey Evans, but it won't change the fact that I still love you, no matter what. I still want to marry you, to start a family with you."

His expression turned even more bleak and wintry, if possible. He shifted to Genevieve.

"You did this, didn't you? This is why you've been so jumpy the last few days. What the hell? You had no right."

"I know." The audacity of her actions was indefensible, and she was suddenly miserable, horrified at what she had set in motion and the additional pain she might have caused the two of them. "It's just . . . you were all alone. I thought . . . I wanted to make you happy. A wonderful Christmas gift."

"More like a Christmas nightmare," he growled.

"Why don't we take this somewhere a little more private where we can talk," Dylan suggested.

"Good idea." Spencer Gregory had come into the room in the middle of the drama. He looked baffled but had obviously picked up enough hints to guess at what might be going on—at least enough to give Genevieve a *you're-in-big-trouble* sort of look.

"What's the point? I don't have one damn thing to talk about. I didn't ask for this. Once, Jenna and I were engaged. We broke things off. End of story."

"*You* broke things off and left without even telling me where you were. You didn't even give me a chance to change your mind—you just ran away."

"I didn't run away. I was transferring to the rehab facility in San Antonio. And what would have been the point of dragging things out? You *can't* change my mind."

"Trey—"

"I don't want to marry you. Is that clear enough for you? I'm sorry you came all this way from Georgia, but it was a wasted trip. I don't want to marry you. I don't love you. I don't know if I ever loved you."

Jenna swayed a little, color leaching from her features. "I . . . see."

Genevieve suddenly remembered the other woman hadn't eaten. She grabbed for her elbow and felt the vibration of her trembling through her sweater and blouse.

Her heart ached at what she had done. Dylan was watching the whole thing with a resigned expression, as if everything had happened just as he'd expected.

She thought of how hard he was pushing her away, just like Trey pushed Jenna away. She wasn't as brave as Jenna. Her feelings were so new, so raw, she hadn't confessed them to Dylan. She probably never would—but she suddenly knew that if she ever did, Dylan would react just as Trey had, lashing out from a place of pain and loss instead of seeing hope and possibilities.

Even as her heart spasmed painfully in her chest, she was furious suddenly, livid with both of them. She had worked too hard for this, spending hours she didn't have on the internet trying to find Jenna and then money she *also* didn't have to fly her here.

It wasn't fair. It wasn't fair and it wasn't right.

"You are a liar, Trey Evans," she burst out, aware of Jenna's trembling fingers in hers. "I heard the yearning in your voice the day you told me about her. How can you deny it? I saw all the emotions in your eyes you now claim you don't feel. You are *lying*. Your feelings haven't changed. You know they haven't. I know they haven't. *Jenna* knows they haven't! I can't believe a man who earned two Purple Hearts in Afghanistan could be such a damn coward."

Dylan heard all the assembled veterans give a collective intake of breath. None of them would take one of their own being called a coward sitting down.

He should have pushed to take this somewhere private when he'd had the chance—though how the hell he had let her twist him up in this whole thing was still a mystery.

He stepped up and laid a hand on her arm. "Gen, that's enough."

She whirled on him. "Shut up, Dylan. You're as bad as he is!"

He blinked at that, not sure how this had become about him.

"Come on, everyone," Spence said with sudden firmness. "Let's give them some space to work this out."

In the few minutes it took to usher everyone out, Genevieve marched right up to Trey.

"I'm sure I know what you're thinking," she said when everyone except the four of them had left.

He aimed a stare at her so hard it would cut through concertina wire. "Oh, I doubt that."

"You think she can't want you now. That you're somehow . . . inadequate."

Dylan froze, wondering just who she was talking to now.

Trey's gaze narrowed. "Look, I appreciate that you thought you had good intentions, but you don't know anything about this."

She darted a quick look at Dylan then jerked her gaze back to Trey. "Maybe not. But I know how lucky the two of you are. Do you have any idea how many women would kill to have the man they love talk about them the way you did when you told me about Jenna? I know you still love her. I heard it in every word you said to me. She must know it, too, or she would never have found the courage to follow you here."

Her voice softened and she touched his arm. "If I were the woman you loved, I would have fought for you, too."

"It's not that easy."

She gave a ragged-sounding laugh. "I'm sure it's not." She paused. "And while I do think you love her, I have to ask myself how you can, when you think so little of her."

"I don't," he protested.

"You think she's weak."

He raked a hand through his hair, genuine confusion on his features. "Where the hell did you get that crazy idea?"

"From you. From your actions. You pushed her

351

away because you must think she's so fragile she can't handle a little imperfection. You seem to think she'll melt with horror if she has to look at some scars."

"I've got more than a few scars! Look at me! I can't walk. Did you happen to notice that little fact? When I realized I wasn't going to miraculously get the strength back, I knew I couldn't go ahead with the wedding. How the hell can I provide for her, can I be any kind of decent father to all the kids she wants? I can't give her what she needs!"

The anguished words resonated inside Dylan. Hell, he had spent the whole summer and fall sitting around at his cabin in Snowflake Canyon, drinking and wallowing in his self-pity, thinking of all he had lost and the options no longer available to him.

Genevieve straightened, fiery, determined . . . and so lovely she took his breath away.

"Are you really going to throw away something beautiful and good because you're afraid she will reject you later? Jenna loves you. She came all this way to tell you. After she stayed with you those long months in the hospital, don't you think you owe her the courtesy of at least listening to what she has to say?"

Trey said nothing, his hands clenching and unclenching the wheels of his chair. His expression, though, was one of stark longing.

Jenna no longer looked as if she were close to toppling over. Color had returned to her cheeks while Genevieve spoke, and now she stepped forward on Trey's other side.

"Oh, you foolish man. I thought I loved you two years ago when I agreed to marry you. I thought I loved you when you left overseas on another deployment. I thought I would die when they told me you were injured, that you might not survive. This last year, watching your strength and courage as you faced this hardest of challenges has only made me love you more than I ever imagined possible."

She touched his face with a tenderness that made Dylan's chest ache. "Please. Don't push me away again, Trey. I don't think I can bear it."

Trey made a sound, a gasp or a sob, Dylan wasn't sure, but after a long, tense pause, he closed his eyes and pressed his face into her hand.

As Jenna leaned down to kiss him, Dylan grabbed Genevieve by the crook of her elbow and yanked her out of the room.

"Well?" Tonya Brooks seized on Genevieve the moment they joined the others out in the lobby.

She gave a strained smile. "They were kissing when we left, but I think it's too soon to say."

The wives all gave a little cheer. Tonya grinned and hugged Genevieve, and Pam and Elena hugged each other and then Genevieve, too.

Women.

Gen wasn't the only one wiping away tears. Nobody would ever accuse her of being a cold bitch if they could see the soft, happy light in her eyes as she shared in the other women's excitement.

Spence, on the other hand, didn't look nearly as happy at this new development.

"What just happened here?" he demanded, in the same tone of voice he probably used against rookies on the ball field making stupid mistakes.

Guilt flashed in Genevieve's eyes and she nibbled her lips. "Um, a sort of . . . Christmas miracle, I hope."

"And what part did you play in this *Christmas miracle?*"

She fidgeted. "Um, not much, really. Okay, a little. Trey mentioned his former fiancée to me and the circumstances of their breakup, and I . . . sort of tracked her down and invited her here."

And helped pay for her airfare, but Dylan decided not to mention that little fact to Spence, who didn't look very happy about what he *did* know.

"We're running a recreational therapy program here, not a matchmaking service."

"I know."

"I hope you haven't seriously compromised the integrity of A Warrior's Hope. We're trying to build a reputation here. What if word gets out that we take personal information our clients offer and interfere in things that are none of our damn business? You completely overstepped."

She looked stricken. "I didn't think. I just wanted to help Trey. He seemed so lonely. Everyone else has a support system but he has . . . no one."

"This isn't some happy-ever-after fairy tale, where the prince and princess ride off on a white charger to their gleaming castle. These men have been through hell. You have no idea what the climb back is like. As somebody once told me, you can't just step into their lives and think you can sprinkle fairy dust and make everything better."

Dylan gave a little inward wince, remembering he had said those very words to Spence another lifetime ago, it seemed, when Spence had first come up with the idea for A Warrior's Hope.

"You and I both know how important reputation is, Genevieve, and how hard it is to overcome a bad one."

"I'm sorry," she whispered. She looked devastated, and he hated seeing her little moment of triumph—premature though it might be—dissolve into despair.

"She thought she was helping him, Spence," he spoke up.

She sent him a shocked look, as if she'd never expected him to step up and defend her. Spence looked just as surprised.

"No doubt. Her motives aren't in question. It's the outcome I find concerning."

"I know. I'm sorry. I . . . I didn't think."

Before Spence could respond, Eden came in from outside. "The sleighs just pulled up. Is everybody ready to go for a ride up to see the elk herd?"

The cute little Brooks girls squealed with excitement and hugged each other.

"Elk and moose and a little romantic drama," their mother said. "What else could we possibly need?"

"Our coats are still in there." Quiet Elena pointed to the closed door of the reception room. "Do you think we dare go get them?"

"Why wouldn't you?" Eden, who had just missed the whole thing, asked.

"It's a long story," Spence said. "I'll explain it to you while we load up the sleighs."

Elena tentatively poked her head through the door and then turned back to face the others. "They're not here anymore. They must have gone out the other door."

"Who?" Eden asked.

"Trey and Jenna."

"Oh, that must be the woman I saw him with. I just bumped into them outside, heading toward the cabins. He said he would skip the afternoon activities and see everyone tonight."

A couple of the women giggled, and Tonya

gave a throaty, knowing sort of laugh that earned her an affectionate pinch from Joe.

As he watched their interaction and thought about Trey and Jenna and what had just happened, Dylan was aware of a sharp spike of envy—and the niggling fear that he was being an even bigger fool.

Chapter Eighteen

All afternoon, while they rode on horse-drawn sleighs on a groomed fire road to a high pasture where a large herd of elk grazed, Genevieve fretted.

۰ She hoped she had done the right thing. It looked as if Jenna and Trey would be able to mend their differences, though she certainly knew one kiss didn't necessarily equate to a happy ending.

The lecture from Spence stung, in part because she knew she had earned it. Her impulsive, heedless actions could have damaged two people irreparably—not to mention stained the reputation of A Warrior's Hope.

Dylan seemed to be avoiding her, especially after her outburst that afternoon. He deliberately chose a seat in one of the other sleighs, and when they climbed out to take pictures of the elk from a safe distance, he didn't approach her.

She tried to tell herself his distance didn't hurt but it was a fairly useless lie.

Eden sat next to her on the way back to the recreation center. As soon as the horses headed down the mountainside, bells jingling, she turned to Gen and started interrogating her.

"Okay, I'm getting all kinds of crazy stories about what I missed this afternoon with Trey. Apparently you're the one who knows the whole skinny. What's going on? Who is she?"

"Her name is Jenna Baldwin. She's a school-teacher in Georgia. They met at church and were engaged until a couple of months ago. Sunday was supposed to be their wedding day."

"No shit?" Eden exclaimed, then winced. "Sorry. I'm trying not to swear. I mean, you're kidding."

"I'm not."

"You said they *were* engaged. What happened?"

"Trey broke things off just before he was transferred to another rehab facility in Texas. I guess he thought Genevieve deserved better than a wounded veteran. She didn't know where he was. He mentioned her to me and I took a little initiative—inappropriately, I realize now—and tracked her down."

"How did you find her?"

Without implicating Dylan, she explained about isolating Jenna's location to Georgia and how she had searched web databases until she found her and then had emailed her.

"It was a thoughtless thing to do. I feel terrible that I've risked the reputation of A Warrior's Hope. It wasn't my intention."

"Wow! That must have taken guts—for you to look for her that way and for this Jenna person to come after him."

"You don't think I overstepped?"

"Well, yeah. But if it works, and you make two people happy, then it was worth it, wasn't it? I mean, what can Spence do? Fire you? Duh. You're a volunteer."

Her surprised laugh turned to stunned disbelief at Eden's next words. "You've done a really great job here, Genevieve," the director said. "Are you sure you wouldn't like to stay on after you finish your hours? We would love to have someone on our volunteer staff with your event-planning skills and your flair for design."

If her circumstances were different, she would jump at the chance, she realized. This past week had been . . . life-altering.

She was flattered and humbled by the request, even as she knew she had to refuse. "I'm sorry, but I won't be in town much longer. I'm trying to fix up my grandmother's house to sell it. As soon as I do, I'll be heading back to France. I have an apartment there and friends and . . . well, I'm starting a business."

"I'm sorry to hear that. Happy for you, if this is what you want, I mean, but sorry for us. We'll miss you."

"I'll miss all of you, too," Genevieve said quietly.

"Tell me about your grandmother's house. I'm in the market for something here in town. I've been living in a condo with a short-term lease until I find something I like."

"You don't want this house. It's horrible. Dark, outdated. The location is really good but the house needs so much more work than I'll be able to finish."

"I don't care about the inside, only the bones. I love a challenge. Maybe I could swing by after dinner and take a look. I would love to sneak in and grab something that's not on the market yet."

The faster she sold the house, the less work she would have to finish. She should be thrilled, but she couldn't help a sharp pang at the idea of leaving.

"Sure. Come by tonight. That will be great. You'll have to look past the remodeling projects. I'm afraid it's a bit of a mess."

"My last house in Seattle was definitely a fixer-upper. I can deal with mess."

When they returned to the recreation center, the plan was to split the group into two, one to go ice fishing in the reservoir, the other to skate on the frozen pond in a meadow near the recreation-center parking lot. Eden assigned her to the skating group, much to her relief, so she spent the rest of the afternoon tying laces and handing out hot cocoa.

Dylan went with the ice-fishing group, managing to avoid her for a few more hours without much effort on his part.

Dinner was to be catered by Alex McKnight's restaurant again. She was starving, she realized, as, like Jenna, she had been too nervous that morning to eat much.

When they came in from outside, cheeks rosy, Genevieve found Jenna and Trey in the two-story lobby of the recreation center. He was in his wheelchair and Jenna sat on a chair next to him, though she might as well have been sitting on his lap. They were holding hands, brushing shoulders, touching arms.

Her nerves immediately settled. The two appeared radiant. For all his affable good nature during the past week, she now realized she hadn't seen Trey truly happy until now. All the lonely edges seemed to have been smoothed away.

Jenna rushed to her first and wrapped her arms around Genevieve, promptly bursting into tears. "I can't thank you enough for what you've done. You have no idea."

"Um. You're welcome." She patted the other

woman's back, somewhat helpless as Jenna sobbed against her.

"I'm sorry. I'm just so happy."

"Are you?"

"Beyond anything I imagined. I can't believe two days ago I felt as if all the color and joy had been sucked out of my life and now it's all back, brighter than ever."

"I'm glad."

Trey wheeled forward and took her hand. "Thank you," he murmured.

"You're welcome."

"You all might as well be the first to know," he said to the group, strangers brought together by circumstances, who had bonded over the past week. "We're getting married after all, just as soon as we can arrange it."

Marisol clapped her hands, and beside her, Claudia jumped up and down. "Married! I want to see them get married!"

Jenna and Trey exchanged looks. "Well, if we can arrange it on such short notice, we were thinking of trying to make it into the courthouse to find a justice of the peace before we leave town."

Of all the unlikely supporters, given how upset he had been a few hours earlier, Spencer Gregory stepped forward. "Why not get married here? We've already had a few people ask to use the facility for that reason. The reception room where we've been sharing meals would be a beautiful place for a wedding, with the fireplace and the windows overlooking the river and the mountains."

"Yes!" Genevieve exclaimed, her mind already racing with ideas. "We could give you *such* a spectacular wedding. Oh, please. Will you let me do this?"

"You've already done so much," Jenna protested.

"Maybe, but I want to do this, too. You don't know this about me, but I'm kind of an expert at planning weddings. I worked on my own for two years."

They exchanged surprised looks. "I had no idea you were married," Trey said.

"I'm not," she said matter-of-factly. "I dumped the cheating bum a few weeks before the wedding. But trust me, it would have been spectacular."

Jenna smiled, even as she looked a little overwhelmed. "I don't want to be a bother. We can just go to the courthouse."

"No bother. I want to do this for you and Trey."

"You have to let us help," Marie Augustine insisted.

"Yes," agreed Whitney Reid. "I work in a florist shop back home. If I can get my hands on some supplies, I would love to do your bouquet."

"Can I be in your marriage?" Marisol asked shyly.

Jenna was obviously a very good teacher, judging by the patient way she knelt down and spoke with the little girl. "Of course you can be in our wedding, darling, as long as your mom and dad don't mind."

"How soon can we arrange it?" Spence asked Genevieve. "Everybody's supposed to go home Monday afternoon."

"Can I have until Sunday evening? That was supposed to be their wedding day anyway."

Jenna burst into tears again. "That would be so perfect. Oh, thank you."

She noticed Dylan hadn't reacted to the joyful announcement. He had retreated to the windows and was looking out, his features as remote as the snowy landscape.

Oh, she did not want to do this.

Genevieve parked as close as she could to String Fever, in the small public lot a block over. On this, the last Saturday before Christmas, downtown Hope's Crossing was clogged with ski-resort tourists and locals trying to squeeze in a little last-minute shopping.

Everywhere she looked she saw people bustling around with packages, bags of takeout from the restaurants around, even a couple of guys carrying a large wrapped parcel in the shape of a bicycle, probably from Mike's Bikes.

She had too much to do to sit in her car here all morning watching everyone else hurry about, but she couldn't seem to make herself move, could only gaze out at the flakes of snow landing on her windshield.

She didn't want to climb out of the warmth into that cold, especially because she expected she would be in for an even colder reception when she reached her destination, String Fever—Claire McKnight's bead store.

She had been beastly to Claire during her lengthy engagement to Sawyer. That was the bald truth of it. She had been her most exacting, her haughty, patronizing worst. She had hired Claire to hand-bead the bodice of her designer wedding gown and had demanded perfection from the outset.

When her original gown had been vandalized through no fault of Claire's, Genevieve had thrown a spoiled, immature tantrum, quite certain Sawyer wouldn't want to marry her now and everything would be ruined.

The memory of it made her cringe. Claire, and everyone else in town, had been mourning the death of a teenage girl—Maura Lange's youngest daughter—and the severe injuries of Brodie Thorne's daughter Taryn.

In retrospect, Genevieve couldn't believe she had ever been so narcissistic that she had even *cared* about her stupid wedding gown in the midst of such tragedy—especially considering her own younger brother, Charlie, had been driving the vehicle in the accident that had killed Layla and injured Taryn.

Oh, how she wished she could go back and relive that time from the perspective she had now. Of course, if that were possible, she never would have been stupid enough to think she could marry Sawyer Danforth.

A sudden rap on the window startled a squeak out of her. She shifted and saw Dylan standing on the other side of the glass and metal, his gaze concerned.

He looked gorgeous with snow melting in his brown hair. He had trimmed away almost all the shagginess—for the wedding? she wondered. The cut made him look younger, somehow.

He continued watching her with concern and she finally sighed, knowing she was going to have to face him eventually, and hit the power button on the window.

"Everything okay? I saw you pull in. You've been sitting here for a couple of minutes without moving."

In the corner of the lot, she spied his beat-up old pickup truck. She must have been too distracted when she arrived to notice it.

"What are you doing here? Why aren't you with A Warrior's Hope?"

"I had a couple of errands to run, so Eden and Mac agreed to let me have a few hours. I'm heading back there. What about you? Why are you just sitting in your car?"

"Trying to gather my nerve."

"Yeah, the tourist traffic can be a real bear on winter Saturdays in Hope's Crossing."

Despite her angst, she managed a smile at his dry tone. "True. I wish that were all that is worrying me. I have to walk over to the bead store and see if I can ransom my wedding dress."

He leaned back a little on his heels. "Something tells me there's a very interesting story behind that particular statement."

With a sigh, she climbed out of her SUV. She didn't want to tell him, as it didn't show her in a very good light.

"I had this really gorgeous wedding dress created by this up-and-coming designer in New York," she finally said. "I wanted hand-beaded accents on it and I wanted Claire McKnight to do them for me. She did a beautiful job, twice, which is a long story in itself. After things fell apart with Sawyer, I never wanted to see that dress again. I told her so."

"She still has it?"

She nodded. "I owe her the last payment for the work she did. I was terrible to Claire. Rude and condescending. I don't want to face her, especially since I am going there to eat crow."

"How?"

She reached into her purse—another she had sewn—and pulled out the envelope that contained the last of her cash, after helping with Jenna's plane ticket.

"This is most of what I still owe her, short a few hundred dollars. I hope to pay her the rest when I sell the house. I should have paid her a long time ago. I know. You don't have to lecture me."

He raised his eyebrow. "I didn't say a word."

"The truth is, I really didn't want to see the stupid dress again. I guess I was hoping my parents would take care of it while I was in Europe but they can be passive-aggressive about some things. I guess this happened to be one of those times."

"Why do you want the dress now?"

She gazed at the mountains. Why had she never noticed how strong and commanding they looked when they were covered with snow? She had always considered them a prison, keeping her in boring little Hope's Crossing, but that was yet another perspective that had shifted.

"It's a beautiful gown," she answered. "Someone should wear it. I want to give it to Jenna. She deserves something magical when she and Trey get married tomorrow."

For only an instant, she thought she saw something in his eye—a spark, a light, warmth that hadn't been there before—but then it vanished, probably a trick of the shifting clouds.

"Right now I need to go to String Fever and face Claire," she said glumly. "I would rather be scrubbing toilets at The Speckled Lizard."

"That can probably be arranged. Pat would probably love to put you to work."

"Figure of speech. I have to go to the bead store. I just don't want to."

"Want some company?" He looked as shocked by the offer as she was.

"You? Seriously?"

He shrugged and held up a bag in his hand. "I bought the last thing on my list and I've got an hour before I'm supposed to be back at the recreation center. I've got time."

Oh, she was turning into such a baby if one tiny gesture of kindness could make her want to burst into tears. "That would be wonderful. I know I shouldn't be so cowardly."

"You made it this far, didn't you? Now all you've got are a few more steps. Anyway, as far as I'm concerned, there's no shame in being afraid. Only in letting the fear win."

Like you're doing by pushing me away? she wanted to say. But he had offered to help her and she didn't want to start a fight.

After he put his parcels in his truck, they started off in the direction of the bead store, sidestepping slushy spots and piles of snow. Usually when they walked together, Dylan seemed determined that she walk on his right side. This time, she was equally determined not to let him try to protect her. She walked stubbornly as close to the edge of the sidewalk as she could manage, where he would have to be in the gutter if he was going to make a point of it.

He had to get over thinking she would freak out if she touched his residual arm—since she hated the word *stump* she decided that was what she was going to call it.

After a few minutes, she decided to push the issue further. "Would it hurt if I held on to you? I'm nervous about the ice. I love these boots but they're not very practical for a Colorado December."

They were gorgeous, she had to admit. She'd bought them in a fabulous shop in the Sixteenth.

He stopped and held out his right arm. "Come on the other side."

She shook her head. "I prefer this side, as long as it doesn't hurt."

"Gen."

She gave him a firm look and grabbed his elbow. After a long, awkward moment when she thought he might yank away and leave her standing there alone, he gave a little sigh and continued on his way.

As they walked, she was aware of the void just below the spot she held. She looked inside herself for any kind of squeamishness and could find nothing like that. She could find plenty of emotions there, thick and heavy. Admiration for what he had been through, as well as sadness that she wouldn't have many more moments like this with him.

"I think I may have sold the house."

Beneath her fingers, his arm tensed slightly then relaxed. "Really?"

She nodded. "Eden is looking for her own fixer-upper. She came over last night to check out Grandma Pearl's place and says it's just what she wanted. It's in the right location and everything. She even likes the pink tile in the bathroom. Go figure. She wants to figure out her budget but so far the signs look positive."

He cleared his throat. "Great. I guess you can shed the dust of Hope's Crossing earlier than you expected."

"I guess."

She should probably try to sound more enthusiastic about returning to Paris—that was what she'd been saying all along she wanted, right?—but she couldn't quite act that well.

Fearing he would correctly guess the reason she suddenly didn't want to leave, she turned the subject to one she knew would distract him.

"Charlotte told me the other day you had surgery some months ago where they implanted an artificial eye."

She could feel the tension in him again. "Charlotte talks too much."

"Why do you wear the patch if you really don't need it?"

"You don't like the pirate look?"

She wanted to tell him he was perfect to her,

just as he was, but she knew he wouldn't believe it. "I just wondered. Does it have anything to do with why you avoid wearing your prosthetic?"

"Which one? I have several. None of them are particularly comfortable. They get in the way and I finally give up in frustration. And no matter how far technology has come, the eye still looks fake. I can't see anything out of it anyway." He paused. "I'm missing a hand and an eye. No prosthetic hand or artificial eye is going to erase that fact. I figure I need to get used to reality, not try to mask it."

"Are you thinking *you* need to face that or everybody else needs to?"

He slanted a look down at her. "Both."

"Can I say something?" she said after a moment.

"Any chance I could stop you?"

She squeezed his arm. "Probably not. I just want to point out that you seem to be the only one focused on what's missing. When I look at you, all I see is a man of strength and courage trying to adjust to tough changes in his life."

He grew silent as they crossed the street and headed for String Fever. Had she overstepped? She really wished she could read him better.

She didn't have time to fret about it for long— she had something else entirely to worry about as they reached the charming little bead store, with its colorful display window and hanging sign.

She used to love coming into String Fever and

had even taken a class or two when the store used to be owned by Katherine Thorne. If she were staying in town, she would certainly consider taking another one.

The store seemed to be busy. She spotted a few people who looked familiar at the worktable and Claire and Evie Thorne standing by the cash register, along with a plump but pretty teenage girl she didn't know.

Claire moved away from the counter and headed toward them, trying unsuccessfully to hide the surprise on her soft, pretty features. "Genevieve. And, er, Dylan. Hello. This is an . . . unexpected pleasure."

She really doubted that. The *pleasure* part, anyway. She tried for a smile. "Hello. I haven't been into String Fever in a while. I like the new paint color."

"Thank you. The walls were looking a little tired. I'm actually glad you stopped by. I owe you an apology."

She hadn't been expecting that. "You . . . do?"

"The other night. My mother. I'm so sorry. What she said was unconscionably rude. I'm sorry you had to hear that."

Oh. That. "Don't worry about it. It wasn't your fault. If I tried to make amends for everything *my* mother did, it would take me hours just to walk through town."

Claire smiled, and Genevieve suddenly

remembered what she *did* have to apologize for.

"Are you two looking for something in particular? We have some nice premade items that make lovely Christmas gifts."

Genevieve turned in the direction Claire indicated, and there, hanging in a glass display case, was her exquisitely designed wedding gown—all that was left of shattered dreams that didn't seem at all important anymore.

She had forgotten how gorgeous it was. Gathered bodice that draped, softly flaring skirt, the Swarovski crystals that gleamed in the light.

Barely realizing what she did, she walked to the case and touched the glass. It was cold against fingers that had been warmed by Dylan's heat.

Jenna would look lovely in it. They were a similar height and measurements, though Gen was a little bigger in the bust. Other than that, she was certain the dress would fit.

She turned and found Dylan at her shoulder, as if he sensed she needed the moral support.

"First, I . . . You apologized for your mother. I need to apologize for myself."

Claire waited, her expression curious.

"I don't need to tell you how terrible I was during my engagement and how I was even worse after things fell apart. I'm ashamed of my behavior and I'm very sorry for the way I treated you, especially when you were nothing but kind to me through everything."

Dylan reached for her hand and curled his fingers around hers. She couldn't look at him or she knew she would start to cry.

"I don't know what to say," Claire said.

"You don't have to say anything. I don't expect you to forgive me. I was awful to you. I know that."

"You wanted things to be perfect. Most brides do."

"Most brides don't treat everyone in town like their personal slaves."

"It's done. It was two years ago. From everything I've seen and heard since you've been back, you're a different woman than you were then."

She desperately wanted to believe that. She still had a long way to go but she wanted to think she was making progress.

"You said you were here for two reasons," Claire prompted. "What's the second one?"

She reached into her purse. "I would like to take my wedding gown now. This is almost everything I owe you, minus a couple hundred dollars, which I'll pay you as soon as I—"

To her shock, Dylan pulled his wallet out and thrust out a debit card. "She'll pay you the rest now, along with whatever you think is fair in interest and storage fees."

Genevieve and Claire both stared at him as if he'd suddenly stripped down to his boxers and started belting out "Jingle Bells."

"Dylan!"

He shifted, not sure why he had made the gesture. He only knew it felt right. It had to have taken her buckets of grit to come in here and face her own mistakes. Beyond that, he found it incredibly sweet that she wanted to give a designer dress worth thousands to a woman she had only just met.

Crazy, yeah, but sweet, too.

"Don't worry about it. I would probably just waste it on Johnnie Walker. Let me do something good with my money for a change."

"Fine." She looked stunned, her eyes soft and shiny. "I'll pay *you* back when I sell the house, then."

A weird ball of *something* lodged in his gut at the reminder that she would soon be selling her grandmother's house and heading across the ocean.

"Do you mind if I ask who the bride might be?" Claire asked.

Genevieve smiled. "It's very romantic. Her name is Jenna Baldwin and she's a schoolteacher in Georgia. The groom is Trey Evans. He's one of the guests at A Warrior's Hope. You might have met him at the welcome reception the other night."

"Oh, right. Is he the good-looking guy with the cute Southern accent? As I recall, he's the only one who didn't have anyone with him."

"He does now." Genevieve beamed with pleasure and pride.

"Gen here did a little matchmaking behind the scenes and brought in his ex-fiancée from Georgia to try to patch things up between them."

"He's a really nice young man and he doesn't have any family to help him through the healing process. It seemed ridiculous to me that any man would turn his back on someone who loved him just because of some silly idea that he's not perfect anymore."

She didn't look at Dylan when she spoke but somehow he felt her words tug between them anyway. He didn't miss the glances Claire and Evie exchanged, both of them careful to also avoid looking at him, until he felt as if he were invisible.

"So you're loaning her your wedding gown?" Claire said after an awkward pause. "How kind of you."

Genevieve shook her head. "Not a loan. A gift."

Claire's expression was clearly surprised. He wanted to tell her to get in line. Gen was full of surprises, when she let down her prickly guard.

"When is the wedding?" Evie asked.

"Tomorrow afternoon," Gen answered. "All the guests are flying home Monday, and Jenna and

Trey wanted them to share in their moment. We've had to hurry to throw everything together."

"How wonderful." Claire's eyes, predictably, turned soft and dreamy. All the other women at A Warrior's Hope had the same expression every time the talk turned to weddings.

"Riley and I had a Christmas wedding, too," she said. "I'm sure everything will be lovely."

"How can we help?" Evie asked.

"You want to help?"

"Yes!" Claire exclaimed. "I can't imagine throwing together a wedding in such short order. You have to let us pitch in."

"Thank you. I don't know what to say. That's . . . very kind of you both."

"Everyone will want to help. You know they will. If Alex finds out we threw a wedding and didn't ask her to take care of the food, she'll never forgive any of us."

"You know," Evie said thoughtfully, "Mary Ella probably has all the decorations from her own wedding lying around somewhere."

"That's right!" Claire exclaimed. "Do you think the bride would mind secondhand decorations? They were so elegant—silver, blue, white. Perfect for a wedding during the holidays."

Gen looked as if she wanted to burst into tears. "That would be great! I was planning something simple, maybe taking some fresh greenery from the grounds and whatever ribbons and ornaments we could swipe from the guest cabins. But if Mary Ella wouldn't mind loaning a few things, I'm sure the bride will be very grateful."

"I'll call her right now," Claire offered.

As she headed into her office, apparently to use the phone, Evie turned to Gen. "You know, I think we have a necklace-and-earring set that would go perfectly with that dress. I created it for the school-dance season around the corner but it always seemed a little old for a teenage girl."

She headed for another jewelry case. When she pulled out a piece, it reflected a swirl of colors.

"Oh. Look at that," Gen exclaimed. "Are those Swarovski crystals like the gown?"

"Yes," Evie said. "The pearls are Swarovski, as well."

"Stunning. Really stunning. I love how light and airy it is, like the gems are suspended there."

"Take it for the bride. It can be a wedding gift from me."

"Thank you. Thank you so much. I know she'll love it."

When Claire returned, she carried a black clothing bag—for the dress, he assumed.

"Mary Ella is *thrilled* to let your bride and groom use their decorations. She and Harry will load everything up tonight in his pickup truck and drop it off at the recreation center. She says for you to use whatever you want and keep the rest in one of the spare rooms at the recreation center.

379

They'll pick it up Sunday night or Monday."

Dylan had a tough time picturing Harry Lange—the wealthiest man in town—delivering wedding decorations for people he didn't know, but apparently marrying Mary Ella McKnight had a mellowing effect, even on the cranky old codger.

"Thank you. I want to give them the most magical wedding they can imagine. This will be wonderful."

"You have to let us help you decorate. Between the Giving Hope gala and all the weddings around here lately, we've become sort of experts at throwing parties."

"Okay. Great." She cleared her throat. "I want to start early in the morning. The earlier the better, no later than eight."

"Perfect. We'll be there. Riley's working tomorrow, so I'll probably have Emma. The older kids will be with their dad. I hope you don't mind. She's a really good baby."

"No. I don't mind."

Claire unlocked the case and pulled out the wedding dress with a sort of reverence he might have found amusing under other circumstances.

"You hold it and I'll zip it in," Claire said.

Genevieve took it. "It really is an exquisite dress. The beading takes it over the top. I knew it would." She touched the edge of the bodice. "You did a really beautiful job, Claire."

"I'm still sorry I didn't get the chance to see you wear it down the aisle," Claire said, swooping the last bit of material inside the bag and zipping it tight.

"I'm not," Genevieve declared. "Sawyer Danforth was a womanizing jerk. If I had married him, I don't think I would have liked myself very much. At least not as much as I'm beginning to now."

Claire smiled broadly and hugged Genevieve, dress and all. In that moment, he wanted to kiss Claire Bradford McKnight right on the lips for being the kind, generous person she was—exactly what Gen needed right now.

"So we'll see you tomorrow bright and early," Claire said, waving as they headed out.

The snow had begun to fall in earnest while they were in the store and he imagined Gen was grateful the dress was protected by the zippered bag.

She didn't take either of his arms this time, too busy carrying the dress.

"That wasn't so bad, was it?" he said.

She gave a soft laugh. "Isn't it funny how the things we dread never turn out as poorly as we imagine?"

Sometimes they were worse—far worse—but he didn't want to ruin her little philosophical moment by being such a downer.

"I guess I'd better get up to the recreation center.

I told Eden and Mac I'd be back for the afternoon of skiing."

"And I have to find Jenna and have her try this on so I can make any necessary alterations tonight."

"You?"

"You don't have to sound so shocked. Yes, I can sew. It happens to be a necessary skill for an interior designer. Grandma Pearl taught me when I was a girl. She was always patient with me. Even when I had to redo a stitch a half-dozen times, she would never raise her voice or call me stupid."

Who had called her stupid? he wondered. They reached her car before he had a chance to ask.

"Thank you for coming with me. You gave me courage I couldn't find for myself."

He couldn't help himself. He reached out and drew his thumb down her cheek. For just an instant, the wonder of skin on skin overwhelmed him. He suddenly missed his other hand fiercely, deprived forever of the chance to touch her completely.

"You've got more strength than you see, Gen."

She leaned her face into his hand for just an instant—very much like Trey had done with Jenna—then she stepped away.

"I hope I'll have enough," she murmured, rather cryptically, before reaching into the pocket of her coat for her keys.

Chapter Nineteen

❄ ❄ ❄

Genevieve plumped the bow on one last silver ribbon and stepped back to admire her handiwork, shaking her fingers out to ease the ache of the repetitive motion.

The room looked like something out of a fairy tale, all silver and blue and magical. After conferring with Jenna and Trey, they had decided to have the ceremony itself in front of the huge wall of windows that overlooked the mountains and river. She had bordered the windows with two of the trees from Mary Ella's wedding decorations, each bare branch covered in yards and yards of twinkly lights. The mantel of the huge river-rock fireplace glowed with evergreens, silver and blue ornaments and elegant silvery branches.

The rows of chairs angled to watch the ceremony had been adorned with elegant silver and blue ribbons entwined with sprigs of evergreens. In one corner, the various colored ornaments on the large Christmas tree she had already decorated once in here had been swapped out with only ornaments matching the rest of the theme—huge blue ornaments as big as bowling balls, silvery icicles, a few crystal snowflakes.

It was truly a winter wonderland.

"Okay, what is missing?" she asked the room in general.

Her large crew consisted of Mary Ella and Maura Lange, Claire McKnight, Alex, Charlotte, Eden, Pam and the wives from the program. Jenna's mother, Patty, who had flown in from Virginia on the last flight into Stapleton the night before, had wanted to help but Genevieve insisted she stay with Jenna to help with her hair and makeup.

Those gathered, though, paused in their various labors to look around.

"I can't see a thing wrong," Mary Ella declared.

"It's going to be exquisite when we're done, Genevieve," Claire said. "I can't believe you put this all together in only two days. It appears as if it was years in the planning."

"I couldn't have done it without all of you—and without Mary Ella's decorations."

"You have such a gift for throwing things together," Tonya Brooks said. "I can't even figure out where to hang my family pictures in our place. Every time we were transferred to a new base, it was the same dilemma."

"I guess we know who to put in charge of the decorations committee for the next Giving Hope gala," Maura said.

She should quickly tell them that by the time the next Giving Hope Day rolled around—held in early June each year—she would be on another continent, probably decorating tiny Parisian apartments. The words clogged in her throat. She only wanted to savor this success, not think about leaving.

The past two hours had been . . . amazing. The women had rushed in with hugs and energy. They had laughed with her, chattered about everything under the sun and worked hard together to create something beautiful and memorable for a couple most of them didn't even know.

"What's left?"

"Only arranging the table decorations for the luncheon," she said.

The six eight-top tables had been set out on the other side of the fireplace. As she was demonstrating how she wanted the tablecloths she had hastily sewn overnight, a familiar figure came inside the room and stood rather uncomfortably in the doorway.

Genevieve's voice trailed off and she stared. After a frozen moment, she hurried over.

"Mom! What are you doing here?"

Laura looked around at the decorations. "We were supposed to go to brunch this morning, remember? You were going to meet us at Le Passe. Your father and Charlie are still there."

Her stomach dived. "Oh. Oh, my word. I

completely forgot. I'm so sorry. I should have called you."

"Yes. You should have."

Between working on the house and filling her community-service hours at A Warrior's Hope—and now organizing a wedding in forty-eight hours—she had barely given her family a thought. "How did you know where to find me?"

"When you didn't answer your cell phone, I was worried about you. I was about to go to Pearl's house to see if you had passed out from the wallpaper-glue fumes or something when Harry and Jackson showed up at the restaurant. When your father asked where their wives were, imagine our surprise when Harry told us Mary Ella and Maura were here helping our daughter decorate for a wedding."

Her mother gave one of her little sniffs that could mean a hundred different things. Disdain. Distaste. Indifference. In this case, she had the sudden, startling insight that her mother's feelings were hurt at being excluded.

Was it possible that Laura felt as isolated and alone as Genevieve did? She saw a flash of something there, just a tiny hint that made her wonder if her mother wore her social position as a shield to keep everyone away.

"Laura. Hello, my dear." Mary Ella stepped up and brushed her cheek against Gen's mother's.

"Mary Ella. How are you?"

"I'm great. Thank you. Look at the fantastic job your daughter has done here. It's all been her. She's incredibly talented. Did you know she sewed the tablecloths herself last night? You must be so proud of her."

"I . . . Yes. Of course we are. We always have been. I just have one little question. Who is the happy couple, if you don't mind me asking?"

"He's one of the guests at A Warrior's Hope, a young man from Alabama," Genevieve answered. "She is a schoolteacher from Georgia. They're very much in love."

She didn't tell her mother about her role in bringing Trey and Jenna together. Perhaps she would someday—but she did have one confession she couldn't avoid.

"Mother, she's going to wear my wedding gown."

Laura jerked her gaze from the decorations toward Genevieve. "I thought it was still at String Fever."

"No. I have it. Actually, Jenna has it. I gave it to her."

She waited for her mother to make some cutting comment, something about irresponsible, thoughtless benevolence. Instead, Laura surprised her.

"Just as well," she said with an airy wave of her hand. "What else could you have done with it?

Sell it, I suppose, but that's about all. It would have been tacky to wear it when you marry someone else."

That question was fairly moot now. How could she ever marry anyone now? No other man could possibly compare to Dylan.

"You're not angry?"

Laura shrugged. "Why should I be angry? It's your dress. You can do as you want with it."

Okay, had she awakened in some alternate universe? First, all the women in Hope's Crossing were being so kind to her, laughing with her, making admiring comments about her flair for decorating. Now her mother was showing remarkable understanding.

Further shocking her, Laura looked around at the little groups of women scattered throughout the room. "Is there anything I can do to help?"

"I'm . . . sure we could use an extra pair of hands."

Mary Ella stepped forward. "Laura, dear, you have such beautiful handwriting. Why don't you help me make place cards for the tables?"

"I *have* always prided myself on my cursive."

Her mother followed Mary Ella. Genevieve gazed after her for only a second—all the time she could spare.

The alternate-universe theory was seeming more credible by the second.

What were the chances she could stay there?

•••

All the predictions came true. It was a truly beautiful ceremony, with a handsome groom and a stunning bride. The love between the fragile-looking Jenna and the damaged soldier was a palpable force that seemed to encircle them, binding them tightly together.

Trey actually stood for the ceremony with the help of his forearm crutches, insisting he wasn't going to take his own wedding sitting down. The sight of him struggling valiantly to his feet before the ceremony even began and standing erect and proud was the first moment Gen cried.

All right. The second. The first had been when Dylan had walked in—without his ever-present eye patch and wearing his prosthetic.

He looked so very different, she couldn't stop stealing glances at him. His left eye drooped slightly more than the right and she could see a network of scars. After all this time of seeing him with the black patch, the absence of it left her disoriented.

He did look gorgeous in a suit and tie. He must have figured out how to tie a Windsor—or found someone to help him. His sister, probably. She was aware of a tiny spasm of pain that he hadn't asked her.

He had given her a brusque nod then slipped into a back row, next to his father and Charlotte and Spence, and then the music started.

Trey had asked Jason Reid to stand up with him, and the sight of two handsome warriors in hastily rented tuxedos—courtesy of Spence, she learned—touched her deeply, especially as she looked around the room at Pam and the others and thought of all they had endured.

While the small string ensemble Spence had also arranged played Pachelbel, the little Brooks girls came in, adorable in matching blue dresses with faux white fur around the wrists and hem. They joyfully skipped up the aisle, scattering glitter and tiny crystals out of winter-white baskets, and then Jenna came in on her mother's arm, glowing with joy and looking absolutely breathtaking in a gown that could have been designed just for her.

When they exchanged vows—Trey in a gruff voice he had to clear a few times to get the words out and Jenna with starry-eyed happiness, Genevieve had to fight back a sob.

Now, the ceremony over, the guests milled around with champagne glasses and small plates of delicious little bites hastily provided by several restaurants in town while the string ensemble played elegant music in the background.

Everything had gone off without a hitch. Maybe she should think about going into the party-planning business instead of interior design. She definitely had a knack.

"Genevieve."

She turned at her father's voice. "Mother. Dad. It's really nice of you to come."

She couldn't have been more shocked when she had seen them walk into the room in time for the ceremony earlier. That alternate-universe theory again . . .

Her father reached in to brush a kiss on her cheek. "It's the first wedding at the city's new recreation center. It's only right that the mayor and his wife attend."

She tried not to roll her eyes at his pompous tone. As much as she loved him, William could certainly be puffed up in his own importance.

"Mother, thank you for pitching in this morning. We needed every single volunteer to make this happen."

Laura preened a little. "If that's the only chance I have to spend a little time with my only daughter, I'll take what I can find."

She squashed down her twinge of guilt. "Everyone is leaving tomorrow. I only have to help clean up after they go and then my community-service hours are finished. I should be free on Christmas Eve. Are we having dinner, like always?"

Her mother nodded. "Actually, we're doing something different this year. We've invited guests. Larry and Joan Billings. Their sons are spending the holidays with their in-laws this year. Oh, and your father has a young new associate in his law firm and he's all alone this holiday season. We thought the two of you might hit it off."

Perfect. Without asking, her parents had decided to start setting her up with eligible men—and on Christmas Eve, no less. She could imagine few things more miserable. She supposed marrying her off to some up-and-coming associate of her father's was one way for them to make sure she stayed out of trouble and didn't rack up more debt.

She could endure for one night. They would find out soon enough that she was close to selling the house and leaving Hope's Crossing for good.

Out of the corner of her gaze, she spied Dylan speaking with his father. Again, she had that disorienting shift at seeing two blue eyes in that rugged face.

When Harry Lange approached at that moment to greet her father, she seized the diversion as the perfect chance to escape. "Thank you again for coming. Will you excuse me for a moment?"

She walked away, fully aware her parents were watching after her. "Dermot," she said when she reached the pair. "Your tarts are a huge hit. Thank you!"

He gave her an embrace and kissed her cheek. "You're very welcome, my darling. You throw a good party."

"This was a team effort. Everybody pitched in."

"I've heard otherwise. Charlotte was telling me

how you were up all night sewing things, making little gewgaws, fixing wedding dresses. Sounds to me like a one-woman show."

"Charlotte exaggerates."

"She has been known to," Dermot said, "but I think in this case she was speaking truth. And you look beautiful doing it. Doesn't she look beautiful, son?"

That muscle she had once pressed her mouth to twitched along Dylan's jawline. "Stunning," he murmured.

"Thank you. Both of you."

She started to ask if they were staying for the dinner being catered by Brazen when Katherine Thorne came over. "Apparently, they're running out of tarts. Alex sent me over to ask if you have more."

To Gen's amusement, color soaked Dermot's cheeks. "Oh, yes. I brought three more trays. I can fetch them."

"Thank you." Katherine smiled, which only made Dermot flush more. "I'll help you."

The two of them walked off, looking completely adorable together.

"Speaking of exaggeration, I thought you were joking about your dad and Katherine."

He looked after his father, his expression slightly amused. "No. Both of them are obviously interested in the other, but neither will make the first move."

"Maybe they just need a push."

He raised his eyebrows. "Oh, no. Get that thought out of your head right now. One success does not make you the town matchmaker, Gen."

"You have to admit, it was a *spectacular* success."

"Yes. But Pop apparently likes to move at his own pace, which is just about as fast as a snail on sedatives. If you step in, you'll only embarrass him."

She watched Dermot and Katherine for a moment, mostly to get her racing heartbeat under control, then she turned back to Dylan.

"You didn't wear your eye patch."

That muscle flexed again. "Somebody implied I was hiding behind it. I figured maybe it was time."

"You look good. Really good."

He made a face. "It feels strange. Kind of naked after all these months."

She flashed him a look, trying to force her imagination not to go there. Pulling off his jacket, loosening that tie, baring all those muscles . . .

She cleared her throat. "You'll get used to it, I'm sure. Or if you prefer the eye patch, wear that. It doesn't matter to me."

I love you either way.

"Or anyone else, I'm sure," she quickly added. "Wasn't it great to see Trey standing for the ceremony?"

"Yes. And Jenna's dress was beautiful. I kept picturing you in it, though."

Before she could respond to that, the couple in question approached them, trailing their happiness like Jenna's train.

The bride embraced her, smelling of hair spray and lilies from her exquisite bouquet. "Genevieve. Oh. I don't even know what to say. It was the most beautiful wedding, in front of those big windows with the mountains in the background and that light snowfall."

She smiled and hugged her back. "I can't take credit for the view or the snowfall."

Jenna eased away. She really did look beautiful in that dress. "Everything else is because of you. We can never repay you for the wonderful gift you have given us. Another chance. You've given us a future."

"You had the courage to grab your own future together. I'm so happy for you both."

Trey, still using his forearm crutches, embraced her next. Genevieve kissed his cheek. "I needed a kick in the ass, somebody to show me I was being a stubborn fool. Thank you for giving it to me."

"Anytime." She managed another smile, though it was edged with sadness. Why couldn't Dylan accept he needed her, as Trey had finally opened his heart and his life to Jenna?

"What are your plans now?" Dylan asked.

"I've got a contract to finish up the school year

in Georgia," Jenna said. "After that, we're not sure where we'll settle."

"I've decided to go back to school to finish my degree. Mac has convinced me I could work in a program like this one or something similar."

"Oh, wonderful," Genevieve exclaimed. "You would be perfect."

The orchestra set their instruments down and the beginning strains of the romantic pop-ballad recording Jenna had requested for their dance together began playing over the sound system.

"Oh! There it is. Our song. We have to go dance."

He rolled his eyes. "I'll look ridiculous trying to dance. I'm going to topple both of us to the ground."

She gave him a dewy-eyed smile. "Don't you know by now, I'm strong enough to support us both, when I have to?"

Gen watched them go out to the small dance floor she had marked by more of those trees with twinkly lights. The lights dimmed as they walked out while Justin Timberlake and the rest of *NSYNC sang about promising to love forever and battles being won.

Trey used his crutches to go to the middle of the dance floor and then handed them to Jason, something that had obviously been planned ahead of time. He took Jenna in his arms and they held each other, not really moving, mostly swaying in time to the music.

She watched them, the handsome battered warrior and his sweet bride in her beautiful wedding gown. She wasn't the only one crying softly before the song was through.

Dylan handed her a handkerchief. "You did a good thing, Gen."

She wiped her eyes, her heart a heavy ache. When she lowered the handkerchief other couples began to move out to join the newlyweds. Charlotte and Spencer moved past them, Alex McKnight and Sam Delgado. Even Mary Ella and Harry Lange.

He said nothing, just watched as the small dance floor began to fill. Finally she decided this was her only chance and she couldn't let it slip through her fingers. "Dance with me," she said softly.

The moment stretched out, awkward and wooden. She could feel his tension.

"I wasn't a good dancer, even before."

"Do you think I care about that?" *I just want one last chance to be close to you.* She thought the words but couldn't say them.

Finally, when she thought he would leave her standing on the edge of the dance floor, he reached for her hand and they walked out among the twinkly trees.

After some quick mental calculations, she switched the way she would traditionally place her arms and curled her right arm around his neck. After a pause, he put his prosthetic hand around her waist. It wasn't really holding her, just resting on the curve of her hip.

This was another romantic ballad from about a decade ago, obviously also picked by Jenna. She closed her eyes and rested her cheek against his chest, trying to savor every moment. It was magical and she never wanted it to end.

But forever wasn't in the cards for them. As soon as the song was over, he stepped away.

"Thank you for the dance," he said, his voice gruff and stiff, his features once more remote.

She had been wrong about the eye patch. Even when he didn't wear it, his expression wasn't any more clear to her.

"You're welcome," she whispered.

He gave her one last look, then turned around and walked away—not simply from her but from the whole reception, working his way through the dancers and the crowd with single-minded purpose.

A wise woman would simply let him go, since he was so determined to put as much distance between them as he could.

She watched his progress for a moment, aching and miserable and filled with sorrow, then screwed her eyes shut. When had she ever been wise about anything? Why ruin a perfect track record of foolish mistakes?

She drew in her courage and rushed after him.

● ● ●

All he wanted was to climb back in his truck, drive up to Snowflake Canyon and climb inside the last bottle of Johnnie Walker in the place.

Emotions were a big, messy snarl inside him, like fishing line that had been left in the bottom of the boat over the winter. He didn't want to untangle them right now; he only knew he had to get away.

He didn't want this. These tender, fragile, terrifying feelings.

This was all Jamie's fault. If his brother had never asked to meet him at The Speckled Lizard that night, he never would have stepped in to help Genevieve Beaumont.

He would have been perfectly happy the rest of his life thinking she was a spoiled, snobby bitch instead of the soft, vulnerable, *perfect* woman he had come to know these past few weeks.

A woman who gave away her wedding dress then stayed up all night making alterations so another woman could wear it. Who cried like a baby as she watched a broken soldier dance with his bride. Who looked at him—screwed up, angry, half-missing *him*—as if he was everything to her.

He reached his pickup, telling himself the ache in his chest was only the cold air hitting his lungs.

Just as he opened the door, he heard a swish of fabric, and some sixth sense had him turning around.

Of course. There she was. He should have known she would come after him. She was so damn stubborn when she wanted to be: punching assistant D.A.s and firing her father out of pique and steaming off layer after layer of wallpaper in a dilapidated old house.

She didn't have a coat and her cheeks were pink and he wanted to bundle her up, throw her in the pickup and take her home with him.

"Why are you running so hard from me?" she demanded.

He loosened the stupid tie his father had tied for him as if he were six years old.

"Can't I just be done with the party? I've spent more time surrounded by people these last ten days than I have in my whole life. Is it so hard to believe I might just want to be alone for a while?"

"Not hard at all. I just think it's me you're eager to escape."

He wanted to deny it. It would make things so much easier, all the way around. The last thing he wanted to do was hurt her, but he had to make her face reality somehow.

He rubbed his hand over his face, hating this, hating himself. Even hating *her* a little for forcing him to face all the things he had never, for a moment, thought he wanted—a wife, a family, a future—and the bitter realization that what he wanted was out of reach to him.

"Gen, I can't be the man you need."

She paled a little but lifted her chin. "How can you be so certain?"

"You need someone who wants the same things you do, who is used to the kind of life you've had. Someone polished and cultured. Someone who has no problem listening to that French jazz crap you like and going to museums and escorting you to the opera. That was never me and it sure as hell isn't now."

"A few weeks ago, I would have agreed with you. The man you're describing is exactly the one I've always thought I wanted. Is it so hard to believe I was wrong—about myself and about so many other things?"

"Gen—"

"I love you."

She said the words quickly, as if afraid she would lose her nerve if she didn't rush through them.

He inhaled sharply as some of those emotions seemed to yank free of the snarl.

Love. Of course. *That* was what this was.

He closed his eyes—the real one and the fake one—as the truth soaked through him like somebody had doused him with that bottle of whiskey waiting at home for him.

He loved Genevieve Beaumont. And she apparently felt the same.

He wanted to savor the words as he had that

dance, to drink them in, swirl them around inside him and just let them soak through.

He couldn't do that, to either of them.

She must imagine they could have a happy ending like Trey and Jenna.

He wasn't like Trey. Trey had been basically a good soldier who had been injured through no fault of his own. He hadn't been responsible for the deaths of five of his closest friends because of weakness and uncertainty.

What did he have to offer her? A broken-down house in Snowflake Canyon, no career. He did have a great dog, but on the list of things Mayor Beaumont wanted for his daughter, a great black-and-tan coonhound likely wouldn't make the cut.

Nor would a washed-up army ranger with several missing parts.

He drew in a sharp breath. "You don't love me. I'm flattered that you would say so—who wouldn't be?—but you're just caught up in the whole wedding romance thing."

"You really think I'm that shallow?"

A few weeks ago, he would have given an unequivocal yes to that question. Not now. She was so much more.

He couldn't let her love him. Two years from now, what would she want with him when she finally realized he couldn't miraculously regrow an eye and a hand? He wouldn't be able to bear that.

He didn't know what to do, what to say. The only thing that seemed certain to convince her was to strike out where he knew she was most vulnerable.

"What if you're not the kind of woman I want?"

He hated himself more in that moment than he had in all the months since his accident, but he didn't see any other choice but to drive her away irrevocably.

Her features grew even more pale. "Is that so?"

He focused his gaze somewhere over her shoulder, unable to lie straight to her face. "You're incredibly beautiful, and if circumstances were different, I would sleep with you in a second. But you surround yourself with perfection. The way you dress, your makeup, your hair. You can't tolerate anything being out of place. You wrap presents with ribbon ends that have to be exactly equal. Even before I was injured and became very much less than perfect, I wouldn't have been the man for you. Eventually, I probably would have wanted to chew my own arm off to get away from all those expectations."

She stared at him, eyes wide, and he could see her curling into herself, pulling all her protective barriers back in place.

"I . . . see."

He wanted to call back every word, but all he could picture was a future with her eventually coming to despise him. He wouldn't be able to handle that.

Yeah, it made him the coward she had called Trey a few days ago. He knew that.

Better to be a coward now than completely wrecked later when she finally realized he wasn't enough for her.

"It's cold. You should go back inside."

"I . . . Yes. I guess you're right."

With each breath, he felt as if knives were carving holes in his chest, but he forced himself to give his best imitation of a casual smile. "It really was a beautiful wedding, Genevieve. Merry Christmas."

"Merry Christmas."

She wouldn't look at him as she turned and fled back to the lights, the music, the fairy-tale ending he could never give her.

Chapter Twenty

"Are you sure you're all right, darling? You hardly touched your dinner, and you've been so pale and quiet all evening."

"I'm fine, Mother." She tried a smile to ease the worry she could see in Laura's features. "I'm only a little tired."

She was working hard to be patient with her parents, trying to remember they had her best interests at heart.

Sometime in the past few days, she had come to the realization that her father had been right to bring her home to Hope's Crossing. She had been aimless in Paris. Oh, she had certainly enjoyed herself but that life had been unsustainable. She had needed to find her purpose—and perhaps the strength inside herself to reach for one.

She could have done without the heartbreak that had come along with it, but blaming her parents for that would be unfair.

"Thank you for dinner. It was delicious. Mrs. Taylor outdid herself."

"Didn't she?" Laura beamed as if *she* had been the one slaving away in the kitchen instead of their longtime housekeeper. "And what did you think of Adam? Isn't he a lovely man?"

"Yes. Lovely." Her father's new associate, Adam Schilling, actually had been quite nice. He was funny and smart and treated her with respect, as if he genuinely cared about her opinion—something of an appealing rarity, in her experience.

She would definitely have been interested in him if circumstances had been different.

Her heart felt achy and sore, as if she had a strange sort of flu. She had cried herself to sleep the past two nights, something she hadn't done once after the end of her engagement.

Having all these tender feelings for a man who didn't want them hurt worse than anything in her life.

Dylan hadn't come to A Warrior's Hope to see their guests on their way the previous day. She had spent the whole night before trying to figure out how she would possibly face him again . . . and then he hadn't even had the courtesy to make all that effort worthwhile.

No one had explained to her where he was, but she had overheard Charlotte tell Eden he'd phoned her that morning and said he had an appointment he'd forgotten about. He promised he would make up the last of his hours after the holidays.

She knew it was a lie. He wouldn't have forgotten an appointment. He only wanted to avoid the awkwardness of facing her again after that last humiliating scene between them.

She sighed, earning a concerned look from her mother.

"Really, darling," Laura exclaimed. "I think you must be coming down with something. And on Christmas Eve, too! Poor thing. Why don't you stay here tonight instead of going back to your grandmother's house? I can tuck you in, just like old times, and make some of your grandmother's Russian tea you always used to like."

"I'm just tired, I think. A good night's sleep will be just the thing."

"You should definitely stay here, then," William piped up. "You'll sleep better in your own bed than at your grandmother's."

She didn't want to argue with them when so far the evening had been conflict-free. Even so, she had a deep yearning to be alone. Pretending to enjoy herself all evening took emotional energy she just couldn't spare right now.

She had done as they asked by coming to dinner, spending time with them, being polite to their guests. That was all she could handle tonight.

"Thank you, but I would rather go back to Grandma's house. All my things are there—my makeup remover, my moisturizer. I'll be more comfortable there."

Her mother, at least, would certainly understand the importance of good skin care.

"You're coming over tomorrow morning, then, for breakfast and to open presents," Laura insisted.

"Yes. Of course. I'll be here bright and early, I promise."

At that moment, her brother, Charlie, came in from outside, stomping off snow. "It's really coming down. I just scraped your windows, but maybe you ought to stay here."

She rolled her eyes, even as she was immensely touched that her previously troublesome, sullen brother had learned to look outside himself and help others. "Not you, too! Give it a rest, everybody. I'll be fine."

Her words were a lie. She wasn't fine and hadn't been for two days. Though it sounded melodramatic, right now she wasn't sure how she would ever be fine again. How was it possible to ache so deeply for something that had never even had the chance to begin?

With hugs and air-kisses, she said her goodbyes to her family and climbed into her little SUV.

The streets of Hope's Crossing were mostly empty. Just after dark each year, Silver Strike ski resort had a Christmas Eve candlelight ski, when they would turn off the resort lights and the only illumination would be the line of tiny lights held by skiers as they traversed the run. Nearly everyone in town usually attended—her family and her parents' guests had watched, hot cocoa in hand, from the deck of their home not far from the resort and then returned inside for dinner.

By now, all those skiers and the bystanders were back in the warmth of their homes, tucked up together to celebrate the joy of the season together.

Her windshield kept up a steady rhythm to beat away the snow as the Christmas lights of Hope's Crossing glimmered. It really was a pretty little town. She had to keep her eyes on the road because of the inclement conditions, but every once in a while, she caught a vignette inside a frosted window of people gathered around laughing, talking, smiling.

Her feelings for Hope's Crossing had changed, as well. Once she had considered it an insular backwater, filled with small-minded people. Working at A Warrior's Hope and seeing the outpouring of support by people in town toward outsiders they didn't even know had given her new perspective.

She might have reconsidered returning to her flat in Paris, if not for Dylan and her aching heart.

As she pulled into her driveway, she noticed fresh tracks in the snow. It looked as if someone had pulled in and then out again while she had been gone. It must have been some time ago as more snow had filled in the tracks.

Someone had left something on the porch, she could see as she drove into the garage. Curious, she parked her vehicle then walked through the house to the front door to find a shiny red gift bag with a clumsily tied gold bow on the porch.

Odd. Who would be leaving her a gift? Perhaps Charlotte had stopped by, or maybe Eden.

She carried it inside and turned on the lights in Grandma Pearl's living room. She couldn't find a gift label or a card. With a frown, she began to pull away tissue-paper layers. Something solid and dark lay inside, she saw. She reached inside and her hand closed around smooth wood.

A figure.

Three wooden figures, actually.

She pulled them out and caught her breath as

her heart started to pound with stunning ferocity.

Three figures: Joseph, Mary, Baby Jesus, each rather roughly carved out of a fine-grained wood, unpainted but stained with a clear finish.

With fingers that trembled suddenly, she set them on the coffee table for a better look. Mary knelt beside the manger, her features in shadow from her head covering. Joseph stood beside her, strong and sturdy, staff in hand, and the tiny Baby Jesus lay in a manger with arms stretched wide.

She looked in the bag again and found nothing to indicate who had left such treasure.

But she knew.

He could have purchased it somewhere, she supposed, or his father or one of his brothers could have made it.

That would have been logical, given his circumstances, but somehow she knew in her heart Dylan had made them himself, to continue the tradition her grandmother had started so long ago.

She pictured him trying with one arm to carve this for her, probably using the prosthetic he hated to hold the wood in place, and she started to sob.

She cried for all he had endured, for her pain the past few days and for the unbearably precious gift he had given her, overwhelming in its magnitude.

When the torrent of tears had slowed to a trickle, she picked up the carving of the baby in the manger. It was raw, primitive, like something out of a folk-art museum, but beautiful in its simplicity, in the young, serene mother, the watchful father, those open arms.

As she looked at it again, the truth washed over her.

He loved her.

Despite what he'd said, all that ridiculous nonsense that had cut so deeply, he loved her. He wouldn't have spent a moment doing this for her otherwise, let alone the hours it must have taken him to painstakingly carve something so lovely.

He loved her and she refused to let him pretend otherwise.

She scooped up all three figures, hugged them close to her heart and hurried back out to her SUV.

Dylan stirred the fire and watched red-gold embers dance up the chimney.

Christmas Eve, and here he was alone at his cabin in Snowflake Canyon with Tucker, a fire and a book he knew would remain unread.

He had done his best. He had dutifully gone with his family to watch the candlelight ski and then had gone to Pop's place for dinner. He had stayed amid the noise and chaos as long as he could, until his nerves felt as frayed as Tucker's favorite rug and he finally made his excuses.

Then he had made the fatal mistake he had been regretting for the past hour.

He poked at the fire again then tossed in another

split log, watching while the flames teased at it for a moment before taking hold.

"I know I'm an idiot, Tuck. You don't have to tell me that."

His dog just looked at him out of those big eyes. Yeah, he had definitely climbed onto the crazy bus. What else would explain the past few days?

The whole thing had started as a whim, just to see if he could still carve. After a frenzied two days with little sleep and countless tries, next thing he knew, he was actually dropping the whole thing off on her porch like the town's do-gooder Angel of Hope.

He couldn't believe he had actually left them, but he had figured, what the hell? What else was he going to do with them?

He supposed on some level, he was trying to atone for his cruel words the other night—which really made no sense at all since he was hoping she wouldn't guess the crappy gift came from him.

Yeah. He was not only riding the crazy bus—at some point in the past few days, he had taken the damn wheel.

He sighed. Nothing for it now but to get through the holidays, wait for her to go back to Paris and then move on with his life.

The snow was still coming down steadily, so he decided to head out to the woodpile to fill up the box on the porch. Few things sucked worse than having to run out in the middle of the night all the way to the woodpile so he could keep the fire going—but even that beat the alternative of waking up to an ice-cold house.

He threw on his boots and his coat but didn't bother with a glove. It wouldn't take him long. In two or three trips to the stack out beyond the house, he could have enough split wood on the porch to last twenty-four hours or more.

"You coming?" he asked Tucker. The dog gave him a "fat chance" sort of look and settled back on his rug in front of the fire.

He was on the second trip to the porch through the snow when he saw a flash of light on the long, winding drive to the main canyon road.

He stopped and stared, the leather wood carrier dangling from his hand. What the hell? Who would be stupid enough to drive up here in the dark in the middle of a storm?

If it was Charlotte or Pop, he was seriously going to have to start yelling. Couldn't they leave him alone for two damn seconds?

He climbed up to the porch and dumped the wood in the bin then waited while the vehicle drew closer.

He recognized it when it was about twenty yards away, and his pulse started pounding in his ears.

Not Charlotte or Pop.

He shouldn't have bothered with a coat. Despite the cold wind that hurled snow at him, his face and chest felt hot and itchy as he watched Genevieve climb out of her SUV.

She looked like a Christmas angel, with her little cream wool coat, red scarf and a jaunty little matching wool cap.

He drew in a sharp breath, aching with the effort not to run down the steps and yank her into his arms.

"I thought *I* was the crazy one, but you are completely insane," he growled.

"Probably." She stopped at the bottom of the steps.

"No *probably* about it," he snapped. "What were you thinking, driving up here in the middle of a blizzard?"

"This?" She made one of her funny little gestures at the snow steadily piling up. "This is just a few inches."

"You have got to leave now if you want to make it back down and not be stuck up here all night."

She looked up at him for about ten seconds then walked up the steps and into his house without waiting for an invitation, untwisting her scarf as she went.

He followed after her. "Genevieve Beaumont. Get back in that SUV and go home. If you don't, I swear, I'll haul you over my shoulder, toss you in my pickup and take you down myself."

She ignored him, instead looking around his house with interest. She hadn't been here, he realized. He tensed even more, wondering what she saw. Yeah, it was pretty bare-bones but it was comfortable and he liked it.

Tucker the Traitor padded right over to her for a little love, and she knelt down with a slight smile and rubbed just behind his left ear, right where he adored.

"Hey, buddy. How've you been? Hmm?"

"Seriously, Gen," he tried again. "This isn't a joke. The canyon roads can be slick and dangerous even when there's not new snow. If you don't believe me, ask your brother."

Her mouth seemed to tighten a little as she rose to her feet and faced him. "I'm not leaving. At least not until you explain this."

She pulled three wooden figures out of her pocket and set them on the table.

His face turned hot again and he could barely look at them. Crazy bus. Definitely. What the hell had he been thinking? How could he ever have imagined it was a good idea to give them to her?

"Well?" she demanded when he said nothing.

He tried for nonchalance. "I don't know. They look like something a third-grader did in art class."

She crossed her arms across her chest. "They do not. They're beautiful. Absolutely beautiful. I can't believe you did this for me."

Her voice caught a little on the last word and he finally had a clear look at her face.

She had been crying.

He could see the red-rimmed eyes, the traces of tears on her cheeks.

His lungs gave a hard squeeze. Damn it. He hated her tears. Why hadn't he just let this whole thing between them die a natural death?

"You think I did that?" He did the only thing he could think of and tried to brazen through. "You *are* crazy. A one-handed carver. That would be something to see."

He saw just a trace of uncertainty in her gaze as she looked at him and then she gave a slight shake of her head.

"You are *such* a bad liar. I can't believe I didn't see it the other day."

She came closer to him, until they were only a few feet apart. Until the scent of vanilla-drenched cinnamon taunted him, seduced him.

"I don't know what you're talking about."

"Oh, stop. I know you made them. Who else would have given such a gift to me? No one knows about Grandma Pearl and our Nativity tradition except you and my parents, and they would certainly never do something like this."

And there was part of their problem in a nutshell. "No doubt that's true. They would probably give you something that should be in a museum, sculpted out of Italian marble or something."

A small smile lifted the corners of her mouth.

"Maybe," she said softly. "That sounds lovely. But it would mean nothing to me. Not compared to this one. I will cherish this gift forever."

Something warm and soft unfurled inside him, pushing away some of his embarrassment. He didn't know what to say, especially not when she moved even closer, just a breath away.

"You lied the other day, too, didn't you?"

"I don't know what you're talking about," he said again, easing away just half a step and hoping she wouldn't notice.

"I was too hurt by everything you said to see clearly but now it all makes perfect sense. You're Mr. Fuzzy."

He blinked. "Excuse me?"

She gave that sweet smile again, looking so stunningly radiant he could hardly breathe.

"Never mind. I'll tell you someday." Before he could react, she reached out between them and grabbed his hand with both of hers. She gazed up at him and the emotion in her eyes sent his pulse racing again.

"I love you, Dylan."

"Gen."

"Let me say this. You said the other day that I need perfection in my life. I suppose there's some truth to that."

He hated thinking about those words he had said to her, the flimsy barriers he had tried to erect.

"But here's the funny thing," she went on. "I

417

once had what some would say was the ideal fiancé—handsome, rich, destined for success—and I was completely miserable, even before he cheated on me."

Her fingers were cool against his, trembling a little, and he wanted to tuck them against his heart and warm them.

"I was miserable because somehow I knew from the beginning that perfect image was all wrong for me. What I needed, you see, was not the perfect man. Just the man who's perfect for *me*. Someone who sees beyond the surface to the person I'm trying to become."

Her fingers trembled a little against his. How much courage must it have taken her to drive up here through the snow, to confront him, to bare her heart like this?

How could he possibly push her away?

He thought of the past two days, how completely wretched he had felt when he drove home from that wedding—more terrible than he ever remembered, even counting the moment he woke up and realized the surgeons had taken his crushed and useless hand.

He had walked into the cabin, grabbed the whiskey bottle and poured three fingers. He planned to get completely hammered so he wouldn't have to think about this ache in his chest, the yawning, endless emptiness that stretched out ahead of him.

He had raised the glass, but before it reached his mouth, an image of her face as he had left her flashed across his mind, devastated and raw, and he couldn't do it.

Instead, he had grabbed Tucker and gone for a long walk in the snow and then had ended up in the run-down barn he used as a workshop. He had seen wood chunks lying there, a leftover piece he had bought to repair a sagging shelf in the bathroom.

He used to spend downtime on deployments playing around, making little toys and knick-knacks to pass out to the villagers they sometimes encountered.

The carving tools he used to keep in his pack were still there, untouched since his accident. He rooted through the pile of screwdrivers and wrenches until he found what he needed, and before he knew it, he had carved a simple Baby Jesus.

For hours, he worked on it, trying again and again to make it just right. It hadn't been as hard as he might have expected. He had figured out ways to hold the wood—with his prosthetic or in a vise.

Okay, it had been a hell of a lot harder than it would have been with two hands, but he had managed it anyway.

Maybe that was some kind of metaphor for his life. He would never be able to do things as easily as he once had. He couldn't change that—and pissing and moaning about it sure as hell wasn't helping the situation.

Maybe it was time to just suck it up and deal.

He thought of the sheer grit it must have taken for his Genevieve to drive up here in the middle of a snowstorm and lay her heart bare for him again after he had already flayed it raw.

It would take guts to climb out of the hole he'd been living in these past months and embrace life again. But he was an army ranger, charging headfirst into the toughest of situations. Once a ranger, always a ranger, right?

Was he really going to let some little cream puff in her beret and scarf outdo him in the courage department?

Hell no.

"Gen."

"Admit it. You have feelings for me, don't you?"

He was tired of lying. What was the point, when she saw right through him anyway? "Feelings for you. I guess that's a pretty mild way of saying I'm crazy in love with you. Yeah."

She gazed at him, blue eyes huge and drenched with emotion. "Oh."

She looked so sweet, so beautiful, he had to kiss her. He had been fighting it since the moment she pulled up and he couldn't do it a moment longer.

With her hands still wrapped around him, it was easy to tug her toward him. She landed against his chest with a surprised oomph, which changed to a delicious sigh when he lowered his mouth to hers.

They kissed for a long time, until he was breathless and hungry.

"Please don't push me away again," she murmured, long moments later. "I can't bear if you do."

"I'm not easy to be around, Gen. I'm trying to be better but I don't expect that to miraculously change overnight. I have moods and I get pissed and sometimes I stay awake around the clock to keep the nightmares away."

Those nightmares had been coming with less frequency the past few weeks. He had figured it was because they had been replaced with heated dreams that left him aching and hard.

"If you're looking for easy," she retorted, "I'm not your girl. I'm the coldest bitch in Hope's Crossing. Haven't you heard?"

He had to smile because he just wasn't seeing that. Not anymore.

"We're quite a pair, aren't we?"

"Yes." She smiled and wrapped her arms around his waist, her cheek against his chest. He held her close, his chin resting on her hair, feeling as if this was the safest, most secure place he could ever imagine.

They stayed that way for a long time, until he had to kiss her again. He had a feeling he would never get enough. He leaned his head down but she eased away before he could find that soft, sexy mouth.

"First I want you to admit it."

"Admit what?"

"You were lying. You made those carvings, didn't you?"

He didn't see any point in denying it anymore. "I don't know why I ever gave them to you. I should have just thrown them away. I'll get better with practice, I promise. I'll try again."

"I don't want another one. This will always be my favorite Christmas gift ever. It came from your heart when the words wouldn't."

She got him. He wasn't sure how, but Genevieve Beaumont—rich, pampered, spoiled—understood him like nobody else ever had.

She kissed him once more while the snow fluttered down outside his little cabin and the wind sighed under the eaves. The fire crackled beside them and the dog snuffled in his sleep.

And everything was perfect.

WALLINGFORD PUBLIC LIBRARY
200 North Main Street
Wallingford, CT 06492

Center Point Large Print
600 Brooks Road / PO Box 1
Thorndike ME 04986-0001 USA

(207) 568-3717

US & Canada:
1 800 929-9108
www.centerpointlargeprint.com

A2170 677347 8

WALLINGFORD PUBLIC LIBRARY
200 North Main Street
Wallingford, CT 06492